The Wickie

and the Umpqua Lighthouse

ALFRED W. BATES

and the Umpqua Lighthouse

ALFRED W. BATES

Alfred W. Bates
THE WICKIE
and the Umpqua Lighthouse
Second Edition

ISBN: 978-0-578-54824-1 Paperback

Author's websites:
AlsLighthouses.blogspot.com
www.franklinscribes.com/alfred-bates/

Publishing services provided by
Franklin Scribes Publishing Consultants

This book was printed in the United States of America.

Author's Note

Although this is a fictional story about the lives of the light keepers at the Umpqua River Lighthouse, the lighthouse itself is in fact a true part of history on the Oregon coast. There were two lighthouses built along the Umpqua River, and both were given the same name. The dates and times mentioned in this book are used to give you a sense of timing for the story only, and enable your imagination. No intent was made to provide dates and times to match events in history or those occurring to characters in the story.

As of the time of this writing, the second Umpqua River Lighthouse still functioned as an active light. It has guided ships from the Pacific Ocean into the mouth of the river for more than 115 years. This lighthouse is located on the Oregon coast near the small town of Winchester Bay.

Both of the towns mentioned in this book, Scottsburg and Gardiner's City, are factual towns. Gardiner's City was the original name of the town now known as Gardiner. They are located only a few miles from the current day small town of Winchester Bay.

The 1857 lighthouse pictured on the book cover and inside is actually a scale model of the first Umpqua River Lighthouse. The river in that picture is in fact the Umpqua River. Since there were no pictures available of that original lighthouse, through creative photography, I was able to bring that first lighthouse back to the banks of the Umpqua River.

My inspiration to write this book began when I learned the keepers of the more recent lighthouse, in the early years, nicknamed each other "Wickie." I knew this name would make a unique title for a book about those lighthouses.

The adventure of writing this book, unknown to me at the time, began after my late wife, Rose, and I retired. We started traveling this great country in our truck and fifth wheel trailer.

The first summer of our travels we left Phoenix, Arizona and traveled to New Jersey to visit close friends. While there, we drove down the coastline to see the Cape May Lighthouse. We walked to the top and enjoyed the beautiful view out over the ocean. Rose was absolutely thrilled with the sights and expressed her great pleasure of being in the lighthouse.

That feeling sparked a desire in her to travel around the country and search for lighthouses. I always teased Rose, and often told people we met along the way, that her love for lighthouses was due to her being bit by a bug while in the Cape May Lighthouse.

My initial thought was if you had seen one lighthouse, you had probably seen them all. However, I soon got caught up in her quest. I learned that each one does have its own personality, architecture, history, and stories about the light keepers and their families. As my excitement about lighthouses grew, and ultimately matched Rose's, we were always eager to find and explore the next one. Our travels in the United States and three provinces of Canada enabled Rose and me to photograph and collect data on 302 lighthouses.

During the summers of 2004 and 2005, we worked as tour guides at the Umpqua River Lighthouse and Museum. That's where I was inspired to write this book.

I hope you enjoy reading *The Wickie* as much as I enjoyed writing it.

Rose M. Bates and Alfred W. Bates
Umpqua River Lighthouse Museum – 2004

Acknowledgments

This author sincerely acknowledges the following individuals for their respective contributions. They were of great help to me in writing and preparing this book for publication.

A special thanks to Gaylyn Bradley, who was caretaker of the Umpqua River Lighthouse and Museum. Thank you, Gaylyn, for granting permission to photograph selected items displayed in the museum. Further, for providing the newspaper clipping of the second Umpqua River Lighthouse tower nearing completion of construction.

Thanks to Colin MacKenzie of the Nautical Research Center in Petaluma, California for building the scale model of the first Umpqua River Lighthouse. Thank you, Mr. MacKenzie, for also donating said model to the Umpqua River Lighthouse Museum at Winchester Bay, Oregon. Your donation allows the public not only to appreciate your work, but more importantly, enables them to have a realistic vision of that first Umpqua River Lighthouse, built in 1857 on the banks of the Umpqua River.

Thanks to the unknown tourist who provided the picture of my late wife and I at the Umpqua River Lighthouse Museum in 2004. Thank you for sharing your visit to the museum and lighthouse by providing us with a copy of your picture.

My deepest thanks to my late wife, Rose, for her encouragement to pursue my idea of writing about the Wickie.

Thanks to members of the Christian Writers Group of Greater San Antonio, Texas, who edited and critiqued my writing and story.

I thank my wife, Linda, and stepdaughter Kathy Johnson for their help in further editing my manuscript.

Contents

Disaster on the Umpqua 1
Aftermath 6
Responsibilities 20
The Move 27
Tower Concerns 34
The Indian Affair 47
Pitch, Sand, and Shingles 52
A Special Guest 58
The Knife 66
An Inspection 73
More than Books 78
A New Beginning 88
Wedding Night 99
The Fatal Blow 107
Dangerous Work 117
The Light is Dark 128
Reunion and a Special Gift 137
Sad Job 145
Reflections 159
There, I Said it 167
A New Home 178
Forever Final 196
The Bread 204
Joy and Sorrow 211
Near Completion 222
Good News All Around 229
She's Beautiful 235
Anticipation 250
Life Saved — Life Given 269
Hard Thing to Do 279

Dedication

This book is dedicated to my late wife, Rose M. Bates.
Her encouragement to me and her love of lighthouses provided the inspiration to write this book. We were married for over fifty-two years when she died in January 2008.
Read more about Rose in the author's note.

Chapter 1

Disaster on the Umpqua

THE FRONT DOOR of the lighthouse opened and Wyatt stepped out into the pouring rain. He walked down the front steps, then waded through the high water surrounding the lighthouse. Wearing a raincoat, hat, and boots, he crept toward the side of the barn facing the river.

Seconds later the front door of the lighthouse opened again and Wyatt's wife, Elizabeth, stepped out. "Wyatt! Come back in here. Let that cow go," she said from the top of the steps.

As Wyatt turned back toward the sound of her voice, a wave swept him off his feet. It carried him into the swift-moving Umpqua River.

"Hold on, I'll get Gus!" Elizabeth turned and reached for the doorknob as a bearded man burst through the front door.

"What's wrong, Elizabeth?" Gus asked.

"Wyatt's in the river!" She grabbed him by the arm. "Help him!"

"Where? Show me!"

Elizabeth pointed toward Wyatt who was struggling to keep his head above water.

"You get back inside," Gus said. "I'm going to the barn to get a rope."

Elizabeth looked back toward the river and screamed. "He's gone! Wyatt's gone! No! No! Oh, God, help Him!" She fell to her knees and sobbed.

***

Five days later at the edge of a small graveyard, a man named Gunther stood under a big pine tree located several yards from a fresh grave he had dug the day before. He watched a horse-drawn wagon roll into the graveyard carrying a simple pine coffin. Gus and Elizabeth, along with her children, followed the wagon. A few mourners followed them in their buggies.

At least it's *good weather today for Wyatt's family to bury him.* Gunther looked to the blue sky and the few powder puff white clouds. *Everyone around here is sure going to miss him, especially Gus and Elizabeth.*

The mourners parked their wagons and buggies, and carried the coffin to the grave. As Wyatt's family and friends gathered around the grave, Gunther moved closer so he could better hear the preacher's comments.

"Friends, we are here today to commit the body of Wyatt Saunders to this place. Elizabeth, we want you and the children to know that we deeply mourn the death of Wyatt with you." He paused for a few seconds as he opened a book he had carried to the gravesite. "Our friend Wyatt was born in Scottsburg on January 12, 1827, and died at the age of only thirty-four. He leaves behind his wife Elizabeth, son Rusty, and daughter Elsie. Wyatt was a very caring man, a good husband and father, and a hard worker. He was respected by everyone who knew him. Wyatt will truly be missed, but we know he's in a better place. May his soul rest in peace. Let us pray ...

"Heavenly Father, as we commit Wyatt's soul to you and his body to this place, we ask for strength and comfort to get us through the coming months. Father, we especially ask this for Elizabeth and the children. Amen."

The preacher turned toward Elizabeth and the children. "Mrs. Saunders I'm so sorry for your loss, and with the children being your responsibility, your challenges will be even greater. I'll pray for you that God will grant you peace, and that you'll seek him for guidance to help you meet any challenge." He looked at the children. "You be good for your mother and help her daily." He patted Rusty on the shoulder before he walked away.

Gus and the others in attendance also expressed their condolences, each one hugging Elizabeth and the children, or holding their hand in sympathy as they spoke softly. After Gus finished, he moved away from Elizabeth to the outside of the group. Gus stood about five feet ten inches with charcoal colored hair and a beard. He wore a black wool P-Coat with dark blue dungarees.

Gunther approached him. “Hi Gus, I’m real sorry about Wyatt.”

“Thanks. I sure miss him. He was the only assistant I ever had, and he was the best. I’m still trying to figure out why he thought he had to save his cow.”

“Will you be able to replace him?”

“I think so, but it could be a few days. I sent a telegram to the Lighthouse Board in Scottsburg.” Gus looked back toward Elizabeth. “Well, it looks like Elizabeth and the children are ready to go. I need to get them back to the lighthouse.” He shook Gunther’s hand.

“Take care of yourself and don’t work too hard,” Gunther said.

Gus walked back to Elizabeth’s side and accompanied her and the children to the buggy.

In a short time, the graveyard was empty, so Gunther shoveled dirt back into the grave and covered the pine box holding Wyatt’s body.

***

During the ride back to the lighthouse, Gus, Elizabeth, and the children said nothing to each other for several minutes. The only sounds that could be heard were the horse’s hooves, the slapping of the harness, and the buggy wheels rolling over the narrow dirt road.

After several minutes of silence, Elizabeth spoke. “Gus, the children and I will be moving out of the lighthouse in a couple of days. I know you’ll need our side of the house for Wyatt’s replacement.”

Gus frowned. “Where will you go?”

“We’re going to Scottsburg. I have relatives there,” Elizabeth said in a sad tone.

“You don’t have to move that soon. Wyatt’s replacement may not get here for several days.”

“The lighthouse has been our home for four years. Without Wyatt, it won’t seem like home anymore. The quicker we move out the sooner the children and I can adjust to a new life.”

“I know you’ll do what you want, but you need to know if there’s anything I can do for you and the children, just let me know.”

They arrived in front of the lighthouse and Gus stopped his horse.

He stepped down from the buggy, and then walked around to the other side and helped Elizabeth and the children down.

“Papa liked working with you,” Rusty said as Gus helped him down. Rusty was nine years of age with light red hair and brown eyes.

“Rusty, I also liked working with your papa. He was honest, dependable, and a hard worker. If you grow up to be like him, your mama will be even more proud of you than she is now.” Gus set the boy down.

Rusty looked back at Gus and smiled. He walked toward the front door with his mother and sister.

Elizabeth stopped suddenly and turned. “There is one thing you could do for me.”

“Just name it,” Gus said.

“Could you arrange for someone to haul our furniture and personal items to Harvey’s Landing? We’ll take the boat up river to Scottsburg.”

“Sure, I’ll go to the Landing in the morning and take care of it.”

“Thanks, Gus.” She turned and walked inside with the children.

***

Gus climbed back into the buggy and drove his horse to the

barn. After unhitching, he put his horse in the stall, then removed the harness and hung it up. By this time, it was 2:00 p.m. "I'm tired before I ever start my night's work," he said to himself. At the age of forty-nine, the last four nights of working sixteen hours were wearing on him. "Since I'll be up again all night tonight, I better go take a nap."

He left the barn and went around to the back of the lighthouse to get a good look at the storm damage. He found part of the ground under the tower's foundation was washed away. *This is worse than I thought, and it could cause big problems. I better notify the Lighthouse Board tomorrow.* Gus went to his quarters to lay down for a nap.

Chapter 2

Aftermath

AT 5:30 p.m., GUS awoke from his nap and started performing the tasks to get the light in the tower ready for operation. He went to the oil house at the rear of the lighthouse and picked up a five-gallon can of whale oil. Gus carried the can back inside through the workroom and continued on to the weight room. There, he began his walk up the 120 narrow steps of the circular stairway in the tower. On the way up, he stopped on the second landing to catch his breath. *This tower really has a feeling of emptiness since Wyatt is gone. It seems more gloomy and chilly in here.* He continued to the top of the stairway which ended at the lantern room. *I must be getting old. This can seems a lot heavier today than normal.*

He poured some oil into the reservoir, then pulled the cover off the lantern, folded it, and laid it aside. Gus unfastened the latch on the lens and pulled it open, enabling him to reach into the lantern burner head. He checked the wicks of the burner and found that one needed to be replaced. He trimmed the other two wicks and returned to the workroom with the empty can.

Gus picked up a new wick and climbed the stairs again to the lantern room. He replaced the burned-out wick and inspected the lens. *It looks good for now—I better get the light working.* Gus lit the wicks and closed the lens. He stepped down a few steps from the lantern room to the watch room and cranked up the cable to wind the clock mechanism. *I've cranked this weight up a lot of times in the past four years.*

After winding the mechanism, he checked the light and clock

mechanism to ensure he had not missed anything. *It looks good.* Gus returned to the workroom, picked up the oil can and took it out to the oil house. *I'm hungry. I haven't had any dinner or supper! That may be why I feel so tired.*

Gus went to his quarters and prepared some food. After eating, he went to the sitting room and sat down in his favorite easy chair. He picked up his pipe, filled it with tobacco, and tamped it with his index finger. He struck a match on a small rock lying on the lamp stand and lit his pipe, being careful not to set fire to his beard.

It sure feels good to sit here and rest. Gus sat there for several minutes enjoying his pipe before laying it down on the lamp stand. He returned to the lighthouse weight room and walked up the stairway to the watch room. He rechecked operation of the light and clock mechanism, then looked toward the mouth of the river to check the status for any ship in distress. All was well, so he returned to his quarters. Throughout the night, about every hour, Gus returned to the watch room to ensure the equipment was operating properly, and to check the status of the lookout. Every three hours, he rewound the clock mechanism.

After daylight that morning, Gus extinguished the flame on the lantern and covered the lens. He returned downstairs to the workroom and sat down at a small desk. He picked up the record book and wrote in it: "February 22, 1861, 8:35 AM – No problems with equipment or lookout." Then he signed his initials: GC.

Gus returned to his quarters and fixed breakfast. After eating he washed his dishes, carried in wood for the stove, then went to the barn and fed the horses and chickens. He harnessed his horse, Jake, hitched him to the buggy, and drove over to the lighthouse to see Elizabeth. He walked inside to the common hallway, knocked on her door and she opened it.

"Morning, Elizabeth," Gus said.

"Morning, Gus."

"I'm going to the Landing to make the arrangements you requested. Do you need anything before I leave?"

"I need wood, but the children can get it." Little Elsie, still in her nightclothes, appeared in the doorway next to Elizabeth. Elsie was seven years old with dark brown hair and brown eyes.

"All right," Gus said. He looked down at Elsie. "How are you this morning, Elsie?"

"I miss Papa," she said sadly. She looked up at Gus with her beautiful brown eyes.

Gus bent over and gently laid his hand on Elsie's shoulder. "I know you miss your papa, Elsie. I miss him too."

Her eyes welled up with tears as she lowered her head.

Gus patted Elsie on the head, then stood up, and looked at Elizabeth. "I've already fed your horse. I hope to be back by middle afternoon."

"Thanks, I really appreciate your help," Elizabeth said.

Gus went back to his buggy and drove off toward the Landing.

***

Gus had driven about a quarter mile when he saw a man on horseback coming down the side road. He took a second look as he passed the intersection. *Looks like Gunther.* He pulled his buggy to a stop and allowed time for the rider to catch up. "Hi, Gunther, I thought that was you."

"Morning. Where are you off to?" Gunther asked.

"I'm on the way to the Landing to get someone to move Elizabeth's furniture. She wants to move tomorrow."

"I sure hate to see her and the children go, but I knew it would happen now that Wyatt is gone." Gunther leaned forward, placing his forearm on the saddle horn. "Gus, I'm free tomorrow. I'd be willing to haul her furniture. You know that whoever you get at the Landing will charge Elizabeth to move her stuff. Besides, Wyatt was always good to me, so this would give me a chance to do something for him and Elizabeth."

"I'm sure Elizabeth will appreciate your time. I'll help you."

"Thanks."

"Thank you. Now, I better get on to the Landing, I still have to send a telegram."

"Hey, that's where I'm headed to order Wyatt's headstone. I'll ride with you."

***

A short time later, they arrived at the Landing and Gus tied Jake to the hitching rail in front of the Landing office. Inside, he was met by an agent who stood almost six feet tall, heavy around the waist, and dark brown hair with thick eyebrows. He was wearing a light-brown plaid shirt with dungarees held up with two-inch wide suspenders.

"Hi, Lloyd. How are you today?" Gus asked.

"I'm fine." Lloyd looked down, then back at Gus. "I'm sorry about Wyatt. That was a nice service Elizabeth had for him."

"Yeah, it was. I need to send a telegram to Scottsburg."

"Who do you want it sent to, and what do you want to say?"

"To the Lighthouse Board," Gus said. He leaned on the counter for a few seconds. "Storm damaged foundation of lighthouse tower. Request inspection for structural damage. Sign it Crosby."

Lloyd counted the words. "That'll be ten cents."

Gus paid him. "Thanks, I'll see you later."

He walked across the street toward the general store.

***

As Gus entered the store, the clerk said, "Hi, Gus. What can I get you today?"

"Morning, Emmit. I need two pouches of tobacco." He pointed to a glass jar sitting on top of the counter. "I want two pieces of that hard candy, too."

Emmit went to the other end of the counter and picked up the tobacco. On his way back he stopped and removed the candies from the jar. "Can I get you anything else?"

"No, that's it. Add it to my bill. Thanks, Emmit."

***

Gus started to climb back into his buggy and just as he took a seat, he was surprised by a stranger's voice.

"Pardon me, sir! Are you Gus Crosby? A lady at the Landing office pointed out your buggy."

Gus turned around to see a clean-shaven young fellow, slender build, average height, and dark hair who looked like a kid. "Yeah,

I'm Gus Crosby. Who's asking?"

"My name is Jesse Fayette. I was hired by the Lighthouse Board to work at the Umpqua River Lighthouse. They told me to report to you and that I'm replacing your assistant. What happened to him?"

"He drowned. I have a question for you, Mr. Fayette. How old are you?"

"Eighteen, Mr. Crosby, and you can call me Jesse. I may look young for my age, but I'm strong and not afraid of work."

Gus shook his head. "I'm desperate for help, so I guess you'll have to do. Where's your gear?"

"It's at the Landing with my furniture."

"Quick, climb in!" Gus motioned with his hand.

Gus drove the short distance to the blacksmith shop where he found Gunther as he was mounting his horse. "Gunther, hold up!" Gus yelled.

Gunther pulled back on the reins and his horse turned. "What's the matter?"

"I want you to meet the new help they sent me. This is Jesse Fayette from Scottsburg. Jesse, this is Gunther Hall, a good friend of mine."

Gunther and Jesse greeted each other.

"Jesse has a few pieces of furniture at the Landing office. Would you haul his stuff back to the lighthouse when you bring Elizabeth's furniture here tomorrow?"

"I can pay you, Mr. Hall," Jesse said before Gunther could answer.

"Just call me Gunther, and yeah, I'll haul your furniture," he said in a firm voice.

"Thanks, Gunther," Gus said. "I appreciate that. So, we'll see you tomorrow. Now, I better get this young fellow back to the Landing office to pick-up his gear."

"All right, see you guys tomorrow," Gunther said. "Now, I'm gonna visit the bathhouse while I'm here."

***

Gus drove his buggy back to the Landing office and stopped.

"Do you need help with your gear?"

Jesse jumped out. "No, I can get it, and I shouldn't be very long."

Gus waited for only a short time before Jesse returned with a suitcase and laid it in the back of the buggy.

"I'll get my trunk and be right back." Jesse turned and went back inside. Three or four minutes later, he returned with a big round-top trunk and loaded it in the back with his suitcase.

A young woman appeared on the front porch as Jesse climbed back in the buggy. She had dark brown curly hair that hung down the back of her light brown dress. Her dress was contrasted by the white apron she wore, and she was smiling.

"You be careful now," she said. "Come back and see us."

"Thanks for all your help." Jesse waived.

Gus picked up the reins and said in a low voice, "I see you met Alice."

"Yeah, do you know her?"

"She's the daughter of Lloyd Harvey, the agent who owns and operates the Landing," Gus said. "You better stay away from her."

"Why? She seemed like a nice girl to me."

"She's a nice girl, but her father doesn't like anyone looking at her."

"Hold up!" Jesse said. "That reminds me, I better tell Mr. Harvey that he'll need to keep my furniture until tomorrow."

"Good idea." Gus pulled back on the reins as his horse was about to move forward.

***

After Jesse and Gus finished at the Landing office, Gus drove them toward the lighthouse. The road was narrow and its base consisted of sand and dirt. To the right, the land cascaded down about twenty yards to the river. The water was so calm that the current could hardly be seen moving down river. To the left, the land rose up gradually away from the road for approximately thirty yards to the base of a hill covered with tall Douglas fir.

"Would I be correct to assume that Elizabeth, who you talked about to Gunther, is the wife of your former assistant?"

"Yeah. His name was Wyatt Saunders, and he was the best wickie I ever worked with."

Jesse turned in his seat toward Gus. "Why did you call him wickie?"

"You know, for a young fellow, you sure ask a lot of questions."

"I guess it's just part of my nature. My dad told me that's how I could learn more."

Gus rolled his eyes. "Well, it's a nickname. You'll find out soon enough."

"Oh, I see." Jesse turned back around in his seat.

They rode in silence for a couple of minutes. "You'll have to stay in my side of the lighthouse for tonight," Gus said. "During the next two nights neither one of us will get much sleep. I'll work with you to teach you the duties."

"I'm looking forward to working with you, Mr. Crosby. Have you always been at the Umpqua River Lighthouse, or did you work somewhere else first?"

"There are no other lighthouses in the Oregon Territory. Both Wyatt and I learned the job right here through experience. I was hired as the head keeper, and then about a week later Wyatt was hired. We were both on the job the first night the lantern was lit, over four years ago."

"Mr. Crosby, what did you do before you started working at the lighthouse?"

"Knock off the Mr. Crosby stuff. It's Gus." He coughed up some mucus and spit it out over his left arm. "I worked at the hotel in Scottsburg. I heard they were building a lighthouse out here, so I talked to one of the officials on the Lighthouse Board and told him I wanted to work in the lighthouse. I was the first one they hired." Gus moved to adjust the way he was seated. "What did you do before you hired on here?"

"I worked two places in Scottsburg at the same time," Jesse said. "One job was working for the agent at the Landing. The other was cleaning up a café each day after it closed. I was tired of that work. I probably would have got a job in the lumber business if my friend Oscar had not turned down the offer to work in the lighthouse. Instead, he recommended me for the job."

"Are you married?" Gus asked.

"No, but I'm sweet on a girl in Scottsburg. She doesn't seem to care anything about me. Are you married?"

"I was married, but my Martha died a short time after we moved into the lighthouse. The doctor said it was her heart."

"Sorry to hear that."

For a while, neither Jesse or Gus said anything, then the lighthouse came into view.

"Oh!" Jesse said. "What a sight. That's beautiful. This is the first time I ever saw a lighthouse."

The lighthouse was painted white with two windows on both sides of the front door. The door was centered on the front of the lighthouse. The tower and lantern room reached skyward and towered several feet above the roof line of the house. The sun sparkled off the river water, adding to the beauty of the moment.

Umpqua River Lighthouse – 1857

"You'll get to know her better in time," Gus said.

"I can hardly wait. This is exciting. How tall is it?"

"Still full of questions, hey? Well, the tower is ninety-two feet tall."

"Why so high?" Jesse asked.

"So the light from the lantern can be seen for eight miles out on the ocean and guide the ships to the mouth of the river."

"Wow, that's interesting."

They arrived at the lighthouse and Gus stopped his horse and buggy by the front steps. "I'll show you where to put your stuff, and then I'll stable my horse and be right back."

"Thanks, Gus."

Gus helped Jesse carry his suitcase and trunk into the sitting room. "Let's set them over here by the daybed. You'll sleep here until you get moved next door. So, make yourself at home. I'll be right back."

"I'll be here."

***

Gus drove Jake and the buggy to the barn, then stabled him and hung up the harness before going back to the lighthouse. He entered the front door, which opened into a common hallway. It ran between the two sides of the lighthouse. Gus walked to Elizabeth's door and knocked. Almost immediately, she opened the door.

"How are you and the children doing?" Gus asked.

"It's hard without Wyatt, but we'll make it. Were you able to find someone at the Landing to haul my furniture?"

"No, but I met Gunther on the way there. He volunteered to move you at no charge. He said it would give him a chance to pay you and Wyatt back for being so good to him over the years."

"Thank you, Gus. That was nice of Gunther."

"You may have noticed I brought someone back with me. He was sent by the Lighthouse Board, but he's no Wyatt. His name is Jesse Fayette."

"Since he rode with you, I gather he doesn't have a horse or buggy."

"No, I don't think so," Gus said. "Why do you ask?"

"Well, I was going to sell mine to the agent at the Landing, but since you already have Wyatt's replacement, maybe he could use them."

"I'll get Jesse and you can ask." Gus stepped across the hallway to his door. "Jesse?"

"What do you need, Gus?"

"Come here."

Gus introduced Jesse to Elizabeth. "Elizabeth has a question for you."

"Oh!" Jesse grinned.

"Do you own a horse and buggy?" Elizabeth asked.

"No, Mrs. Saunders," Jesse said.

"I'm moving tomorrow, and I'd like to sell my horse and buggy. Would you like to buy them?"

"Well ... yeah. How much do you want?"

Elizabeth turned toward Gus. "Do you think sixty dollars is too much?"

"They're worth more than that, Elizabeth." Gus turned toward Jesse. "If you want them, give her seventy-five dollars."

"Sounds like I just bought myself a horse and buggy." Jesse paid her.

"I'm going to leave you my kitchen table and the remaining food stuffs. They were provided by the Lighthouse Board."

"Why are you leaving your table?" Gus asked.

"I'll be moving in with my brother and his wife at the hotel in Scottsburg, so I'll have no use for the table. After I telegraphed him the other day about Wyatt's death, he offered me a job in the hotel and a place for the children and me to live."

"Thank you, Mrs. Saunders, I appreciate your generosity."

"You're welcome. Now, I must get back inside and continue packing. I'll see you men later."

Gus and Jesse stepped over to Gus' side of the lighthouse. "We need to eat and get some sleep," Gus said.

"I'm hungry, but I don't know if I can go to sleep this early in the day."

Gus pointed a finger at Jesse. "Listen to me. You have a long night ahead of you, so you better get some sleep."

Jesse's eyes widened. "All right."

"While I fix us something to eat, you might want to take a look around in the tower. It'll help you start getting familiar with her layout."

"That's a good idea. How do I get up there?"

"Go back out this door into the hall and turn left. The door at the end of the hallway is the entrance to the tower. I should have something fixed in about twenty minutes."

"I'm anxious to climb up to the top." Jesse opened the door to the hall. "I'll be back in a few minutes."

***

Jesse walked down the hallway and entered the tower workroom. To the right of the door sat a small table. On the floor on the other side of the room were wooden boxes of various sizes containing supplies. Several tools hung on the wall, and next to them was an open door leading to an adjacent room. He stepped toward the room and saw what appeared to be a weight fastened to a cable in the center of the room.

Something moved in the shadows in the adjacent room. *What was that?* He stopped and tried to focus on the object.

"Who are you?" A soft voice spoke from the shadows.

"I … I'm Jesse." His heart pounded. "Who are you?"

A young boy stepped out of the shadows. "Whee!"

Jesse sighed.

"I'm Rusty. My papa was the keeper of this lighthouse."

"What are you doing in here?" Jesse asked.

"I was playing on the weight. My papa let me climb in here."

"Oh, I see."

"Are you taking my papa's job?"

"Yeah, that's why I'm here. In fact, I was just going up the stairs for my first time. Would you like to go up with me?"

Rusty hurried up the stairs ahead of Jesse.

They stopped on the second landing to catch their breath, then continued their climb up to the watch room where Jesse looked out the window.

I have never been up this high before in my life. Wow! ... I think I can see all the way to the end of the river. Jesse turned around and looked at the clock mechanism. *All those gears, that big drum, and the cable – it all looks so complicated. I have a lot to learn.*

Rusty remained in the watch room while Jesse climbed the stairs on up to the lantern room. Jesse stood there in front of the windows enjoying the beautiful view of the Umpqua River and the blue sky dotted with a few white clouds. The water in the river flowed past the lighthouse and beyond for about a half mile, until it merged with the incoming waves of the Pacific Ocean.

This is beautiful. I think I can see the ocean ... my first time. Jesse turned and stepped toward the lantern. He lifted up one side of the cover and revealed the lens. *I wonder why this is covered? It smells horrible up here. Guess I better get back downstairs. Gus will probably get upset with me if I'm late for dinner.*

Jesse walked down one level to the watch room. "Rusty, I should get back. Gus will think I got lost. Are you ready?"

"Yes." The boy quickly walked down the steps ahead of Jesse.

Upon returning to the weight room, Rusty climbed back on top of the weight. "I'm gonna be a lighthouse keeper, just like my papa."

"Rusty, if you put your mind to it, you can be anything you want to be. Be careful, and don't fall off there. I'll see you later." Jesse returned to Gus' quarters.

***

"You're just in time," Gus said. "It's ready. You sit there." He pointed to a chair at the side of the table. "Go ahead and help yourself. My cooking is not as good as my Martha's was, but it'll keep you from starving. Anyway, after you move next door, you'll cook for yourself because we'll be working separate shifts."

Jesse took a couple of bites from the potatoes and ham Gus set in front of him. "Good thing for me that I learned to cook a little from my mother. But there's nothing wrong with your cooking,

Gus. This is really good." He reached for a slice of bread. "Gus, can I ask you a question?"

"Why stop now? You've been asking ever since I met you!"

Jesse grinned. "Why is the lantern covered up, and what is that awful smell up there?"

"The lens must be covered during daylight hours to prevent a fire. Those lenses magnify light. So if the sun would be allowed to shine through the lens when the lens is not turning, it could actually set fire to the grass or trees around here. This would depend, of course, on the angle of the sun. As far as the smell, that's the whale oil. You'll get used to that smell after you're around it for a while."

They continued to eat and Jesse told Gus about his encounter with little Rusty.

When Gus finished eating, he got up from the table. "We better try and get some sleep. Our work tonight will only allow for a few cat naps,"

"I'll try," Jesse said. He pushed his chair away from the table. "But first, I need to use your outhouse."

Gus pointed. "It's on that side of the lighthouse, toward the barn. Be careful with the door. The storm almost tore it off and I haven't had time to fix it. When you're done out there, clear these dishes off the table. I'm going to bed."

"Where should I put them?"

"Stack 'em on the counter, and we'll wash them tonight during one of the breaks."

Jesse put on his coat and walked outside. After he finished in the outhouse he headed back toward the lighthouse. *While I'm this close to the barn, I may as well look at my new horse.* He turned and walked into the barn where he found two horses. He remembered that Gus' horse was a black gelding with one white leg. The other horse was a sorrel mare with a long white streak down the middle of her forehead. Jesse walked into the stall and started rubbing his horse's neck and head.

"Hi, girl. You know, you're beautiful. You don't know me, but I'm your new owner. We'll get to know each other better. Right now, I have to get some sleep."

On his way back to the lighthouse Jesse looked at the foundation. *That must have been an awful bad storm for enough water to wash away that much dirt from under the foundation.* He went back inside the lighthouse, hung up his coat, and then lay down on the daybed. In less than five minutes, he fell asleep.

Chapter 3

Responsibilities

GUS WALKED OUT from his bedroom about 5:00 that afternoon. "Jesse, get up!" He said in a firm voice.

Jesse raised himself up from the daybed and rubbed his eyes. "I didn't think I could go to sleep in the middle of the day like that. Guess I was more tired than I thought."

"Traveling can make a body tired," Gus said.

"Before I went to bed, I noticed a lot of damage to the foundation back there." He pointed. "Did you know about that, Gus?"

Gus rolled his eyes. "Yeah. I've already notified the Lighthouse Board."

"Guess I should have known you'd know." Jesse rubbed his eyes, then stretched one arm as though it were asleep. "Oh, before I forget, do you know the name of my horse?"

"Wyatt called her Molly, and speaking of Molly, we better go feed the animals and get ready to light the lantern in the tower."

They finished in the barn and went to the lighthouse workroom.

Gus looked Jesse in the eyes. "Now is when you start learning the job and your new responsibilities. Everything you do to keep the light burning as bright as possible can save lives. The lantern must be lit thirty minutes before dusk and stay lit until sunrise. The captain of every ship who comes to this coast depends on this light to help guide him into the mouth of the river. Dusk is fast approaching, so we need to get to work."

"I want to learn as fast as I can. You show me what needs to be done and I'll do it to the best of my ability."

"You better. It takes two good men to do this job. For starters, let's go out back to the oil house and get some oil."

When they entered the oil house, Jesse could see several round brass five-gallon cans neatly lined up in rows across the floor.

Gus pointed to the right of the door. "These are the empty cans here, and those over there are the full cans."

"What happens to the empty cans?" Jesse asked.

"They're sent back to be refilled when we receive new shipments of oil. Now, pick up a full one and let's get up to the lantern room."

Jesse picked up a can and followed Gus back into the lighthouse.

When they came to the tools hanging on the wall in the workroom, Gus stopped and picked up a pair of scissors before going on into the weight room. They started their climb up the narrow spiral stairway to the lantern room.

As they entered the lantern room Gus pointed to the reservoir under the lens. "You'll need to pour part of that can in there. First, remove the can lid, but be careful not to spill any of the oil when you pour it. That stuff's hard to clean up."

Jesse did as he was told.

"We need to trim the wicks, so I'll remove the cover," Gus said. He carefully pulled the cover from the lens and showed Jesse how to fold it. "Lay the cover over there out of the way." Gus pointed to the selected spot.

Jesse laid the cover down, and reached up and ran his fingers across the lens. "This is the thickest glass I've ever seen."

"Yeah, but they're called prisms and they were made thick so they'd magnify and reflect the light. Tomorrow, we'll probably have to clean them. We'll start early in the afternoon to ensure enough time to finish before we have to light the lantern. But for now, let's check these wicks."

Gus turned the latch that fastened the two halves of the lens together and pulled on one side of the lens. It opened like a clamshell sitting on its side, and then exposed the burner head which sat centered in the lower part of the lens enclosure. Gus narrowed his eyes as he trimmed the wicks using the scissors.

"Each day before you light these wicks, check to see if any are burned enough to need replacing. We have to keep the black trimmed from the wicks, otherwise the flame will burn yellow and that puts off black smoke and soot. The grease in the soot blackens the lens and then it won't reflect the light as well. This also will create a need to clean the lens more often.

"Huh, that's interesting," Jesse said. He leaned toward the burner with Gus.

Gus turned toward Jesse. "Step back; it's time to light the lantern." He struck a match and lit the wicks, then closed the lens and fastened the latch. "Let's go down to the watch room, and I'll show you how to start the lens turning."

They walked down about eight steps to the watch room where the clock mechanism was located. The room also contained one window that faced toward the ocean.

Gus pointed to the handle on the mechanism. "Turn that handle to the right. It will wind the cable around that drum and pull up the weight that's fastened to the other end of this cable downstairs. After the crank is released, the weight slowly pulls the cable back down and causes the drum to turn. It powers the gears and turns the lens around."

"That weight must be heavy. This is difficult to turn."

"It's about 200 pounds," Gus said.

A few minutes passed and Jesse finished cranking up the weight. When he stopped, the lens started turning. He stepped back and wiped his brow.

"There's more to running this lighthouse and doing the job than what you have seen so far. In addition to keeping the lens clean and trimming the wicks, we have the responsibility to keep the lighthouse clean. You'll be sweeping the floor, cleaning windows, removing a lot of spider webs, as well as soot and dirt that collects on the inside of the tower walls. We also need to paint almost every summer. We never know when we'll get an inspection by the Lighthouse Board." Gus moved to the window and motioned for Jesse to come over. "Another important job is the lookout." He pointed down river toward the ocean.

The water was calm and clear as it flowed down river to mix with the ocean's surf. "Unless it's very foggy you can see the mouth of the river from here." Gus said. "Besides the lantern room, this is the other location where we can watch for ships that may be in distress at the mouth of the river. Sometimes when the mariners try to maneuver into the river, they can get stranded on the sandbar out there in front of the river."

Jesse frowned. "How do we know from up here that a ship is in distress?"

"The ship's captain will usually signal distress by having his crew wave a lantern back and forth, and ring the ship's bell."

"What do we do to help?" Jesse asked.

"You help by ringing the bell that's mounted on top of the pole at the north side of the lighthouse yard. Pull the rope and continue ringing the bell for at least five minutes. That's the signal to the lifeboat men to provide assistance."

"Lifeboat men?" Jesse asked. "Where are they?"

"The boatmen are up river between here and Harvey's Landing. They have a thirty-foot lifeboat for rescue service."

"Why can't they hear the bell ringing from the ship?"

"Sometimes they can, but it depends on wind direction," Gus said. "We're closer to the mouth of the river, so it's our responsibility to signal distress. Those lifeboat men are volunteers who have lost family or friends to the sea. When they hear the bell ringing, they launch their boat and row to the ship. They try to rescue the passengers and crew, but not the ship. Sometimes, due to the size of their boat, they have to make several trips back to shore with survivors. Like this lighthouse, those men have saved many lives in more than the four years that I've been here."

"What happens to the ship?" Jesse asked.

"It's up to the captain to get another ship or larger boat to pull his ship off the sandbar. Sometimes ships break up before they're rescued. I remember hearing about the schooner Bostonian from out of Boston. It wrecked on the sandbar and then broke up. That was about seven years before the lighthouse was built. Fortunately, most of the crew survived the disaster. They were able to salvage most of the ship's cargo, and then took it north to what is now named Gardiner's City."

"What happens if a ship gets in trouble during daylight hours?"

"One of us will still come up here every hour or so and check the lookout." Gus said. "If we're outside, we usually can hear the ship's bell."

"There's a lot more involved in working here than I ever thought there'd be." Jesse shoved his hands in his pockets and avoided eye contact with Gus.

Gus took one more look toward the mouth of the river. "Well, for now, it all looks good. Let's take that partial can of oil down to the oil house."

Jesse picked up the can.

They walked back down the stairway to the workroom and Jesse took the can out to the oil house. When he returned, Gus picked up a book from the table and handed it to him.

"Another one of your duties is to record your activities in this record book. Each shift you're on duty, you must log entries to indicate the lookout status and operating condition of the equipment." Gus pointed to the chair next to the little table. "Sit down there and take a look through here. You'll see the types of entries you'll be making." Gus pointed to a box under the table. "There are several more record books in there that Wyatt and I filled up over the years."

Jesse took a seat and flipped through the record books, including a couple he pulled from the box.

Gus gave him ten minutes to get a feel for the types of entries he would need to make, and then they returned upstairs to the watch room and checked operation of the light and status of the lookout. They didn't identify any problems so they went back down to Gus' sitting room.

Gus picked up his pipe, lit it, and sat down in his chair. "We have a few minutes, Jesse, so if you want to lay down there on the daybed and take a nap, I'll wake you when it's time."

Jesse wiped the side of his face. "I don't know if I can go to sleep, but I'll take advantage of the opportunity to lie down."

***

"Ready to go back to work, Jesse?" Gus asked an hour later.

Silence.

"Jesse! It's time to go to work."

Jesse sprung up on the side of the daybed. "I'm ready."

Gus chuckled. "You weren't sleepy, huh?

"I didn't think so."

They returned to the watch room to check for any problems with the equipment or the lookout. Every three hours they wound the clock mechanism. Throughout the night, they continued those procedures. Soon after daylight, it was time to extinguish the flame in the lantern, so they returned to the watch room.

"Before you can extinguish the flame, you have to stop the lens from turning." Gus pointed to a metal lever on the clock mechanism. "See this? Turn this lever to the 'stop' position and that'll keep the gears from turning the lens around."

Jesse turned the lever as Gus instructed and the lens stopped.

They climbed up the few steps to the lantern room and Gus showed Jesse how to extinguish the flame on the burner head and cover the lens.

Jesse wrinkled his nose. "It sure smells in here."

Gus rolled his eyes. "Like I told you, you'll get used to it. One more thing to do and we're done up here."

"What's that?"

"I'll show you when we get back down to the watch room. Don't forget we need to clean the lens this afternoon and also inside of the tower walls."

Jesse grinned. "I'll be ready."

"After we finish this one last thing, we better get breakfast. It won't be long until Gunther will be here. I want to be ready to help him load Elizabeth's furniture."

"I want to help too, and I need to find out how much he's going to charge for hauling my stuff."

As they entered the watch room Gus pointed to the clock mechanism. "After you extinguish the light, come down here and turn that lever back to the 'run' position. That allows the cable to continue unwinding until the weight rests on the floor down in the weight room. It keeps the cable and drum from having the weight pulling on it twenty-four hours a day."

Jesse nodded. "Oh."

"This only applies if you're working the second shift."

They returned to Gus' quarters and he started to fix breakfast. "I don't remember ever having to cook for Wyatt."

"I'll fix it, if you want." Jesse stood up from the chair he was sitting in.

Gus shook his head. "I got it, but you can go get some wood for the stove."

"Sure."

A short time later, Jesse returned with an armload of wood and placed it in the wood box. "Is that enough?"

"Yeah."

"When we need more wood, where do we go to cut it?"

"Don't worry about the wood," Gus said. "The Lighthouse Board hired a man to cut and deliver the wood."

Jesse grinned. "That's great."

"Take a seat," Gus said a few minutes later. "This is almost ready. After we eat, we'll need to feed the animals. Now that you're a new horse owner you have to take care of her."

"Oh, you're right! I forgot all about my horse."

"She's your responsibility."

Jesse nodded. "I know."

Chapter 4

The Move

AFTER BREAKFAST, GUS and Jesse went to the barn and fed the animals. As they walked back to the lighthouse, they saw a team and wagon approaching.

"Look, there comes Gunther already," Gus, said.

"Yeah, he's early."

They arrived in front of the lighthouse as Gunther pulled his team to a stop.

They exchanged greetings.

"I knew you would get here early," Gus said.

"Well, I wanted to make sure Elizabeth gets to the Landing in plenty of time to get her stuff loaded on the boat before it leaves for Scottsburg."

The front door opened and Elizabeth stuck her head out. "Morning, gentlemen."

"Good morning, Elizabeth," each man said.

"Gunther, I have everything ready," Elizabeth said.

"All right, I'll get started. We don't want to miss that boat."

Gus turned toward Jesse. "While I help Gunther, go up and check the lookout."

"All right." Jesse went inside.

Gunther and Gus walked into Elizabeth's quarters. They were greeted by Rusty and Elsie.

Looks like both the children are in a sad mood. "Are you two ready to move to your new home?" Gus asked.

They shook their heads and Elsie crossed her arms.

"This is our home and we don't want to leave," Elsie said.

"I know how you both feel, but you are young and you're both strong," Gus said. "Once you get moved into your new home, you'll forget all about this place."

"I'll never forget about my Papa and this lighthouse," Rusty said.

"Now children, don't bother Gus," Elizabeth said. "He's trying to help Gunther load our things."

"Gunther, that lamp table and those chairs go also." Elizabeth pointed to the corner of the sitting room.

A few minutes later, Gunther and Gus were in the bedroom figuring what to load next.

"Are you ready for us to take the bed?" Gunther asked.

"Yes," Elizabeth said.

Jesse returned from the lookout. "Everything looks good up there, Gus. What can I do to help?"

"There's the bed, a big trunk and those boxes to load," Gus said. "Elizabeth said they contain clothing. After that, I think we've got everything."

"I'll help carry them," Jesse said. "Lead the way."

Gunther and Jesse carried out the bed and big trunk while Gus carried the boxes, and that finalized the loading.

Standing next to the wagon, Gus turned toward Gunther. "Could you use Jesse to help unload Elizabeth's stuff at the Landing?"

"Yeah, but there's not enough room in the wagon for all of us."

Gus turned toward Jesse. "You need to drive Elizabeth and the children to the Landing in your buggy."

"I'd be glad to." Jesse grinned. "I'll go hook up Molly."

"Good," Gus said.

Gus and Gunther went back inside to be with Elizabeth and the children.

"Elizabeth, Jesse will drive you and the children," Gus said. "He should be ready in a few minutes."

Elizabeth touched her hand to her mouth and bit her lip. "Gus, I want to thank you for everything you've done for Wyatt and me these past four years," she said in a shaky voice. Her eyes started tearing up. "If Wyatt had not gone after that stupid cow, he would still be alive and we wouldn't have to move." Tears trickled down her cheeks. "Thank you for recovering Wyatt's body and helping me with his funeral."

"You're welcome." Gus hugged Elizabeth. "I have wished many times that I could have saved him. I know you miss him. I miss him, and now I'm going to miss you and the children. Since Martha died, your family has kept me from being lonely, and now I feel like I'm losing the rest of my family."

Elizabeth wiped her tears. "The children and I will miss you too, Gus."

"You're a strong woman, and a good mother. You'll do fine in your new life."

Jesse knocked on the door. "Elizabeth! Gunther! I'm ready to go."

"We're coming!" Gunther said.

"Gus, it's time for us to go." She turned toward the children. "Say goodbye to Gus."

Gus kneeled down. Rusty and Elsie darted toward him and hugged his neck.

Rusty's eyes teared up. "I'll miss you a lot. Thank you for letting me play in the lighthouse. You and Papa were my best friends."

"I'll miss you too, and you'll always be my friend," Gus said.

Elsie stood silent with tears running down her cheeks.

Gus turned and kissed Elsie on the forehead. "I'll miss you a whole lot, but you're going to be all right. You're a strong little girl. I want you to help take care of your mama and Rusty."

Rusty pulled out of Gus' arms. "I'm grown up and I can take care of myself!"

Gus reached inside his coat, pulled out two pieces of candy, and held them out. "I was going to give each of you one of these, but since you're all grown up Rusty, you probably don't want any."

Rusty's eyes lit up. "Yes, I do."

Gus chuckled and gave the candy to both Rusty and Elsie. They smiled, said thanks, then put the candy in their mouth.

"Children, we have to go now," Elizabeth said. "We can't miss the boat. Come on."

Everyone walked outside. Gunther climbed up on the wagon and picked up the reins. He looked around at Rusty. "How would you like to ride up here with me?"

"I sure would." Rusty turned toward his mother and pointed toward the wagon. "Mama, can I ride up there with Gunther?"

"Yes, but you hold on," Elizabeth said.

Rusty had already started climbing up to the wagon seat.

Elizabeth and Elsie walked to Jesse's buggy and he helped them in.

"Goodbye." Gus waved as the wagon and buggy moved away from the lighthouse. He stood there until they were down the road a ways. Once they disappeared, he lowered his head and crept back inside the lighthouse. He entered his sitting room, went to the lamp table, and picked up his pipe. As he sat down in his chair, he wiped a tear trickling down his cheek, then tamped tobacco in his pipe before lighting it.

I feel so lonely. It's like the feeling I had after Martha died. Guess I never realized how much Wyatt and his family meant to me. This lighthouse really feels empty now. I should stay busy. I'll fix that outhouse door. Oh, and empty the chamber pot.

Gus finished smoking his pipe, and then went to the bedroom and took his pot out to the outhouse and emptied it. He set the pot down by the outhouse, and then went to the barn and got a few tools and a couple of boards. A short time later, he finished repair of the door. Feeling numb, Gus headed to the lighthouse with his pot. *I better refill my lamp. The oil was low this morning when I blew out the flame.* He took his lamp out to the oil house, filled it, then returned it to the lampstand in the sitting room. He was still fidgety, so he went to the lighthouse weight room, climbed the stairs to the lantern room, and checked the status of the lookout. *Everything looks quiet. I may as well get started cleaning the inside of the tower. Hopefully, Jesse will be back in time to help clean the lens. He needs to learn that job.*

He went back down to the workroom and picked up a pole,

about six-feet long, with a brush attached to one end. He cleaned spider webs from the walls in the workroom, the tower, the weight room, the watch room, and the lantern room. About an hour and a half later, Gus finished and went back down to the workroom and hung up the brush.

Gus returned to his quarters and saw Jesse through the front window, driving his horse and buggy toward the barn. *"Jesse and Gunther are back."* Gus went out to help Gunther unload Jesse's furniture.

"You made it back in good time," Gus said. "Did you get all of Elizabeth's belongings loaded in time?"

"The two guys helping Lloyd at the Landing made my job easy. They unloaded everything from my wagon onto the boat."

"How were Elizabeth and the children doing?" Gus asked.

"They were sad to leave, but Elizabeth told me she knew she had to do it, so there was no use putting it off."

"I didn't think I would miss them so much," Gus said.

Jesse arrived from the barn carrying something wrapped in brown paper. Gus pointed to the package. "What've you got there?"

"I bought myself a new oil lamp. I almost forgot that mine got broke while I was packing."

"Was all your furniture still at the Landing?" Gus asked.

"Yeah, Mr. Harvey and his daughter took good care of it.

Gunther picked up a small box from the wagon and started toward the door.

"Let's just set this stuff inside," Jesse said. "Later, I'll figure out where I'm going to put it."

"Sounds good," Gunther said.

"When you're ready to arrange furniture, let me know," Gus said.

Jesse grinned. "Thanks, Gus."

A short time later, the three men finished carrying the few items of furniture into Jesse's side of the lighthouse.

"Looks like that's all of it," Gunther said. "I better get on back to the house."

"Hold on!" Jesse said. "How much do I owe you for hauling my furniture?"

"That'll cost you one of your freshly baked apple pies," Gunther said. "The next time you bake, remember me."

"It's a deal, and thank you for hauling my stuff."

Gus shook Gunther's hand. "I want to thank you too, especially for all you did to help Elizabeth and the children."

Gunther waved them off. "Ah, you're both welcome. I may need a favor sometime."

Gus and Jesse followed Gunther outside and watched him climb up on the seat of his wagon.

"See you guys later," Gunther said. He picked up the reins and drove away.

Gus and Jesse went back inside the lighthouse to the common hallway.

Gus turned toward Jesse. "That was a big surprise!"

Jesse frowned. "What?"

"I didn't know you could bake!"

"I told you I learned to cook a little from my mother. I didn't mention that she taught me how to bake a pie. Gunther and I were talking while the men were unloading Elizabeth's stuff. He asked me if I was going to make it on my own. That's when I told him about Mom teaching me how to bake pies."

"Speaking of eating, we need to eat now, so we can clean the lens. I'll fix us something. Meanwhile, you can move your gear over to your side of the lighthouse."

They took the few remaining steps down the hallway to Gus' quarters. He went to the kitchen and started preparing their meal.

Meanwhile, Jesse moved his gear over to his side of the lighthouse. After finishing, he looked around at his small rooms and tried to picture where to set the furniture. *Gus offered to help me, but I can set this up by myself.* Jesse returned to Gus' quarters.

"Well, did you figure out where you want to put everything?" Gus asked.

"Yeah, I think so, but my few pieces of furniture won't begin to fill those rooms. I probably won't use the children's bedroom."

"Sit down and eat while it's hot." Gus set down two plates of beef, beans, and potatoes on the table. "I don't know about you, but I don't like my food cold."

"Me, neither. It smells great."

They took a seat and dug in.

"You were talking about your furniture," Gus said between bites. "I don't have much furniture in that room either. Martha and I wanted to have a baby, but that never happened. In fact, she was so sure we were going to have one that she had me build a crib. It's still sitting in there along with Martha's spinning wheel. The only rooms I use are my bedroom, the sitting room, and kitchen. You'll probably do the same."

They ate in silence for a couple minutes and Gus ate quicker than Jesse. Jesse paused and looked at Gus. "Where do I get my water?"

Gus pointed outside. "The well is out there on the south side. When we're done eating, we'll stack these dishes on the counter. We need to get started on the lens." He finished the last few bites on his plate.

"I'm almost done," Jesse said.

A few minutes later they stacked their empty dishes.

"Come on; let's go clean the lens," Gus said.

Chapter 5

Tower Concerns

ONCE GUS AND Jesse were inside the workroom, Gus pointed to two boxes in the corner. "Get five or six rags from that box and grab the box of brushes too. I'll get the can of rouge and the brass cleaner." Gus looked around. "That's it, we're ready."

They climbed the narrow circular stairway to the lantern room. "I'll show you how to clean the lens and then you can join me," Gus said. "This will take longer than normal since you're learning."

"You only have to show me once, and I'll have it down," Jesse said.

"It's not a single brush and rag operation," Gus said. "You see all those different sized brushes in the box? Each of them cleans a different size prism of this lens." He started cleaning the lens and showed Jesse how to use some of the brushes.

After a few minutes: "I've been watching every move you've made Gus, and I think I'm ready to help you."

"Go ahead and start. I'll be the judge of that."

Jesse picked up one of the smaller brushes. "Is this the right one to use where the prisms join each other?

"Yeah, that's the one." *Maybe he'll catch on sooner than I thought.*

They cleaned the lens for the next hour and a half.

***

"While we're here, we'll trim these wicks," Gus said.

"Could I trim them this time?" Jesse asked.

"Yeah, you have to start sometime."

With little supervision from Gus, Jesse trimmed the wicks, then closed the lens.

Gus checked the lookout status. "All's well here. Let's gather up this stuff and go down to the watch room."

"When do we use the brass cleaner?" Jesse asked.

"We'll use it to clean these rails." Gus pointed to the brass rails at the side of the stairs and then showed Jesse how to polish and clean them. "Now, you try it."

"There's a lot of brass to polish" Jesse said. "Why are the rails made of brass?

"Not sure, but they don't rust from saltwater like some of the other metals do."

Ten minutes later, they finished with the rails that stretched from the watch room back up to the lantern room.

"Good job," Gus said. "Now let's polish the rails on down the tower to the workroom."

They picked up the cleaning materials, took them down to the second level of the tower, and started polishing rails back up to the watch room.

"How often do we have to polish these rails? Jesse asked.

"Twice a week."

After they finished, they went back down to the second level and moved their cleaning equipment to the first level of the tower. They repeated the polishing process until they had polished every rail that led down to the weight room.

"Starting tomorrow night, we will work separate shifts," Gus said. "You seem to catch on fast, so you take the first shift and I'll relieve you at midnight."

"Thanks for your confidence in me. I won't let you down."

"We better get a couple hours of rest. It won't be long until it's time to light the lantern. Do you need me to wake you at 5:30 p.m.?" Gus asked.

"No, I'll wake up."

Gus and Jesse entered the common hallway and then parted toward their respective quarters. Within a short time, Gus was in bed. Jesse, however, had to unpack his blankets and make his bed. It was about thirty minutes before he could lie down.

***

Two hours after Gus fell asleep, he awoke and put on his shoes. *I wonder if I'm going to have to wake Jesse. I hope he'll be as dependable as Wyatt.*

He finished dressing and went to the kitchen for a drink of water, and then to his chair and lit his pipe. After a few puffs, he laid his pipe down and walked to the hall door. As he stepped into the hallway, there stood Jesse.

"I'm ready." Jesse yawned.

"How long have you been waiting?"

"I just got here about a minute before you came through the door."

"We better get started. Dusk will be here before we know it."

Again, Gus showed Jesse how to light the lantern, operate the clock mechanism, and they reviewed what to look for during the lookout phase.

They worked together through the night without any unusual events. This included watching two ships safely enter the mouth of the river. After they finished that morning, Jesse made entries in the record book to reflect operation of the equipment and status of the lookout.

"What are you going to do today?" Gus asked as they entered the common hallway.

"I'm going to try out my stove and do some baking."

"All right, but remember you have the first shift tonight, so you better include some sleep in your day."

Jesse opened the door to his quarters and turned around. "I won't forget."

"If you need my help tonight, don't hesitate to wake me," Gus said.

"Thanks."

***

A couple of hours later Jesse was baking pies when he heard a knock on the front door of the lighthouse. He went to the door and there stood a man about fifty years of age with a gray beard and mustache.

"I'm Frank Yonkers. Are you Gus?"

"No, I'm Jesse, his assistant. What can I do for you?"

"I'm here to inspect the lighthouse."

"Come on in."

Jesse led the way down the hall to Gus' door and knocked. After a short wait, he knocked again.

A short time later, Gus opened the door. "What's going on, Jesse? I was catching a few winks."

"Sorry for waking you, Gus, but I thought you would want to know that Frank Yonkers is here. He wants to inspect the lighthouse."

Gus rubbed his eye. "I'm glad you woke me." He introduced himself to Frank. "You've not been here before. Are you new on the Lighthouse Board?"

"I'm not on the board. They hired me to inspect some damage to the lighthouse."

"Good, hold on and I'll get my coat."

Gus returned a couple of minutes later. "Follow me. You too, Jesse."

"I'll get my coat and catch up to you," Jesse said.

Gus and Frank went around back of the lighthouse.

"You arrived earlier in the day than I expected." Gus frowned.

"Well, I have to be back in Scottsburg tonight. I came on the boat yesterday so I could leave this afternoon. I rented that horse and buggy from the agent at the Landing."

Jesse caught up with them.

Gus pointed to the foundation. "Here's our problem, Frank."

"Wow!" Frank said. "The storm must have been much worse for you guys than what we had in Scottsburg."

"I wasn't here when this happened," Jesse said. "I was still in Scottsburg."

"Yeah, Jesse hasn't been here but a few days," Gus said. "He replaced my previous assistant, Wyatt, who was taken by the same storm."

"Oh, no!" Jesse said. "I forgot about my pies." He turned and ran back to his quarters.

Frank kneeled down to enable his inspection and measurements of the damaged foundation. He said words such as "deep," "wide," "sandy," and "too close." Several minutes passed and he stood back up. "I believe the foundation is still structurally sound. However, this cavity needs to be back filled as soon as possible to keep water from further undermining the foundation."

"We'll take care of it," Gus said. "I'm just glad the damage was not as bad as I thought." They walked to the front of the lighthouse. "Would you like a cup of coffee?"

"Yeah, I could use a cup. I have some time before I have to leave."

"Good, come on in."

As Gus and Frank drank their coffee, there was a knock at the door.

"Gus! It's me."

"Come on in, Jesse."

Jesse sat down at the kitchen table. "Is the damage as bad as you thought, Gus?"

"Frank said the foundation is sound."

"That's good news," Jesse said. "Another reason I came over was to let you know I'm going to Gunther's. I thought I would pay my debt to him as soon as possible."

"Hold on, I need to ask Gunther to borrow his team and wagon, so I can take your pie over with me and give it to him."

"Well, I guess so, but I could ask Gunther to borrow the team," Jesse said.

"Yeah, you could, but Gunther doesn't know you well enough, yet. He's more likely to loan the team to me. We need them to haul some soil to fill that cavity out there."

"All right," Jesse said. "I'll check the lookout and, if all is well, I'd like to take a ride to the Landing."

"Sure. Remember you've got the first shift."

Jesse stood up. "I won't forget."

"Well, I better get back to the Landing," Frank said. "You know if this lighthouse hadn't been built so close to the water, you wouldn't be having this problem."

"You're right," Gus said.

"Thanks for the coffee," Frank said. He and Gus stood up from the table.

"I'll walk out with you, Frank," Gus said. "I'm going to the barn anyway." He turned toward Jesse. "After I hitch up my horse, I'll stop out front and pick up that pie for Gunther."

"All right. I'll have it ready." Jesse turned to go back to his quarters. "Goodbye, Frank, good to meet you."

"Same here," Frank said. He headed for his buggy.

"Have a good trip back to Scottsburg," Gus said.

Frank nodded his thanks and climbed up inside the buggy and drove off.

Gus went to the barn, hitched Jake to the buggy, and drove over to the front of the lighthouse. Jesse came out the front door carrying the pie. It was wrapped in a towel.

"Here's the pie," Jesse said. "Tell Gunther I hope he is as happy with this payment as I was with his moving job."

"If it tastes as good as it smells, he should be very happy."

Jesse smiled. "I'll see you at midnight, if not sooner."

"Right." Gus drove away.

Jesse went back inside the lighthouse and up the tower stairs to check the lookout. *Everything looks good. I better get ready to go to the Landing.* He returned to his quarters and grabbed his coat before going to the barn and hitching his horse and buggy. Jesse drove over to the front of the lighthouse, then went inside. A couple of minutes later he returned to his buggy with a small basket, then climbed back in and drove off.

***

Jesse arrived at the Landing office and tied Molly to the hitching rail. He picked up the basket, and walked to the office. As he stepped inside, he was met by the agent, Lloyd Harvey.

"Hi, can I help you?"

"Well, I was hoping to see Alice. I have something for her."

Lloyd frowned. "Aren't you the new assistant keeper that took Wyatt's place?"

"Yes sir, I am."

"Why do you want to see my daughter?" Lloyd asked.

Jesse slightly lifted the basket.

Lloyd put his hands on his hips. "What's that?

"Just a pie, sir."

Lloyd rolled his eyes. "Hold on. I'll get her." He walked to the door leading to the back room. "Alice, there's someone here to see you."

A few seconds later Alice appeared in the doorway, then smiled when she saw Jesse. "Hi, what brings you back?"

"I brought you something." Jesse stepped toward Alice and set the basket on the counter, close to her.

"What's that?" Alice asked.

Jesse reached in the basket and lifted out his pie still wrapped in the towel.

"Whatever it is, it sure smells good!" Alice said as Jesse pulled the towel back.

He handed the pie to Alice. "This is an apple pie I baked for you. I hope you like it."

Lloyd shook his head. "Young fellow, if she doesn't like it, I'm sure I will. It smells good."

"Thanks for your kindness," Alice said. "I'm sorry, but I forgot your name."

"Jesse Fayette. Remember, you and your father helped me with my furniture several days ago."

"Yes, I remember your face, but I'd forgotten your name," Alice said.

"Well, I better go. I need to get back to the lighthouse."

"Thanks again, Jesse Fayette." Alice smiled. "I'm sure I'll enjoy your pie."

"You're welcome, Alice, and I look forward to seeing you again." Jesse turned to leave. "Hope to see you later, Mr. Harvey."

Gus arrived at Gunther's home and knocked on the front door.

Gunther opened the door. "I didn't expect to see you today!

This is a surprise."

"Yeah, me neither," Gus said.

Gunther took a step back. "Come on in."

"Here, this pie is from Jesse."

"It smells good. Jesse didn't waste any time keeping his end of the bargain. I'm curious why he didn't bring it himself."

"He wanted to, but I told him I would bring it since I needed to come see you anyway."

"What's wrong?" Gunther asked.

Gus told Gunther about the inspection.

"Do you want to try a piece of Jesse's pie with me?" Gunther asked.

Gus' eyes widened. "Sure!"

Gunther unwrapped the pie and cut two pieces.

Gus continued to tell Gunther about the inspection and the need to haul soil. "I figure it will take a wagon load of soil, and as you know, I don't have a wagon. I came to ask if I can borrow yours. I'll get the Lighthouse Board to pay you for the use of it."

"Maybe we can work something out. Didn't you tell me the Lighthouse Board furnishes you with wood?"

"Yeah, but what's that got to do with me using your wagon?"

Gunther finished chewing a large bite of his pie. "I would rather have a few armloads of wood than the money in exchange for the use of my team and wagon."

"Son of a gun. That's a good idea. I'm sure the board would go along with that trade."

Gunther took the last bite of his piece of pie. "You know that kid sure bakes a good pie."

"Yeah, I haven't had pie like this since my Martha died."

"All the years I've been a bachelor, I never learned to bake a pie," Gunther said. "Anyway, back to the team and wagon situation. To save time, you take them with you and leave your horse and buggy here for tonight."

"I'll bring your wood back with me when I return your wagon."

Gunther went to the barn while Gus went to the front of the

house and drove his horse and buggy around to the barn. He arrived at the barn and Gunther had already started harnessing his team of horses.

Gus started unhitching Jake.

Gunther pointed to an open stable door. "You can put your horse in there."

When Gus came out of the barn, Gunther had finished harnessing the team and backed them up to the front of his wagon.

"Let me help you hitch up," Gus said.

"All right. I've got this side."

In a short time, they finished hitching the team.

"Thanks for use of your wagon, Gunther."

Gunther grinned. "You're welcome. I think I got the better end of the deal."

"I'll be back sometime tomorrow afternoon." Gus waved as he drove away.

***

Gus arrived at his barn, stabled the horses, and went to his quarters. After hanging up his coat, he went over to Jesse's and knocked on the door.

Jesse opened the door. "Hi, Gus, come in."

"I won't stay long. I wanted to let you know that Gunther really appreciated your pie. He gave me a piece, and I must say, you make a good apple pie."

Jesse grinned. "Thanks, Gus."

"The other reason I stopped by was to let you know I got Gunther's team and wagon. Tomorrow morning, we need to get a load of soil. Plan on leaving right after we feed the animals, say … around 8:00."

"I'll be ready."

Gus started for the door. "First, I'll see you tonight at midnight."

"I finished trimming the wicks a few minutes ago."

"Good." Gus returned to his quarters.

***

Later that afternoon Jesse put on his coat, then walked over and knocked on Gus' door. "I'm going to the barn to feed Molly. Do you want me to feed the other animals while I'm there?"

"Sure, if you want to."

"I'll take care of them," Jesse said.

After Jesse fed the animals, he returned to his quarters and fixed himself something to eat before starting his shift. Shortly after he had lit the lantern and got the lens turning, it started to rain. At first it was a light rain, but after ten minutes it began raining harder. Later, when he finished checking the lookout and operation of the light, he returned to his quarters for a few minutes. Less than an hour later, Jesse went up to the watch room and checked the status of the lookout and operation of the light. Everything was well with the light, but the rain continued to beat against the window. *The rain sure makes it hard to see.*

He extended his time at the lookout to satisfy himself that he had not overlooked anything, and then returned to his quarters. Each time Jesse checked the operation of the light and the lookout, he found no problems until around 10:30 p.m. He started checking the lookout again, and saw a light. It *appears to be coming from the mouth of the river. Yes! No doubt about it. There's a ship in trouble. It must be stuck on the sandbar.*

Jesse hurried down the steps, then outside, breathing hard as he began ringing the bell. He continued for at least five minutes and during this time the rain slowed to a drizzle. Curious about the ship, Jesse returned upstairs to the watch room and looked toward the distressed ship. *I hope the lifeboat men could hear the bell.*

Suddenly, Jesse reached for the wall to keep from falling. *What was that?* His heart skipped a beat. "What's going on?" He said. *I could swear the tower moved.* The movement stopped and Jesse took his hand off the wall, catching a glimpse of light coming from up river. *That light is coming from the direction where the lifeboat men would come from. They did hear the bell.*

The lifeboat men moved past the lighthouse and continued downriver toward the ship. By now it was 11:30 p.m. and the rain had stopped.

I feel like I really helped someone tonight who needed help. Jesse snapped his fingers. "Darn it! I almost forgot to wind the clock mechanism." He walked over to the mechanism and cranked up the cable and weight. *I haven't made any entries in the record book either.* He walked down to the workroom and wrote entries in the book regarding the tower moving, and the ship stranded at the mouth of the river.

I wonder what time it is. He got up from the desk and went to his quarters. "Wow, it's almost time for Gus to take over," he said. He returned to the workroom to wait for Gus.

A short time later, Gus arrived. "Sounds like you had a busy night!"

Jesse frowned. "Yeah, but how did you know?"

"I always hear that bell. I'm not a sound sleeper."

"The night seemed to go faster by me being busy. Maybe because of what I experienced.

"Experienced?" Gus asked.

"Something weird happened up there tonight." His voice trembled.

"Your experience probably seemed weird to you because you're new at this."

Jesse shook his head. "I don't think so. I was standing lookout and all of a sudden I felt the tower move."

Gus' eyes widened. "The tower moved? I hope you're wrong. We don't need that kind of problem. Maybe it's a good thing we're filling in that cavity tomorrow morning."

"Yeah, and all the rain we had probably didn't help."

"You're right, but there's nothing we can do about it tonight. I'll take over. You go get some sleep"

"All right. I'll see you in the morning, Gus." Jesse retired to his room.

"I better check to see if Jesse recorded his eventful night," Gus said. He checked the record book. "It looks like he covered everything. This kid is detailed and I can read his handwriting better than I could Wyatt's." He sat the book back down on the table and went upstairs to the watch room.

He checked the operation of the light and status of the lookout. As he looked out the watch room window, he saw a light move slowly from the shore to the area in the mouth of the river. *The lifeboat men must still be transferring people to shore.* For a short time, Gus continued to watch the movement. *I can't do any more than Jesse has done. I may as well go back downstairs.*

Gus worked through the rest of the night with no events. At sunup, he made a final trip up to the lantern room, extinguished the light, and covered the lens. He recorded his entries in the record book, and went to his quarters to prepare breakfast.

After breakfast Gus went to the barn to feed the animals. As he entered, he bumped into Jesse. "I wasn't expecting to see you, yet."

"I wanted to make sure I got Molly fed before we started hauling that dirt."

"Have you had breakfast?" Gus asked.

"Yeah. As soon I finish with Molly, I'll be ready to go. Do you want me to feed the chickens?"

"Go ahead, Jesse. I'll feed the team and harness them."

Gus and Jesse finished their chores and hitched the team to the wagon.

"Where are we getting the dirt?" Jesse asked.

"Not too far from here there's a piece of bare ground along the hillside. The water drains good there, so I figure it will be easier digging and the dirt won't be so wet. That reminds me, we'll need the shovels. They're sitting next to the workbench in the barn. How about you get them."

Jesse retrieved the shovels and loaded them in the back of the wagon.

They drove to the spot Gus picked out to get soil, and began shoveling dirt in the wagon.

Ten minutes later, Jesse stopped. "Each shovel full gets heavier.

Gus leaned on his shovel handle. "I've noticed that too, but we have to keep going."

They finished loading the dirt and drove back to the lighthouse. While they were unloading, Gus stopped and picked up a handful of soil from the wagon. "This soil is about half sand, like most of it around here." He opened his fingers and let the soil sift down between his fingers.

"Yeah, I noticed that. I hope this don't wash out too."

They finished unloading the wagon.

"We need more dirt," Gus said. "That cavity was deeper than I thought. First, let's take a break and get something to drink."

"Sounds good to me! I found some muscles in my back I didn't know were there."

"Me, too. Leave the horses here. We'll water them when we come back."

A few minutes later, Gus and Jesse returned from their break and took the wagon back for more soil. They returned with the second load and shoveled it into the cavity, filling it.

Gus turned toward Jesse. "Glad that's done.

"I'll sweep the residual soil out of the wagon bed."

"When you finish, put the tools back in the barn and I'll start loading up the wood. I need to take Gunther's team and wagon back. After that I'll go to the Landing and send a telegram to the Lighthouse Board. I need to tell them about the trade I made with Gunther, and request extra wood."

"I'll meet you at the woodshed and help with loading."

A short time later, Jesse arrived at the woodshed. "I need to buy a chamber pot, Gus. After I had to run out to the outhouse in the rain last night, I'm convinced I need a pot. Since I have to go to the Landing to buy the pot, I could send that telegram and save you the trip."

Gus nodded. "Good idea, but check the lookout before you go."

"Sure."

Chapter 6

The Indian Affair

AFTER JESSE AND Gus finished loading the wood, Gus climbed up on the wagon. "I'll see you when I get back from Gunther's."

Jesse went back inside the lighthouse, climbed up the stairs to the watch room, and checked the lookout. *Everything looks good.*

He returned to his quarters and put more wood in the stove before going to the barn. He started to harness Molly and hitch her to the buggy, but noticed a saddle hanging in the corner of the stall. *If Molly is saddle broke, I'll ride her instead of taking the buggy.* Jesse picked up the saddle blanket and gently placed it on Molly's back. She didn't flinch, so Jesse placed the saddle on her back and again she stood still.

"Molly, old girl, I do believe you've carried Wyatt and this saddle before." Jesse tightened the cinches and walked Molly outside. He put his foot in the stirrup and threw his leg over the saddle. *So far, so good.* He eased down in the saddle, and Molly responded to every one of his commands. It was as though they had always ridden together. Jesse rode her around the barnyard a couple times to assure himself she would allow him to ride, then he rode off toward the Landing.

***

Alice glanced out the office window and saw Jesse coming. When she realized he was not going to stop at the office, she hurried outside to him. "Where are you going?"

Jesse pulled back on the reins. "Hi, Alice," he said smiling. "Nice to see you again."

"What's your hurry?"

"I'm on my way to the general store." Jesse dismounted.

Alice's face was glowing. "I'm glad I saw you. This gives me a chance to thank you again for your thoughtfulness. Your pie was very good. In fact, my daddy ate three pieces himself."

"Oh, I'm glad you liked it."

Two Indians on horseback suddenly raced past Jesse and Alice. Their hair flew straight back behind them.

Jesse flinched. "They're sure in a hurry!"

"About once a week those two race each other up and down the side of the river. One of the officers from Fort Umpqua told Daddy as long as they're not hurting anyone, they wouldn't do anything about it. The Indians have been peaceful, so the Army doesn't want to antagonize them. They aren't hurting anything."

"Well, except for maybe running their horses too hard." Jesse looked at Alice. "What do you do for fun and relaxation?"

"Read books when I'm lucky enough to get them from Scottsburg. I like to knit if I have time. Daddy keeps me pretty busy here at the Landing though."

"What do you do with the books after you've read them?"

"If Mrs. Watson at the general store doesn't want them, I usually send them back to Scottsburg. Do you like to read?"

"Yeah, but there's nothing to read at the lighthouse. I left Scottsburg in such a hurry I didn't think to bring anything to read."

"I have a couple of books I've finished. Would you like to have them?"

"Hey, that would be great!"

"Wait here." Alice hurried back inside the office. She returned in a couple of minutes and handed Jesse two books. "Here are a couple to get you started."

He took the books. "Do you have any time when you're not busy?"

"Not much." Since mother died three years ago, I do all the cooking, cleaning, and help Daddy in the office."

"I'm sorry you lost your mother."

Alice lowered her head. "I've missed her every day and some

days it's very hard. She was not only my mother but also my best friend. Don't get me wrong, I love my daddy, but I have never been able to talk with him like mother and I did."

"Do you mind if I stop and visit sometime? I enjoy talking to you."

"No, I don't mind." Alice tried to conceal a smile.

Jesse shook her hand and looked into her beautiful hazel eyes. "I better go, and thanks again for the books." He hesitated before releasing her hand and she made no move to pull away.

Alice looked back at Jesse. "I hope you enjoy the books."

"Guess I'll have to read these in a hurry, so I can come back sooner." He released Alice's hand, pushed a book down in each of his lower coat pockets, and climbed back up on his horse. "I hope to see you soon, Alice."

"Be careful," Alice said.

***

Jesse visited the general store and came out a few minutes later carrying a burlap bag with the top twisted. He tied the bag to the saddle horn and mounted his horse. After riding a short distance, he realized he forgot to send Gus' telegram. He turned Molly around and rode back to the Landing office.

He entered the office with hopes of seeing Alice again, but, instead, her father was there.

"Mr. Harvey. How are you today?"

"Well, not bad, except for my mouth," Lloyd said.

Jesse frowned. "What's wrong with your mouth?"

Lloyd grinned. "My tongue is still watering from your pie."

"Shoo" Jesse sighed. "You had me worried for a second. I thought maybe you were sick."

"No, just my way of saying I really enjoyed your pie." Lloyd chuckled.

"I'm glad you liked it. Anyway, I came to send a telegram for Gus."

Lloyd stepped behind the counter. "Step over here and I'll take care of you. Who do you want to send the telegram to, and what do you want it to say?"

"Send it to the Lighthouse Board in Scottsburg. It should read, 'Request full wagon load of wood on next delivery. Needed to pay for use of wagon and team to haul dirt to fill cavity made from storm damage.' Sign it Crosby."

"Are you sure you're allowed to sign the telegram, Crosby?"

"Gus authorized me to send the message on his behalf."

"All right." Lloyd counted the words. "That'll be fifteen cents."

Jesse paid him.

"Can I help you with anything else?" Lloyd asked.

"No, thank you. I need to get back to the lighthouse."

"All right, Jesse. See you later."

***

As Jesse approached the lighthouse, he saw Gus by the barn unhitching Jake from the buggy. Jesse rode to the barn, dismounted, and walked Molly inside. "It looks like we returned at the same time."

"Did you get my telegram sent?"

"Sure did," Jesse said.

"What's in the bag?

"It's my new chamber pot."

Gus and Jesse finished hanging the harness and saddle in the barn.

"We may as well go ahead and feed while we're out here," Gus said.

"I was thinking the same thing."

Gus fed the horses while Jesse fed the chickens.

"Do you ever eat any of the chickens?" Jesse asked.

"Once in a while, Wyatt and I would kill a couple. I'm not good at cooking chicken and Elizabeth knew it. She would cook 'em and then send Wyatt over with some for me."

"I'll make a deal with you," Jesse said. "The next time you want chicken, you kill it and I'll cook it."

Gus frowned. "You know how to cook chicken, too?"

"I think you'll find that I make the best fried chicken west of Scottsburg."

They finished feeding the animals and approached the front door of the lighthouse.

"I saw a couple of Indians riding their horses like a streak of lightning today," Jesse said. "I was surprised when they rode so close to the Landing office. Have you ever had any trouble with them here at the lighthouse?"

"Not personally. However, during the building of the lighthouse, the construction crew had trouble with them."

"What kind of trouble?" Jesse asked.

Gus motioned toward the door. "Let's get inside; it's much warmer there."

They entered the lighthouse and stopped in the hallway.

"I was still in Scottsburg when it happened," Gus said. "The story I heard was the Indians were stealing construction materials. After a while the foreman got tired of it. So, one day he lit a stick of dynamite and threw it in the direction of the Indians. The explosion scared them away. After that, the foreman and crew didn't have any more trouble with them. Anyway, I haven't had any trouble with them since I've been here."

"That's good to hear."

"It's been some time since either of us checked the lookout," Gus said. "I'll go up and check it."

Jesse started to open the door to his quarters then turned back. "Hey Gus, do you like to read?"

"Yeah, I read the Bible. That's the only book I have around here."

Jesse pulled the books out of his coat pocket. "Alice gave me these books today. I can't read both of them at the same time. Would you like this one?" He handed Gus a book.

"Sure. Thanks."

Chapter 7

Pitch, Sand, and Shingles

JESSE WORKED THROUGH his shift that night without any incidents. At midnight Gus relieved him, and he had no incidents until morning. At 6:30, it started to rain. A half an hour later, Gus walked from his quarters to the hallway to go back up in the tower. As he arrived at the door leading into the tower, he saw water running from the ceiling down into the hallway. *Jesse was right, the tower did move. It must have pulled away from the house. Now we have a mess. Who knows if we can fix it?* Gus shook his head. *Well, there's nothing we can do right now. It'll have to wait until the rain stops.*

Gus went on up the tower steps and after a short time he shut down the light. He returned to the workroom and recorded the events of the night, then completed his shift. He returned to his quarters for breakfast. After eating, he washed his dishes and headed for the barn. As he opened his door to the hallway, Jesse came out of his quarters.

Gus pointed down the hallway. "Did you see the leak there at the end of the hallway?"

"No." Jesse looked around.

"You were right about the tower moving the other night. I think that's why we have that leak."

"I didn't notice any leaks on my side of the house," Jesse said. "How about yours?"

"None on my side, either. For now, the leak appears to be contained at the end of the hall. After it quits raining, we'll need to fix it before it gets any worse. For now, let's go take care of the feeding."

"All right," Jesse said.

The rain continued to fall, so they ran to the barn.

"Do we have the materials to fix the leak?" Jesse asked.

"We have some materials, but first I need to determine how big a separation there is between the tower and the roof. After we finish feeding, I'll get up there and take a look."

***

"Jesse, could you give me a hand with the ladder?"

"Sure, where is it?"

Gus pointed. "It's there in the corner of the tool shed."

They picked up the ladder and carried it to the back of the lighthouse. It continued to rain as they set the ladder up against the house roof, but close to the tower.

"Steady this ladder. I'm going up to see how bad the damage is."

"I've got it. Be careful. That roof may be slippery."

Gus arrived at the top of the ladder. "I won't have to get on the roof. I can see pretty good from here."

"How bad is it?"

"Just like I thought. The tower has pulled away from the house about two inches." Gus stood on the top of the ladder observing for a minute longer, then climbed back down. "I think maybe we can fix it. Let's leave the ladder here. As soon as it stops raining, we'll need it again. Let's get out of this rain."

They hurried to the back door of the lighthouse, and as they entered, both shook water from their raincoats.

"Should we write anything in the record book about the leak?" Jesse asked.

"Good thinking. I'll make the entry, and if we can fix it, we'll need to make another one later." Gus moved over to the table and wrote in the record book. "We may as well take a break and hopefully it will quit raining soon."

"I may use this time to start reading the book I got," Jesse said.

"Have you looked at yours?"

"I read some last night, but the first few pages were dull. I was about ready to quit when I read about horses that were gathered in the English camp, and two of them appeared to be for female riders. That got me curious."

"What's the book I gave you?"

"*The Last of the Mohicans*, but if it don't get better soon, I won't be reading much more."

Jesse wiped the side of his face. "I hope *Rip Van Winkle* is more interesting."

A slow rain continued to fall for the next hour while Jesse and Gus sat reading in their respective quarters. Shortly thereafter, the rain stopped. Gus laid his book and pipe down on the lamp stand and walked over to Jesse's door and knocked.

"I'll be right there." In a few seconds, Jesse opened his door. "Are you ready to work on the roof?"

"Since it stopped raining, we need to get started. It won't be long 'till dinner time."

Gus and Jesse went out to the barn and carried roofing materials to the back of the lighthouse. Gus climbed up the ladder and onto the roof.

Jesse climbed the ladder right behind him to see the damages for himself. "Where do we start?"

"First, I want to make a support and install it in that opening." Gus pointed to a two-or-three-inch gap between the roof of the house and the tower wall. "Then we'll need to work some of those repair shingles up under the existing shingles to extend the roof over to the tower. The only problem I see is, we don't have enough pitch to finish the job."

"Where do we get more pitch?"

"They have it at the general store. I need you to make the trip there while I work on this. Maybe we can finish this by supper time."

Jesse grinned. "Sure, I don't mind"

"You'll need to take your buggy. Those gallon pails are hard to carry on horseback. To make sure we have enough, you better get two pails. Put it on the Lighthouse Board's tab and they'll pay for it."

Jesse started back down the ladder.

"Since we haven't had dinner yet, you better grab something to eat before you leave," Gus said. "Otherwise you're going to get hungry by the time we finish this."

"All right." Jesse went inside the lighthouse.

Gus stayed on the roof and took several measurements and continued planning for the repairs. Several minutes passed before he climbed down the ladder and went to the barn for tools. When he arrived at the barn, Jesse was already hitching Molly to the buggy. Gus shook his head. "It sure didn't take you long to eat."

"I didn't want to hold you up." Jesse climbed into the buggy and picked up the reigns. "I'll be back as soon as possible."

Gus picked up the tools he needed and returned to the back of the lighthouse. He made some cuts on the wood he was using to make a support, and then climbed up the ladder to check the fit. Gus placed the support in the opening. *That fits pretty good. I just need to cut some of these shingles back to make room to fasten the support to three of those rafters.*

Gus continued work on the roof until he had positioned the new support. *That looks good and I think it'll work.* He scratched his head. *I better take a break and get something to eat.* He climbed down from the roof and went back into the lighthouse for dinner.

***

Jesse finished his purchase at the general store and was loading the pitch into his buggy when he heard Alice's voice.

"Hi, Jesse, what brings you back so soon?"

Jesse turned to see Alice approaching his side of the buggy. He smiled. "Hi, Alice, it's great to see you again. I'm here to get this pitch. We have a leaky roof at the lighthouse. I had no idea that I would be coming over here today, but I was thinking about you this morning."

Alice blushed. "That's odd. I was thinking of you, too."

"You were!" Jesse took a few steps toward her.

"Yes, I have another book for you."

"While it was raining this morning, I enjoyed reading one that I kept, and my thoughts turned to you." I gave the other book to Gus."

"I'm glad you're enjoying them. If you have time to wait, I'll go get the other book. I came to the general store to see Mrs. Watson."

Jesse touched Alice on the shoulder. "I really would like to spend more time with you, but I have to get back to the lighthouse with this stuff. I'll get the book the next time I'm over here, but for now I better go."

Alice nodded. "That's all right. It'll be good to see you again."

Jesse turned and stepped up into the buggy and picked up the reins. "I'm looking forward to seeing you again, Alice. You take care." He drove off toward the lighthouse.

***

A few minutes later, Jesse arrived at the lighthouse and drove his horse around to the back where Gus was working. "I'm back." He stepped down from the buggy.

"It won't be long until I'll be ready to use that stuff. I have just a few more shingles to put in place. However, before that pitch is ready to use it has to be heated."

"I'd like to unhitch Molly first and put her in the barn. Then I'll come back and heat this stuff up on the stove."

"All right, but be sure you remove the lids first." Gus pointed. "Don't forget that partial can sitting over there. I want to use that one first before we use any of the new stuff."

"I won't forget." Jesse drove to the barn.

Gus picked up a few shingles and carried them up the ladder and over onto the roof. He worked several minutes carefully placing shingles over the gap, then climbed down the ladder and carried up some sand.

After Jesse unhitched and stabled Molly, he returned to the lighthouse and started heating the pails of pitch on the stove. He walked out the back door of the lighthouse and looked up toward Gus on the roof. "Can I help you up there?"

"I just laid the last shingle down, but as soon as that partial pail of pitch is runny enough to pour, bring it out."

"All right. It shouldn't take very long." Jesse went back into the lighthouse and returned with the pail five minutes later. He handed the pail to Gus at the top of the ladder. "What are you going to do with that sand?"

"After I pour the pitch, I'll put sand over it to keep the pitch from running away from the area where the roof joins the tower. When that pitch dries, the sand will give it more strength."

"I learned something I didn't know," Jesse said.

Gus poured the pitch from the partial pail. "You were right. It didn't have much in it."

"I'll go check on the others heating on the stove." Soon, Jesse returned with one of the pails. He climbed up the ladder and handed it to Gus. "Do you need more sand?"

"Just a little."

"I'll get it."

A short time later, they finished repairing the roof and started picking up the scrap wood and shingles.

Jesse rubbed the side of his face. "I don't know much about roof repair Gus, but the job you did up there looks good to me. I'll bet that roof doesn't leak there anymore."

"I hope you're right, but we won't know until it rains again. Do you want these scrap pieces of wood for your stove?"

"Yeah, I'll take 'em," Jesse said.

"I'll take these tools to the barn, but when I get back, I'll need your help to carry the ladder and that leftover can of pitch."

"What do you want to do with the scrap pieces of shingles?"

"Put 'em out back of the barn."

They finished cleaning up and as they set the ladder down in the barn Gus said, "It's late enough that we may as well feed while we're out here."

"Sure. This has been a busy day so far, and I feel good about it.

Gus nodded. "That's good, but the day's not over yet."

Chapter 8

A Special Guest

GUS AND JESSE headed back to the lighthouse after feeding the animals.

"How was everything at the Landing?" Gus asked.

"Good, as far as I know. I saw Alice as I was about to leave the general store. She said she had another book, but I told her I didn't have time to wait."

"I'm glad you didn't linger or we wouldn't have finished the roof in time for supper."

"Speaking of supper reminds me—I'm getting low on supplies," Jesse said.

"Can you hold on for a couple days? We're due for a delivery of dry goods from the Lighthouse Board day after tomorrow."

Jesse nodded. "I can make it 'till then."

They entered the front door of the lighthouse.

"You know, some fried chicken would help stretch those supplies," Gus said. "Is your offer to fix chicken still good if I kill it?"

"Sure, but to make good fried chicken I need flour, and I don't think I have enough left."

"I'll give you as much flour as you need. In fact, let's get it right now. Come on in." Gus opened his pantry door and removed a container of flour. He started scooping flour into a pan. "Tell me when you think it's enough. As you can see, I have plenty."

"Two more scoops will do it," Jesse said.

Gus finished and placed his container back in the pantry. "I'll kill the chicken in the morning right after I feed."

"That's early enough. I'll have time to get the chicken done for dinner."

Gus raised his eyebrows up and down. "I'm looking forward to it."

"I better get back and fix myself something to eat. It won't be long until I start my shift."

"I'll see you at midnight."

***

Jesse started his shift performing his usual duties to prepare for and light the lantern in the tower. He worked through his shift with no incidents. Shortly before midnight he was in the workroom writing in the record book when Gus walked in.

"Any problems?" Gus asked.

"Everything was normal."

"I hope it stays that way the rest of the night. My knees are so sore from kneeling on the roof. I had trouble getting out of bed."

"Would you like me to work part of your shift?"

"I'm not that bad. These knees will be limbered up by the time I get up to the watch room. Go get some sleep and I'll see you in the morning."

"If you need me, give a shout." Jesse turned and opened the door.

"I'll be all right." Gus walked slowly up the stairs of the tower. Throughout the night he took care of the light and equipment with no incidents. At daylight, he extinguished the light, covered the lens, and walked down to the workroom and made an entry in the record book. Gus returned to his quarters and fixed biscuits, gravy, and coffee for his breakfast.

After Gus had eaten, he put on his coat and headed out the front door to the barn. He was ten feet from the front step when he stopped in his tracks and his eyes widened. Th*at's the biggest bull I think I ever saw. Looks like he has about twelve tines.* Just then the elk bolted and ran up the hill toward the forest. Gus walked to the barn and started feeding. He was almost done when Jesse walked in.

Gus smiled. "You sure missed a beautiful sight a few minutes ago. I saw the biggest elk bull I've ever seen. He was standing in front of the barn as I came out to feed."

"I would like to have seen him. How big was he?"

"I didn't get a long look at him, but I'm pretty sure he had twelve tines."

"Wow! Have you seen many elk around here?"

"Yeah, over the past four years I've seen several, but none as big as that guy." Gus shook his head. "Guess I should quit talking about that elk and go catch a chicken."

"I'm almost done feeding. Do you need some help catching the chicken?"

"No. We made a deal, remember?"

Jesse waved. "I'll see you back at the house."

Gus picked up the ax and stuck it in a big block of wood. He crept among the chickens and then, quick as a wink, he reached down with his left hand and caught one by the leg. With his other hand, he grabbed the other leg of the chicken and also placed it in his left hand. The chicken flapped its wings trying to get away. Gus carried it over to the block of wood and picked up the ax with his right hand. Holding the chicken's legs with his left hand, he laid the chicken down so its neck was out across the block of wood. He raised the ax and with one quick chop, the chicken's head was off. He released the chicken to flop around and bleed out while he returned the ax to the barn.

Returning from the barn, Gus picked up the chicken and carried it to the back door of the lighthouse and laid it down before he went inside. Several minutes later he returned with a pan of hot water. Gus soaked the chicken in the water, plucked out the feathers, then took the chicken inside to Jesse. "Here's the chicken. Would you like some biscuits to go with it?"

Jesse chuckled. "That sounds good to me."

"I'll bake some later so they'll still be hot for dinner."

"When it comes time to eat, bring your biscuits over here and we can eat at my table."

"All right. I better go clean up the feathers and bring in my pan."

A short time later, Gus finished the cleanup and went out to get some wood. He carried in one armload and returned for another. As he approached the back door, he heard something. *Sounds like a team and wagon. I wonder who that could be?* He went inside and unloaded the wood and hurried to the front door. As he poked his head outside, the wagon came to a stop. Gus smiled. "Well, hi Mansel! I didn't expect to see you for a couple of days, yet."

"Hi, Gus." Mansel released the reins.

"You've got a full load there."

"Gosh, they told me you needed extra wood. I figured you must be gettin' low."

"It's to replace what we used for barter. We probably had enough to last a couple of days."

Mansel started climbing down from the wagon. His hair and beard were gray and his beard long enough that it touched the front of his denim jacket. He wore a red and black checkered hat. His teeth showed yellow from smoking the pipe he held in his mouth. Mansel shook hands with Gus. "Now you guys won't have to worry about running out of wood. Where's Wyatt?"

"I thought you knew! Wyatt was killed in that bad storm we had."

"Gosh, I'm sorry, Gus. No one told me. How are Elizabeth and the children doing?"

"The last time I talked to them they were doing as well as could be expected, under the circumstances. You probably don't know that Elizabeth and the children moved to Scottsburg."

"I really feel bad about Wyatt. I really liked that guy. He was a gem. Gosh, I'm gonna miss him and little Rusty. I got a kick out of Rusty. He always wanted to help me unload the wood, so I would pick out a few of the smaller pieces and let him carry them into the woodshed."

"You're not the only one who misses them. I didn't know how much they meant to me until they were gone."

The front door opened and Jesse stepped outside.

"Come here Jesse. I want you to meet Mansel Carter. He's the man who brings our wood."

Jesse moved down the stairs.

"Mansel, this is Jesse Fayette—my new assistant keeper," Gus said.

Mansel shook his hand. "It's good to meet you, Jesse."

"Same here, Mr. Carter."

"Just call me Mansel."

"I heard voices so I came out to see who was here. Gus told me you would be bringing wood, but I thought you'd be a much younger man."

"Gosh, a man's thoughts can sometimes lead him to the wrong conclusion."

"I didn't mean that you're old, but I—"

"I better get this wagon unloaded." He turned and climbed back up to the seat of the wagon.

"I'll see you before you leave," Gus said.

"Gosh, I hope so." Mansel picked up the reins and drove around to the woodshed.

Jesse frowned. "I feel like I insulted Mansel. I really feel bad about what I said to him."

"He's a tough old guy and it'll take more than that to get him upset. Now, I better get started on my biscuits or they won't be done in time for dinner."

"I've got everything else started, but I still have to fry the chicken. I'll have it ready by the time you make the biscuits."

Both Gus and Jesse returned to their respective kitchens.

***

As Gus was preparing to put his biscuits in the oven, he heard a knock on the door. It was Jesse.

"Come on in."

"How many biscuits are you making?" Jesse asked.

"A dozen or so. I like the leftovers. Why do you ask?"

"Well ..." Jesse rubbed his forehead. "I was thinking. With all your biscuits and everything else I've fixed, we have enough to share with Mansel. Would you care if I invited him to stay for dinner?"

"I don't care, but he'll probably say no."

"I'll go ask him."

Jesse went back to his quarters for his coat, and then went out to the woodshed. He met Mansel at the back of his wagon as he was loading another armload of wood.

"You need wood?" Mansel asked.

"No. We were wondering if you would like to eat with us. I'm frying chicken for dinner."

"Thank you, but I better not."

"After handling all that wood, you have to be hungry. We have plenty, but maybe you don't like fried chicken?"

"Gosh, I guess I could eat a piece."

Jesse nodded. "Good. When you finish unloading the wagon, tie your team over by the barn and come on inside. Dinner is almost ready."

"Thanks. I won't be much longer."

Jesse returned to the house and told Gus that Mansel would be joining them. "As soon as your biscuits are done bring them on over. Mansel's almost finished."

Gus shook his head. "I never thought he would say yes. He always seems to be in a hurry."

A short time later, Jesse looked out his front window and saw Mansel coming.

"Mansel's here," Jesse said. He opened his door into the hallway just as Mansel came through the front door of the lighthouse.

"Come on in." Jesse stepped back, enabling Mansel to enter. On the way to the kitchen, Jesse pointed to a chair. "You can throw your coat and hat there."

"Glad you decided to eat with us, Mansel," Gus said.

"Everything is ready and on the table," Jesse said. "You can wash up over there." He pointed to a pan of water.

After Mansel washed his hands he stepped over to the table.

"You sit here, Mansel." Jesse pointed. "Gus you can sit there at the end." Jesse sat down at the side of the table. "Dig in before it gets cold. Gus, you may have to pass the gravy and mashed potatoes. I don't think Mansel can reach 'em."

The men dug in without saying anything for a couple of minutes.

"Wow!" Gus said. "This sure is good fried chicken. It's the best I've had in a long time!"

"Thanks," Jesse said. He turned toward Mansel. "What do you think of those biscuits?"

Mansel looked away from the table, then back at Jesse. "Gosh, for a young fellow, you bake a pretty good biscuit, but a few more years of baking and yours can be as good as mine."

Jesse grinned and looked at Gus, then back at Mansel. "Well, I can't take credit for the biscuits. Gus baked these."

Mansel closed his eyes, then opened them, looking at Gus. "Gosh, I'm sorry, Gus. I thought Jesse baked 'em."

Jesse sat up straight in his chair and looked at Mansel. "A man's thoughts can sometimes lead him to the wrong conclusion."

Mansel scratched his beard, looked back at Jesse and chuckled. "You're a pretty sharp fellow. Gosh, I guess the laugh is on me." Mansel reached for another biscuit. "This is very good food and I really appreciate you guys asking me to share your table."

"We're glad to share it with you," Gus said. "But I'm curious. Wyatt asked you several times to eat with him and Elizabeth, but you always turned them down."

"I felt uncomfortable around Elizabeth. You know—well—gosh—she's a real lady and has a lot of class. I was always so scruffy and dirty when I got here. I felt she was embarrassed to be around an old coot like me."

"I know Elizabeth pretty well," Gus said. "I agree she has class, but she would never treat anyone that way. Remember what you told Jesse earlier about a man's thoughts. You know, we can't always judge a person's qualities by their exterior appearance. For example, the first time I met Jesse, I thought he looked like a kid. However, I soon found out he wasn't a kid. He's carried his share of the work around here like a man, not to mention that he's also a good cook." He laughed.

"I appreciate that," Jesse said.

"Gosh, you may be right," Mansel said. "I could have been wrong about Elizabeth."

By now they finished eating.

"That sure was a good meal," Mansel said. "I haven't eaten like that for a long time."

"We're glad you liked it," Jesse said.

"I don't like to eat and run, but I do need to get going. Thanks again." Mansel pushed his chair back from the table.

"You're welcome," Jesse said. "Have a good trip."

Mansel picked up his coat and hat, and walked to the door.

"Take care, and thanks for the wood," Gus said.

Gus and Jesse returned to the kitchen. "I better get this cleaned up." Jesse said. "Do you want a piece of this chicken to take with you?"

"Sure! Do you want any of these biscuits?"

"Yeah. You know, I think Mansel has a different opinion of Elizabeth than he did before, thanks to you Gus."

"At least I found out why he always said no to Wyatt and Elizabeth's invitation to eat with them."

After they finished the dishes Gus picked up his food. "I'll take this stuff over and put it away. Maybe I'll read some more of that book you gave me."

"I'm going up to get the light ready. I hope it's a good night. It's sure been a good day.

Chapter 9

The Knife

SEVERAL WEEKS LATER, Jesse was in the lantern room preparing the light for operation that evening. He pulled the lens cover off, and as he laid it aside, he glanced outside. *It looks like it's going to blow up another rain out there.* He opened the lens and started trimming the wicks. *This wick looks like it needs to be replaced.*

He finished trimming the other wicks, and then removed the one burnt out. He took the empty oil can downstairs and out to the oil house. Returning to the workroom, he picked up a new wick and went up to the lantern room. He started to install the new wick in the lamp, but struggled for a couple of minutes with the wick. *There must be something wrong with this wick. It doesn't want to go in.*

Jesse started down the stairs. As he did, it started to rain. He knocked on Gus' door. After several seconds of no response, he knocked again.

"I'm coming." Gus opened the door looking sleepy-eyed. "I was reading and fell asleep in the chair."

"Sorry to wake you Gus, but I'm having trouble with a new wick I tried to install. I can't figure out why it won't go in."

Gus rolled his eyes. "Well, let's go take a look at it." As they started up the stairs he asked, "Is this the first time you've had to replace a wick?"

"I've changed one before, and when I took this one out, I tried to pay close attention so I would know how the new one should go in. But for some reason it won't go in."

They entered the lantern room.

"It's raining again," Gus said.

"It's been raining for a few minutes, but not hard."

They moved in front of the lantern and Gus leaned in closer to the burner head. He pulled the new wick back out, and then looked down into the channel that was holding the wick. "I see the problem."

"What's wrong?"

"There's a piece of the old wick still in the channel. That channel has to be clear before the new wick will go in. When this happens, you have to take your pen knife, or something strong and slender, and slide it under the wick to pull it out."

"I don't have a knife anymore," Jesse said.

"I'll use my knife this time. In the future, there's a small knife hanging down in the workroom." Gus pulled out his penknife and worked the blade under the old wick and pulled it out. He handed it to Jesse. "Now watch. This new wick should go right in here with no problem." Gus finished installing the new wick and turned toward Jesse. "Why don't you carry a knife anymore?"

"I've carried a Barlow knife since I was about six years old. However, I gave it to little Rusty when we were at the Landing."

Gus frowned. "Why in the world would you give your knife to Rusty?"

"I guess I was trying to cheer him up. I kind of took a liking to him. While we were talking, I told him he had to be a big boy now and be the man of the family. I showed him my knife and told him that only big boys can handle one of these. I asked him if he thought he was a big boy. He said yes, so I gave him my knife."

Gus rolled his eyes then closed and latched the lens. "Did Elizabeth know you gave Rusty the knife?"

"Yeah, she was standing right there with us. I looked at her to get her reaction before I gave it to him. She smiled and nodded, so I knew it was all right."

"That was good of you, Jesse."

"Thanks, but there have been a couple of times since then that I've had second thoughts about whether or not I should have given him the knife."

"Why?"

"That Barlow was special to me. My father gave it to me and it had a white bone handle." Jesse started down the steps.

"Now I understand why you've had second thoughts. However, you may have helped Rusty better handle his father's death."

"I hope you're right."

A few minutes later they arrived in the workroom while the rain continued outside.

"Thanks for fixing my wick problem," Jesse said.

"Glad to help, Wickie. Now if it happens again, you'll know how to fix it."

Jesse smiled. "You know, that's the first time you've called me Wickie."

"I know, but you've earned the name. You're doing a good job."

"Thanks, that means a lot to me."

Gus pointed to the tools on the wall. "There's that knife I told you about." He stepped to the workroom door and opened it. As they walked down the hall back to their quarters Gus said, "The rain sounds like it's coming down harder. I hope it stops by feeding time."

"Yeah. In the meantime, I'm going to read."

"If I can stay awake, I may read too," Gus said.

***

Later that afternoon, Jesse was sitting in his chair reading when he was interrupted by a knock on the door.

"Jesse, are you awake?" Gus asked.

Jesse jumped up and opened the door.

"I'm going out to feed," Gus said. "If you want, I'll feed Molly. There's no sense of both of us getting wet."

Jesse rubbed the side of his face. "Like you said once before, it's my horse and I have the responsibility to take care of her. If anything, I should do the feeding and let you stay in."

Gus shook his head. "Well, I guess we're both going to get wet."

"I'll get my raincoat and catch up to you."

Gus walked out into the pouring rain. *Seems to me it's raining harder, but the air sure smells fresh and clean.* He hurried to the barn to get out of the rain, and started feeding. A couple of minutes later Jesse opened the barn door, and darted inside with water running off his raincoat.

"I think it's raining harder than it has all afternoon," Jesse said.

"I agree."

Jesse finished feeding Molly. "Let me give you a hand with the rest of the feeding."

"I'll make you a deal. You gather the eggs, and I'll finish my feeding."

"All right." Jesse walked to the back end of the barn and picked up a small basket and started checking the nests for eggs. Five minutes later he finished gathering the eggs and went back with Gus. "I only gathered six eggs."

"We ate one of the egg layers. That's why you didn't get the usual seven eggs."

Jesse nodded. "I forgot."

Gus walked to the barn door and opened it. "We may as well get back to the house, but watch your step. With all this rain the water could have made some new holes or trenches." He closed the barn door behind them, and as they hurried back to the lighthouse, they had to step over a few pot holes filled with water. Once inside, Gus and Jesse stamped their feet and shook the water off their raincoats.

"Since we only have six eggs, I'll take three," Gus said. "That'll give me enough for breakfast."

Jesse reached in the basket. "I can get by with two eggs if you'd like four."

"Three are enough."

Jesse took three eggs and handed the basket to Gus.

As Gus opened the door to his quarters he said, "I'll see you at midnight."

"All right." Jesse entered his quarters and put the eggs in the kitchen.

Ten minutes later he started his night of work. Throughout the night it continued to rain. Jesse and Gus each worked their shifts without any incidents and noted this in the record book at the end of their shifts. By the time Gus shut down the light at daylight the rain had stopped.

Later that morning, Gus and Jesse finished feeding the animals and were walking back to the lighthouse. Gus pointed to the ground off to the left. "The rain has made some new gullies. That one goes toward the back of the lighthouse. I want to see what it looks like there."

"I'll go with you."

They waded several puddles to get around to the back of the lighthouse.

"Oh, no!" Gus said. "That's what I was afraid would happen. Too much water running through here, and it washed some of the soil away that we just hauled in here."

"Will it affect the foundation?"

Gus shook his head. "Not sure, but it's disgusting. In such a short time, part of our work has been washed out to the river. If the erosion doesn't get any worse, maybe the foundation will be all right."

"I'm glad to hear that."

"We'll have to watch and see what happens. For now, I'm going into the house and have another cup of coffee." Gus started toward the back door of his quarters then turned toward Jesse. "Just a reminder, we're due for a delivery of stores and oil, today."

"What time will they be here?"

"They usually come between 1:30 and 2:00 p.m."

"I'll be ready.

***

Gus was reading when he heard a voice from outside the lighthouse.

"Hold up there, boys!"

Sounds like our delivery is here. Gus laid his book down on the lamp stand and went over by the door and grabbed his coat and hat. As he entered the hallway, Jesse was also coming out of his quarters.

"Is this our delivery?" Jesse asked.

"Yeah. The way Wyatt and I usually handled these deliveries was that he helped unload one wagon while I helped with the other one. I'll give you your choice. Do you want the oil wagon or the stores wagon?"

"It makes no difference to me."

They walked down the front steps of the lighthouse and approached the wagons. They exchanged greetings with Alex and Jim.

"Fellows, I want you to meet Jesse, my new assistant keeper."

"Hi Jesse, good to meet you," Alex waved.

"Morning," Jim nodded at Jesse, then looked back at Gus. "Before I forget, I have a letter for you from Elizabeth." He leaned down from the wagon seat and handed the letter to Gus. "Elizabeth gave it to me just before we loaded on the boat."

"Thanks, this is a pleasant surprise." Gus placed the envelope in his coat pocket. "I'm looking forward to reading it, but we better get this stuff unloaded first. He turned toward Alex. "Jesse will work with you and I'll work with Jim."

"Jesse, climb up here," Alex said. "You can ride around to the oil house with me."

As Alex and Jesse pulled away, Gus and Jim started unloading the wagon of stores and carried them into the hallway of the lighthouse. About an hour later, both wagons were unloaded and the empty oil cans were loaded on Alex's wagon.

When they finished, Gus asked, "Would you fellows like a cup of coffee before you leave?"

"We need to get back to the Landing, so we'll have to pass this time," Jim said. "But thanks for the offer."

The men said their goodbyes and parted ways.

Jesse brushed the side of his face. "Gus, I know you're anxious to read the letter from Elizabeth. I'll go up and check the lookout and leave you alone for a few minutes."

"Thanks. When you get back, we'll divide these stores and put them away."

"Sure thing." Jesse headed toward the tower.

Gus went to his quarters and sat down in his easy chair, then lit his pipe. He pulled the letter from his pocket and opened the envelope. A few minutes later, he finished reading it and laid it on the lamp stand. He sat there reflecting on the letter for a few moments and enjoyed his pipe.

Jesse knocked. "Gus, I'm ready to work on those stores!"

"Be right there!" Gus laid his pipe down and walked out to the hallway.

"Is everything all right with Elizabeth and the children?" Jesse asked.

"Yeah. She said her and the children are adjusting to their new home. She wrote that she's learning her new job at the hotel, and is settled in. She said that although she's busy working, she still misses Wyatt a lot. She wanted to know if the marker had been placed on Wyatt's grave. Elsie started going to school. Elizabeth said to tell you that Rusty is very proud of his new knife. He shows it to everyone, and passes a lot of his time by carving."

Jesse grinned. "That's good to hear."

"You did a good thing when you gave Rusty your knife." Gus pointed to the stores. "We better get this stuff put away. Let's roll that barrel of flour into your pantry. You use more than I do. We'll split the beef, pork, rice, beans, potatoes, coffee, laundry soap, stationary, and the brooms and mops."

Jesse picked up an odd-looking bundle of paper. "What's this?"

"That's what our toilet paper looks like when we get it." Gus grinned then pointed to other items. "That's the Brilliant Shine we use for polishing the brass. It goes in the workroom along with those bundles of rags over there."

Gus and Jesse continued storing the items until everything was put away.

Chapter 10

An Inspection

FOR THE NEXT several months, work at the lighthouse was pretty normal. Jesse was feeling good about the job he was doing and liked his work. One morning he walked out the front door and headed for the barn to hitch Molly to the buggy. A few feet away from the front steps he stopped when he saw a man approaching on horseback.

The man rode up to Jesse and stopped his horse. "Morning. Are you Jesse?"

"Yeah." *I never saw this guy before. How does he know me?*

The rider dismounted and stepped toward Jesse. "I'm Tyler Bronson from the Lighthouse Board. I'm here to do an inspection."

"All right, but how did you know me?"

"Process of elimination," Mr. Bronson said. "I knew you weren't Gus or Wyatt, so I figured you had to be Jesse."

"Oh, I see. Hold on Mr. Bronson; I'll get Gus."

Jesse turned and started up the front steps just as Gus stepped out the front door. "Gus, I was coming to get you. Mr. Bronson is here from the Lighthouse Board."

"Hello, Mr. Bronson. I figured we were about due for another visit. Let's take your horse to the barn before you get started."

Gus turned toward Jesse. "I know you were going to the Landing, but I need you here for this inspection."

"That's fine. I've been looking forward to this."

Gus and Jesse went to the barn with Mr. Bronson while he stabled his horse. After he finished, Gus asked, "What do you want to look at this time?"

"I'll start with the woodshed, then the outside of the lighthouse before I move inside."

They walked over to the woodshed.

"It looks like you're in good shape for wood," Mr. Bronson said. "Did Mansel deliver the extra wood?"

"Yeah. His wagon was full this time," Gus said.

As Mr. Bronson walked toward the lighthouse, he looked at the side of the house and tower. He was silent until he moved around the corner of the lighthouse. "This appears to be where the foundation was damaged."

"Yeah," Gus said.

Mr. Bronson pointed to the cavity, then looked around at Gus. "I thought there was an exchange of wood for use of a wagon to haul dirt to backfill this cavity?"

"Mr. Bronson, we hauled almost two wagon loads of dirt and had all this filled in," Jesse said.

"Like Jesse said, this was filled in before the last rain, then, it washed out part of the fill."

"I understand," Mr. Bronson said. "I just didn't realize the foundation was undercut that much." He walked around the rest of the lighthouse and finished outside. "I'm ready to go inside."

They entered the workroom.

"I'd like to look at the record book," Mr. Bronson said.

Gus picked up the book from the table and handed it to him.

Mr. Bronson opened the book and began reading through some of the entries. He frowned.

Jesse rubbed the back of his neck and looked at Gus.

Gus cleared his throat.

Mr. Bronson leafed through several pages before he made any comment. "According to this, you had more damage to the lighthouse than just the foundation. This entry says the tower moved. Is that correct?"

"Yes sir," Jesse said. "I felt it move."

"As a result of the tower moving, we also had to repair a bad leak in the roof," Gus said.

Mr. Bronson flipped back a page. "Yeah, I read about the leak. Is that what the pitch was used for that you charged at the general store?"

"Yeah. You know about that?" Gus asked.

"The board approved payment of that some time ago."

"Oh," Gus said.

Mr. Bronson closed the record book and handed it to Gus. "Have you been getting your supplies delivered on time without any problems?"

Gus nodded as he laid the book on the table. "Oh, yeah. The deliveries are always on time and they include most everything we need."

"That's good to hear. Now, I'd like to take a look at the tower and lens."

Gus and Jesse followed Mr. Bronson up the tower's narrow winding stairway. Mr. Bronson walked slowly up the steps, looking at the condition of the tower walls. He made no comments. They continued up the stairs to the watch room. Mr. Bronson inspected the clock mechanism and remained silent. Gus and Jesse stayed in the watch room while Mr. Bronson climbed on up to the lantern room and inspected the lens, the burner head, and the windows of the lantern room. He returned to the watch room and met up with Gus and Jesse. "Let's go back outside. I want to look at the oil house."

"Sure," Gus said, leading the way to the stairs.

When they were outside, Mr. Bronson turned toward Jesse. "How do you like your job? You've been here almost a year already."

"I like it and Gus has been great to work for. I'm glad to be working here."

They arrived at the oil house and found the door open about four inches.

Mr. Bronson pulled the door open wide, walked inside, and looked around. He came back out the door and looked at Gus. "That door should be kept locked to prevent theft of our oil, and to help keep animals out of here."

Gus frowned and nodded.

Jesse stepped forward and locked the door.

The three men began walking toward the front of the lighthouse.

"Mr. Bronson, what else do you want to look at?" Gus asked.

"I'm finished with my inspection, and as usual most everything looks pretty good. I only found three items that need attention. The oil house door being left open and the paint that's peeled off the west end of the barn. Do you have paint to take care of that?"

"No," Gus said.

"I'll have some sent out on a future delivery. The third item is the water that runs off the hill back there. The way it washed away the dirt from under the foundation, I think the board has to get someone out here to change the grade of the land at the bottom of that hill to divert the runoff away from the lighthouse."

"That's a good idea," Gus said.

Mr. Bronson began walking toward the barn. "Gus, keep up the good work, and Jesse you pay close attention to Gus. He'll teach you how to be a good keeper."

"I know what you mean, Mr. Bronson. He's already taught me a lot."

"I'll see you next time," Mr. Bronson said.

Gus opened the barn door while Mr. Bronson walked his horse out.

"I'll try to get the board to take action on that grade work as soon as possible." Mr. Bronson mounted his horse and rode off down the road.

Jesse turned toward Gus. "Man! He sure doesn't say much while he's inspecting."

They started walking toward the lighthouse.

"He's always been that way," Gus said. "I learned a long time ago not to talk to him while he's doing the inspection. He gets upset, so I'm glad you held your tongue. Anyway, before long we'll have some painting to do. As far as the oil house, it's my fault for not telling you that we have to keep that door locked."

"It won't happen again, Gus." Jesse opened the front door of the lighthouse. "I'm going to grab something to eat, and then go to the Landing to trade books with Alice. Do you need anything while I'm there?"

"Nothing I can think of. I'm going fishing, and that's all I want to think about right now." Gus started to open his door then turned toward Jesse. "Well, you could tell Alice I appreciate the books."

"Sure." *It seems like such a long time since I've seen her. I hope she'll have time for me.*

Chapter 11

More than Books

JESSE RODE UP to the front of the Landing office, dismounted, and quickly tied Molly to the hitching rail. He entered the office and found Alice leaning on the counter with her head down. She glanced up at Jesse and he greeted her with a smile. "Hi, Alice, it's sure good to see you again."

"Hi, Jesse," she said in a low tone with a frown on her face.

Jesse reached for Alice's hand. "What's wrong?"

"Mr. Watson died and his wife, Nellie, is selling the general store."

"Oh, I didn't know that. I'm sorry about Mr. Watson. I didn't know him very well, but I liked him. Why are you so sad about Mrs. Watson selling the store? It would be a big responsibility for her to run that store by herself."

"Yes, but if she sells the store she'll probably move away. She's the only woman around here who I can talk to."

"How's she taking his death?" Jesse asked.

"Actually, for several years Mr. Watson has been mean to her, so I don't think she's grieving very hard. Daddy is over there right now trying to help her any way he can."

"That's good," Jesse said. "At least she'll know that she has some support."

"I probably shouldn't tell you this, but I think Daddy has liked Nellie for quite some time."

"That's interesting. Maybe your father will talk her into staying."

"Gee whiz! I never thought of that, but I hope you're right." Alice smiled. "You didn't come here to listen to my problems. How can I help you?"

"I don't mind listening to you." Jesse reached in his coat pocket. "In fact, I use these books as a reason to come here and talk with you."

Alice smiled and looked Jesse in the eye. "I'm glad you do."

They chatted for a few more minutes and exchanged books. Sensing her openness to the idea, Jesse leaned forward and kissed her on the cheek. "I really have to go now. I have first shift."

"I understand. Come back soon."

Jesse went outside to his buggy. He started to pull away when he saw Gunther coming with his team and wagon. He pulled back on the reins and stopped Molly. "Hello, Gunther, I didn't expect to see you."

"Good to see you. What brings you to the Landing?"

"Reading materials. How about you?"

"I came to pick up the marker for Wyatt's grave," Gunther said.

"Gus received a letter from Elizabeth the other day, and she was asking about the marker."

"It will be taken care of within a day or so. Tell Gus I'll write to Elizabeth."

"All right, Gunther. I need to get back to the lighthouse."

"Oh! I haven't had a chance to tell you how good your pie was. Thanks."

"Glad you liked it." Jesse waved and drove away.

***

Jesse arrived back at the barn, unhitched Molly, and put her in the barn. He went to the lighthouse and knocked on Gus' door. "Gus, it's me."

"Come on in."

Jesse stepped inside. "I just got back from the Landing, and I saw Gunther. He said he picked up the marker for Wyatt's grave and he will write to Elizabeth."

"That's strange. Just before you knocked, I was thinking of

going to Gunther's tomorrow. I was writing a letter to Elizabeth, so now I can tell her that Gunther has taken care of the marker, and she'll be getting a letter from him."

"It's funny how things work out." Jesse pulled a book from his coat pocket. "I got you another book."

Gus nodded and took it.

"Well, I'll leave you alone. I want to get started trimming the wicks for tonight." He turned to leave, then stopped. "Oh! I almost forgot to tell you. Alice told me Mr. Watson died, and his wife, Nellie, is selling the general store."

"What? I never knew him to ever be sick. How did he die?"

"Alice told me he died in his sleep more than a week ago."

"We never know when it's going to happen."

"Yeah," Jesse went to his quarters.

***

Six months later, on one of many trips Jesse had made to see Alice, he tied Molly to the hitching rail and walked toward the front door of the Landing office.

Alice came out with a big smile on her face. "Oh, Jesse, I'm so glad you're here."

"Well, you certainly look cheerful today."

"You were right about Daddy. He not only talked Nellie into staying, but he asked her to marry him. They were married day before yesterday."

"I wasn't thinking of marriage as a way for him to talk her into staying. What do you think about them getting married?"

"The timing was a surprise, but I knew he felt something for her. I like her. Daddy's happy, so I'm happy for him."

"Did Nellie sell the store?"

"A man by the name of Potter from California bought the store about a week ago."

"Sounds like everything is working out," Jesse said.

"It's strange. Only a few months ago I thought I was going to lose my friend. Instead, my friend became my stepmother." She smiled.

"I guess you'll get some help now with the cleaning and cooking."

"Yes. Nellie started helping almost immediately after she moved in."

"That takes a worry off my mind," Jesse said.

"Why would you worry about Nellie cooking and cleaning?" Alice asked.

"I haven't been worrying about Nellie. I was worried your father depended on you so much that you would say no."

Alice put her hands on her hips. "What are you talking about? Say no to what?"

"How would you feel about living in the lighthouse?" Jesse asked.

"What?" Alice lowered her hands.

Jesse took Alice by the hand. "I love you and want you for my wife. Will you marry me?"

"Oh, Jesse. I love you too, but I'm not sure I'm ready to get married. This is so sudden."

"I think about you all the time."

Alice lowered her head. "I need more time to think about it."

Jesse lifted Alice's chin with his finger. "All right, but how much time do you need?"

"I'm not sure … a few weeks, maybe."

"I'm willing to wait." He gently pulled Alice close to him and kissed her.

She pulled away. "Jesse! Everyone will see us."

"I don't care. I love you and you make me so happy." Jesse kissed her again.

"I love you, too. Now, I better get back inside. I promised Nellie I would help her bake bread for supper." Alice turned and walked back toward the office.

"I love you, Alice! I'll be back soon."

***

Jesse returned to the lighthouse and entered the front door. As he started to enter his quarters, Gus stepped into the hallway.

"You're back just in time."

Jesse's eyes widened. "Time for what?"

"We're going to clean the lens this afternoon?"

Jesse shook his head. "Oh! I forgot."

"It appears that you have your mind on something else. Anyway, you're back, so we need to get started."

"I'm ready, Gus."

They entered the workroom and picked up cleaning brushes and other materials before they climbed up the stairs to the lantern room. Gus pulled the lens open and looked inside. "It looks like we also need to trim these wicks while we're here."

"Should we trim the wicks before we clean the lens?"

"You trim the wicks, and I'll start cleaning the outside of the lens. After you finish, then you start cleaning the inside of the lens."

"All right, Jesse said."

For several minutes, the only sounds that could be heard were those of Gus and Jesse working. Then, Jesse broke the silence. "Gus, is there a church around here?"

"The closest church is in Gardiner's City." Gus grinned. "Are you figuring on going to church?"

"I just wanted to know where I could find a preacher."

"Sounds like your trips to the Landing have developed into more than just a book exchange."

"I've been in love with Alice for several months. I've wanted to ask her to marry me, but I knew she probably would say no, because she had to take care of her father. You know, she does all the cooking and cleaning?"

"I don't think Lloyd will let Alice go. She does an awful lot to help him at the Landing."

"That has changed. There's something I haven't told you about Lloyd."

"What's that?" Gus' eyes widened.

"Lloyd got married."

"He got married! To who?"

"Nellie Watson."

"Well, I'll be switched," Gus said. "That sure is a surprise."

"Yeah, it was for me, too, but it was great news."

"Have you and Alice set a date?"

"Alice wants to think about it, but I believe she'll say yes."

"Do you love her enough that you could spend the rest of your life with her?"

"Oh, yeah." Jesse smiled. "I think about her all the time."

"I see." Gus nodded. "That explains why you haven't had your mind on things around here the last several weeks."

"You may be right."

They finished cleaning the lens and picked up the cleaning materials.

"Do you mind if I get married?" Jesse asked.

Gus chuckled. "I don't mind. In fact, I'm glad for you and Alice. This reminds me of when I was trying to get up the nerve to ask Martha to marry me." They walked down the stairs and Gus asked, "Do you mind if I make a suggestion?"

"No, I respect your opinion."

"First, you might want to ask Lloyd if you can marry his daughter. That'll start you out on the right foot with him."

They arrived in the workroom.

"Thanks, I sure don't want to get sideways with her dad."

***

A week later, Jesse drove back to the Landing, and when he entered the office, he found Lloyd standing in front of the counter. "Good morning, Mr. Harvey. Congratulations on your marriage to Nellie."

Lloyd smiled. "Well, thank you Jesse. Nellie is a fine woman, and I'm a very lucky man.

"Is Alice here?"

"Yeah, she's in the back with Nellie. I think Nellie is showing her how to use the spinning wheel. I'll get her."

A couple of minutes later Alice came out by herself.

Jesse moved toward her and greeted her with a kiss. "Is there some place where we can go that is more private?"

Alice's face was beaming. "We can go outside, but I need to tell

Daddy I'll be gone for a few minutes."

"All right."

A couple of minutes later they walked outside holding hands. When they arrived at the back of the building Alice said, "I didn't expect you back this soon."

"I couldn't wait any longer. These last few days have been really long for me." Jesse's eyes lit up. "You're all I think about."

Alice smiled. "Well, I've thought a lot about you too, and I've also talked to Daddy about us. I'm not sure he'll allow me to leave."

He stroked her hair. "Alice, I love you so much. Your daddy has to let you go. Let me worry about him. Right now, my question is, will you marry me?"

"Yes, I love you, too, but Daddy will be upset with us."

"Don't worry about your father." Jesse held Alice in his arms and pulled her close as he kissed her with compassion and tenderness.

When they released their embrace, Alice looked at Jesse. "I think this is the happiest I've ever been in my life."

"I'm so happy that I feel like my chest is going to burst. I'll be even happier if your father gives us permission to marry." Jesse kissed Alice again. "Let's go talk to him."

"I hope Daddy is in a good mood."

They entered the front door of the Landing office, and Alice's father was standing next to the counter. "What have you two been up to?"

Jesse scratched his brow. "Uhh … Mr. Harvey, I need to talk to you."

"What's on your mind, Jesse?" Lloyd asked.

"Well … Mr. Harvey, I love Alice and she loves me. We want to get married, so … I'm asking your permission to marry her."

"Why should I let Alice marry you?"

Jesse looked down at the floor and then back at Lloyd. "I love her and I'll be good to her. I have a steady job and a good place for us to live. A few weeks ago, I knew you wouldn't have let Alice marry me. But now, you have someone to take care of you."

Lloyd didn't say anything for a few seconds. He looked at Alice.

"Do you really love Jesse?

"Yes Daddy, I do."

"Well then, I hope the two of you will be as happy as Nellie and me."

Jesse's eyes lit up and a big smile came over his face. He shook Lloyd's hand. "Thanks, Mr. Harvey!"

Smiling from ear to ear, Alice hugged her father around the neck. "Yes, Daddy, thank you. I love you."

As Alice hugged her father, Nellie walked into the room. "What's all the hugging about?"

"Nellie, come here," Lloyd said. "You're just in time to congratulate Alice and Jesse. They're getting married!"

Nellie approached Alice with outstretched arms and hugged her. "I'm so happy for both of you." She released Alice, turned toward Jesse, and hugged him. "When's the big day, Jesse?"

He was still blushing from the hug. "Well, Alice and I haven't had time to talk about that yet."

"Nellie, we better leave these two love birds alone so they can make plans." Lloyd said. They wandered off toward the back room.

"Thanks again, Mr. Harvey. I promise to take good care of Alice," Jesse said.

Lloyd turned. "You better, or you'll hear from me."

As soon as Lloyd and Nellie left the room, Jesse embraced Alice.

"Jesse, I love you."

"I love you too and I think we should get married as soon as possible. I'll talk to Gus and find out if I can get away from the lighthouse day after tomorrow. We'll get married in Gardiner's City. Is that all right with you?"

"Yes." Alice touched his cheek.

"Can you be ready around 8:00 a.m.?"

Alice frowned. "Well, yes, but why so early?"

"I'm anxious."

"So am I, but the boat won't get here until about 12:45," Alice said.

"Well, then we'll go in my buggy."

"But there's no road from here to Gardiner's City."

"Oh, that changes things," Jesse said. "Can we get back here on the boat the same day we're married?"

"No, the *Melissa* only docks here once a day."

"Oh man!" Jesse rubbed his forehead. "That means we'd have to stay overnight."

Alice blushed. "What's wrong with that?"

Jesse reached for Alice's hand. "Honey, I can't ask Gus to stay up all night to work my shift and his too. He told me there was a preacher in Gardiner's City, but he didn't say anything about me being gone overnight. I had this all planned out in my head, but now I'm not sure what to do."

"I just got an idea."

"What is it?

"Daddy and Nellie got married right here in the Landing office. We could do the same."

Jesse smiled from ear to ear. "That's a great idea." Then his smile disappeared. "But who would marry us?"

"We can do what Daddy did. Send a telegram to the preacher in Gardiner's City and ask him to come here and marry us."

"Let's do it!"

Alice went to the back room and returned with her father. He walked over to the telegraph key and was about to send a telegram when Jesse stopped him.

"Mr. Harvey, tell the preacher I'll pay for his expense of coming here in addition to his charge to marry us."

Lloyd sent the telegram. "You may not get a reply until tomorrow."

"That's all right." Jesse grinned. "This will be better than me having to be gone overnight from the lighthouse. I'll come back tomorrow to check on a reply."

"While we wait to find out, we can go ahead and make plans to move," Alice said.

"After we're married, we can take a few of your things with us to the lighthouse. Then later, we'll come back and pick up the rest of it."

"I don't have much, but you're right; it won't all fit in your buggy." Alice turned toward her father. "Daddy, could you haul my stuff in the wagon?"

"Sure," Lloyd said.

"That would be great, Mr. Harvey." Jesse turned toward Alice. "You know I don't have much furniture either. We can get more later on, if you want."

"I'm not worried, we'll get by."

Just then a man walked in the front door of the office. "Morning," Lloyd said. "Can I help you?"

"I need to find out when the boat leaves for Scottsburg," the man said.

Lloyd took care of his customer while Jesse pulled Alice aside.

"I need to be going," Jesse said to her. "Will you step outside with me?"

Alice took Jesse's hand.

Outside, Jesse turned toward Alice. "I love you." He pulled her to himself and kissed her. "I hate to leave."

Alice's face beamed. "I love you, too."

They walked to his buggy. "I'll see you tomorrow."

"All right, but you be careful."

Jesse picked up the reins. "I'm sure glad you thought of having the preacher come here."

"Me, too," Alice said. She waved as Jesse drove away.

***

Jesse returned to Harvey's Landing the next afternoon for a response to his telegram. Preacher John Haley wrote that he would be happy to perform the marriage ceremony the following day.

Chapter 12

A New Beginning

JESSE ARRIVED AT the Landing office the following day for his wedding to Alice. In addition to the preacher, witnesses included Lloyd and Nellie, and Ike and Seth who both worked for Lloyd at the Landing. Both men were accompanied by their wives.

Jesse stood with Preacher Haley and the other witnesses in the office. He was dressed in a dark frock suit with a white shirt and black bow tie.

At one side of the room, Ike was playing his guitar while they all waited on the bride. A couple of minutes later, Nellie said, "Here comes the bride."

Alice was holding on to her father's arm as they entered into the Landing office through the back-room door. Alice wore her late mother's long-sleeved white dress. Her brown curly hair flowed from under her little white hat and glistened against her dress trimmed in lace around the collar and sleeve ends. She carried a small bouquet of dried flowers that Nellie gave her. They stepped across the room and stopped in front of the preacher.

"Who gives this woman to marriage?" Preacher Haley asked.

"I do," Lloyd said. He took Alice by the arm and gently handed her over to Jesse. Lloyd joined Nellie

Alice and Jesse looked at each other.

Preacher Haley glanced at the two of them. "You ready?"

They nodded.

"Beloved, we're here to join Jesse Fayette and Alice Harvey in holy marriage. If there's anyone here who has just cause why these two should not be married, speak now or forever hold your tongue." Preacher Haley looked around the room and then opened his Bible. "From the book of Genesis, we know God created Adam and then He created Eve for him from Adam's rib. Reading from chapter 2:23 of God's holy word.

"And Adam said, 'This is now bone of my bones, and flesh of my flesh: she shall be called Woman, because she was taken out of Man. Therefore, shall a man leave his father and his mother, and shall cleave unto his wife: and they shall be one flesh.'"

Preacher Haley looked up from his Bible at Jesse. "Do you, Jesse, take Alice to be your wife, and do you promise to love and protect her as long as you both live?"

"Yes"

"The ring."

Jesse pulled a ring from his coat pocket.

"Take Alice's left hand and place the ring on her finger."

Jesse held Alice's hand. He put the ring on her ring finger, but the ring was too big, so he slid it onto her middle finger.

"Repeat after me," Preacher Haley said. "This ring symbolizes our unending love.

Jesse repeated the words after the preacher.

Preacher Haley looked toward Alice. "Do you, Alice, take Jesse to be your husband, and do you promise to love and protect him as long as you both live?

"Yes"

Preacher Haley closed his Bible. "I now pronounce you husband and wife. What God has joined together, let no man take apart. Jesse, you may kiss your bride."

Jesse kissed Alice and when they pulled apart, he whispered, "I'll get you a ring that fits."

"This one still symbolizes our love."

Lloyd stepped forward and hugged Alice. "Honey, you remind me so much of your mother in that dress. I'm very happy for you, and I hope you and Jesse will be happy."

At the same time, Nellie hugged Jesse. "Congratulations, Jesse. I wish you and Alice a long and happy life together." She released Jesse, then hugged Alice. "You are such a beautiful bride, and you are lucky to have Jesse."

Alice's face beamed with joy. "I think so, too."

Lloyd shook hands with Jesse. "Congratulations, Jesse. Alice will be a great wife. She's a good woman and a hard worker. You take care of her."

"I know. Don't you worry."

After everyone had congratulated the bride and groom, Nellie said, "Could I have your attention please. We have cake and coffee back in the kitchen. You're all invited to help us celebrate Alice and Jesse's wedding."

Lloyd pointed to the door leading back to the kitchen. "Follow me, and let's go eat some cake."

After they arrived in the kitchen, Jesse approached the preacher. "I want you to know I really appreciate you coming here to marry Alice and me." Jesse handed the preacher some money. "Count this to be sure it's enough to pay your expenses and your fee."

"I'm sure it's all right," Preacher Haley said. He pushed the money down inside his pants pocket. "I was glad to do it, Jesse. I enjoy performing marriages."

"Did Lloyd tell you where you'll be staying tonight?" Jesse asked.

"Yeah, with Seth and his wife. I stayed with them before when I came to conduct Wyatt Saunders' funeral."

"Gus told me about Wyatt," Jesse said.

Preacher Haley frowned. "I felt bad for the children."

"I know what you mean. I didn't know them very long, but long enough to know they were taking their father's death very hard."

Nellie approached with the coffee pot. "Preacher, would you like some more coffee?"

"No, but thank you. I've had enough for today."

"Coffee, Jesse?"

"I'm full. Thank you, Nellie for all the work you've done for this reception today, especially for baking the cake."

Nellie smiled and looked Jesse in the eye. "You're welcome. I enjoyed doing it."

Jesse turned and set his cup on the kitchen table. He approached Alice and put his arm around her waist. "Could I have your attention. Alice and I want to thank you for coming to help us celebrate this special day in our lives. We especially thank Preacher Haley for putting himself out to help us." Everyone applauded. "I hate to break this up, but Alice and I need to get on to the lighthouse."

Lloyd approached Jesse. "I'll have Ike and Seth load the rest of Alice's things in the wagon, and they'll follow you later."

"I sure thank you, Mr. Harvey. That'll be a big help to Alice and me."

Jesse and Alice went to her bedroom and picked up a few items that she and Nellie had packed that morning. They walked out the front door to load the items into the buggy and everyone started throwing rice on them.

They arrived at the buggy and Lloyd approached Alice. "Ike and Seth will be along in the wagon with the rest of your stuff as soon as possible. Now, when they arrive, you'll find a few extra things in the wagon from Nellie and me."

Alice's smile broadened. "Extra things?"

As Nellie arrived holding a dish, she patted Alice on the arm. "Yes, you know I had extra dishes and furniture after your father and I got married. We have more than enough for us, so that's our wedding gift to you."

"Thank you." Alice hugged Nellie. "You and Daddy have been so good to us. That's the nicest wedding gift anyone could get."

Nellie smiled. "You're welcome, Alice. We just want you to be happy. And here's the rest of your cake."

Jesse helped Alice climb up into the buggy. They said goodbye to everyone, and Jesse drove off toward the lighthouse.

***

A short time later, the lighthouse came into view.

"This is the first time I've seen the lighthouse up this close," Alice said. "It is so beautiful with the river in the background, and the white tower reaching toward the blue sky."

"Yes, I remember the first time I saw it. I was amazed at its beauty and character." Jesse turned in the seat toward Alice. "I hope you like it inside."

"I'm sure I will."

They pulled up in front of the lighthouse. Jesse climbed down from the buggy and hurried around to the other side to help Alice down.

The front door of the lighthouse opened and both Gus and Gunther came out smiling. Everyone exchanged greetings, and Gus and Gunther congratulated the newlyweds.

Gunther, how did you know Alice and I were getting married today? Jesse asked.

"I came over the other day to visit with Gus and he told me what you'd planned."

"This is a pleasant surprise," Jesse said.

"Yes." Alice said.

"I wanted to be here with Gus to welcome Mr. and Mrs. Fayette to their home."

Alice looked at Jesse. "That sounds strange. I'll have to get used to hearing that name."

"I like the sound of it," Jesse said. He took Alice by the hand. "Mrs. Fayette, would you like to see the inside of your new home?" They arrived at the top of the front steps, and Jesse turned toward Alice. "I hear a team and wagon coming. I can't believe Ike and Seth are here already.

Seth pulled the team to a stop. "Hello, everyone."

"Hi, Seth. What brings you here? Gus asked.

"We have a few furniture items from Lloyd and Nellie," Ike said.

Gus nodded.

"Now that everyone knows why we're here, where do you want this stuff unloaded?" Ike said sarcastically.

"Don't get excited, Ike! Seth said. "Can't you see these kids haven't even got in the house yet?

Jesse waved. "It's all right, Seth. We need to get inside."

"If we all pitch in, we'll have the wagon unloaded in no time," Gus said.

Jesse reached down and picked Alice up in his arms and walked into the lighthouse.

"Oh, Jesse!" Alice said.

Jesse opened the door to his quarters and carried Alice inside. As they entered the sitting room he stopped. "Honey, welcome to your new home."

"I love you, Jesse, and I know we'll be happy here. I already feel at home." She kissed him.

Their kiss was interrupted by a knock on the door.

"Jesse, Alice, we have your furniture," Gus said.

Alice and Jesse ended their kiss, and Jesse lowered Alice down to the floor. "Come on in, Gus!" Jesse said.

"Alice, you tell us where you want the furniture placed and we'll put it there for you."

"Well, I'm not sure. I haven't been here before, so I don't know the house."

"I'll help you, honey," Jesse said. "You name the room where you want each piece of furniture placed, and I'll tell them where to take it. Later, you and I can straighten it out"

They worked out the furniture situation, and in a short time Gus and the others completed unloading the wagon. As Seth and Ike set down the dresser, Seth said, "That's the last piece. Since it's fixing to rain, Ike and me better get back to the Landing. I wish the two of you a happy life together."

"Me, too," Ike said. They moved toward the door.

"Thanks, guys," Jesse said. "We sure appreciate everything you've done for us."

Seth and Ike departed.

Gus turned toward Alice and said, "Welcome to your new home. I hope you and Jesse will be very happy here."

"Thank you, Gus."

Gus winked at Gunther. "We need to get out of here and let these two have some time alone."

Gunther grinned. "Yeah."

They moved toward the door and Gus stopped. "Jesse, I'll take care of your horse and buggy.

"Oh! With all that's been going on, I forgot about Alice's items in the buggy."

"I'll take care of them," Gus said.

"Thanks," Jesse said.

Gus and Gunther left the room.

Jesse turned toward Alice and put his arms around her waist. He drew her close to him, kissed her and said, "I love you so much, Alice."

"I love you too. I'm so happy you came into my life." Alice jumped as thunder clapped.

He held her. "It's all right, honey."

"I have always been afraid of thunder and lightning."

Jesse released Alice. "I'll light the lamp; it's beginning to get dark in here."

A knock at the door. "Jesse, Alice, it's me."

"Come in, Gus," Jesse said.

Gus and Gunther both entered carrying items.

"Oh, no." Alice said. "What are you men up to?

"We have some wedding gifts for you," Gus said.

Gunther handed a blanket and a wash tub to Alice. "These are from me. I hope they will make your life together warmer and easier."

Gus moved a baby crib and a spinning wheel closer to Alice. "Jesse mentioned that you were learning to use the spinning wheel, so I thought you might be able to make good use of this one. As far as the baby crib, well, I know you two don't need it right now. But maybe you can use it sometime down the road."

Alice's face got red. She looked at Jesse and then looked back at Gus and Gunther. "Thank you both so much. This was very sweet of you men to think of us."

Jesse nodded. "We really appreciate the gifts and your

thoughtfulness."

"You're welcome," Gus said. "It's not much, but we wanted to give you something to help celebrate your new beginning."

They shook hands with Gus and Gunther.

Gunther turned toward Gus. "I better get going."

"Could you stay longer?" Gus asked.

"For what?"

"I need your help to carry dinner over here for Alice and Jesse."

"You've fixed dinner, too?" Jesse asked.

"Gus, you didn't have to do that." Alice said. "I was going to make something for Jesse and me."

"You'll have plenty of meals to fix from now on, but this one is on me." Gus said.

Alice smiled. "This is a pleasant surprise."

"I'll stay and help," Gunther said.

Gus looked at Jesse. "All you have to do is set your table for two, and we'll take care of the food."

Gus and Gunther moved toward the door.

"We'll be back in a few minutes with dinner," Gus said.

"We'll be waiting," Jesse said. He turned toward Alice. "I hope you don't mind eating off my dishes." He moved to the kitchen and took dishes from the cupboard and placed them on the table. "Honey, these aren't very good dishes, but they're all I've got."

"Don't worry. They're fine. When we get time to unpack, we'll have more dishes that Nellie gave us. Tell me where you keep your utensils, and I'll set the table."

"In there." Jesse pointed to a drawer.

Gus and Gunther returned and each one was carrying a kettle of food, which they set on the table.

"There's more, so we'll be right back," Gus said. "Oh! You'll need to fix yourselves something to drink."

Alice picked up the lid on one of the kettles. "That pork roast looks and smells so good."

Gus smiled. "Thanks, there's biscuits in the other kettle." He and Gunther hurried out and returned a few minutes later with mashed potatoes and gravy. "Well, that's all the food. You two enjoy the meal and your time together." They moved toward the door and Gus stopped. "Oh, I almost forgot. I want you to take the second shift tonight. That'll give you and Alice more time together before you have to start back to work."

"I'll see you at midnight and I appreciate you doing this for me and Alice. Thanks again to both of you for everything you've done."

"Yes, thank you so much," Alice waved. "This was so sweet of you men."

Gus and Gunther went back to Gus' quarters.

***

"Well, I better get going," Gunther said. "It won't be long 'till feeding time."

"Hey, it's still raining hard out there," Gus said. "Stay and have dinner. By the time we finish eating, maybe the rain will at least have slowed down. I have enough food."

"Well, you talked me into it, but after dinner, I'll have to leave regardless of the rain."

They sat down, ate dinner, and talked about events of the day. The rain continued to fall but finally slowed to a drizzle.

Gunther pushed his chair back from the table. "Thanks, Gus. This has been a great afternoon. I'm glad you asked me to come and be a part of Jesse's wedding day."

"I think it meant a lot to Jesse and Alice."

Gunther put on his raincoat and shook hands with Gus. "I'll see you later."

"All right, but you be careful going home. There's been a lot of rain out there."

"I'll be fine," Gunther said.

Gus closed the front door and headed back to his quarters. *I better go up and check the lookout.* He went up to the lantern room and looked out toward the mouth of the river and scanned the area for any ships that may be in distress. *Everything looks good out there. I better get back and wash those dishes.*

He walked down to the workroom and made an entry in the

record book before going to the kitchen. After finishing the dishes, Gus settled down in his easy chair enjoying his pipe. His eyes welled up, and a tear trickled down his cheek. *I remember the day Martha and me got married. She was so beautiful and we were so much in love. We were very happy. I thought we would be together forever.*

Gus wiped his eyes. *It's almost feeding time. I hope the rain stops soon. The foundation concerns me. That last rain wasn't as hard as this one and it didn't last as long, but it still washed a good-sized gully through the dirt Jesse and I hauled in. When I go out to feed, I better check the foundation.* For a short time, Gus read his book and smoked his pipe, then laid them on the lamp table. *Well, I can't put off the feeding any longer, rain or not.* He moved by the door, put on his coat, and went over to Jesse's and knocked.

After a short time, Jesse opened the door. "Hi, Gus." Alice and I washed your kettles. We were about to bring them back to you."

"I stopped to tell you I'm going out to feed, and I'll take care of Molly. As for the kettles, just set them on my counter."

"Sure. I feel guilty about you going out in this rain to feed my horse."

"I won't make a habit of this. You enjoy your evening." Gus moved toward the front door.

"Thanks, Gus."

Gus hurried to the barn while trying to dodge big puddles of water. He fed the animals, gathered the eggs, and headed toward the back of the lighthouse. Suddenly, he changed direction. *I better take these eggs to the kitchen, first. Can't chance getting any broke. Jesse will need more eggs now.* Gus arrived in the kitchen and placed the eggs in a dish on the counter. *They left me a piece of cake. I'll eat it after I look at the foundation.*

Gus went to the back of the lighthouse and his suspicions were confirmed. *The gully under the foundation is bigger than it was before.* He shook his head. *I think Tyler Bronson's idea of changing the grade of the land around here may be the solution to the problem. I just hope the board doesn't wait too long. It won't do any good to haul in more soil. It will just wash into the river again at the next big rain.*

Gus went to his quarters to rest until time to light the tower lantern.

Chapter 13

Wedding Night

JESSE AND ALICE sat in the sitting room talking about their wedding day, the gifts, and the meal Gus prepared for them. A short time later, Jesse reached out his hand. "Alice, come sit on my lap."

Alice got up from her chair and moved to Jesse's lap. From time to time they would stop talking, and kiss. They told each other how much they loved one another. After a while, Alice got up from Jesse's lap and walked to the other side of the sitting room. "Would you show me around the lighthouse? I haven't seen all the rooms, yet."

"Sure. The rooms aren't very big, but I think we'll be comfortable here." Jesse took Alice by the hand and walked her into the bedroom. "This bed is really comfortable. Do you want to lie down and try it?"

"Well, yes, but … not now."

They moved into the second bedroom. "These rooms aren't very big, but I like them." Alice said. "I think we'll be very comfortable." She touched the curtains. "Did you put these up?"

"Elizabeth left them, but we can redecorate. Someday, this can be our nursery."

"Sure." Alice smiled. "Now that I've seen our home, could I go up in the tower? I've been watching the light from the Landing every night for a long time. I'd like to see it up close."

"Sure, come with me." Jesse took Alice by the hand, and they went to the workroom to begin their walk up the tower steps. "Honey, get ready for a long hard climb."

"Why do you say that?" Alice asked.

"We have 120 narrow steps to climb before we get up to the lantern room. The first time I climbed these stairs my legs were hurting, and I was short of breath. If you need to, we can stop and rest on the way up, or if you want, I could carry you."

Alice chuckled. "If you climbed up by yourself, I can too."

"All right. I'll go first, but if you need to stop and rest, let me know."

They climbed about halfway up the stairway then Alice stopped him. "I need to stop and rest. Now I know what you meant about a hard climb."

"You want me to carry you the rest of the way?"

"No way. I'll be fine. I just need to rest my legs. It's amazing to me how these steps spiral up along the inside of these walls."

"Yeah, somebody worked hard to build these."

A minute or so later, they continued climbing up the stairs until they arrived in the watch room. Jesse showed Alice the clock mechanism and explained how it worked, then they climbed up to the lantern room.

As they entered, Alice turned up her nose. "What's that awful smell?"

"That's whale oil in the reservoir, honey."

Alice stepped over to the windows. "Oh, my! The water looks so beautiful from here. The river looks like it just disappears into the ocean waves. This is spectacular. It's such a fantastic view."

"You're right, and you can see a lot further now that it has stopped raining. I remember the first time I came up here with little Rusty. My first look over the river and ocean that day was very special for me. It was my first time to see the ocean."

"It's my first time, too. Maybe that's why it's so spectacular." Alice turned away from the windows. "Could I see the light?"

Jesse frowned. "I can't really show you the light because the burner is not lit. But I can show you the lens which projects the light coming from the burner head when it's lit." He removed the cover from the lantern.

"That's a beautiful piece of glass." Alice ran her fingers across one of the prisms.

"It sure is. Gus told me it's a third order Fresnel lens, made in France." Jesse opened the lens. Here is the burner head."

"So, that's what makes the light?"

"Yeah. I won't light it now, but sometime when I'm working you can see it burning."

"I'm looking forward to it," Alice said.

Jesse closed the lens and put the cover back on before they went down the stairs to their quarters.

"It sure smells better in here," Alice said.

"Yeah." Jesse put his arms around Alice and hugged her. "It will take awhile for you to get used to that smell up there. It did me. Anyway, right now I don't smell anything but you, and you smell wonderful."

"I don't think I'll be going up there very often." Alice giggled. "You're tickling my neck."

"Are you ready to try your new bed?"

"Well, … later." Alice grinned. "I could use some coffee. I'll make it, and that'll help me get acquainted with the kitchen."

"Let's have another piece of cake with our coffee."

"That'll be easy to fix," Alice said.

Jesse sat at the kitchen table and watched Alice fix the coffee and cut the cake. "I like the way you move around in the kitchen. You look so comfortable and in charge."

"All I did was make coffee and cut some cake. That was easy. I may not look so comfortable when I have to find food in the pantry."

***

Jesse finished his coffee. "That was excellent. It looks like I not only got a beautiful wife, but also a wonderful cook."

Alice blushed. "Mother taught me how to make coffee, and since she died, I've had lots of experience cooking and making coffee for Daddy."

"Before your father married Nellie, I knew he wouldn't have let you go."

"You may be right." Alice got up from the table. "I better get these dishes washed. It's getting late."

Jesse reached over and gently took Alice by the hand as she started to clear the table. "Honey, there are only a few dishes. Can you let them go 'till later? You still haven't lain on the bed to see if you're going to like it."

"After I do the dishes, then the bed. I have a thing about leaving dirty dishes sitting around."

While Alice washed the dishes, Jesse interrupted her with a kiss every so often, and they talked about how much they loved each other. By the time Alice finished the dishes it was dark outside.

Jesse took her by the hand and gently pulled her close to him. He kissed her, picked up the lamp, and walked her to the bedroom. Jesse set the lamp down on the stand next to the bed. When he turned around, Alice was standing at the foot of the bed. He reached out to her. "Honey, don't be afraid. Come lie down and try the bed." He held her hand as she stepped forward and sat down on the edge of the bed. "It's comfortable, isn't it?"

"Yes."

Bam! Clang! Rattle!

Alice jumped up and grabbed Jesse around the neck. "What's that?"

"I'm not sure. It's coming from in front of the lighthouse." Jesse's heart pounded as he held Alice closer. "I'll go check." He picked up the lamp and Alice followed him into the sitting room. "That rattling sound is coming from something rubbing against the window. I can see a lantern and someone moving around out there. Why can't they leave us alone? I'll bet it's a *chivaree*."

"You may be right. I remember that sound from the night daddy and Nellie got married. It sounds like someone is banging kettles with sticks and slamming pan lids together.

"I'll try to get rid of them."

"It's probably Daddy and some of the people from the Landing."

Jesse opened the front door of the lighthouse and the noise stopped. He stood in the doorway and could see Lloyd and Nellie, as well as Ike, Seth, and their wives in the light of their lanterns. "Well, this is unexpected. What brings you all here tonight?"

"We came to help you celebrate your wedding night," Lloyd said.

Jesse rubbed the back of his neck. "Well, we don't really need help, but come on in."

As they all filed into the hallway, everyone was smiling, laughing, or jesting in some way as they shook Jesse's hand, and then blew out their lanterns. They followed Jesse into his quarters where Alice greeted each one with a hug. "If I had known you were coming, I could have made a cake or something. I don't have anything to eat, but I could make some coffee."

"We've all had our fill of coffee and cake," Nellie said. "We came to celebrate the two of you and help you remember this night."

"We wish you the very best in your marriage," Lloyd said.

"Well, thanks," Jesse said. "I just can't figure out how you arrived without Alice or me hearing you drive up."

"We tied the team and wagon to a tree down the road and then we walked the rest of the way." Lloyd grinned.

"Oh, I see," Jesse said.

"Well, Alice how do you like your new home?" Nellie asked.

"It's different than I'm used to, but I already feel very comfortable."

Someone knocked on the door. Jesse answered it. "Hi, Gus, come in and join friends and family."

"I was up in the tower and saw the lights coming up the road. I heard all the noise, so I thought it might be a *chivaree*." Gus entered the sitting room. "I just wanted to take time to say hi to everyone. Except for Ike and Seth, the rest of you have never been to the lighthouse. It's good to see everyone here."

They were all joyous and visited with each other over the next hour.

"Well, I need to get back to work, so I'll say good night," Gus said.

"I think we should leave also," Lloyd said. "We've accomplished what we came for, so we'll leave you two alone."

"Yeah, let's go," Ike said.

Ike's wife nudged him with her elbow. "You're always in a big hurry."

"We didn't expect to see any of you tonight, but it was very nice of everyone to think of us," Alice said.

"Yeah," Jesse stood ready to close the door.

Lloyd grinned. "Now, you two have a good night."

Everyone filed out the front door and said good night

Alice moved toward Jesse. "You know, when Gus said he had to get back to work, it reminded me that you have to relieve him at midnight. You aren't going to get much rest. It's already 9:00."

"I'll be all right. I may be able to take a couple of catnaps during the night, and that'll help me get through."

"I hope you're right, but we should go to bed now so you can get some rest."

They went to bed and talked about how different but wonderful it was to lie next to each other. They cuddled and enjoyed each other's company. After a time, both drifted off to sleep.

***

A little after 11:30 p.m., Jesse's alarm clock rang. He got up and lit the lamp, then dressed to go relieve Gus. He stepped around to the other side of the bed and kissed Alice on the cheek. As he did, she opened her eyes.

"Is it already time for you to go to work?"

"Yes, but you go back to sleep. I'll see you in the morning. I'll leave the lamp here for you and I'll use a candle to light my way to the workroom."

Jesse went to the kitchen and added more wood to the stove, and then warmed up some left-over coffee. *This sure tastes good, and I need it to help me stay awake.* After Jesse drank a few sips he went to the workroom to relieve Gus.

"Hi. I bet you didn't get much sleep."

"Not much." Jesse rubbed his eyes and then stretched his arms.

"You're young. You'll recover. I remember my wedding night with Martha. She was so soft and beautiful. I'll never forget that night." ... Gus stared off in the corner then looked back at Jesse. "Except for your noisy visitors, it's been a quiet night. The equipment worked good and there's been no problems on the river."

"That's good to hear. Now, it's time for you to go get some sleep. I'll see you tomorrow."

"Sure thing, it's all yours." Gus stood up and went to his quarters.

Jesse worked through his shift that night and the equipment operated normally. There were no problems with the lookout. At daylight he shut down the light, and after making his entries in the record book, he returned to his quarters and found Alice in the kitchen already.

She stood there in a long blue robe, her hair pulled back with a blue ribbon. "Good morning, darling. Breakfast is almost done. By the time you wash up, it'll be ready."

Jesse walked to the kitchen. "Do I smell fresh coffee? He put his arms around Alice, and kissed her. "Honey, this is so nice to walk into the kitchen and you have breakfast ready. I've been used to fixing my own food. This is a real treat."

"I made you bacon, eggs, and biscuits to go with the coffee you smell."

"It all smells good," Jesse washed his hands. "Thanks, darling."

Jesse sat down at the table and started to eat. "I came in about 3:00 a.m. for another cup of coffee, and you were sound asleep. Did you sleep good?"

"Oh, yes. I was so relaxed when I fell asleep last night. I slept like a baby until I woke up a little before 6:00. I got right up because I wanted to have your breakfast ready."

Jesse grinned. "You were so warm and soft last night. I didn't want to take my hands off you, but I knew I had to go to sleep."

"After breakfast, you should go back to bed and get more sleep to make up for last night."

"I may take a nap later on, but first I have to take care of

Molly."

They finished eating, and Jesse leaned over and kissed Alice. "That sure was a good breakfast."

"Thanks, darling."

Jesse pushed his chair back from the table to go to the barn.

"There is one thing you could do for me before you leave," Alice said.

"What's that, honey?"

"I would like the chamber pot emptied every morning and cleaned. It'll make it more pleasant to use at night, and will help keep the odor to a minimum in the bedroom."

"I'll take care of it." Jesse walked to the bedroom and took the chamber pot out with him as he went to the barn.

Chapter 14

The Fatal Blow

ALMOST THREE YEARS passed and everything at the lighthouse was running smoothly. Gus was happier than he had been since Wyatt's death. Jesse and Alice were happy and their love for each other grew stronger every day. At least once a month, Alice would cook extra food and invite Gus over to share the meal with her and Jesse. During this time, Jesse and Alice returned to the Landing now and then to visit with Lloyd and Nellie. On one of the trips, Jesse got Alice another ring at the general store. They continued to get reading materials that Nellie received from Scottsburg.

One morning in October 1864, Gus and Jesse finished feeding the animals, and were on their way back to the lighthouse. Gus pointed to the sky. "Wickie, it looks like another storm is coming,"

"The wind is starting to make white caps on the river."

"Since the Lighthouse Board hasn't done anything yet to change the contour of the land, we don't need any more heavy rains."

They entered the front door of the lighthouse.

"Good thing we finished out there when we did," Jesse said. "It's starting to rain."

"I need to bring in more wood before it gets any worse."

"That's a good idea. I'll get my raincoat and get some, too."

***

"Wickie, we need to clean the lens this morning," Gus said as they walked in the back door with their second armload of wood.

"After I dump this load in my wood box, I'll meet you in the workroom."

They picked up the materials in the workroom they needed to clean the lens. After climbing the stairs, they entered the lantern room.

"It's raining twice as hard out there now as it was when we carried in the wood," Jesse said.

"Yeah." Gus laid down his cleaning materials next to the lens. "Go ahead and pull the cover off, and I'll open the lens."

Jesse laid his materials down. "Do you want me to clean the inside of the lens?"

"Yeah. You've been doing a good job in there. I'll clean the outside."

***

"It's a good thing we're almost done," Jesse said. "Those clouds are so black that it's hard to see in here."

"I don't like the looks of them, and that wind has really picked up."

Lightning flashed and thunder rumbled as they finished cleaning the lens. They replaced the cover and carried the cleaning supplies back downstairs to the workroom.

"We could be in for trouble if this storm gets worse," Gus said.

"This is the worst storm we've had since I've been here."

The rain continued to fall in torrents.

Gus frowned. "It's bad out there, but it's still not as bad as the storm back in sixty-one that took Wyatt's life. Let's stop for now 'cause we need to keep an eye on this storm."

"Good." Alice is afraid of lightning, so she'll be glad when I get back."

"See you later, Wickie."

***

Alice jumped up from her chair as Jesse walked into the sitting room. She greeted him with a hug. "Honey, I'm scared! This storm is bad."

"It's all right. I'm here now. We'll be fine."

"I had to light the lamp. It was getting so dark in here I could hardly see to knit."

"It did get dark fast. Gus and I had trouble seeing up there as we cleaned the lens."

Lightning flashed again and thunder roared.

Alice jumped.

Jesse reached out to her and held her close to him. "Honey, we're fine. We've seen lightning before." After comforting her, he sat down in his chair. "Let's have a cup of coffee."

"Do you hear that rain?" Alice asked as she got up to make the coffee. "It's raining much harder than it was before."

"Yeah, I hear it." He got up from his chair, and walked to the front window. "It's coming down in torrents. That wind must be blowing fifty miles an hour."

Jesse moved from the front window to the spare bedroom window where he had a better view of the river. *The waves are bigger and they're splashing over the river bank. If this continues, the water will spill out of its banks before long.* Jesse returned to the sitting room with Alice. "This is the worst storm I've ever seen. It's really bad out there."

Alice put her arm around Jesse. "It's as bad as the storm we had three years ago at the Landing."

A knock on the door.

"Jesse, Alice, it's me."

"Come in, Gus," Jesse said.

Gus stepped inside and closed the door. "The storm has gotten worse. I came over to tell you not to go outside for any reason. I don't want to lose you, too." He lowered his head.

"Don't worry, I'm not letting him go out in this mess." Alice held on to Jesse's arm.

"I know who you're referring to, Gus. I'll be right here. I was just looking out the window in the spare bedroom, and if the storm keeps up, the river is going to be out of its banks before long."

"That's what happened almost three years ago," Gus said. "With the river flooding and the water running off the hill, that's what washed the cavity under the foundation. There's nothing we can do now, except wait and see."

"Would you like a cup of coffee?" Alice started to move toward the kitchen.

"No, thanks. Think I'll try to read." Gus walked out.

Jesse shook his head. "I couldn't read with this storm raging."

"I'll try to fix dinner. We still have to eat."

***

After dinner, Jesse returned to the window in the spare bedroom to look at the river. Water was now overflowing the river banks and crashing against the back of the lighthouse. He walked back to the kitchen. "Honey, I'm going over and talk to Gus."

"All right, but whatever you do, don't go outside."

"I won't." Jesse stepped across the hall and knocked on Gus' door. "Gus, it's me."

"Come in," Gus said from his easy chair.

Jesse stepped inside. "Did you know the river is out of its banks and the waves are crashing against the back of the lighthouse?"

Gus walked to his kitchen window and looked out back. He frowned and held his chin. "The flooding is worse than it was three years ago. I'm afraid to think of what that foundation is going to look like when the water recedes."

Jesse pointed to the kitchen wall. "Look! Water is running in."

"It's going to be a mess in here, real fast. The tower must have moved again, or the wind has torn off the shingles where we repaired the roof."

"I'm going back to check my side of the house."

Jesse entered his sitting room, and Alice ran toward him. "I was just coming to get you. We have an absolute mess in the kitchen. There's water running everywhere."

"Oh, no! I better tell Gus about this. He has water leaking in his kitchen, too."

Alice stood with her palms out in front of her. "What are we going to do?"

"I'll be right back, honey, and we'll figure out something."

Jesse ran back to Gus' side. "I have water running in my kitchen, too."

Gus shook his head and put his hand on his forehead. "We've

got big trouble."

"The rain and the wind seem to have slowed."

"I hope it stops soon," Gus said. "Almost three hours of this torrential rain and wind has been too much for the foundation."

"I need to get back. Alice is upset about all the water."

"No use worrying about the water until the rain stops, Wickie. I think we are in for big trouble, and it's more serious than just cleaning up water. The tower must have moved more than the last time."

"What do you mean big trouble?" Jesse's eyes widened.

"The tower is ninety-two feet tall, and sixty-five feet of that is above the roof line of this house. Since the tower is no longer standing vertically straight, it may not have to lean very far before it tips over."

Jesse let out a breath. "I didn't think about that."

Gus grabbed Jesse by the arm. "You probably shouldn't say anything to Alice just yet. No sense worrying her."

"You're right. I better get back and help her with the mess."

Jesse returned to his quarters and found Alice holding a mop in one hand and her other hand on her hip.

"I've been working on this mess ever since you left. This is terrible. We can't live like this!"

"I know. The weather is getting better though. The rain is slowing and the wind is not as strong. That should give us a chance to make some progress in cleaning this up. However, the leaky roof is another problem. Gus and I were able to fix the roof the last time the tower moved, but he doesn't sound very hopeful this time."

"I don't want to live here if I have to mop up water every time it rains."

Jesse remained silent and continued to mop up water.

A little while later the wind subsided and the rain stopped. Jesse and Alice finished mopping up the water in their kitchen.

"Let's go over and help Gus with his clean up," Alice said.

"I'm sure he won't want our help, but we can offer."

They walked in with two mops and a bucket.

"We came to help you mop up the water, Gus," Alice said.

"I just started, so there's still lots of water," Gus said. "I appreciate your help." They began mopping. "Although the storm stopped, we are going to have to wait until the water recedes before we can go out back and check on the foundation. If we're very careful, we may be able to get to the barn to check on the animals and feed them."

"What about getting to the oil house?" Jesse asked. "The last time I looked out it was surrounded by water."

"We'll just have to wait and see if the water goes down enough that we can get in there by the time we have to light the lantern. There may even be enough oil left in the reservoir from last night to get through tonight."

Alice mopped up the last of the water in the pantry. "Do you think you and Jesse will be able to fix the roof?"

"I'll have to look at it first to see if it's something we can fix."

"I hope so," Alice said. "This is no way to live. We can't go through this mess every time it rains."

Gus nodded. "We'll just have to wait and see what damages there are."

"I understand," Alice said. "I know both of you will do your best to fix it, if possible."

"I'm going to the barn and check on the stock," Gus said.

"As soon as I help Alice with the bucket and mops, I'll go with you."

"Sure, I'll meet you in the hallway," Gus said.

***

They walked through shallow water to the barn and found it had been damaged. "Look Gus, three of the siding boards blew off the barn."

"Let's hope the animals are all right," Gus said.

They entered the barn.

"Molly looks all right," Jesse said. He rubbed his hand down her neck.

"Easy, boy," Gus said. He laid his hand on Jake's back as he was shifting his weight back and forth from one foot to the other. Gus reached for the halter and pulled Jake's head toward him so he could rub his neck and head. "Jake's still a little spooked from the storm."

"I'm just glad they're not injured. That was a bad storm."

"Yeah." Gus continued to rub his horse, and after a few minutes, they returned to the lighthouse and entered the hallway.

"I'm going up to the lantern room to see what the flooding looks like from up there," Jesse said.

"That's a good idea. I'll go up with you."

When they arrived in the lantern room, Gus stepped over to the windows. "Looks like the river flooded worse on the other side than it did three years ago."

"It does look bad out there. By the river flooding like that, it makes the ocean look like it moved in closer to the lighthouse.

"We better get back downstairs. With both of us moving around up here, it could cause the tower to move even more since it's already leaning off center."

"Since the tower is leaning toward the mouth of the river, will that change the distance that the light can shine?"

"That's a good point. I didn't think of that."

They started down the stairway a few steps and Gus stumbled.

"Watch out!" Gus yelled. He scrambled to recover his balance.

"Hold on Gus!" Jesse grabbed the handrail and recovered his balance.

"The tower moved!" Gus said. "That was bad! Now I know for sure, we've got a big problem."

"Are you all right?"

"Yeah, I am now," Gus said.

They crept down the steps toward the workroom.

"You know, being up there in the tower when it moved like that, gave me a sick feeling in my stomach," Jesse said as they entered the workroom.

"Me, too. I need to get a telegram to the Lighthouse Board as quickly as possible. I think this tower is unsafe, and it could tip over at any time."

"Do you want me to go to the Landing?" Jesse asked.

"No, I'll go. You stay here with Alice, but don't go back up inside the tower, even if I don't get back in time to light the lantern."

"I won't. And don't worry about the feeding. I'll take care of it."

Gus nodded. "I better get ready to go to the Landing. I want an answer back today, so I may be a while."

"You may want to take your lantern if you're going to be late. And be careful." He entered his quarters and was met by Alice.

"I heard you talking. Why is Gus going to the Landing?"

"He's wants to send a telegram to the Lighthouse Board about the storm damage."

"Does that mean he doesn't think the two of you can fix the roof?"

"I think so."

A few minutes later, Jesse and Alice watched from their sitting room window as Gus drove away from the barn.

***

Gus arrived at the Landing office and tied Jake to the hitching rail. He entered the office and found no one there, so he rang the bell on the counter.

In a short time, Lloyd entered from the back room. "Hi Gus. What in the world brings you out in this water?"

"The storm hit the lighthouse real hard. I need to send a telegram to Scottsburg."

Lloyd touched Gus on the shoulder. "Are Alice and Jesse, all right?"

"Oh, yeah, they're fine."

"I was concerned they may have been hurt in the storm. Now, about your telegram. Is this to the board?"

"Yeah. The message is: 'Severe storm hit lighthouse. Damage to foundation is fatal. Tower teetering and may fall. Request immediate instructions. Standing by for reply. Crosby.'"

"I'll send this right now. The telegrapher there in Scottsburg is very conscientious about his job. If it's possible, he will deliver your message immediately after he receives it."

"I hope so." Gus reached for his coin purse. "How much do I owe you?"

"Let's see here." Lloyd counted the words. "That's fifteen cents."

Gus paid him.

"Since you have to wait a while, how about a cup of coffee."

"Thanks, I could use one."

Lloyd went back to his kitchen, and returned with their coffee. "How are Alice and Jesse doing with the situation?"

"I think they're doing good, under the circumstances. Alice was upset because of all the water leaking into the house."

"What will happen to Alice and you guys if the lighthouse gets shut down?"

"To be honest Lloyd, I haven't thought that far ahead. Jesse and I haven't even told Alice how bad things really are with the tower. She only knows there's a problem with the roof leaking." Gus took a couple of sips from his coffee mug.

"I don't want to get in your business, but I know my daughter. Other than being afraid of lightning, she's a strong woman. She's been through a lot of hard times, so if you let her know there's a problem, she'll work with you to help get through it."

"It's my fault she wasn't told. I suggested to Jesse that we not tell her what really happened. I just didn't want her to worry."

Lloyd shook his head. "I know what you're saying, but you guys are being too protective of her."

The telegraph key began clicking and Lloyd started writing down a message. After the telegraph silenced, Lloyd turned and handed the message to Gus. "Here's your answer, and I think the board is asking an awful lot of you."

Gus read the telegram silently: 'If possible, remove lens and mechanism for use in another lighthouse. We'll pay for help. Advise board when removal is completed.' Gus shook his head. "I better get back. We've got lots of work to do." He pushed the telegram down in his trouser pocket.

"Maybe Gunther could help you guys," Lloyd said. "He told me a couple of days ago he hasn't been very busy."

"Thanks, I may ask him." He shook Lloyd's hand.

***

Gus drove back toward the lighthouse, and then turned on the road that led to Gunther's place. He tied Jake to the hitching rail, and knocked on the front door.

A few seconds later Gunther opened the door. "I sure didn't expect to see you this time of day. Come in. Is anything wrong?"

"Yeah, this storm hit us hard at the lighthouse."

Gunther frowned. "Was Jesse or Alice hurt?"

"No, they're in good shape," Gus said. "It's the lighthouse." He went on to explain the damage to the lighthouse, and the telegram he received from the board. "Could you help us with removal of the lens and clock mechanism?"

Gunther rubbed his ear. "Sounds like the job could be risky."

"Yeah, it could be."

"If you can take the risk, so can I. When do you want to start?"

Gus patted Gunther on the shoulder. "We'll start first thing in the morning."

"I'll be there as soon as I can after feeding the stock."

Chapter 15

Dangerous Work

BACK AT THE lighthouse, Jesse had finished feeding the animals and was back in his quarters reading. Alice finished washing the supper dishes and sat down to knit.

"Will you light the lamp?" Alice asked. "I'm having trouble seeing."

"Darkness seems to have come early tonight." Jesse got up to light the lamp.

"Gus is not back yet. Shouldn't you light the tower lantern for him?"

"No, he said to wait until he gets back."

That's odd. Ever since I've known this lighthouse, the light has always been visible every night around dusk. "Jesse, is there something you're not telling me?"

Jesse looked away and then back at Alice. "Well, ... Gus and I didn't want to worry you, but the tower has moved so much that the light probably won't shine to the mouth of the river, let alone out over the ocean. He believes the tower is unsafe."

"Is he trying to get someone to fix it?"

"To be honest, I don't know what Gus was going to say in his telegram."

"Well, if the tower is unsafe, I'm glad you're not going up there to light the lantern."

Jesse rose up from his chair. "I just saw Gus pull up to the barn. Now we'll find out what the board had to say."

Jesse and Alice waited patiently in the sitting room, and in a short time they saw Gus approach the front door of the lighthouse. Anxious to hear the news, they walked out to the hallway and met Gus as he entered the front door.

"Did you get an answer from the board?" Jesse asked.

"Yeah, but I'll tell you later."

Alice looked Gus in the eye. "Gus, I already know about the tower being unsafe. So, you don't need to talk behind my back."

Gus' eyes widened. "I'm sorry, Alice. I know from talking to your father I made a mistake by trying to protect you from the situation."

"I forgive you," Alice said. "Now, come in and sit down, and let's talk about this."

"I want to change out of these boots first and hang up my coat."

"When you finish, come on in," Jesse said.

A short time later, Gus returned.

"Come, sit here." Alice pointed toward a chair. "Would you like a cup of coffee?

"I sure would," Gus said. "Thanks."

Jesse rubbed his hands together. "I'm anxious to hear what the board had to say."

"We're faced with a very dangerous situation. As you know, the tower is unsafe. However, the board has directed us to remove the lens and clock mechanism. We'll start the job in the morning, as soon as we're done feeding. In fact, we need to get up early enough that we can start at daybreak. I have also asked Gunther to help us, and the board will pay him."

"Sounds like it will be dangerous work," Alice said.

"Yeah, there will be risks involved," Gus said.

"Well, regardless of the risks, I still want to help," Alice said.

"I need your help Alice, but in a different way. You would be of great help if you could take care of the cooking for all of us. This will enable me to work longer, because I won't have to stop and cook for Gunther and me."

"Would you like me to start with breakfast?" Alice asked.

"That would be great. I'll give you some of my stores, so you don't run short."

"How long do you think it will take us to complete the job?" Jesse asked.

"Four or five days, maybe. I figure at least three days just to disassemble the clock mechanism into small enough pieces to carry down the stairs."

"What happens after the lens and mechanism are removed?" Alice asked.

Jesse leaned forward in his chair. "That's a good question."

"To be honest with you both, it's not good." Gus took a drink of coffee and stared off into the distance. "I gave this some thought on the way back from Gunther's place. I think we'll have to move out of the lighthouse. The roof is already severely damaged, and if the tower should fall over while we're in here, it would be extremely dangerous. So, be thinking about where you can go."

Alice wrung her hands. "I'm not so concerned about where to go right now as I am about you guys working and moving around up there in the tower. Won't that increase the chances of the tower tipping over?"

"It could," Gus said. He drained the rest of his coffee. "We'll have to be very careful, and pray that our movements don't cause it to tip over while we're in it."

Alice shook her head. "It sounds so dangerous. More coffee, Gus?"

"Yeah, thanks."

"Will Gunther be staying over?" Jesse asked.

"He'll go home every night because he has to feed his stock, and I understand."

"Will we start by removing the lens first?"

"Yeah, and I want you to work on the lens while Gunther and I work on the mechanism."

"Where are we going to put the lens and mechanism after we get them down from the tower?"

"Well, it will be tight, but we'll put the pieces out there in the hallway to start with. As soon as possible we'll move them to the barn. I'm afraid to store them in both the workroom and the weight room. If the tower should fall, then the lens and mechanism would probably still be destroyed before we could find out what the board wants us to do with them. They said to let them know when removal is completed. I think they'll want the lens and mechanism shipped to Scottsburg for storage until the tower can be rebuilt.

"That all makes sense," Jesse said.

Gus got up from the chair. "Well, unless you have more questions, I'll see you two in the morning. Oh, thanks for the coffee Alice."

"You're welcome, Gus. Now, you get some rest."

"See you in the morning," Jesse said.

***

The next morning everyone got up early, as planned. Alice began preparing breakfast while Gus and Jesse went to the barn to feed the animals and gather the eggs.

They finished their chores and were headed back to the lighthouse when Jesse looked up and pointed to the tower. "Look, Gus, even from here you can see the tower is leaning toward the river."

"Yeah, I see. It's sad. You know, last night was the first night in seven years that the light was not lit." Gus' voice trembled. "To see it leaning is a hard reminder that our work up there is going to be dangerous."

"I remember how my stomach felt when we were in the tower and it moved. I'm not looking forward to working up there."

"Me either." Gus pointed to the eggs. "Don't drop those."

They entered the lighthouse and went to Jesse's quarters.

"Get washed up fellows, breakfast is ready," Alice said. "There are eggs, bacon, biscuits, gravy, and coffee."

"Sure smells good," Jesse said. He carefully laid the gathered eggs on the counter.

The men washed up and sat down at the table to enjoy breakfast.

***

After Gus finished eating, he slid his chair back from the table. "That was real good, Alice. Thank you."

"Yes, it was, honey." Jesse turned toward Gus. "I'll go up and get started on the lens."

Gus nodded. "I'll be right behind you."

"Jesse.... I know you're anxious to get started, but didn't you forget something?" Alice asked.

Jesse turned back toward Alice with his brows furrowed. "What did I forget?"

"The chamber pot."

"I'll take care of it right now." Jesse looked at Gus and grinned.

As Jesse returned from the outhouse, he saw Gunther coming with his team and wagon. Jesse entered his quarters. "Gunther is here."

"I'll go out and help him unhitch and stable his team," Gus said. "We'll meet you upstairs, Jesse."

Jesse took the chamber pot to the bedroom, and returned to the kitchen with Alice. "Sorry about the pot. I just wanted to start in the tower as soon as possible to get that job done."

"I understand, but we still live here, and that pot needs to be emptied every day."

"Sure." Jesse kissed her. "Now I better get to work."

He stopped in the workroom and picked up some tools on his way up to the lantern room. Jesse had been working on the lens for about fifteen minutes when he saw Gus and Gunther arrive below him in the watch room. "Good morning, Gunther."

"Morning, Jesse."

Gus looked up to the lantern room at Jesse. "Listen up. I want to emphasize to both of you, the importance of not making any quick movements or sudden stops up here. We need to be very cautious, or we could end up in the river inside this tower."

"Don't worry, Gus," Gunther said. "I'll move like I was walking on eggs."

Jesse waved down at Gus. "Me, too."

The three men continued through the day and the next with no problems. By the end of the third day, they were making good progress with disassembly of the lens and clock mechanism, and carrying the pieces down to the hallway.

***

"I should be able to finish with the lens this morning," Jesse said to Gus after breakfast on the fourth day. "Do you want me to start removing the burner unit next?"

"You might as well," Gus said. "Hopefully, Gunther and I can finish by the end of the day. Speaking of Gunther, I just saw him drive by the window going to the barn. He's right on time again today."

Jesse grinned. "He's in a hurry to get this job done."

"I know he doesn't like working under the constant threat of the tower possibly falling over, but neither do we." Gus walked toward the front door.

"That's for sure." Jesse moved over to where Alice was standing in the kitchen. She was holding her stomach. "Honey, what's wrong?"

"I'm just a little sick to my stomach."

"It's probably from worrying about our situation."

"You may be right." Alice kissed him. "Now, we should get to work. I have dishes to wash, and you have work to do in the tower."

"I love you. I hope you're feeling better soon."

"I hope so, too." Alice touched Jesse's cheek. "Now, you be careful up there."

Jesse walked out into the hallway still feeling the tips of Alice's fingers on his cheek. He arrived as Gus was greeting Gunther at the front door.

Jesse and Gunther greeted one another and the three of them crept up the narrow winding stairway toward the top of the tower. Gus and Gunther stopped in the watch room, while Jesse continued up the steps toward the lantern room. The moment his left foot touched the top step, the tower moved as if to teeter back and forth. Jesse gasped and grabbed the railing with both hands.

"Everyone stand still!" Gus said.

"It's going to fall!" Gunther grabbed Gus' arm.

"The foundation must have settled more during the night," Gus said.

They all stood still as Gus fixed his eyes on a big rock at the far side of the river bank for a reference point to determine additional movement of the lighthouse. They stared at each other, remaining silent for three or four minutes. "It hasn't moved anymore," Gus said. "Hopefully, it's done moving. Let's go to work, but move easy."

Gunther held the back of his head. "Gus, are you sure this thing isn't going to fall over?"

"I'm not sure, but I'd like to keep going. We're close to finishing the job."

"I don't like this," Gunther said. "My stomach is in my throat!"

"Me neither, but the job has to get done. If you can't work up here, I understand. Jesse and I will finish it by ourselves."

"Well … I don't like it, but if you've got the guts and loyalty to the board to keep going, I guess I'll stay.

Gus put his hand on Gunther's shoulder. "Thanks. With your help, we might be able to finish this by dinner time."

Jesse started disassembling the burner unit while Gus and Gunther returned to disassembling the clock mechanism. They all were careful and worked at a slow pace to prevent additional movement of the tower. After a few hours, Jesse had completed disassembling the lens and burner unit. Each time he carried the parts downstairs, he announced his descent to Gus and Gunther as he approached the watch room. "Coming through."

"How much longer will it take you to finish?" Gus asked after Jesse made several trips.

"This is the last of the burner unit," Jesse said. "I have to come back and pick up the tools,"

"When you come back, I'd like you to relieve Gunther."

"Sure," Jesse said. He continued down the steps.

"I told you I would stay," Gunther said. "Jesse can help me finish. We have to move all those parts that are downstairs in the hallway out to the barn. If you agree, we'll use your wagon to move everything out there for temporary storage. If you would, hitch up your team and start loading the smaller items in your wagon. It shouldn't take Jesse and me too long to finish up here, and then we'll be down to help."

"Don't you need my help to carry that drum and cable downstairs?" Gunther asked.

"Jesse and I can do it. Only the drum will have to be carried down. We'll unwind the cable and unfasten the end from the drum, then lower the cable down with a rope to the weight room floor. We can pick it up from there."

Gunther grinned. "Well, that will save a lot of heavy lifting."

They returned to work, and a few minutes later Jesse returned to the watch room and relieved Gunther.

An hour later Gus and Jesse finished disassembling the mechanism, and carried the last of the pieces down to the hallway. As they headed back through the weight room to go back up in the tower to get their tools, Jesse pointed to the floor. "That's a lot of cable when it's lying there loose like that."

"Yeah." Gus said. "But lowering it down like we did saved our backs."

A few minutes later they returned with the tools. "I'll be right back, Gus. I'd like to check on Alice."

"All right, but don't be long."

Jesse entered the kitchen.

"How are things going up there?" Alice asked.

"We've got everything down, and Gunther already started moving some of it to the barn." Jesse got a drink of water. "The real reason I came in was to see how you're feeling."

Alice smiled. "I'm feeling fine. Tell Gus dinner should be ready in an hour."

"That's good. Now I better get back to work."

Jesse returned to the hallway as Gus and Gunther picked up a larger piece of the clock mechanism.

"You're back just in time," Gus said. "Hold that door open for us."

"I'll prop it open until we're done," Jesse said.

"That's a good idea," Gus said. "Since Gunther has already carried out the lens and part of the burner assembly, it won't take the three of us long to finish in here."

"Alice told me dinner will be ready in about an hour."

"I'd like to get the rest of this to the barn and unloaded before dinner," Gus said. "It might take us a little longer than an hour. You should tell Alice."

"I'll be right back."

***

After Jesse returned, the three men loaded the balance of the burner assembly and clock mechanism into Gunther's wagon and headed for the barn.

They unloaded the wagon as quickly as possible. When they finished, Gunther said what they all had been thinking. "Well, Gus, we did it, but I have to admit I was scared to death up there a couple of times."

Jesse walked back to the wagon. "I was afraid too."

"That makes three of us," Gus said. "Hey, we better get this team unhitched, and go eat. Alice will be upset with us for being late."

"I'll be leaving for home right after we eat," Gunther said. "Let's just leave the horses hitched, and I'll give them some water before I go in."

"Sounds good, we'll help you," Gus said.

After watering the horses, they went back to the lighthouse. As they walked down the hallway toward Jesse's door, Gus stopped.

"You know, all at once it feels like the lighthouse is empty and has no spirit," Gus said. "It's as if her heart has been removed. It's sad. I've been here almost seven years, and it's like I just lost another friend."

Jesse opened the door to his quarters. "I have that same feeling, and I haven't been here but three years."

Alice met them as they entered the room. "Go wash up. Dinner has been ready for a time. If you don't eat soon, it's going to be burnt up."

Gus closed his eyes and shook his head. "Sorry we're late, Alice. It's my fault. I wanted to finish the job before dinner and with Gunther's help, we did."

Alice began placing food on the table. "I just wanted to serve you men a good meal."

The men washed their hands and sat down at the table. Jesse

passed the mashed potatoes to Gunther.

"Alice, I sure have enjoyed your cooking," Gunther said. He spooned out some potatoes. "This is the best food I've eaten in my life, except for maybe an apple pie Jesse gave me a few years ago. I will miss your cooking, Alice, but I won't miss working up in that tower."

Alice smiled. "Thank you, Gunther, I'm glad you like it."

"Gus, please pass Gunther the gravy," Jesse said.

Gunther took the gravy. "Now that the tower is unsafe, and the light has been removed, what are you guys going to do?"

Gus cleared his throat. "We agreed that we can't live here much longer. We haven't talked about specific plans. It really depends on the Lighthouse Board and their plans for us. If they don't have work for me and a place to live, I probably will go to Gardiner's City and get a job there."

"That's strange," Jesse said. "Alice and I decided to go there also, unless the board has something for us."

"What'll you guys do in Gardiner's City?" Gunther asked.

"I'm not sure," Gus said. "But I worked at a hotel in Scottsburg before I came here. I'm good with my hands, and I'm not afraid of work. I'll find something."

"I think I can get work in the lumber business," Jesse said. "Before I came here to the lighthouse, I almost worked in lumber." He took a bite of his potatoes.

Gunther pointed his fork at Gus. "How long do you think it will be before you know when you'll be moving?"

"I'm going to send a telegram to the board this afternoon. I'll tell them the lens and mechanism have been removed. I'll also advise them the lighthouse is unsafe to live in."

"Would anyone like more coffee?" Alice asked. "Gus, have another helping of that pork."

"Yeah, I'll have more coffee," Gunther said.

Alice got up from the table to get the coffee.

"Now, if there's anything I can do to help you guys, let me know," Gunther said.

"Well," Jesse said. "Now that you brought it up, when it comes time to move, we'll need help hauling our stuff to the Landing.

"We may also need you and your wagon to help haul the lens and mechanism to the Landing," Gus said.

"You fellows just let me know, and I'll be glad to help," Gunther said.

They finished eating their meal and got up from the table.

"Thank you, Alice. Another great meal. I'm like Gunther. I'll miss your good cooking."

"As long as we're living here, plan on eating all your meals with Jesse and me. It's really no bother, and I enjoy cooking."

Gunther looked at Gus. "It sounds like you're done cooking for a while."

Gus smiled. "Yeah. Alice, I really appreciate that."

"Well, I am going to head for home," Gunther said. "I have a few things around there to catch up on." He stood up. "When you guys are ready for my help, just let me know."

"All right," Gus and Jesse said in unison.

Gus followed Gunther toward the door, then stopped. "Wickie, I'm going to the barn with Gunther, and then to the Landing to send that telegram. I'll be back before feeding time."

"Is there anything I can do to help?" Jesse asked.

"Yeah, there is. Get a count of the oil cans we have left. I'll also give that information to the board."

"Sure. How about the wood?"

"There's not that much out there. We'll give it to Gunther, unless the board tells us to do something different."

"That's a good idea. All right, I'll meet you out front with the can count."

Chapter 16

The Light is Dark

GUS ARRIVED AT the Landing and asked Lloyd to send the following telegram to the Lighthouse Board: "Removal of lens and mechanism complete; eleven cans of oil remain; lighthouse unsafe to live in; standing by for instruction. Crosby."

***

Two hours later, Lloyd's telegraph key started to click. He wrote down the message and handed it to Gus.

Gus read the telegram to himself, then looked at Lloyd. "Well, it looks like I'll see you again tomorrow."

"Yeah, I thought so," Lloyd said. "If you can, get Alice to come and stay with Nellie and me. I don't like her being in the lighthouse if you say it's unsafe."

"I think that can be worked out. But I have another problem that maybe you can help me solve."

"What's that?" Lloyd asked. He leaned on the counter with his elbows.

"Since I have to ship all this stuff to Scottsburg, it would help me if I could hire your team and wagon."

"Sure, Gus. Three dollars a day. When do you want to start?"

Gus scratched his head. "Well, since I have to get all that stuff back here and then loaded on the *Melissa* by tomorrow afternoon, I need to take the team with me today. If I do that, I'll need to board my horse with you until I return your team and wagon."

"That's all right," Lloyd said. "I'll take good care of your horse."

"Thanks, Lloyd."

"I'll have Ike hitch up the team for you. They should be ready in a few minutes. Don't worry about payment now. We can settle up when you return them."

A few minutes later Gus had unhitched Jake from the buggy and put him in the corral.

Ike finished hitching the team and approached Gus. "They're all ready to go."

"Thanks, Ike." Gus climbed up into the wagon seat and picked up the reins. "I should have these guys back tomorrow afternoon."

"I'll be here," Ike waved.

Gus drove away toward Gunther's home.

***

An hour and a half later, Gus arrived back at the lighthouse. He unhitched the team and stabled them in the barn.

Jesse and Alice met Gus in the common hallway of the lighthouse as he walked in the front door.

"I saw you drive in with a team and wagon. What's up?" Jesse asked.

"Let's go inside and I'll fill you in," Gus said.

"All right, come on in," Jesse said.

"I'm anxious to hear what the board had to say," Alice said. She sat down in a chair.

"Me, too." Jesse sat down on the edge of his chair and leaned toward Gus.

Gus told Jesse and Alice about everything that had to be shipped to the Landing. Then he added, "Jesse, the board wants you and me to go with all the items to Scottsburg."

Jesse shook his head. "I don't like that. It means Alice would be left here by herself."

"I'm not afraid," Alice leaned over and touched Jesse's arm. "I'll be just fine."

"I don't feel good about it either, Jesse, and neither does Lloyd. He suggested that Alice stay with him and Nellie while we're gone to Scottsburg."

"Who's going to take care of the animals if I stay with Daddy and Nellie?" Alice asked.

"The chickens will be the only animals left here to feed," Gus said. "Molly will be with us at the Landing, and Jake is already there. I've asked Gunther to come by and take care of the chickens."

Jesse frowned. "Gus, how are we going to get the lens, clock mechanism, and all those cans to the Landing in time to load them on the *Melissa* before it leaves?"

"Well, I've also asked Gunther to come haul some of those items to the Landing with his team and wagon."

"That was a good idea." The deep worry lines in Jesse's forehead diminished.

"Alice, Jesse and I could be gone for a couple of days."

"Why that long?" Alice asked.

"Since the board wants us to go along with the lens and mechanism, I figure we will have to unload everything and move it to a designated storage area. Also, I'm not sure how soon the *Melissa* will return to the Landing."

"I know from working with Daddy, the *Melissa* gets to the Landing around 12:45 p.m. In the morning, I'll fix some sandwiches for you fellows to take with you."

"Thank you, Alice," Gus said. "Now, I better get back out to the barn and feed."

Jesse got up from his chair. "I'll go with you. I haven't fed Molly yet."

"I've already started supper. It should be ready when you get back."

***

After Gus and Jesse finished in the barn, they returned to the lighthouse and ate supper.

Following the meal, Gus pushed away from the table. "Guess I'll go back to my side of the house. It's been a long day. Thanks for supper, Alice."

Jesse sat down in his sitting room and began to read while Alice washed the dishes.

When Alice finished, she sat down in her chair next to Jesse.

"I'm so tired tonight."

Jesse looked up from his book. "Honey, you do look a little pale."

"Oh, I've been tired before." Alice picked up her book. "I'll be all right."

"I hope you get rested tonight. Tomorrow's going to be tiring for you."

Alice and Jesse read for a time, and then Alice laid her book down. "Darling, I'm going to pack a few things to take with me to Daddy's. It'll be bedtime by the time I finish."

"All right. I'm going to read for a while longer, and then I'll be in." Jesse looked up at Alice. "You know, it feels so strange not to have to light the tower lantern."

***

The next morning, they awoke and started their morning activities. Alice started preparing breakfast while Jesse went to the barn to feed Molly. When he returned to the lighthouse, he took the chamber pot out to empty and clean it. He returned the pot to the bedroom, and went to the kitchen area to wash his hands. He noticed Alice standing in front of the stove holding one hand over her mouth and the other hand over her stomach.

"What's wrong?" Jesse asked.

"I'm so sick to my stomach. I don't think I can finish cooking breakfast."

"Go sit down. I'll finish it."

Jesse had breakfast almost prepared when he went over to Gus' and knocked on the door. "Breakfast is ready, Gus!"

"Be right over!"

When Gus entered the sitting room, he saw Alice sitting there in a chair, and Jesse in the kitchen putting food on the table. Gus looked at Jesse and then back at Alice. "Are you all right, Alice?"

"For some reason, the smell of bacon made me sick to my stomach. But I'm starting to feel better." Alice motioned toward the kitchen. "Jesse finished cooking breakfast, so sit down and eat while it's still hot."

"The bacon sure smells good," Gus said. "Is this the first time you've been sick in the morning?"

"No, this is the second time."

Gus looked back at Alice. "Oh, I see."

Jesse and Gus sat down and began to eat.

"Honey, if you're feeling better, you should try to eat," Jesse said. "You can't go until dinner without something to eat."

"You're right." Alice got up from her chair in the sitting room and moved to the kitchen and sat at the table.

After a short time, Jesse and Gus finished their breakfast and pushed their chairs back from the table.

"I just saw Gunther drive up in front of the barn," Alice said.

"That man is never late," Jesse said.

"Yeah, you're right, but I'd rather that he be early than late," Gus said. "I'm going to the barn. I'll see you out there Jesse."

"I'll be right out."

"I've got dishes to wash, and I need to fix something for you men to take with you to eat, so I better get to work, too," Alice said.

"Honey, are you sure you feel like doing that?"

"Yes, I'm feeling fine, now."

"I'm glad," Jesse said. "After we finish loading the lens and the other items, I'll come back and help you carry out the things you packed to take with you."

"I also packed a few things for you to take with you to Scottsburg."

"Between you and me, I hope Gus and me won't be gone two nights. I'll miss you."

"I'll miss you too, darling."

Jesse kissed Alice on the cheek.

***

Two hours later, Gus, Jesse, and Gunther finished loading the lens and the other items into the wagons.

Jesse harnessed Molly and hitched her to the buggy. "Gus, I'm going to get Alice, and then I'll be ready to go."

"I have to get my bag, and then I'll be ready," Gus said.

"Gunther, you may as well come on in."

"I could use a drink before we go," Gunther said.

Gus and Gunther went to Gus' quarters while Jesse went to his. A few minutes passed, and Alice and Jesse walked out into the hallway and met Gus and Gunther. They started toward the front door.

Gus shook his head. "You know, this is only the third time the lighthouse has stood empty since I moved in here about seven years ago. The first time was for my Martha's funeral, and the second was for Wyatt's."

"It'll only be a few days now until life in the lighthouse will come to an end," Jesse said.

Gus's shoulders slumped at the thought.

"There'll be no one here," Alice said. "Should we lock the doors?"

"I'll take care of it," Gus said.

***

After Gus locked the doors, he met the others in front of the lighthouse. Gunther was leaning against Jesse's buggy.

"Well, Gus, how does it feel to not have to operate the light?" Gunther asked.

Gus lowered his head. "Like part of my life is gone, and I'm not needed anymore. I've been so restless. I wake up at my usual time to relieve Jesse, but then realize the light is dark. I really feel bad for the mariners." Gus looked at Gunther. "Without the light, their navigation will be very hazardous and challenging." Gus shook his head. "Well, we better go. I don't want to miss that boat."

"We're ready," Jesse said. "We'll follow you guys."

"All right," Gus said. He and Gunther climbed up onto their wagons.

***

When they arrived at the Landing, they stopped in front of the office. Jesse helped Alice down from the buggy, and they walked up ahead to Gus' wagon. Alice and Jesse got to the wagon as Lloyd came out of the office.

"Hi, Daddy," Alice said. I've come to stay with you for a couple of days."

Lloyd smiled and hugged her. "I wouldn't have it any other way. Put your stuff in your old room. I have to prepare some documents for the items Gus is shipping to Scottsburg."

"Thanks, Daddy."

"Gus, I'm going to help Alice carry her stuff inside," Jesse said. "I'll be right back to help."

"Go ahead," Gus said.

After Jesse helped Alice, he returned to the wagons. A short time later, the men were ready to load the items onto the *Melissa.*

"Just give this paperwork to the first mate, Webster, and he'll tell you when to load your stuff," Lloyd said. "I'll get Ike and Seth to give you a hand; otherwise, you may cause the boat to be late."

"Thanks, Lloyd," Gus said. "We appreciate your help."

"Glad to help. I'll see you men when you get back."

"Oh, Lloyd, I almost forgot about your team and wagon," Gus said.

"Don't worry about that, Gus. I'll have Ike take care of them." Lloyd waved and headed to the office.

***

Jesse walked the several yards to where the *Melissa* was docked, while Gus and Gunther drove the wagons from the office over to the dock. Gus gave the paperwork to the first mate.

Webster looked over the paperwork and gave the three men instructions on where to place the items on the boat. "You need to start loading immediately. We have a schedule."

The three men began carefully loading the lens pieces on the boat. Soon, Ike and Seth arrived and helped finish loading all of the other items.

"If that's all, Gus, I'll take care of the team and wagon for you," Ike said.

"Yeah, we're done," Gus said. "Thanks to you and Seth for your help."

Jesse turned toward Gus. "Do you think I'd have time to go to the Landing office and say goodbye to Alice?"

"I don't know. You better ask the first mate."

Jesse hurried over to Webster.

"We cast off in ten minutes young fellow, with or without you," Webster said.

Jesse quickly turned and went back to where Gus and Gunther were standing. "I'll be right back, Gus." Jesse ran to the office and found no one there, so he walked toward the back room and met Lloyd.

"Aren't you going with Gus?" Lloyd asked.

"Yeah, but I have a couple of minutes, so I came to say goodbye to Alice."

Lloyd grinned. "She's in the back with Nellie. Come on in."

They entered Lloyd's sitting room and found Alice and Nellie standing in the middle of the room.

Jesse walked toward Alice and embraced her. "I only have a couple of minutes before the boat leaves. I wanted to say goodbye and tell you that I'm really going to miss you."

"I'm going to miss you, too."

"Jesse, I don't want to break this up, but if you don't get out of here, you're going to miss that boat," Lloyd said.

"I'm going." Jesse kissed Alice. "I love you and wish I didn't have to make this trip."

Nellie placed her hand on Jesse's shoulder. "Don't worry, Jesse. Lloyd and I will take good care of Alice while you're gone."

"Darling, you better go," Alice said. "You don't want to be late."

Jesse released Alice's hand and hurried toward the door, then turned toward Alice. "I'll miss you."

"I'll miss you too, darling." She blew him a kiss from across the room.

Jesse started out the door but stopped suddenly. "Oh, no!"

"What's wrong?" Lloyd asked.

"I just remembered that Molly is still hitched out front."

Lloyd waved Jesse off. "Don't worry about Molly. I'll take care of her. Now you get out of here!"

Just then the *Melissa's* whistle blew.

Jesse ran to the boat and boarded just as the crew was about to raise the gangplank.

Gus and Jesse waved goodbye to Gunther as the *Melissa* steamed away from the dock.

Jesse looked back in the direction of the lighthouse and touched Gus on the arm. “Look, Gus! You can see part of the lighthouse tower from out here.”

“Yeah.” Gus nodded and sighed. “It’s a beautiful view, but it sadly reminds me that the light is dark and won’t shine again from the tower.”

“We should talk to the Lighthouse Board about building a new lighthouse as soon as possible,” Jesse said.

Chapter 17

Reunion and a Special Gift

THE *MELISSA* STEAMED up the Umpqua River toward Scottsburg with Gus and Jesse on board. They enjoyed the quiet river and the forest of tall green pines covering the mountains adjacent to the river. After two and a half hours, darkness set in and all that could be seen was the *Melissa's* bow light reflecting off the water. Half an hour later, the boat was nearing Scottsburg. From a distance, Jesse and Gus could see lanterns and a couple of people standing on the Landing. As the boat drew closer to the Landing, its whistle blew.

"I recognize Tyler Bronson from the Lighthouse Board, but not the other guy," Gus said.

"That's Mr. Bronson, all right," Jesse, said. "The other man may be Sam Waters, the Landing agent. I used to work for him."

"I think you're right. It does look like Sam."

The *Melissa* docked, and the crew tied her lines and lowered the gangplank. Gus and Jesse walked off the boat and Tyler Bronson and Sam Waters greeted them with a handshake.

"Did you men have a good trip?" Mr. Bronson asked.

"No problems," Gus said. "In fact, it's been a long time since I've been to Scottsburg. I had forgotten how beautiful the mountains are along the Umpqua."

"We saw some great sights on the river," Jesse said. "Before it got dark, we saw a bald eagle swoop down from the top of a tall pine tree and snatch a big fish right out of the water."

"I'm glad to hear you enjoyed the trip," Mr. Bronson said.

Sam Waters joined the conversation. "Gus, it's good to see you again. I haven't seen you for several years. You still look fit as a fiddle."

Gus grinned. "Thanks, it's good to see you again too."

"Jesse, you're a sight for sore eyes," Sam patted Jesse on the shoulder. "I sure have missed your help around here with the lifting of cargo and such."

Jesse grinned. "Mr. Waters, I've thought about you several times since I left here. But Gus has kept me so busy at the lighthouse that I really haven't had time to miss being here."

"Gus, were you able to bring everything with you?" Mr.

Umpqua River

Bronson asked.

"Yeah. We brought the lens, burner head, clock mechanism, and the eleven cans of whale oil, just like you said. We also brought the boxes of record books that were prepared over the past seven years."

"That's good," Mr. Bronson said. "I've made arrangements with Mr. Waters, here, to receive those items and hold them. We'll come back in the morning with wagons and more help to haul the stuff to our warehouse."

"Sounds good," Gus said. "At least we'll be able to get some rest before we start in again."

"I'll see you men later," Sam said. "I need to go check with the first mate about your cargo and any others the *Melissa* may have brought with her." He walked away.

"Get your gear and come with me," Mr. Bronson said. "My buggy's over there." He pointed to the other side of the Landing office. "The board has arranged hotel rooms for both of you. I'll drop you off there, and then come by in the morning with the other wagons and pick you fellows up."

They loaded in the buggy and headed to the hotel.

***

Gus and Jesse walked into the hotel lobby and were greeted by the desk clerk. "Can I help you gentleman?"

"I'm Gus Crosby and this is Jesse Fayette. Tyler Bronson of the Lighthouse Board said you have rooms for us."

"Indeed, I do," the clerk said. "I've heard the name Gus Crosby mentioned lots of times around here. I feel like I already know you. My sister, Elizabeth, speaks highly of you."

"So, you're Elizabeth's brother," Gus said. "Well, I'm glad to meet you." Gus reached across the counter and shook his hand. "What's your name?"

"I'm Ken Johnson. Just call me Ken."

"Ken, I must say, it was good of you to take Elizabeth in after Wyatt's death."

"She's my sister, and family has to help family. Regardless, she has worked hard ever since she arrived, so I really haven't given her anything."

"Is Elizabeth here now?" Jesse asked.

"Yes, but she's already put in her time today and was very tired," Ken said. "By now, she has already put the children to bed and will retire shortly herself. I know she'll be glad to see both of you in the morning."

"We're tired too," Gus said. "We'll wait till morning to say hello to her."

"I can't wait to lie down," Jesse said.

"Just sign the register, fellows, and your rooms are right up those stairs." Ken pointed.

Gus signed the register. "If you see Elizabeth in the morning before we do, would you tell her we're here, and we'd like to see her."

"I sure will," Ken said.

Gus and Jesse walked up the stairs to their rooms. Gus opened his door, and then turned toward Jesse. "We better get up at 6:00. Mr. Bronson will be here to pick us up at eight."

"The restaurant is just across the street." Jesse's brow curled. "Do we need that much time before Mr. Bronson gets here?"

"Not if breakfast is all we have to do before he gets here. I would like to visit with Elizabeth before we get away from here though. I'm not sure how long we'll be in town."

"Oh, I understand," Jesse said. "I'm also looking forward to seeing her and the children again. I'll see you in the morning."

***

The next morning, they got up as planned and went across the street to the restaurant. After breakfast, they returned to the hotel, packed their gear, and met back in the hallway.

"Let's go see if we can find Elizabeth," Gus said.

They headed for the stairs.

"Maybe she's not up yet," Jesse said. "I noticed there was no one at the desk when we went to breakfast, nor when we came back through the lobby."

"Me, too."

As they approached the bottom of the stairs, Jesse spotted Elizabeth across the lobby. He whispered, "She just entered the room."

Gus looked up and smiled.

She saw them at the same time and smiled as she moved toward them.

With her brown hair rolled up in a bun and the sound of her mint colored dress rustling across the floor, Elizabeth reached out with both hands and firmly held Gus' hands. "Gus, it is good to see you again. You look well."

"You also, Elizabeth. I'm so glad to see you." He released her hand.

Jesse shook her hand. "It's nice to see you again, Elizabeth."

"Nice to see you too, Jesse." Elizabeth turned toward Gus. "Who's taking care of the lighthouse?"

Gus lowered his head. "We had to shut the lighthouse down. That last storm washed the soil out from under the foundation. The tower is leaning badly, and it's unsafe to be up there."

"That's why we're here," Jesse said. "We brought the lens and clock mechanism to the Lighthouse Board."

"I'm so sorry. I didn't know." Elizabeth touched Gus's arm. "That's very sad to hear. I can't imagine the lighthouse not being lit up at night. What's going to happen to all those ship captains who depend on the lighthouse to guide them into the river?"

Gus shook his head. "I think there will be a lot more shipwrecks."

"That's terrible. How soon will the board get the lighthouse fixed?"

"They probably can't fix it," Gus said.

"They may have to build a new one," Jesse said.

"That's such a shame, but I am glad it brought you here. How long will you be in town?"

"We're not sure," Gus said. "It depends on Mr. Bronson." Gus looked into Elizabeth's eyes. "How are you and the children doing?"

"We're doing just fine. Elsie and Rusty will be thrilled to see you both. In fact, if you have time, I'll go get them right now."

Gus grinned. "Yeah, we have a few minutes before Mr. Bronson gets here."

"Have a seat." Elizabeth pointed to the lobby chairs. "I'll be right back."

"We'll be here," Gus said.

It wasn't long before Elizabeth returned with the children. Gus and Jesse stood up as they entered the room. Elsie and Rusty ran toward Gus and threw their arms around his waist.

Elsie loosened her hug and smiled as she looked up at him.

"Oh, Gus, I'm really glad to see you."

"I thought I would never see you again." Rusty smiled.

Gus bent over and hugged both of them. "I sure have missed you children. I'm glad to see you." Gus looked at the children as they released their hug. "Well, you both have grown like weeds. How do you like your new home?"

"I like it just fine," Elsie said. "I like going to school, and I'm getting good grades."

"Well, that's good! Gus turned toward Rusty. "How about you?"

"Our home is good." Rusty frowned. "But I don't have a weight to play on like I did at the lighthouse. I still miss it." He reached in his pocket and then swirled around toward Jesse. Rusty's face lit up. "See, Jesse I still have the knife you gave me. I use this almost every day. None of my friends at school have one like this one."

Jesse nodded. "What do you use it for?"

"I carve things."

"What do you carve?" Gus asked.

"Different things," Rusty said.

"One of the things he carved was a likeness of the lighthouse," Elsie said. "I think it's pretty good."

"The lighthouse!" Jesse said. "I'd like to see your lighthouse, Rusty."

"I'll go get it." Rusty ran out of the lobby.

"Elizabeth, I'm glad you and the children are doing well," Gus said. "They seem to have adjusted to their new home. I'm so happy for you."

"Thank you," Elizabeth said. "I'm proud of Elsie and Rusty. They've not only adjusted to their new home, but they have also helped me to adjust."

Rusty ran in holding his carving of the lighthouse and handed it to Jesse.

"Oh, my!" Jesse ran his finger over the carving. "Rusty, this is a beautiful piece of work. You have done a great job on this." Jesse turned toward Gus and held out the carving. "Look at the detail on this lighthouse, especially the lantern room."

Gus took the little lighthouse in his hand. "Elsie, you were right about your brother. You recognized his talent, but this is better than pretty good. This is great work. I'm so proud of you both."

The front door of the lobby opened and Mr. Bronson walked in.

Gus turned back toward Elizabeth and the children. "It looks like it's time for us to go to work."

"Will we see you before you leave town?" Elizabeth asked.

"I'm not sure. I'll ask Mr. Bronson." Gus turned toward him. "Good morning, Mr. Bronson. Do you think we will finish everything today?"

"I believe we will. However, the *Melissa* already left the Landing and headed down river to Gardiner's Landing. You won't be able to leave until tomorrow morning."

"I understand. Could we have a couple of minutes before we go to work?" Gus asked.

"Sure," Mr. Bronson said. "I'll wait for you out by the wagon." He tipped his hat toward Elizabeth and walked out.

"That's not good news," Jesse said. "I was hoping we wouldn't have to stay another night." He rubbed his hands together.

"It sounds like you didn't like your room last night," Elizabeth said.

"There was nothing wrong with the room. Guess I'm just anxious to get back home to Alice."

"Alice!" Elizabeth said. "Is that the same Alice who worked at Harvey's Landing?"

"Yes," Gus said. "Jesse forgot to tell you that he and Alice got married."

Elizabeth smiled. "Congratulations, Jesse. I like Alice. She's such a sweet girl and a hard worker."

"Thank you," Jesse said. "Well, I guess it's time for us to go. It was good to see you and the children again." He touched Rusty on

the head. "Rusty, I'm glad to see you are doing good things with that beautiful knife."

Rusty smiled. "Thanks, Jesse,"

Jesse looked at Elsie. "You keep up the good work in school. Who knows, you may grow up to be a school teacher someday."

"I don't want to be a school teacher. I want to be just like mama. A smart lady and a good mama."

Gus nodded. "Well, Elsie you still need schooling to make you as smart as your mother." Gus looked at Elizabeth. He reached over and took her hand. "It has been really good to see you and the children. I'm glad things are going well for you. Now, we have to go, but since we're staying another night, we'll see you sometime this afternoon."

Elizabeth hugged Gus then stepped back. "I'm glad I had this time with you. I want to thank you again for everything you did for me and the children after Wyatt's death."

"I'm glad I was able to help. I never told you, but when you and the children left, I felt like I had lost my family."

Elizabeth touched Gus' hand. "Thank you for saying that."

Just then Gus felt a tug on his trousers. He looked down and Rusty held up the miniature of the lighthouse he carved.

"Here Gus, this is for you," Rusty said.

"For me!" Gus said. "You don't want to give away that beautiful lighthouse."

"Yes, I do, and I want you to have this 'cause you were good to my papa and he liked you, too."

Gus teared up as he leaned over and hugged Rusty. "I guess I can't turn down your gift." He released Rusty and looked him in the eye. "I will cherish this lighthouse for the rest of my life." Gus stood up and placed the carving in his coat pocket. "Elizabeth, I hate to leave, but we can't keep Mr. Bronson waiting any longer."

"I understand," Elizabeth said. "Now, you both be careful, and I hope to see you later."

Chapter 18

Sad Job

GUS AND JESSE joined Mr. Bronson at the wagon in front of the hotel.

"It's a little chilly out here," Mr. Bronson pulled his coat collar up. "If you fellows had been much longer, I was going to go back inside and wait for you there. Climb up, and let's get to work."

Gus climbed into the seat. "Sorry we kept you waiting, Mr. Bronson."

"No problem," Mr. Bronson said. "I knew you guys hadn't seen Elizabeth and the children for a long time."

Jesse sat down in the wagon seat just as Mr. Bronson shook the reins. "Get up there." He drove toward the Landing.

***

Jesse leaned forward in the seat and looked over at Mr. Bronson. "You should see the lighthouse Rusty carved and gave to Gus."

Gus reached into his coat pocket and pulled out the carving.

Mr. Bronson shook his head. "That boy did a good job of carving a likeness of the lighthouse."

"Yeah, I'm real proud of those kids and how they've grown physically and mentally. I know if Wyatt were here, he would be proud of them too." Gus shoved the carving back inside his pocket.

"I'm sure he would," Mr. Bronson said.

Except for the sounds that came from the team and wagon, there was silence for a couple of minutes.

Jesse leaned forward in his seat again. “Mr. Bronson, last night you said there would be another wagon.”

“I sent two men ahead with the other one to the Landing. They should arrive before us.”

In a short time, Mr. Bronson’s wagon turned the corner at the end of the street.

“I see the Landing,” Jesse said.

“And there’s the other wagon by the Landing office.” Mr. Bronson drove his team up alongside the wagon and stopped.

***

They climbed down from the wagon as three men walked out of the Landing office.

“Morning, Sam,” Mr. Bronson said. “Do you still have my cargo from the lighthouse?”

“Yep, I sure do,” Sam said. He approached with the other two men.

Mr. Bronson turned toward Gus and Jesse. “I’d like you to meet Cecil and Delmar. They’ll be helping us haul the lens and the other items to the warehouse.”

The four men exchanged greetings.

Sam pointed to a small building. “Mr. Bronson, if you’ll pull your wagons over there by the shed, you can start loading. Last night I had all your cargo put in there.”

Mr. Bronson looked at Cecil. “Let’s pull our wagons over there, and we’ll get started,”

They positioned their wagons by the shed and went inside to start loading.

“Mr. Bronson, would you mind if Jesse and I work together loading the lens?” Gus asked.

“Well … no. But I’m curious as to why you think the rest of us can’t handle it. Someone else handled those pieces last night.”

“It’s not that we think no one else can handle the lens. It’s just that this will be our last time to hold them. We have polished those prisms a lot of times over the years, and have come to appreciate what they’ve done to help the mariners. They’re like an old friend that you hate to say goodbye to."

Mr. Bronson nodded. "I understand." He turned toward Delmar and Cecil. "You guys help me start loading the clock mechanism."

They all worked steadily loading the wagons and when they finished, Sam came out to the shed. "I need your signature to show that you received these items."

Mr. Bronson signed the document. "Thanks, Sam, for all your help."

"Glad I could, but I was just doing my job," Sam said.

Mr. Bronson started getting his team ready. "Cecil, you and Delmar follow us. We're going to the warehouse."

Gus and Jesse climbed up on the seat next to Mr. Bronson.

"How far do we have to go?" Jesse asked.

"It's only about ten minutes from here to the warehouse on the other side of town."

The wagons started moving and for a couple of minutes no one said anything. Then, Gus looked at Mr. Bronson. "I feel like I'm going to the cemetery again to bury an old friend. I never thought I would feel this way about a lens and clock mechanism."

"Well, hopefully we won't have to store the items very long," Mr. Bronson said.

Jesse leaned forward in the seat. "Is the board planning to rebuild?"

"As soon as we can get the money."

"I hope they don't plan to rebuild in that same location," Gus said. "That ground next to the river is not solid enough to support a lighthouse when those fierce storms come in from the ocean."

"What if we still changed the contour of the grade to divert the water runoff from the hill?" Mr. Bronson asked.

"I thought about that during the last storm, but to have changed the landscape wouldn't have made that much difference. Those waves crashing in from the river did the most damage."

"How soon will the board start rebuilding?" Jesse asked.

Mr. Bronson shook his head. "I don't know. We're trying to convince the legislature of the importance of the lighthouse, and that we need money right away to rebuild it. In fact, from what you just told me, we may have to also consider a new location for the lighthouse."

"Jesse and I are anxious to go back to work."

"You fellows will get your jobs back, just as soon as the lighthouse is rebuilt."

"What about a job between now and then?" Jesse asked. "Is that a possibility?"

"I'm sorry, but the board doesn't have a job for you until another lighthouse is built.

Gus shook his head. *It's a good thing Jesse and I talked about a plan for other work.*

It's still three weeks until the end of the quarter, but we did agree to pay your wages for the entire quarter, and we'll reimburse you for any expenses you had at the general store."

"Thanks. That's good of the board."

***

They arrived in front of the warehouse, and Mr. Bronson pulled his team and wagon to a stop. He climbed down from the wagon and looked back up at Gus. "What are your plans?"

Gus turned both of his palms up. "Well, now that I know there's no job for me here, I guess I'll go to Gardiner's City."

"Me, too," Jesse said.

Mr. Bronson frowned. "I'll be right back." He opened the warehouse doors, then returned to the wagon and drove the team inside. As he stopped, he turned toward Gus and Jesse. "I wish we had work for you here. I hate to lose good workers to Gardiner's

City. When we're done unloading this stuff, we'll go to the board office, and I'll get you fellows your money."

Cecil and Delmar arrived and pulled their wagon into the warehouse behind Mr. Bronson's. Everyone worked steadily, unloading all the items from the lighthouse. They carefully covered each item as they prepared it for storage. When they finished unloading and storing everything, they pulled the wagons outside and locked the warehouse doors.

"Cecil, you and Delmar follow me back to our corral," Mr. Bronson said. "You guys can unhitch that team when you get there.

Cecil waved. "All right, Mr. Bronson."

***

On arrival at the corral, Mr. Bronson tied his team to the hitching rail. "Come with me, and I'll get you men your pay."

The three of them walked across the street, and entered the Lighthouse Board office. Mr. Bronson pointed to a table with chairs around it. "You fellows have a seat, and I'll be right back."

"Thanks," Gus said.

Jesse pulled out a chair. "I guess our next job will be to get our stuff moved out of the lighthouse."

"Yeah. Oh, that reminds me. I better ask Mr. Bronson about the leftover stores."

Mr. Bronson returned to the room. "Gus, here is your wages of $137.50, plus payment for those telegrams." He counted the money as he handed it to Gus. "We never expected we would ever have to make payment to you fellows like this and shut down the lighthouse."

"Thanks, Mr. Bronson."

Mr. Bronson turned toward Jesse. "This is yours," and he counted out $110.25.

"Thanks, Mr. Bronson."

"I have a question," Gus said.

Mr. Bronson frowned. "Didn't I give you enough money?"

"It's not about the money," Gus said. "It's all here. I wanted to ask you about the unused stores at the lighthouse. Since Jesse and I will be moving, what do you want us to do with them?"

"Bronson looked at the floor for a few seconds then back at Gus. "Since you both had to do all the extra work, I believe the board would agree with me. You've earned ownership of those items. Take them with you."

"Thanks," Gus said.

"You talked about stores, now I'm hungry," Jesse said.

"Let's go up the street to the café," Mr. Bronson said. "I'll buy."

***

After they ate, they came out of the café and climbed back into the wagon.

"Sure do thank you for dinner, Mr. Bronson," Gus said.

"Me, too."

Mr. Bronson picked up the reins. "It's the least we could do for you fellows since we don't have jobs for you. I want both of you to know, the board really does appreciate the work you've done for us. We wish you the best of luck in finding jobs."

"Whatever jobs we get, hopefully we'll only need them for a short time," Gus said. "The board needs to replace the lighthouse as soon as possible. Not just because Jesse and I need jobs, but because the lighthouse is desperately needed to help the mariners navigate the mouth of the river. The lighthouse saves lives and ships."

"I know exactly what you're saying," Mr. Bronson said. "I, for one, will do everything in my power to get the lighthouse rebuilt as soon as possible."

Jesse leaned forward in his seat. "The board should consider building in a different spot."

"The current location is extremely vulnerable to storms," Gus said.

"You fellows seem adamant about a different location. I just had a thought. Do you have more time you could give me this afternoon?"

"Sure," Gus said. "What can we do to help?"

"Let's go back to the office." Mr. Bronson shook the reins and the team moved forward. "I've got a map I'd like you fellows to look at."

Jesse's brow curled. "Well, I'm not much on reading a map."

"Same with me," Gus said. "But I'd still like to see one of the area."

***

They arrived back at the board office, and Mr. Bronson tied the team to the hitching rail, then they went inside.

Mr. Bronson pointed to the table. "Have a seat, fellows, while I get that map."

Gus and Jesse took a seat. A few moments later, Mr. Bronson returned with the map and rolled it out on top of the table.

"Let me show you where the lighthouse is located." Mr. Bronson pointed to a spot on the map. "Now, with the purpose and functionality of the lighthouse in mind, where do you think would be a better location for the lighthouse?"

"Like I said, I'm not good at reading a map," Gus said. "But just from being familiar with the lay of the land and the river around there, I think the lighthouse should be built on that higher ground south of where it stands now." Gus pointed to a spot on the map about 2,000 yards up the hill from the current location.

"Do you think the lighthouse would be as effective if it were located that far away from the river?" Jesse asked.

Mr. Bronson looked at Gus. "That was my first thought, too."

"I sure do," Gus said. "The mariners could see the tower light just as well from that high ground as they could from a tower alongside the river. Second, if the mariners were notified that the light was located on a different azimuth reading in reference to the mouth of the river, then they should be able to see the lighthouse and find the river. Third, the tower could withstand the storms better because it would be built on more solid ground away from the water. It wouldn't be subjected to the erosive power of the water." Gus rubbed the side of his face. "Fourth, by the lighthouse being located on higher ground, the tower wouldn't have to be built as tall in order for the light to be seen from out on the ocean."

Jesse looked at Mr. Bronson. "Gus may be right. Think about it. The height thing he talked about would mean less building materials, and probably less money to build the tower."

"You fellows have some good ideas," Mr. Bronson said. "I'm glad I asked you to come back here and look at this map. This will give the board some new information to discuss at our next meeting."

Gus rubbed his palms together. "I appreciate you asking for our ideas."

"The Board has more experience now than we did when we had this lighthouse built," Mr. Bronson said. "I'm sure we'll do a better job the next time." He rolled up the map and laid it back on the table. "Unless you fellows have any other ideas, I can take you back to the hotel, if you like."

"I did have one other suggestion," Jesse said.

"What's that?" Mr. Bronson asked.

"I'm not sure you're ready to think about this right now, but I'd still like to mention it for planning operation of the new lighthouse. If I were a mariner, I think it would be very helpful to have the lamp burning in the tower, even during daylight hours on rainy days."

Gus rubbed the back of his neck. "I think Jesse has something there. There have been several times in the past in which I've had the same thought about rainy days."

"I'll add that to my list of ideas to present to the board," Mr. Bronson said. He folded up the map and started to return it. "Anything else?"

"No more ideas on the lighthouse from me," Gus said. "But before you take us back to the hotel, could we stop at the general store? I left my pipe at the lighthouse, and I've gone as long as I can stand it without a smoke."

"Sure," Mr. Bronson said. "I'll be right back." He left the room.

"Gus, I noticed you were a little nervous," Jesse said.

"I don't really smoke that much, but I do enjoy my pipe. I've never gone this long without smoking. I guess that's why I'm nervous."

Mr. Bronson returned. "I'm ready."

***

They left the office and Mr. Bronson drove them to the general store. Gus went inside to get a new pipe while Jesse and Mr. Bronson waited on the wagon.

"Mr. Bronson, did you know I got married?" Jesse asked.

"No, I didn't. Who did you marry?"

"Alice Harvey."

Mr. Bronson's eyes widened. "Is that Lloyd Harvey's daughter?"approached

"Yeah."

"You got yourself a beautiful girl there."

"Thanks, Mr. Bronson. I think so, too."

Gus returned and climbed back up on the wagon seat.

"Did they have what you wanted, Gus?" Mr. Bronson asked.

Gus nodded. "Yeah, but now I have to break in a new pipe before it tastes right." He started packing tobacco in it.

***

Mr. Bronson shook the reins. "Get up there." He looked at Gus. "Is there any place else you fellows would like to go before I take you back to the hotel?"

"None I can think of," Gus said.

"Me neither."

"All right," Mr. Bronson said. "Our next stop will be the hotel, and it's just around the corner. I'll come by in the morning and take you to the Landing."

"We appreciate that," Gus said. "What time will the *Melissa* leave?"

"She almost always leaves the dock at 8:00. I'll pick you up at 7:30. That should give us plenty of time to get to the Landing before she leaves."

***

Mr. Bronson's wagon came to a stop in front of the hotel

"That didn't take long," Jesse said.

Gus and Jesse climbed down from the wagon.

"I'll see you fellows in the morning," Mr. Bronson said.

They waved and watched as Mr. Bronson drove his team and wagon away. A few seconds later Jesse turned toward Gus. "It looks to me like we have some free time on our hands. What are we going to do for the rest of the day?"

Gus shook his head. "I'm not sure. Let's go in the lobby and see what's going on. If Elizabeth gets off work in time, maybe we could visit with her until it's time to eat supper."

"That's sounds good," Jesse said.

***

Elizabeth was working behind the desk when Gus and Jesse walked in.

“Good to see you back,” Elizabeth said. “Did you get everything done that you came to do?”

Gus smiled. “Yeah, now we have about an hour or so of free time before supper.”

“I wish I didn’t have to work,” Elizabeth said. “I’d be able to visit with you and help you pass the time. I really feel bad about this. To make matters worse, as soon as I get off work, I have to prepare supper for the children, and help them with their school work.”

“Don’t you feel bad,” Gus said. “I know you have responsibilities. I’m just happy we got to spend some time this morning with you and the children.”

Elizabeth smiled. “Oh, so am I. You know, that reminds me of our conversation about the lighthouse being shut down. You never said what kind of work you’ll be doing.”

“We’ve made plans to go to Gardiner’s City and get jobs,” Gus said.

“Gardiner’s City! That’s ironic,” Elizabeth said. “There’s a young man staying here tonight, and he works in Gardiner’s City. He said he came here to attend a funeral tomorrow morning. If you could

talk to him maybe he could give you and Jesse a lead on jobs around Gardiner’s City.”

“That’s a great idea,” Gus said.

“Can you give us the man’s name and a description? Jesse asked.

Elizabeth picked up the register and browsed down the page at the guests’ names. “His name is Oscar Struthers. He stands about six feet tall and—"

“Oscar!” Jesse said. “I know him. He’s an old friend of mine.”

Gus turned toward Jesse. “Is he the fellow you told me was going into the lumber business?”

“That’s him.”

Elizabeth laid the register down. "He's been gone most of the afternoon, but he never said where he was going, or how long he would be gone."

"We'll just have a seat here in the lobby and wait for him," Jesse said. "Maybe he'll be back before too long."

"Thanks for the information, Elizabeth," Gus said. "Now we'll get out of your way and leave you to your work."

Gus and Jesse sat in the lobby reading the newspaper and observing everyone that came through the door.

Thirty minutes later, a man walked in and Jesse looked up from his paper. "Here he comes, Gus." Jesse got up from his chair and took a couple of steps toward the door.

At the same moment, Oscar saw Jesse and smiled. "Hi, Jesse, it's a surprise to see you here." He shook Jesse's hand. "What are you doing here? I thought you worked at the lighthouse."

"I did until we had to shut it down." He frowned "Come here, I want you to meet my boss."

Gus stood up.

"Oscar, this is my boss, Gus Crosby. Gus, this is Oscar my friend I told you about."

Gus and Oscar shook hands.

Oscar turned toward Jesse. "What's this about shutting down the lighthouse?"

"To make a long story short, the foundation of the lighthouse was undermined by storms. Now the tower is leaning over so far that it's unsafe to be inside her. That's why Gus and me are here. We just finished storing the lens and clock mechanism from the lighthouse. Officially, we are out of work as of now. We plan to look for work in Gardiner's City. In fact, it was no coincidence that we were here when you came in. We heard that you arrived in town today from Gardiner's City, and we wanted to talk to you about the job situation there."

"Lumber jobs are good right now," Oscar said. "I don't know about other work, but you shouldn't have trouble getting work in lumber."

Jesse smiled. "That's good news."

"Sure is," Gus said. "Oscar, would you join us for supper at the restaurant?

"I'd sure like to, but I've already made plans for the evening. I'm in town for my father's funeral. I still have some things to help Mother take care of."

"Oh Oscar, I'm very sorry," Jesse said. "I didn't know."

"I'm sorry about your father," Gus said. "How did he die?"

"Mother said he died peacefully in his sleep."

"That's the way to go," Gus said. "He probably didn't suffer because it happened so quickly."

Jesse laid his hand on Oscar's shoulder. "We'll let you go. Again, I'm sorry about your father. You take care of yourself, and maybe we'll see you in Gardiner's City." Jesse shook his hand.

"I'm looking forward to it, Jesse." Oscar turned and shook Gus' hand. "Gus, it was good to meet you. Watch out for this guy so he doesn't get in any trouble in Gardiner's City."

Gus chuckled. "Since we're both going to be new to the city, we'll probably have to watch out for each other."

Oscar grinned. He departed for his room.

Gus and Jesse moved over to the registration desk.

"I see you found the man," Elizabeth said.

"Yeah. It was great to see him again," Jesse said. "Thanks for letting us know he was here."

"We're going over to the restaurant for supper. I know you'll be gone when we return, so I want to say goodbye now." Gus reached

out for Elizabeth's hand. "It was really good to see you and the children again. I wish you the best in everything."

Elizabeth smiled. "I appreciate that, and it was good to see you and Jesse again. I hope you men find jobs real soon."

"It was good seeing you and the children." Jesse shook hands with Elizabeth.

Gus and Jesse left the hotel and went to the restaurant. After supper, they returned to the hotel and their rooms for the night.

***

The next morning, they got up and by 7:15 they had finished their breakfast. They returned to their rooms, picked up their bags, and went down to the lobby to wait for Mr. Bronson.

"I hope Mr. Bronson isn't late," Jesse said. "I don't want to miss that boat."

Gus grinned. "Just be patient. We'll have enough time if he gets here within the next ten minutes or so."

Jesse paced back and forth as he watched out the front windows of the lobby. "I'm starting to get worried."

Gus stood with his hands behind his back. "Something must have gone wrong. It's unlike Mr. Bronson not to keep his word."

A couple of minutes later Jesse pointed up the street. "Here he comes."

They picked up their bags and walked out the front door of the hotel. By now it was 7:45.

Mr. Bronson pulled his team and wagon to a stop. "Sorry I'm late fellows. I fell while harnessing the horses this morning. I turned my ankle and it hurt so bad that I thought it was broken."

"We figured something must have happened," Gus said. "Sorry to hear you busted your ankle."

Gus and Jesse placed their bags in the back of the wagon and climbed up onto the seat.

"Get up," Mr. Bronson said. The team moved forward. "I don't really think it's broken. I had to sit down for a while to rub it and twist my foot around until it got to feeling better. Anyway, I made

it. Now let's get you fellows to the Landing." He flipped the reins. "Get up there. A little faster."

Jesse leaned forward and looked over at Mr. Bronson. "Your team responds well to the reins."

"Yeah, I've had this team now for about three years. They've done a good job for me. At the pace we're going now, we should get to the Landing in three or four minutes."

***

Branson stopped the team and wagon in front of the Landing office and everyone climbed down. He tied his team to the hitching rail, and they all walked toward the office.

"It looks like we got here none too soon." Gus's brow curled. "The *Melissa* looks ready to leave."

"You never know for sure when she'll depart," Mr. Bronson said. "I guess it depends on the amount of cargo and number of passengers they have to load. Let's check in with Sam Waters and find out how long before she departs."

They started to enter the Landing office as Sam walked out the door. "Morning, men. Mr. Bronson, you got Gus and Jesse back here just in time. The *Melissa* is about ready to cast off."

"I'd walk you fellows to the gangplank, but I probably should stay off this ankle as much as possible." Mr. Bronson stood balancing his weight on one foot. "Here's money to take care of your fare," He shook hands with Gus and Jesse. "Thanks again for all your hard work, and stay in touch with us about the lighthouse situation."

"Don't worry, Mr. Bronson, we will," Jesse said.

"It was good to see you again, Jesse." Sam said. "Take care of Gus.

"He doesn't require much care." Jesse moved to catch up with Gus.

Gus and Jesse approached the gangplank, and the first mate, Webster, hollered from the deck. "Are you men coming aboard or not? We're ready to raise the gangplank."

Gus waved, then he and Jesse boarded. They took up positions on deck where they could see Mr. Bronson. They had just got in place when the *Melissa's* whistle blew. The crew pulled up the gangplank, and the boat started moving away from the Landing. Gus and Jesse waved goodbye to Mr. Bronson. As they waved, Sam Waters walked to the edge of the dock and waved goodbye as well.

Chapter 19

Reflections

THE *MELISSA* HAD been underway for only a short time when the first mate, Webster, approached Gus and Jesse. "We have another nice morning on the Umpqua. No rain, and as soon as the sun burns through that fog it's going to be a beautiful ride. Did you fellows get all your cargo stored away that we hauled up here yesterday from Harvey's Landing?"

"Yeah," Gus said. "I just hope the lens and lantern don't have to stay in storage for very long. They were made to help the mariners navigate their ships safely, not to sit idle in a warehouse."

"We don't take the *Melissa* out on the ocean," Webster said. "But if we did, I bet that light would be a big help for us to find our way back into the river at night." Webster turned to leave. "Well, I've got work to do. You fellows enjoy the trip."

"We are," Jesse said.

After the fog lifted, Gus and Jesse walked around the bottom deck watching the river and surrounding sites slowly pass by.

"We're getting to see things we didn't see on the way up," Gus said.

"This is really a beautiful river. I wish Alice were here to enjoy it with us."

Gus grinned. "We've only been gone two nights and you miss her already."

"Yeah, I do. I've also been a little worried about her. She's been sick."

"Has Alice said anything to you about what might be causing

her sickness?"

Jesse shook his head. "She's only been sick for a few mornings, and it doesn't last long. After a while, she says she's fine."

Gus grinned. "Well, I don't think you have anything to worry about. You'll find out that Alice is just being a normal woman."

"I hope you're right," Jesse said. He reached out and grabbed the deck railing.

Umpqua River with Fog

Gus and Jesse were silent for some time as they continued to enjoy the water, the pine trees standing tall on the side of the mountains, eagles, and other wildlife as they fed on the Umpqua.

***

Jesse looked toward Gus. "Do you remember the comment I made back in Scottsburg about the next job we have to do?"

Gus frowned. "Yeah, but what are you trying to say?

"We have some time before we get back to Harvey's Landing. I was thinking maybe we should use the time to make plans on how we're going to accomplish the move from the lighthouse to Gardiner's City."

"Good idea, Jesse. Let's sit down and talk about it. In fact, I was thinking about that at the Landing during my last look at Mr. Bronson. Ever since he said, "We don't have jobs for you," that statement has echoed in my head. I believe it might be better for us to go to Gardiner's City first. We should look for a house and job before moving any furniture over there."

Jesse rubbed the side of his face. "All right, but there's one factor we should keep in mind."

"What's that?"

"We don't know how much time we have to get our stuff out of the lighthouse before the tower could fall over."

"I'm willing to take that chance. What would we do with our furniture and stores if we took them with us first, and then didn't find a place to put them?"

"I don't know about the furniture and other stuff, but as far as Alice, though, I want to take her with me. She could stay at the Gardiner's Hotel while I look around."

"I forgot about the hotel," Gus said. "That would take care of a place to stay, and then we could move our belongings at a later time."

"At least we can try to find someplace to live first, and then check out the job situation. I just hope the lighthouse tower stays put until we can get this all settled."

Gus nodded. "I agree."

"When do you think we should go to Gardiner's City?"

"The sooner the better. How about tomorrow?"

"Sure."

They were silent for a few minutes. All that could be heard was the sound of the *Melissa's* paddle wheel as it turned through the water.

Jesse turned toward Gus. "By the time we get back to the Landing, it's going to be dinner time. Alice doesn't know for sure that we're even coming back today. I should have sent a telegram to Lloyd before we left Scottsburg."

Gus shook his head. "I didn't think of it, either. My mind has been on all the things we've had to do to shut down the lighthouse. Another concern I've had is for the mariners. They will experience fear and anger when they have to navigate the mouth of the river without the lighthouse."

"One thing we forgot to do was notify the lifeboat men so they would know we weren't going to be there in the near future."

Gus lowered his head. "We didn't have time to notify them. We barely had time to finish loading the lens and mechanism before the *Melissa* was ready to leave the dock."

"Lloyd probably told them." Jesse rubbed the side of his face. "I'm sure the lighthouse is now the big topic of discussion around the Landing."

"Yeah. The lifeboat men probably knew about the condition of the lighthouse the day we left."

They got quiet again, and Jesse turned his attention back to the mountains rising up from both banks of the river. A few minutes later, he looked back at Gus and was surprised to find he had fallen asleep. *He must be tired. I could go to sleep too, if I let myself. The whole thing about disassembling the lighthouse and this trip has been more stressful than I could have ever imagined. It's been hard for me, so I know it has been even worse for Gus. He's been emotionally involved with the lighthouse much longer than I have, and to experience its death is very stressful. We have a ways to go yet, so I won't wake him until we get in. He needs the rest.*

Jesse's thoughts were interrupted by the *Melissa's* whistle. She began to move closer to the river bank. *We're not back yet. Why are we slowing down?*

The sound of the whistle woke Gus. "I must have fallen asleep. I can't believe we're there already."

"We're not!" Jesse stood up and pointed down river. "Look, it's a schooner headed up river to Scottsburg! The *Melissa* moved over to make room for it to pass."

Gus stood up. "That's the schooner *Katie Mae.* Wow! She looks a lot bigger from here than from the top of the lighthouse.

"She sure does." Jesse smiled. "Look how tall those masts are!"

Gus and Jesse waved at the crew and passengers of the *Katie Mae* as they watched her safely pass by. Once she was past, the *Melissa* moved back out into the middle of the river and continued steaming down river.

A few minutes later, Jesse turned toward Gus. "It's hard to believe this river could be so vicious and destructive—especially when we've seen how calm and beautiful it has been on this trip."

"Hearing you say that reminds me of how calm the river was before it took Wyatt's life that morning."

"I'm sorry, Gus. I didn't mean to upset you. I wasn't thinking of Wyatt. I was thinking about the lighthouse."

"It's all right. Now that I think about it, the river took Wyatt's life and the lighthouse's life. Both of those deaths have been sad occasions for me."

Jesse brushed the side of his face. "I didn't know Wyatt, but I know the lighthouse. I feel sad for Elizabeth and the children, and I'm sad about the lighthouse. I know it's only half the hurt you must feel."

"I found out several years ago that life can be tough. Losing Wyatt and the lighthouse were tough enough, but those losses don't compare to the hurt I felt when I lost my Martha."

"I would be crushed if anything happened to Alice." Jesse shaded his eyes with his hand as he looked toward Gardiner's. "I see the Landing up ahead."

Anxious to watch the activity when the *Melissa* docked, Gus and Jesse moved toward the bow of the boat. The boat's whistle blew to notify everyone at the Landing of her approach. They watched patiently as she slowed down and pulled into the dock.

The crew threw ropes from the bow to tie the *Melissa* to shore. While everyone waited for the gangplank, two men and a woman came forward from aft of the boat and stood near where the gang-plank would be lowered. The woman wore a tan colored bonnet.

Gus frowned. "I didn't know those people were on here with us."

"Those men walked by us while you were taking a nap." Jesse frowned. "But I don't remember seeing the woman."

"She reminds me of the woman we saw eating in the café yesterday."

Jesse looked back at her. "I think you're right."

The gangplank was lowered and the two men walked off the boat. Before the woman walked down the gangplank, she looked back toward Gus and Jesse.

Jesse tapped Gus on the arm. "Did you see her look at you?"

"Me? It was just a glance."

"Guess so. Wonder how long we're going to be docked here?"

"I don't know, but here comes the first mate, I'll ask him," Gus said. "Excuse me. How long will we be docked here?

"Just long enough to take on more wood for our boiler. Not more than fifteen to twenty minutes." Webster pointed at Gus. "If you fellows go ashore, I advise you to stay close to the Landing, or you could miss our departure for Harvey's Landing."

"Thank you," Gus said. "We'll be back on board before you raise that gangplank."

Gus and Jesse exited the boat but stayed within earshot. They stood looking at the buildings of Gardiner's City.

Jesse pointed to a little white church located on the side of the hill. "There's where I think Alice would have preferred to be married instead of at Harvey's Landing."

"It's a smaller church than the one where Martha and I were married in Scottsburg. But if you and Alice had gotten married in that little church, she wouldn't love you any more than she does. I think she looked very much in love when the two of you came to the lighthouse after your wedding."

"Are you fellows new in town?"

They turned toward a man who was watching them from about ten feet away.

"We are," Jesse said. "But we're coming back tomorrow to look for a place to live and to get jobs."

"I can get you jobs at the mill." The man approached them. "My name is Morgan Usher and we're looking for good workers."

Jesse looked at Gus. "Did you hear that?"

The *Melissa's* whistle blew.

Gus nodded and shook Mr. Usher's hand. "We have to get back on board right now. Where can we find you tomorrow?"

"In the hotel lobby, the saloon, or here around the Landing."

They thanked him and headed for the boat.

***

Soon after Gus and Jesse boarded the boat the gangplank was raised and the mooring ropes pulled. Once again, the *Melissa* steamed slowly away from the dock and out into the middle of the river. Gus and Jesse sat on a bench watching the river bank and the mountains go by.

Jesse turned toward Gus. “It looks like we won’t have to look very hard for jobs.”

“I guess we were in the right place at the right time.” Gus pulled out his pipe and filled it with tobacco. “That Morgan fellow just said he could get us jobs. He didn’t say what kind of work we would be doing.”

“I guess we’ll find out tomorrow. Wow! It would be nice if we could find a place to live that easy.”

“It would take the pressure off.” Gus puffed on his pipe. “The sooner we can get our stuff moved out of the lighthouse, the better.”

“Alice and me don’t have a lot to move, but I hope the tower doesn’t fall before we can get it out.” Jesse frowned. “Replacing everything would make starting over in a new place even more difficult.”

“We just have to believe that this will all work out,” Gus said.

They sat silent, enjoying the river scenery until the first mate came by.

“You fellows will be home shortly,” Webster said. “We should be getting to Harvey’s Landing in about fifteen minutes.”

“That’s good news,” Gus said. “I feel like I’ve been gone for a week.”

“Me, too,” Jesse said.

“How soon before you fellows can get moved out of the lighthouse?” Webster asked.

“We’re not sure,” Gus said. “We’re going to try to find a place to live first, and we hope it happens soon.”

“I wish you well.” Webster said. “I need to finish my round and get ready for docking."

Ten minutes later, the whistle blew and the *Melissa* pulled into the dock.

The gangplank was lowered and Gus and Jesse walked off the boat. Lloyd and Alice greeted them. Jesse and Alice kissed and hugged each other, while Gus and Lloyd shook hands.

"Lloyd, how did you know we were coming back today?" Gus asked.

"I sent a telegram to Scottsburg and asked Sam Waters if he knew whether you boarded the *Melissa* today."

Gus grinned. "Ahh."

Jesse and Alice joined Lloyd and Gus.

Alice hugged Gus. "Let's all go to the house. Nellie has dinner ready."

Gus smiled. "Jesse and me thought we might miss dinner,"

"When Nellie found out you fellows were coming back today, she insisted we wait to eat until you got here," Lloyd said. "Let's go eat. I'm hungry. I just have to tell the first mate that I don't have any cargo to load, and then I'll catch up to you."

Alice gently pulled Gus' arm. "Nellie's a good cook, so you fellows are in for a treat."

Jesse held Alice's hand as they walked to the Landing office.

Chapter 20

There, I Said it

BY THE TIME they reached Lloyd's quarters behind the Landing office, Lloyd had caught up with them. As they entered the sitting room, Lloyd pointed to an open area next to a big chair. "Just lay your stuff there, guys."

Nellie entered from the kitchen. "Welcome back, fellows! Gus, did you and Jesse have a good trip to Scottsburg?"

Gus grinned. "Well, it was both good and bad."

"What do you mean?" Nellie asked.

"The good part was that we did get the lens and clock mechanism safely stored in the board's warehouse." Gus rubbed the back of his neck. "But we found out that we don't have jobs, and the board has no idea how long it will be before the lighthouse can be rebuilt."

"Mr. Bronson did say that when the lighthouse is rebuilt, we'll have jobs," Jesse said.

"I'm sorry to hear you fellows don't have a job." Nellie placed her hands on her hips. "Maybe a good meal will help take your mind off the situation for at least a few minutes. I have everything ready. Alice, you show Jesse and Gus where to wash up."

After they washed their hands, everyone sat down at the table. Lloyd looked across at Gus. "While you were gone to Scottsburg,

Alice told Nellie and me about your job plans in case the board didn't have work for you. When will you start looking for new ones?"

Nellie pointed to the dish of mashed potatoes. "Alice, start those potatoes around."

"Jesse and me talked about this on the trip back," Gus said. "We figured it would be best for us to leave tomorrow for Gardiner's City."

"We don't know how long the tower will remain standing," Jesse said. "Should it fall with anyone inside the house, it would be extremely dangerous. So the sooner we can find a place to live and get moved, the safer for everyone."

"Gus, some bread?" Nellie asked and held up the plate.

"Thank you." Gus took a piece of bread.

"Since the lighthouse is so dangerous to stay in, and you're leaving for Gardiner's City tomorrow, I think you all should stay right here for tonight," Lloyd said.

Gus frowned. "You don't have room for all of us."

"We have room!" Nellie said. "Jesse and Alice can sleep in her old room, and you can sleep on the daybed there in the sitting room."

Jesse looked at Gus. "If that daybed sleeps as firm as yours, then you should sleep really good tonight."

"Thank you, Nellie," Gus said. "Now, since I didn't pack extra things for the trip to Scottsburg, I'll need to go back to the lighthouse this afternoon and get some things for tomorrow. By staying here tonight, it will save a little travel time in the morning."

"What about me?" Alice asked. "I want to go with you."

"I'm sorry, Alice." Gus said. "I didn't mean that you weren't going with us."

"I hope not," Alice said.

Jesse reached over and gently touched Alice on her arm. "Honey, I planned for you to go with me. I need you along to help pick out a place for us to live."

Alice smiled. "I'm glad."

After everyone had eaten their meal, Gus got up from the table. "Thank you, Nellie, for the good meal and the invitation to stay tonight."

"Lloyd and I are glad to help. You, Jesse, and Alice have had enough things happen to you lately. It's the least we can do."

They all moved to the sitting room and after the men sat down Alice looked at Jesse. "I'll be back as soon as Nellie and I finish the dishes."

"I'll be right here in this chair." Jesse yawned. "After eating all that good food and being tired, I might be asleep when you get back. If so, wake me."

Alice turned and went with Nellie back to the kitchen.

"I hope you fellows can find work right away and a place to live," Lloyd said.

"I'm not sure about a place to live," Jesse said. "But on the trip back from Scottsburg today, I overheard two men on the boat talking about jobs in Gardiner's City. The one guy said he heard they were hiring at the lumber mill and that's where he was going."

"I didn't even know those two men were on board with us until we were about ready to dock at Gardiner's City," Gus said.

"There are a lot of places to hide on that boat." Jesse said. "We didn't walk around on the top deck. After you fell asleep those guys showed up on our side of the boat. Before then, I didn't know they were on the boat either."

Jesse looked at Lloyd. "We also talked to a man at the dock in Gardiner's City about work."

"Well, he approached us about working at the mill," Gus said.

"It sounds to me like you may be getting jobs pretty quick," Lloyd said.

"We hope," Gus said. I better get ready to go to the lighthouse and pack some fresh clothing to take along tomorrow."

"I should do the same," Jesse said. "I don't have enough clean stuff with me, either. In fact, Alice will probably want to gather up more clothes to take with her. I'll go ask her and if she doesn't want to go, then we'll just take one buggy."

"Whether Alice goes or not, I'll go out and hitch up mine," Gus said.

"All right," Jesse headed for the kitchen.

"My bell just rang," Lloyd said. "I have a customer out front. Gus, when you're ready to go hitch up the horses, just make yourself at home. You know where your horse and buggy are located. I'll see you later."

Gus waved. "Thanks, Lloyd."

Jesse returned from the kitchen. "Well, just as I said, Alice wants to go along. I told her we would go out and hitch up the horses, so when she's finished with the dishes we can go."

"All right." Gus stood up.

They went to the corral and after hitching their horses, Gus and Jesse both drove to the front of the Landing office. Alice came out carrying her bag.

"I forgot my bag is still inside," Gus said.

"Mine too." Jesse climbed down from his buggy to help Alice get in.

"What's wrong?" Alice asked.

Jesse shook his head. "We left our bags inside. We'll be right back."

Gus and Jesse returned with their bags, and they drove away toward the lighthouse.

***

Gus shook his head as everyone stood silently looking at the lighthouse. A moment later they all went inside to pick up the clothing they needed. In a short time, Gus came back outside and walked around to the back of the lighthouse. He looked up at the tower. *It doesn't look like it has moved very much. But the angle at which it's leaning, it won't have to move very much more to cause the tower to fall over.* Gus returned to his buggy just as Jesse was helping Alice back into theirs. "Looks like we're ready to go back to the Landing."

***

They pulled up in front of the office. After carrying their bags inside, Gus and Jesse returned to their buggies and unhitched the horses at the corral, then went back inside Lloyd's quarters. For the remainder of the afternoon they visited with Lloyd and Nellie, and ate supper together.

As they got up from the table, Gus remembered the horses. "Jesse, we better go take care of the horses. Oh! Lloyd, that reminds me. I owe you for feed and board."

"Don't worry about the horses," Lloyd said. "You fellows go on into the sitting room and rest. I had Seth take care of your horses just before we ate. As far as settling up, we can take care of that in the morning."

Jesse smiled. "That was sure thoughtful of you. Now all we have to do is get a good night's rest."

"Gus, do you plan on taking your horse and buggy with you to Gardiner's City?" Lloyd asked.

"We never talked about that." Gus scratched his beard. "It would make it easier to get around after we get off the boat."

"If I were you, I would take 'em. It will only take a few minutes to load them on the boat, and likewise to unload."

"Should we take both buggies?" Jesse asked.

Lloyd shrugged. "Well, that's up to you and Gus."

"Jesse, if you want to leave your buggy here, we should be able to get by with mine," Gus said.

"All right," Jesse said. "I can owe Lloyd for the feed and board."

Nellie and Alice entered the sitting room. Alice walked over and sat down on the floor next to Jesse's chair and Nellie sat next to Gus on the daybed.

Alice looked up at Jesse. "Honey, since we have to move out of the lighthouse, I'm really anxious to find a new home and get moved as quickly as we can."

"Me, too." Jesse yawned.

Nellie looked at Lloyd. "It's getting dark in here. I think it's time to light the lamp."

Lloyd got up. "I was just talking to Gus and Jesse about their trip tomorrow. They plan to take a horse and buggy with them on the *Melissa*."

"That's a good idea," Nellie said.

Jesse leaned forward in his chair. "We talked to a guy about jobs, but he didn't offer to pick us up when we arrive at the dock. So, it would be good to take the buggy."

Alice looked up at Jesse. "I'm glad you thought of that. Now I feel better about making the trip."

Jesse patted Alice on the shoulder. "It was your father's idea, not mine."

"Gus, I'm curious about the lighthouse," Lloyd said. "Did it look any worse when you were over there today?"

"The tower was still standing, and it didn't look like it was leaning any more than before."

"Did you go around back of the lighthouse while we were there?" Alice asked.

"Yeah," Gus said. "Why do you ask?"

"I told Jesse on the way back here that I thought you had gone behind the lighthouse to look at the tower, but he disagreed."

Jesse turned his palms upward. "Gus, when I saw you coming to the buggy from around that side of the lighthouse, I thought you were returning from the outhouse."

Everyone burst out laughing.

"You know, this reminds me of what Mansel Carter said to me once," Jesse said. "'A man's thoughts can sometimes lead him to the wrong conclusion.' Remember that, Gus?"

"I sure do. I always enjoyed talking to Mansel. Maybe we'll get to see him since we're moving to Gardiner's City."

"I hope so," Jesse said.

"The way you fellows go on." Nellie smiled. "I bet you could sit up and talk all night long. I think it's time we all go to bed though, so you can get some rest for your trip tomorrow."

"That sounds like a good idea," Jesse said.

"I agree," Alice rose up off the floor.

Everyone except Gus got up from his or her seat and began moving toward the bedrooms.

"I'll wake everyone in the morning," Lloyd said.

***

The next morning, at 6:00, Lloyd awoke and then awakened Nellie. After he got dressed, he went to Alice's bedroom door and knocked. "Alice, Jesse, time to get up!"

"All right, Daddy," Alice said.

Lloyd went to the sitting room and found Gus already up and dressed. "Morning, Gus."

"Morning."

Did you have trouble sleeping on that daybed?"

"It slept just fine. I'm just used to getting up in the middle of the night to relieve Jesse. Now I have to adjust to sleeping different hours."

"I wondered why you were up already," Lloyd said. "You probably heard me wake Alice and Jesse. They should be out shortly."

"As soon as Jesse gets here, I'd like to go feed the horses." Gus said. "You'll need to show us where you keep the feed, and then figure up what we owe you for it and board."

"Well, that's easy," Lloyd said. "All together it's going to be seventy-five cents."

Gus reached for his change pouch as Jesse walked into the room. "Here's the seventy-five cents," Gus said. "I really appreciate you taking care of Jake."

"Good morning, everyone," Jesse said. "Lloyd, I want you to know that I also appreciate you taking care of Molly. How much do I owe you?"

"Your cost is the same, Jesse. Seventy-five cents."

Jesse handed the money to Lloyd. "Are you sure that's enough?"

"Oh yeah, and I thank you both. I'm just glad I could help."

"Well, Jesse, I think we should go feed the horses," Gus said.

"I'm ready." Jesse moved toward the door.

"I'll show you fellows where the feed is located," Lloyd said.

Meanwhile, Alice was in the bedroom packing her personal items for the trip. Just as she closed her bag, a sick feeling came over her again. *I'm sick to my stomach again. What's wrong with me?* Alice frowned and went to the kitchen to help Nellie with breakfast.

Nellie looked at Alice. "Good morning. Are you all right?"

"Not so good." Alice held her hand over her stomach. "I'm sick again."

"What do you mean, again?" Nellie asked.

"Well, it's not every morning, but almost every morning now

for over a week."

"What do you think is causing it?"

"I have no idea."

"Do you want to know what I think?"

"Yes."

Nellie turned away from the stove and moved over toward Alice. She put her arm around Alice's shoulder. "Sweetie, I think you're sick because you're going to have a baby."

"A baby!" Alice said in disbelief.

"I'm pretty sure," Nellie said.

"Oh, my! I wonder what Jesse will say when he finds out."

"If I know Jesse, he's going to be very happy." Nellie moved back to the stove and turned over the bacon frying in the skillet.

"I can't stand the smell of food right now," Alice said. "I think I'm going to vomit." She started to leave the kitchen.

"I understand dear. You don't worry about breakfast. I'll take care of it."

Alice went back to the bedroom.

A few minutes later the men returned from feeding the horses and Lloyd walked into the kitchen. "Nellie, you've done it again. Another great smelling breakfast."

Nellie looked at Lloyd and grinned. "Alice doesn't agree with you."

Lloyd rolled his eyes. "What do you mean?"

"Don't say anything to Jesse just yet, but Alice is sick again this morning. The smell of this food made her worse."

"Oh, you mean she's—"

"Pregnant. Alice told me she's been getting sick now for several mornings, but she doesn't know why. I don't think Jesse knows either. You need to break the news to him, and also let him know that Alice may not be able to go with him to Gardiner's City."

Lloyd shook his head. "I'll try, but I'm not sure how to tell him. Is breakfast ready?"

"Yes, tell Gus and Jesse to come to the table."

Lloyd walked part of the way to the sitting room. "Gus, Jesse, breakfast is ready. Come and get it."

Except for Alice, they all sat down at the table.

Jesse looked at Nellie. “Where’s Alice? I thought she was helping you with breakfast.”

“She wasn’t feeling good, so she went to lie down. Now you fellows start eating or it’s going to get cold.”

“Nellie, is Alice sick to her stomach again?” Jesse asked.

“Yes.”

Jesse shook his head. “I can’t figure out why she’s been getting sick.”

Gus took a sip of coffee and looked at Jesse with a big grin on his face. “Well, Wickie, knowing you like I do, I bet it won’t be long until you solve that mystery.”

“I agree,” Lloyd said. “In fact, Jesse, after you finish your breakfast, I think you should go talk with Alice. I’m sure she’ll be able to explain things now.”

“Since she’s sick, she may not be able to go with us,” Jesse said. “I hate the idea of leaving her here.”

“Don’t you worry about that,” Nellie said. “If Alice doesn’t feel like going, we’ll be glad to have her stay with us.”

Jesse finished his breakfast and slid his chair back from the table. “Thanks for the breakfast Nellie, it was very good. I better go check on Alice.” He turned toward Gus. “I was really looking forward to Alice going with us.”

“You take care of her,” Gus said. “We’ve got plenty of time before we have to leave. She may feel better by then.”

“I hope so.” Jesse headed for the bedroom.

Nellie waited until Jesse was out of hearing range. She chuckled. “He hasn’t figured out yet that he’s going to be a father.”

“I thought that was the situation,” Gus said. “Jesse told me several days ago that Alice was having morning sickness, but I never told him of my suspicions.”

Jesse entered the bedroom and found Alice lying on the bed. He sat down next to her. “Nellie told me you were sick again.”

“I’m feeling a little better, now.”

“I’m glad, but we need to find out why you’re getting sick all the time. I need to get you to a doctor. We have a lot of work to do with house hunting and moving, and you can't do anything if you're down sick."

Alice grinned and raised herself up on one elbow, then placed her other hand on Jesse's cheek. "Honey, you worry too much. I said I was feeling better. Besides, I know now why I've been sick."

Jesse reached up and touched Alice's hand. "You do! What's wrong?"

Alice smiled. "Nothing's wrong. We're going to have a baby."

"What? A baby?" A baby!" He smiled from ear to ear. "Are you sure?"

"Yes, I am."

"Oh! A baby! That's great!" Jesse kissed Alice. "I love you."

Alice smiled. "I'm feeling much better now. Let me up, and I'll get ready to go."

Jesse stood up alongside the bed and helped Alice off the bed. "I'm not sure about you going along, even though you say you're feeling better."

"I'll be just fine. Now that we know why I've been getting sick, it'll be easier for me to bear it."

"All right," Jesse said. "But you have to eat your breakfast before we go."

They moved toward the bedroom door.

"Oh! I can hardly believe it, we're going to have a baby," Jesse said. He stopped and kissed Alice again. "This will be a big surprise to everyone. I know it was to me."

Alice smiled. "Well, do you want to tell them now?"

"Sure, I can't wait."

They entered the kitchen and found Nellie by herself clearing the table.

Nellie smiled. "Well Alice, you must be feeling better."

"I feel much better, and I think I can eat some breakfast now."

"You sit down, dear, and I'll fix you a couple of eggs. Gus and Lloyd ate yours. They didn't think you were going to eat. I did manage to keep some bacon warm for you. Jesse, would you pour Alice some coffee?"

"Sure."

"What time is it?" Alice asked. "I don't want to make us late."

"We're not going to be late," Jesse said. "We have plenty of time. The boat probably won't get here until 12:45 p.m. or so. You eat your

"We thought we heard you, Alice." Gus said. "We came in to see how you're feeling."

"Thank you. I'm feeling much better now."

Lloyd noticed Jesse's face was beaming, yet his hands were clasped and his thumbs rubbing each other in a circular motion. "You seem nervous Jesse. Are you still concerned about Alice going with you to Gardiner's City?"

Jesse grinned. "Oh, no. She's feeling better, so she can go if she still wants to. I'm not nervous, but Alice and me have something to tell you. I've been trying to think of the best way to say it."

"It will be easier if you just come out and say it," Lloyd said.

Jesse wrung his hands. "Alice and me are going to have a baby. There, I said it!"

Lloyd chuckled, then reached over and slapped Jesse on the shoulder. "Well, congratulations to you and Alice."

Gus walked around the table and shook Jesse's hand. "Congratulations. I'm happy for both of you. This is good news."

Nellie hugged Alice. "I'm so happy for you, and I know you're going to be a good mother." She turned toward Jesse. "How do you feel now that you're going to be a father?"

"I guess I have mixed feelings. I'm excited, but I'm concerned about Alice. Considering the move, we have to make. I'm afraid she may do something wrong and hurt herself or the baby."

Nellie grinned. "Don't worry about anything going wrong. Alice is strong, healthy, and smart. She'll do just fine."

"Honey, I'll be all right. You worry too much." Alice looked up at Jesse and got up from the table. "Nellie, I'll help you with these dishes."

"I'll take care of the dishes," Nellie said. "You take it easy for now. You've got plenty of work ahead of you with the move."

"All right, but I'll help you cook dinner and wash up those dishes before we get on the boat this afternoon."

Chapter 21

A New Home

AFTER DINNER, THEY were enjoying good conversation with each other in the sitting room when Gus got up from his chair. "It's time. We need to get ready to go. I'll go hitch up the buggy."

"All right." Jesse turned toward Alice. "I'll take our bags out with me and put them in Gus' buggy, and then you won't have to carry anything."

Alice shook her head. "There you go worrying about me again. It will take us forever to get moved out of the lighthouse if you aren't going to let me lift anything."

"I just don't want you to lift anything that might hurt you." Jesse went to get their bags.

"Alice, I have a jug of water and a blanket I want you to take with you," Nellie said. "It's cool out there and the blanket will help keep you warm."

"Thank you, Nellie. That's sweet of you."

***

Alice and Nellie walked outside and over to the dock to meet up with Lloyd, Gus, and Jesse. Seth and Ike had finished securing the *Melissa's* mooring ropes to the dock. The crew lowered the

gangplank, and three soldiers returning to Fort Umpqua were the first to walk off the boat.

"Good to see you men back," Lloyd said. "Hope you got rested up while you were on furlough."

They all smiled. "We had such a good time we didn't want to come back," one soldier said. They approached another soldier who was waiting with horses for them to ride back to the fort.

As soon as all the passengers and cargo were unloaded, Seth and Ike guided Gus as he drove Jake and the buggy up the ramp onto the *Melissa.* They blocked the wheels to prevent them from rolling. Gus tied up Jake, then turned toward Seth and Ike. "Thanks for your help." He went back to the top of the ramp and waved goodbye. "Thanks, Lloyd."

Jesse and Alice met Gus at the top of the gangplank.

"You're welcome," Lloyd said. You watch out for those two. Nellie and I hope you all have a good trip. We'll see you when you get back."

"We'll see you in a couple days," Gus said.

Jesse and Alice waved and said goodbye.

***

The *Melissa's* whistle blew. Jesse turned toward Gus. "Let's find a place to sit down so Alice can get off her feet."

"There you go again, worrying about me," Alice said.

"Well, we don't know how long we may have to stand around after we get to Gardiner's City," Jesse said.

"You know Jesse may be right," Gus said. "We probably should sit down on one of those benches while we can."

The *Melissa* slowly steamed away from the dock. About thirty minutes after she had been underway, Webster, the first mate approached Gus. "We've got a few minutes yet, but when you hear the whistle, prepare your horse and buggy to unload when we dock."

Gus nodded. "I'll be ready."

Webster turned and walked away.

Jesse looked at Gus. "I'm anxious to get to Gardiner's City. I hope we can find that fellow Morgan Usher without any trouble."

"Yeah."

***

Twenty minutes later the *Melissa* steamed into the Gardiner's City dock. As soon as the ramp was lowered, Gus drove his horse and buggy off the boat. Jesse and Alice followed on foot, then climbed into the buggy with Gus. He drove to the hotel on Main Street and stopped out front. Gus and Jesse climbed down, and while Gus tied Jake to the hitching rail, Jesse helped Alice down from the buggy. The three of them went inside the hotel.

"Welcome to the Gardiner's Hotel," the clerk said. "How can I help you?"

"We'd like two rooms," Gus said. "One for my friend here and his wife, and one for me."

"Sure. How many nights will you be staying?"

Gus glanced at Jesse then back at the clerk. "Well, we're not real sure. We're here to look for jobs and a place to live. We'll be here for at least tonight."

"I have two rooms that face the river, if you'd like them," the clerk said.

Gus looked around at Jesse and Alice.

Alice smiled. "That would be nice."

"Well, it's settled, then," Gus said. "We'll take those rooms."

The clerk turned the registration book around. "Just sign here to register for your rooms." After Gus and Jesse signed the register, the clerk looked at the book and said, "Mr. Crosby, your room will be fifty cents, and Mr. Fayette, you and the Mrs. room will be one dollar."

They paid for the rooms.

"Sir, are there towels in the room?" Alice asked.

"Yes ma'am," the clerk said. "And there's also a wash basin with a pitcher of water. If you need more water, you'll have to fetch it from the well out to the side of the hotel."

"Thank you, sir."

The clerk handed Gus and Jesse keys to their rooms.

Jesse leaned on the desk. "Do you know anyone around town who we could talk to about a more permanent place to live?"

"According to what I hear, there probably aren't any vacant homes," the clerk said. "Homes are scarce with all the hiring that's been done at the mill." He scratched his ear. "I heard yesterday, that two men were hired on at the mill, and they took rooms at the Sawtooth Boarding House. You might ask a fellow by the name of

Morgan Usher. He'll know a lot more than I do about the house situation."

Jesse's eyes widened. "Morgan Usher! He's the same fellow we came here to see about jobs."

"Do you know where we could find Mr. Usher?" Gus asked.

"He normally has supper at the Axe Handle Restaurant. Sometimes, he'll stop in here to say hello, as he says, and then sit for a spell. I think he does it to get away from the pressure of the job."

"Where's the Axe Handle Restaurant? Gus asked.

The clerk pointed. "Right there across the street,"

"Thank you." Gus turned toward Jesse and Alice. "This is good. We have a little time before trying to catch up with this Morgan fellow. Let's take our bags to the rooms, and then we'll have time to look around Gardiner's while we wait to eat supper."

"All right," Jesse said."

Gus turned back to the clerk. "Where can I water my horse?"

"You'll find a watering trough out back of the hotel."

"Thanks."

They took the bags to their rooms, and then met back in the lobby. "I'm going to water my horse. I'll be right back," Gus said.

"If we're not here in the lobby, we'll be on the front porch," Jesse said.

"Sure. I shouldn't be gone long." Gus turned and walked out the front door.

Alice looked at Jesse. "I'd like to sit on the porch while we wait."

"All right, honey."

They sat down on two of several chairs lined up across the porch. Alice ran her hand through her hair and straightened it.

"Honey, how are you feeling?" Jesse asked.

"I'm fine." Alice smiled. "Now, you quit worrying about me." She patted her foot. "I just wish there were some way we could talk to that Mr. Usher before supper. I feel like we're wasting time waiting until then."

"We do have about two hours. When Gus gets back, I'll talk to him about going to find Mr. Usher."

Alice nodded. "We'll have time later to look around Gardiner's City." She smiled at a mother and her two children walking by the hotel.

"The one place we need to look is that Axe Handle Restaurant there across the street. That's probably where we'll eat and I hope they have good food."

"We'll find out this evening." Alice stood up. "There comes Gus now."

Gus tied Jake to the hitching rail and walked up on the porch. "Are you ready to have a look around Gardiner's?"

Jesse moved toward Gus. "Alice and I were just talking about how much time we have before supper. What do you think about trying to find Morgan Usher now, instead of waiting until after suppertime?"

Gus looked down at the porch then back at Jesse. "It's fine by me."

"Do you remember the places where Mr. Usher said he could be found?"

"Yeah. The saloon, hotel, or the Landing. We know he's not here at the hotel, so we could look in the saloon."

They stepped off the porch.

"Hey, that looks like Morgan Usher coming up the street now!" Jesse said.

Gus turned his head. "Yes, it does."

A few seconds later Usher's buggy stopped in front of the hotel. Before Mr. Usher could get out, Jesse approached him. "Hi Mr. Usher. Do you remember talking to Gus and me yesterday about jobs?"

"Yes, and I wanted to be at the Landing to meet you when you came in, but I got tied up and couldn't get there in time. I figured you would come to the hotel first if you did come in today."

Jesse turned slightly toward Alice. "Mr. Usher, this is my wife, Alice. Honey, this is the Mr. Usher that Gus and I told you about."

Mr. Usher tipped his hat. "I'm very glad to meet you, ma'am."

Alice grinned. "Thank you, Mr. Usher. I'm pleased to meet you."

"Just call me Morgan." He climbed down from his buggy.

Gus shook Morgan's hand. "Do you still have those jobs available?"

"If you have time, I'd like to talk to you about that now."

"Oh, we have time," Gus said. "In fact, we were about to go try to find you when we saw you coming up the street."

"Where are you from?" Morgan asked.

"We're from the lighthouse," Gus said. "I was the head keeper, and Jesse here was my assistant."

"Didn't you fellows like that kind of work?"

"We liked it a lot," Jesse said. "But the last storm damaged the lighthouse so bad that it's unsafe to be inside. We were forced to shut it down. That's the reason we have to move and get new jobs."

"I'm sorry to hear that," Morgan said. "I heard talk about the lighthouse from some of the men that come here on ships to load lumber. They say the lighthouse was a big help to find the mouth of the river."

Gus nodded. "Yeah, without the lighthouse, their jobs are going to be more stressful at night as they try to navigate the mouth of the river."

"How long would it be before you fellows are ready to start work?"

"Probably three or four days," Gus said. "We've already closed down operation of the lighthouse, and moved its light and other equipment to Scottsburg. We're ready to move our personal items, but first, we need to find a place to live."

Morgan looked at Gus. "I can get you people a place to live. Unfortunately, there is only one house available, but there is the Sawtooth Boarding House. I can probably get you a room there. Since expanding our operation at the mill, homes in Gardiner's City are scarce. The owner of the mill has been talking about building a bunkhouse for the workers instead of building more homes."

Gus rubbed his bearded chin. "How many rooms are in the house?"

"Three," Morgan said.

Gus looked at Jesse. "I'll take a room at the boarding house.

There's only one of me, and the house will give you and Alice room to grow."

Alice touched Gus on the arm. "Thank you, Gus."

"You're welcome."

"Morgan, what kind of work do you have in store for us?" Jesse asked.

"We need help in our staging area."

Jesse frowned. "What's that?"

Morgan grinned. "That's the area where the logs come in, then are prepared for movement into the saw mill. You'll be rolling and stacking logs."

"It sounds like a job that would build muscles on a fellow," Jesse said.

"Yeah, and I guarantee you'll be tired at the end of the day."

"Morgan, could we look at the house you mentioned?" Jesse asked.

"Sure thing, and I also want to take Gus to the boarding house. After that, if you have time, I'd like to introduce you to our mill foreman."

"Sounds good," Jesse said.

"Yeah."

Alice looked at Morgan. "I'm anxious to see the house."

Morgan nodded and asked. "How are you traveling?"

"We've got my horse and buggy, right there," Gus pointed.

"Well, if you'll follow me, I'll show you that house."

***

Morgan led the way as they went up the hill on Mill Street, and turned right onto First Street. One block later they stopped in front of a little white house.

"Honey, this is beautiful!" Alice said. "Such a pretty house."

"Yeah, but not as big as the lighthouse." Jesse helped Alice down from the buggy.

Morgan unlocked the front door. "Here it is. Take a look around." He walked to the center of the kitchen and pointed out the window. "There's a good well out there on the side of the house."

He turned toward Alice. "As you can see, the people who lived here before kept it clean."

"I noticed, and that will make it easier for us to move in."

Morgan tapped Jesse on the arm and motioned him toward the back door. "The outhouse is right there." He pointed toward it. "And there's a small barn beyond that."

"Care if I go take a look at the barn?" Jesse asked.

"Help yourself."

"I'll go with you," Gus said.

Alice walked through the rooms, and looked out the windows at the surrounding area before arriving back in the kitchen. "Looks like most of the town sits on the side of this hill."

"A good part of it does," Morgan said. "Most of the homes were built on the hill because the majority of the flat land down by the river was needed for the mill." He pointed to a small room off the kitchen. "Did you notice the pantry?"

"Yes," Alice said. "It's not as big as the one at the lighthouse, but I'll make it work."

"When you need supplies, the general store is only a couple of buildings down the street from the hotel."

Jesse and Gus returned from exploring the barn.

"The barn is well built, and although smaller than we're used to, it's big enough for our needs," Jesse said.

Gus looked at Alice. "I think you and Jesse can make a good home here."

Alice smiled. "I do too."

Jesse rubbed the side of his face and glanced at Morgan. "How much do you charge a month for this house?"

"It's $18.00. The house is owned by the mill, so if you want, we can arrange to have that cost taken out of your pay."

"I guess that would be all right, but I don't know if I'll make that much a month."

"I can't tell you how much you'll make off the top of my head, but you'll make more than $18.00," Morgan said.

"That sounds good," Jesse said.

"Gus, are you ready to go see the boarding house?" Morgan

asked.

"I sure am."

***

They had walked part way up the front steps of the boarding house when Morgan stopped and turned toward the others. "Gus, there are a couple of things I should tell you before we go in. The owners of the Sawtooth, Mr. and Mrs. Franks, also operate it. They have rules and you are expected to follow them. First, they require their boarders to keep their rooms clean. They don't allow any rough housing, and they expect everyone to be on time for meals."

Gus nodded. "I shouldn't have any trouble living by those rules."

"I hope not," Morgan said. "If you do, Mrs. Franks will be the first one to tell you about it. She's more particular than her husband." Morgan turned and led everyone up the remaining steps to the front porch. He opened the front door, which rang a small bell that hung above it. They entered into what appeared to be a large sitting room. On one side of the room was a stairway leading up to a hallway on the second floor. There were several chairs located around the room and a fireplace at one end. Next to the fireplace was a wooden box partially filled with wood.

Alice looked at Gus. "This is nice."

A man entered from a large connecting dining room.

"Hi, Tucker." Morgan took a step toward him. "I brought you another boarder."

"That's good, but I didn't expect to see you again so soon."

"These fellows told me a couple of days ago they were coming to town. I didn't say anything to you because I didn't know for sure what day they would show up. Do you have any rooms left?"

Tucker nodded. "Two."

"One is all I need for Gus here." Morgan turned toward Gus. "I don't remember your last name."

"It's Crosby."

"He needs a room," Morgan said.

Gus shook Tucker's hand. "I'm glad to meet you Mr. Franks."

"It's good to meet you too, Mr. Crosby, but I'd just as soon that we not be so formal. Just call me Tucker."

Gus smiled. "Hey, that's fine with me, and you can call me Gus." He gestured toward Jesse. "This is my good friend, Jesse, and his wife, Alice."

Tucker nodded. "I'm pleased to meet you people. Are you staying in town?"

"Yeah," Jesse said. "Morgan also gave me a job at the mill and a place for my wife and me to live."

"It's a beautiful home, not too far from here," Alice said.

Tucker looked at Morgan. "Only a couple of days ago, I heard that all the homes in town were taken."

"This was the last one we had," Morgan said. "It was supposed to be taken by a couple who came here from Boston. However, just before they were to move in, he changed his mind about working at the mill. He said they were going to southern Oregon to try mining for gold."

Jesse grinned. "Lucky for us they changed their minds."

"We're glad you came to Gardiner's City," Tucker said. "I think you'll like it here."

"Tucker, do you have time to show Gus his room?" Morgan asked.

"Sure." Tucker looked at Gus. "In fact, you can pick the room you want since there are two. Come along and I'll show you."

Tucker led the way. Suddenly, he stopped and looked back at the others. "You can come along too, if you want."

Jesse took Alice by the arm. "Thanks, we'd like to see Gus' room."

"I'll wait here," Morgan said. "I've seen the rooms."

Tucker led them to the adjacent room. "This is our dining room where our boarders eat their meals."

"This is big," Jesse said.

"It's the most popular room in the house." Tucker chuckled. "Probably because my wife, Mary, and her help serve such good meals in here."

"That's a big table. How many can you seat around it?" Alice asked.

"We can seat twelve if we need to. Come along and we'll go upstairs."

They walked up the stairway and Tucker stopped at the top of the stairs. "Gus, this is the first room." He opened the door.

Gus looked inside. "It's a good-sized room. Even with the furniture that's in here, it doesn't seem crowded."

"We try to provide the basic items that a person needs to be comfortable." Tucker pointed to items in the room. "You can see, you would have a closet, bed, dresser, oil lamp, a couple of stands, washbasin with a water bucket, a writing table with chair, and a heating stove with a wood box. Then, of course, you will also have use of the sitting room downstairs. When you want to do more than wash up, there's a bathtub in the back room downstairs. If you go on down this hallway, another stairway takes you to that back room. The outhouse is behind the hotel, and it has three holes."

"This is a very nice room," Alice said. "I'm surprised it's still available."

Tucker looked at Alice. "There could be a couple of reasons. This room faces up the hill and it can get a little noisy because of the foot traffic going up and down the stairs. Whenever I put boarders in here, they always want to move as soon as another room becomes available."

Gus nodded. *I could probably handle the noise if I had to.*

Tucker stepped back. "Let me show you the other room. It's at the other end of the hall and faces the street." They headed down the hallway. "This room has a better view. Besides facing the street, you can see the river and the mill from here." Tucker opened the door. "Now, you can see for yourself what I said about the view."

Alice walked in. "Oh, Gus, this is a much nicer view!"

Gus smiled. "Yeah."

"This room will enable you to also see some great sunsets," Tucker said. "You can see there aren't many trees in front of us, and because the Sawtooth sits on this hill you have a good view of the surrounding area."

"Is this room larger than the other one?" Jesse asked.

"They are the same size. This one just looks bigger because the view gives it a more open feeling."

"I like this room better," Gus said. "But Morgan never told me how much a room here would cost."

"All of our rooms are $0.95 a day. That includes breakfast and supper. On Sunday, dinner is provided. Morgan probably told you about the dinner meal during the week."

"No, he didn't. What's that about?" Gus asked.

"The mill has its own mess hall. So you'll eat dinner there."

Gus held the back of his neck. "The price sounds reasonable."

"How soon will you be moving in?" Tucker asked.

"We think three or four days," Gus said. He looked at Jesse. "If we go back on the *Melissa* at noon tomorrow, do you think we can have everything ready to move out of the lighthouse day after tomorrow?"

Jesse shrugged. "Well, all we can do is try."

"I won't hold you fellows to the four days," Tucker said. "Did you say you were from the lighthouse?"

"Yeah," Gus said. "How much do you need to hold this room for me?"

Tucker shook his head. "Nothing. If Morgan wants you to have a room here, that's good enough for me to hold it."

Gus smiled. "Thanks Tucker. I really appreciate that."

"You're welcome. Do you have any other questions?"

"I do have a couple. You have furniture in here, but I was wondering if it would be all right if I brought my favorite chair with me?"

"Sure, if you don't think you'd be too crowded."

"I'll make it work," Gus said. "I was also wondering how many boarders you have now."

"There are eight other boarders." Tucker looked around at Jesse and Alice. "Anyone have more questions? If not, we probably should get back downstairs."

They approached the top of the stairway.

"You fellows said you were from the lighthouse," Tucker said. "I'd think that kind of work would be much easier than working at the mill."

"I'm sure you're right," Jesse said. "But we were forced to close down the lighthouse." He filled Tucker in on the rest of the details.

"That's too bad. I'm real sorry to hear about shutting down the lighthouse. I've heard stories about the shipwrecks that occurred before the lighthouse was built. So

I know the lighthouse has made a big difference in helping the captains find the mouth of the river."

They made their way downstairs and approached Morgan in the sitting room.

"What did you think of the room?" Morgan asked Gus.

"It's big enough, and it has a good view. It's just that I've been so used to all the space in the lighthouse. This will definitely be an adjustment, but I'll make it work."

"I like your attitude." Morgan stood up and looked at Tucker. "If you're finished, I need to take these people down to the mill. The day is gettin' on."

"I've covered everything except for meal times and the house rules, but that's all right. Mary can cover those with Gus when he comes back."

"Sounds good," Morgan said. "Speaking of Mary, I haven't seen or heard from her today. Is she all right?"

Tucker grinned. "Mary's fine, but thanks for asking. She's back in the kitchen helping to prepare supper."

"Thanks for inviting us to go along and see Gus' room," Alice said.

"Oh, you're welcome."

Gus turned toward Tucker. "I'll see you in a few days,"

"We're looking forward to having you as a boarder," Tucker said.

They walked out the front door and down the steps to the buggies.

"That was good of Tucker to let you bring your favorite chair," Jesse said.

Gus nodded. "At least I'll be able to keep one piece of my furniture."

"Tucker and Mary are good people," Morgan said. "As long as

you live by their rules, you shouldn't have any problems."

***

As they walked into the mill office, they were met by a man sitting behind a table. He saw Alice and stood up. His size made Alice look tiny. The man looked to weigh 250 pounds and stood about six feet tall with black hair and thick mustache. "Good to see you're back, Morgan."

"I brought you some more help," Morgan said. He turned toward Gus, Jesse, and Alice. "This is our foreman, Ivan."

"We're glad you men decided to come to work for us." Ivan looked at Alice. "I'm always glad to meet a pretty lady." He shook hands with them. "Are you ready to start work in the morning?"

"Well, ... not in the morning," Jesse said. "We need three or four days."

"Three or four days?" Ivan raised his hands to his hips and looked at Morgan. "I told you we need help right away!"

"I know. But we also need good workers, too. If you'll give these men at least the four days, I feel certain you won't be sorry."

Ivan lowered his hands then turned toward Gus and Jesse. "Why do you fellows need so much time?"

"We haven't moved here yet," Jesse said. "All of our belongings are still at the lighthouse."

"Lighthouse? You're from the lighthouse?"

"Yeah," Gus said. He filled Ivan in on the details. "That's why we need four days, so we can get our stuff moved up here from the lighthouse. There's no road from there to here, so we have to make the move by boat."

"For a minute or so there, I thought you men were a couple of quitters," Ivan said. "Now I know better. All right, we need the help, so if you men can be here to start work in five days, you've got a job."

Gus shook his hand. "Thank you. We appreciate you giving us a chance."

Ivan grinned. "We'll see if you still feel that way after you've worked here a few days."

"How much does the job pay?" Jesse asked.

Ivan looked at Jesse. "$1.35 a day." He stroked his mustache "If there's no other questions, I'll see you fellows in five days." He looked at Alice. "It's been my pleasure to meet you, ma'am."

Alice nodded. "Thank you and we appreciate your understanding our situation."

Outside the office, they untied their horses.

Jesse turned toward Morgan. "I really appreciate the confidence you showed in us in there."

Morgan glanced at Jesse. "Oh, I don't think you fellows will disappoint me. Somehow I believe you'll do a good job."

Gus climbed into the buggy. "We'll try hard not to disappoint you, Morgan,"

Jesse helped Alice up into the buggy. "How are you feeling, honey?"

"I'm a little tired, and I could use a drink of water."

"Morgan, are we going back to the hotel now?" Jesse asked.

"Yeah, we're done here."

***

At the hotel, Jesse and Alice joined Gus at the side of Morgan's buggy.

Jesse shook hands. "Thanks, Morgan. We appreciate all your help."

"I hope your move goes smooth," Morgan said. "I'll see you after you get back." He waved and drove away.

The three of them walked into the hotel lobby.

"Alice would like to freshen up," Jesse said. "How about we meet back here in an hour and go eat."

"That's good," Gus said.

***

They entered the Axe Handle Restaurant and were approached by a waitress.

"Sit wherever you want, and someone will be right with you."

Alice turned toward Jesse. "Can we sit over there?" She pointed to a table by the window.

"Sure," Jesse said. "How about you, Gus?"

"That's good."

They took a seat and soon their waitress came to the table.

"Hi. I'm Jennifer and I'll be taking care of you." Her smile was surrounded by her shoulder length brown hair. She was maybe thirty years of age and wearing a light brown and white checkered dress.

They smiled back at her.

"We have a special tonight. It's steak, mashed potatoes with gravy, beans, bread, butter, and desert for thirty-five cents."

"I'm not that hungry," Alice said. "Do you have any soup?

"We have vegetable beef or just plain vegetable."

"I'll have a bowl of the vegetable beef with a slice of bread with butter," Alice said.

"That's a good choice," Jennifer said. "Would you like something to drink?"

"Water."

"What can I get you fellows?" Jennifer smiled.

"I'll have that special with a cup of coffee," Jesse said.

"The same for me."

"Thank you. I'll be right back."

Jesse rolled his eyes at Gus. "Isn't that the same lady we seen get off the boat the other day?"

"That was my thought when she first came to our table."

Alice frowned. "You know her?"

"No," Jesse said. "Only saw her on the boat."

In a short time, Jennifer returned with their drinks. "Here you go. Your food should be coming up soon." She pointed at Gus and smiled. "You look familiar, but I don't remember seeing you in here before."

Gus shook his head. "This is our first time. We just got here today looking for jobs, but you may remember us from the boat."

"That's where I've seen you. I never forget a face." She glanced around. "I'll be right back. The soup's ready."

"Sounds like she has a watchful eye for strangers in town," Gus said.

Jesse nodded. "Since Gardiner's City is growing, I suppose she has seen several new faces in here."

Jennifer returned to the table. "Here's your soup, ma'am. Have you fellows talked to anyone about jobs yet?"

"We talked to Morgan Usher earlier this afternoon," Jesse said. "He got us jobs at the mill."

"He's the man to talk to if you hadn't talked to anyone yet." Jennifer held up the palm of her hand. "Hold your thought. I'll be right back."

"Sounds as though she knows what's going on around here," Gus said.

Jennifer returned with their food. "Here you go, fellows. Enjoy your meal. Where are you from?"

"We're from the lighthouse," Gus said. "We were the keepers."

"Didn't you like that kind of work?"

"We liked it a lot," Jesse said. He went on to tell her the details about the storm and shutting down the lighthouse

"I'm sorry to hear you lost your jobs, but at least you found new ones."

Alice looked up at Jennifer. "I think they're very lucky to have found jobs and places to live so quickly. By the way, my name is Alice, and this is my husband Jesse and our good friend Gus."

Jennifer smiled. "Nice to meet you all. My grandmother's name was Alice, so it'll be easy for me to remember yours. Where in Gardiner's are you moving?"

"Well, if I remember correctly, it's the last house at the end of First Street." Alice said. "Jesse and I will move in there, and Gus will move into the boarding house."

"We're almost neighbors!" Jennifer said. "I live just two houses from there with my mother. How soon are you moving in?"

"In four or five days," Alice said.

"I think you'll like Gardiner's City. Well, I better get back to work before my other customers get upset with me. I'll be back with your dessert."

A short time later, Jennifer returned. "Can I get you anything else?"

Gus looked at Jesse and Alice. "We'll be full by the time we get this pie down."

"I hope you liked everything. When you're finished, you can pay over there at the counter." Jennifer pointed. "Alice, I'm looking forward to talking with you again."

Alice smiled. "Thank you. Me, too."

They finished their pie, then moved toward the counter to pay the bill. Just then, Morgan walked into the restaurant.

"Well, what do you think of the food here?" Morgan asked.

"It's very good," Gus said.

"That's why I eat here a lot."

"We'll get to eat breakfast here in the morning," Jesse said.

"If you like biscuits and gravy, you'll love these. They're the best I've ever eaten."

Gus paid his bill and moved away from the counter. "After hearing that, I'm looking forward to breakfast."

Morgan moved toward his favorite table. "Have a safe trip."

***

Jesse held the front door of the restaurant open for Alice and Gus. "What are we going to do between now and bedtime?"

"I think we need to put our heads together and plan our move," Gus said. "We can't afford to waste any time once we get back to the lighthouse."

"That's a good idea," Jesse said. "Come to our room and we can talk there."

Chapter 22

Forever Final

AT NOON THE next day, Gus, Jesse and Alice boarded the *Melissa*. After traveling down river for about an hour, they arrived at Harvey's Landing. The gangplank was lowered and Lloyd greeted them.

"Good to see you all back." Lloyd said. "Alice, how are you feeling?"

"I'm fine, Daddy." Alice grabbed Lloyd by the arm. "We found a beautiful little house."

"That's good news." Lloyd hugged Alice and turned toward Jesse. "What about a job?"

"We got jobs too," Jesse said. "But we don't have a lot of time to get moved. He put a hand on Gus' shoulder. "I'll go hitch up Molly, then Alice and me will leave for the lighthouse."

"All right. As soon as I talk to Gunther, I'll be there to start packing."

"Sounds like you already have a plan worked out for the move," Lloyd said.

"Yeah, but we need Gunther's help tomorrow," Gus said. "We figured it'll take almost two days just to move everything from the lighthouse to here."

"If you need more help, I could let you use Seth along with my team and wagon."

"That would be great," Gus said. "Then maybe we could get everything moved in one day. We'd be ready to load it all onto the boat day after tomorrow."

"Do you have anyone lined up to help you after you get to Gardiner's City?"

Gus nodded. "Mr. Morgan will provide help."

"That's good," Lloyd said. "I couldn't do without Seth for three days."

Gus frowned. "Three days?"

"Yeah. A day to move your stuff from the lighthouse to here, and more than a day from here to your new home. Then the *Melissa's* schedule would require Seth to stay an extra night."

"We sure appreciate your help Lloyd," Gus shook his hand. "I better go."

"What time do you want Seth in the morning?" Lloyd asked.

"If possible, 8:00." Gus climbed into his buggy and drove away.

***

Jesse and Alice traveled toward the lighthouse and before long it came into view.

"This view reminds me of the first time I saw the lighthouse," Jesse said. "It was the day Gus brought me here. It's still a beautiful sight to see the house with its white tower reaching up toward the blue sky, and the sun sparkling on the river in the background."

"That is a beautiful view. I'm going to miss it."

They pulled up at the lighthouse and Jesse helped Alice down from the buggy.

"I'll unlock the door and be right back after I unhitch Molly."

"I'll be in the kitchen, honey."

Jesse placed his hand on Alice's shoulder. "Remember, you promised you wouldn't lift anything heavy."

She patted his hand. "I'll leave all the heavy things for you."

***

Gus arrived at the lighthouse. As he entered the front door, Jesse was there to meet him.

"Will Gunther be able to help us?" Jesse asked.

"He said he would be here by 8:30. When I was talking to

Lloyd earlier, he volunteered his team and wagon along with Seth."

"That's great," Jesse said.

Gus nodded. "I better get to packing. With all this help coming in the morning, I don't want to waste their time by them having to wait for me to finish packing."

"We'll be over to help you pack as soon as we finish."

"Thanks."

***

An hour after Jesse and Alice had been helping Gus pack, Alice said, "You men are probably getting hungry. I know I am. I'll go fix some supper." She headed for the hallway and heard a knock at the door. "Gus, someone's at the door."

He opened the door and there stood Ike holding a basket.

"Come on in, Ike." Gus shook his hand. "What brings you here this time of day?"

"Nellie sent you these sandwiches and some peach cobbler." He held up the basket.

Gus smiled. "That's what I call good timing. Alice was just on her way to fix us something to eat."

"Nellie wants you to plan on eating supper with her and Lloyd tomorrow," Ike said.

"That was thoughtful of her," Jesse said. "Tell her we appreciate the food and her thoughtfulness."

Ike handed the basket to Gus. "Enjoy the food. I'll see you later."

After they enjoyed their meal and fed the animals, they finished packing Gus' belongings by bedtime."

***

Alice awoke in the middle of the night. She grabbed Jesse by the arm and shook him. "Jesse, wake up. Did you hear that?"

"Hear what?" He rubbed his eyes.

"That noise from the back of the house."

"I didn't hear anything, but I'll go check." Jesse slowly pulled the covers back, got up, and lit the lamp. He walked into the common hallway and as he closed the door Gus came out of his door.

"You heard it too?" Gus asked.

"I didn't hear anything, but Alice did."

They walked down the hallway to the door leading to the tower. Gus held his lamp up high and looked at the ceiling where the tower had previously pulled away from the roof of the house. "It looks like that gap in the ceiling is wider. I have a feeling the sound was from the tower settling more. I hope it doesn't fall tonight."

Jesse shook his head. "I'm glad we're moving out of here tomorrow. I don't want any harm to come to Alice and the baby."

"If it's any consolation, when I looked at the angle of the tower the other day, I think if it falls, it will fall away from the house. It will probably rip off part of the back of the house and roof with it, but it shouldn't fall into the house."

"After I tell Alice about this, she'll lie awake the rest of the night listening for more sounds."

"Seems to me things are stable for now. We may as well go back to bed."

"Good. See you in the morning." Jesse returned to his bedroom.

Alice sat up in bed. "Did you find out what made that noise?"

Jesse set down the lamp. "Gus thinks the noise was from the tower settling. It's nothing to worry about. Go back to sleep. You need your rest."

"The noise scared me, and I wasn't able to go back to sleep. Do you think we'll be safe tonight?"

Jesse blew out the lamp then slid into bed next to Alice. "Honey, there's nothing to worry about. Gus said the tower stabilized, so let's go to sleep." He put his arm over her. "We have a big day ahead of us, and you need your rest." He kissed her on the cheek.

"I'll try, but I'm still nervous."

***

The next morning Alice fixed breakfast for everyone while Jesse and Gus went to the barn to feed the animals.

"We have to remember to load the tools and other stuff out here." Gus opened the barn door. "You may end up with a lot of this stuff. I won't have room for it in the boarding house."

"Now that we have two wagons to haul everything, how many trips do you think we'll have to make to get everything moved to the Landing?"

"Initially, I thought four." Gus looked around. "But it may take five. There's more out here than I remembered."

They finished feeding and went back in the house.

***

"Wash up," Alice said. "I've got everything ready to put on the table."

"Alice, after we move, I'm sure going to miss your good cooking." Gus sat down at the table.

Alice grinned. "Well, just because we won't be living under the same roof doesn't mean we can't have you over to eat."

"That's good to hear." Gus smiled.

"You'll always be welcome in our house," Jesse said.

"Thanks," Gus took a sip of coffee. "Did either of you hear any more noise last night?"

Jesse shook his head. "I didn't."

"Me neither and I hope we don't," Alice said. "Honey, would you pass me the biscuits?"

"I've been thinking," Gus said. "Because the tower settled more last night, I think we should move everything away from the back wall of the house that we aren't going to load right away. Then, if the tower should fall before we get those items loaded, we won't lose as much of our stuff."

"That's a good idea," Jesse said.

"While you fellows start moving, I'm going to fix some sandwiches for our dinner. Remember, we'll eat supper tonight with Daddy and Nellie."

"If things go like we planned, we should have everything

moved to the Landing by that time," Gus said. "Then we can sit down and enjoy the meal."

They finished breakfast and Alice moved their plates to the sink and started washing them.

"Let's get your stuff moved away from the back wall first," Gus said.

Jesse looked at Alice. "Honey, do you need anything out of the pantry before we move the contents to the sitting room?"

"If I need something, I'll go in there and look for it."

Gus moved toward the window. "I just saw Ike pull up out front. I'll go get him to help us move this stuff."

Jesse nodded.

***

The three men were loading Ike's wagon when Gunther drove up.

"Morning everyone," Gunther said. "Where do you want me to park my wagon?"

Gus pointed. "Back it up here next to Ike's."

The four men worked steadily and in less than an hour finished loading both wagons.

"Let's make sure everything is tied down good," Gus said. "We don't want to lose anything on the first trip."

"Trust me," Gunther said. It'll be tied good."

They checked all the ropes and were satisfied they would hold their belongings in place.

"Alice, you sit up there on the seat with Gunther and I'll sit in back of the seat," Jesse said.

***

They drove to the Landing and unloaded the wagons, then made two additional trips to the lighthouse to reload. While they were unloading the wagons from the third trip, Gunther stopped. "Did you hear that?"

"Hear what?" Gus asked.

"It was a dull thud and it came from the direction of the lighthouse."

Jesse frowned. "I heard it, too."

Gus shook his head. "The tower may have fallen."

***

They finished unloading, and on the fourth trip back to the lighthouse, as it came into view Alice pointed. "Look. The tower is gone! It *did* fall!"

Jesse put his hands over his face. "This is not good. I hoped we could get everything out before it fell." He waved at Gus in the back wagon and pointed toward the lighthouse.

Gus didn't say anything. He could not express words to sum up how he felt upon first glance.

***

They parked their wagons in front of the lighthouse and everyone hurried to the back of it to see the damage.

Gus shook his head. "Look how the tower broke apart. The lantern room is almost lying in the river."

"Look Gus." Jesse pointed to the back of the house. "You were right about the tower pulling away part of the siding."

"I see." Gus lowered his head. "All the work and money they spent to build it, and now it's destroyed. This is a disaster."

"Now we know what made that strange sound I heard," Gunther said. "I never thought I would ever see the lighthouse like this."

Gus pointed to the tower. "Look. Part of the stairway is sticking out through the side of the tower." He shook his head. "I felt the lighthouse was dead when we stored the lens and clock, but now … to see the tower like this makes its death forever final.

Alice laid her hand on Gus' shoulder. "They'll build another one, and you'll love it too."

"But we don't know when that will be." Gus turned away from the wreckage. "We better get back to moving or we won't finish today."

Everyone went inside to Gus' side of the lighthouse to load his remaining items.

"It looks like none of your stuff was damaged when the tower fell," Jesse said to Gus. "That was a good idea you had to move things away from the back wall."

"Thanks. I think we may have some room left on one of the wagons this trip that we could load a few items from the barn. That way, we should be able to finish this part of the move in one more trip.

"I'll be glad when we're finished," Alice said. "I'm tired."

Jesse moved over close to Alice. "When we get back to Lloyd and Nellie's, I think you should stay with them."

"All right. Maybe Nellie could use my help fixing supper. That would be more restful than bouncing around on that wagon."

***

They completed the move from the lighthouse to the Landing as planned, and everyone enjoyed supper with Lloyd and Nellie. After the meal, Gunther went home but Gus, Jesse and Alice stayed the night to be ready to load their belongings on the *Melissa* the next day.

Chapter 23

The Bread

THE *MELISSA* DOCKED a short time after the noon hour and the gangplank was lowered.

Lloyd approached the first mate. “Webster, did you get the telegram I sent to the Scottsburg Landing about the extra cargo for today?

“Yeah, and we appreciate you doing that. It helped us plan our return trip and to know that we’ll be later than normal. You can have ’em start loading now.”

“They’re ready.” Lloyd moved down the gangplank and directed Ike and Seth to help Gus and Jesse load their furniture and other belongings.

***

Webster approached Gus. “We need to get underway as soon as you can finish.”

Gus nodded. “A couple more boxes and we’re done.

Five minutes later, Ike and Seth loaded the last box.”

We better go say goodbye to Lloyd and Nellie,” Gus said. “Webster is pacing back and forth.”

They headed down the gangplank.

“We’re leaving in five minutes,” Webster said.

“We’ll be right back,” Jesse said. “We don’t want to get left behind.”

At the bottom of the gangplank they met Ike and Seth. “Thanks for all your help.” Gus said. “You fellows cut our loading time in half.”

Ike grinned. "You're welcome. That's what we're here for."

Gus and Jesse joined Alice standing on the dock with Lloyd and Nellie. "Time to say goodbye," Gus said.

"Well, Daddy, we have to leave." Alice turned toward Lloyd and hugged him. "I'm going to miss you and Nellie."

"You come back and see us as soon as you can. Take care of yourself, and I hope your baby is a boy."

"A boy?" Alice asked.

Lloyd chuckled. "I want a grandson, but it really doesn't matter as long as your baby is healthy."

"Don't worry, Daddy. My baby will be just fine." She turned and hugged Nellie.

"I'm going to miss you." Nellie wiped a tear from her cheek. "You write and let us know how you're doing. We're anxious to know how you like your new home, and if everything is all right with you and the baby. Seven months is a long time for Lloyd and me to wait."

"I'll write, and I'll miss you too," Alice said. She pulled Nellie close.

"Thanks for everything," Jesse said as he shook Lloyd's hand and hugged Nellie.

Gus shook Lloyd's hand. "You and Nellie are special people." He reached out to shake Nellie's hand.

"You can do better than that," Nellie said. "Give me a hug."

Gus hugged her.

They boarded the *Melissa,* bound for Gardiner's City.

***

Three days later, while Alice was unpacking, she was interrupted by a knock at the door. She opened the door and a big smile came over her face. "Hi, Jennifer. It's so good to see you again. Come in."

Wearing a beige cotton dress, Jennifer stood smiling and holding what appeared to be a loaf of bread. She stepped inside. "I hope I'm not bothering you, but I couldn't wait any longer to come see you."

Alice shook her hand. "You're no bother. I'm happy to see you!"

"Mother told me she saw you guys move in a couple of days ago, but I couldn't get here until today. It's my day off at the restaurant, so I wanted to welcome you to town and give you this." She handed Alice a loaf of bread.

"That was very thoughtful of you to bake bread for us." Alice pointed to a chair. "Here, have a seat."

"The truth is, mother made the bread. I just asked her if I could bring it to you."

"Thank you, and thank your mother."

"I saw your husband leave this morning for the mill. How does he like his job by now?"

"He's learning that it's hard work. He comes home very tired and hungry, so I'm sure he'll also enjoy your mother's bread. What's her name?

"Lucille. During our conversation at the restaurant, I didn't get to ask you if you had any children."

"Not yet, but we're expecting." Alice's face beamed.

"Oh, I'm so happy for you." Jennifer reached over and held Alice by the arm. "If you need anything, let me know. My mother has been a midwife several times, and she'd be glad to help you."

"Thank you. I haven't said anything to Jesse, but I've been a little concerned about how I would handle things when my time comes."

"According to mother, you always experience more pain with the first one, so you don't want to be by yourself."

"I hope I won't, but after talking to you, I know more of what to expect."

Alice and Jennifer visited for a while longer. A few minutes later, Jennifer stood up. "I better get back home. I have washing to do for mother and me."

"I'm glad you came to visit. You've made me feel welcome here, and I'm glad you're my neighbor."

"Me, too." Jennifer smiled and moved toward the door. "Remember, if you need anything, let me know."

"I will, and thank you again for the bread."

***

That afternoon Jesse walked in after work with his shoulders slumped, and kissed Alice. "Hi, honey. How was your day?"

Alice smiled. "I had a good day. Got more things unpacked, and I had a good visit from our neighbor, Jennifer."

"From the Axe Handle Restaurant?"

"Yes. Today was her day off, so she came to welcome us as her neighbors. And she told me her mother's a midwife."

"Well, that eases my mind. I've been wondering who we could get to deliver our baby if the doctor wasn't available."

"I like the idea of having a friend with me who knows what to do." Alice took Jesse's hand. "How was your day?"

"I'm tired, but I didn't have any problems. It's just hard work. Do you remember when the foreman told Gus and me the work would be harder than at the lighthouse?"

"Yes."

"Well, he was right. Some of those big logs are almost impossible for me to roll."

Alice laid her head on Jesse's shoulder then reached back and rubbed his neck. "I know you're tired, and you must be starving. Supper will be ready soon. Get washed up."

***

Alice passed the pork roast to Jesse. "How is Gus holding up on the job?"

Jesse shook his head. "I know he has to be tired, but I've not heard him complain even once. I saw him at dinner, and I made a remark about how sore my muscles were. He just grinned and said, 'The sooner they get a new lighthouse built, the better for both of us.'" Jesse took a bite of his pork. "Honey, this meat is so tender, and it has such a good taste."

"I'm glad you like it. Besides seasoning it with salt and pepper, I slow cooked it four hours." Alice took a sip of coffee. "Getting back to Gus. I miss him. We should invite him for supper some evening."

"Good idea. It would give me time to talk to him about the Lighthouse Board building a new lighthouse."

"How about Friday?" Alice asked.

"I'll ask him tomorrow." He took a bite of bread.

Alice watched as he ate. "What do you think of the bread?"

Jesse grinned. "It's the best bread you've ever baked."

"It's not my bread. Jennifer gave it to us."

Jesse's face turned red. He reached over and took Alice by the hand. "I'm sorry, I didn't know. I love your bread, and I love you. I've never told you this, but each night before I go to sleep, I can't wait until morning so I can be with you again."

"That's very sweet of you, honey. I love you too, but I wasn't upset that you liked Jennifer's bread better than mine."

Jesse finished eating and got up from the table. "That was a very good meal. I better go feed Molly before I get in more trouble."

***

Friday afternoon Alice began to bake a pie for supper and was interrupted by a knock at the door. She opened the door and there on the porch stood the preacher who had married her and Jesse. Alice smiled. "Well, it's so nice to see you again, Preacher Haley."

He stepped closer and shook Alice's hand. "I heard you and your husband moved to town, so I wanted to come and invite you to church Sunday."

"That's nice of you. We haven't been attending church because there was no church around Harvey's Landing."

"Everyone in town would love to see you at church. I think you'll enjoy the people and the Spirit of God. The service starts at 10:30."

Alice smiled. "I'll talk to Jesse."

"Hope you can make it. I look forward to seeing you there."

***

"It's good to be at your table again," Gus said. He took a bite of mashed potatoes. "The food at the boarding house is good, but it doesn't match up to yours."

"Thank you. More coffee?" Alice asked.

"Yeah. Thanks," Gus said.

Jesse set down his coffee cup. "Gus, I thought this would be a good time to talk about a new lighthouse."

"It's strange you brought that up. Just yesterday I was wondering if the Lighthouse Board has made any progress towards construction of a new lighthouse."

"I may sound anxious about this, so don't get me wrong." Jesse rubbed the side of his face. "I'm glad I've got a job, but I don't want to work in the mill for the rest of my life."

Gus nodded. "I understand where you're coming from. I feel the same. It's harder work and much more dangerous than working in the lighthouse. I've already seen one man break his leg when he slipped and fell between rolling logs."

Alice's eyes got bigger. "Oh my." She placed her hand on Jesse's arm.

"Yeah, I heard about that," Jesse took a sip of coffee. "About the lighthouse, do you think we should go to Scottsburg to talk to the board, or send a telegram to them?"

"Our presence there would show the board we're serious about a new lighthouse, but I don't think we could get off work right now."

"You're probably right." Jesse sopped up his gravy with a piece of bread. "Do you want me to send the telegram?"

"I'll take care of it," Gus said. "In the morning I'll stop by the telegraph office on my way to work."

Alice got up from the table. "Are you fellows ready for some apple pie?"

"You know I love the taste of *your* pie and you serve big pieces." Jesse grinned. "Did you bake it?"

Alice chuckled. "With my own two hands."

Gus grinned. "I'm not sure what just happened, but I'll have a piece."

Alice cut the pie and dished it up. "This afternoon, as I started to roll out the crust for this pie, the preacher stopped by. He invited us to church on Sunday. I didn't invite him in because I was afraid he would stay too long and my crust would dry out."

Jesse took a bite of pie. "This is good and the crust is really moist."

"You make the best apple pie," Gus said. "There are two or three people at the boarding house who go to church. I've thought about going myself, now that I'm closer to the church."

"We haven't talked about it yet." Jesse looked at Alice.

"I think it would be the right thing to do," Alice said.

Jesse took another sip of coffee. "Since I work six days a week, that only leaves me one day to get stuff done around here and catch up on a little rest."

Alice leaned her head to the side. "But it would be a good way for us to meet the people in Gardiner's. Church doesn't start until 10:30. That would give you time to sleep in, if you wanted to."

Jesse rolled his eyes. "Well, maybe we could try it."

Gus took the last bite of his pie. "Guess I'll see you Sunday."

Chapter 24

Joy and Sorrow

AFTER GUS GOT off work Monday evening, he stopped by the telegraph office at the Landing. "Did you receive a telegram for me?" he asked the telegrapher.

"Yes. It came in this morning. It's here somewhere." He looked through a few papers on his desk. "Here it is, but I don't think it's the answer you wanted."

"Thanks." He exited the office, stood next to his horse, and read the telegram. *I better go tell Jesse about this.*

***

Gus knocked on Jesse's door with the telegram in hand.

Jesse opened the door. "Come in Gus." He pointed to a chair. "Have a seat."

"We got an answer from the Lighthouse Board, but they've not made much progress." Gus handed the telegram to Jesse. "Here, read it for yourself."

After Jesse read the telegram, he threw up his hands. "They're still waiting for money?"

"I hope those financial people don't take a lot of time to approve the funds. The mariners need that lighthouse *now*."

"I think we should contact the board every three or four weeks to help them stay on top of the situation." Jesse handed the telegram back to Gus.

"I agree." Gus shoved the telegram in his shirt pocket, and then stood up as Alice entered the room.

Alice smiled. "Hi, Gus. I didn't expect to see you so soon."

"I just stopped by to let you know we heard from the Lighthouse Board, but they're not ready to start building yet."

Alice shook her head. "That's too bad." She looked at Gus. "What did you think about the preacher's sermon yesterday?"

Gus touched the side of his beard. "I dozed off a couple of times, but what I heard was good."

"Jesse had the same problem." Alice smiled and took Jesse by the arm.

"I did doze off, but I heard part of his sermon. Especially the part when he talked about the slave asking for his master's patience so he could repay him."

"Yeah, I heard that part, too." Gus said.

Jesse touched the back of his neck. "It got me to thinking about how anxious I am to get a new lighthouse built, and how maybe I should be more patient with the board."

"You *were* listening to the sermon." Alice smiled and squeezed his arm.

"I'm also guilty of being impatient with them." Gus stepped away. "I better go. I don't want to be late for supper. Mrs. Franks will get upset with me."

"Goodbye, Gus. You take care." Alice hugged him.

"Thanks for bringing the telegram," Jesse said. "See you later." He closed the door and turned toward Alice. "I'm glad Gus admitted he's also impatient with the Lighthouse Board."

"Honey, you know the two of you can't build the lighthouse, so you'll just have to be patient and let the board do its job." Alice rubbed her hand across Jesse's shoulder.

"You're right, but I still can't help that I'm anxious."

"I am too, but more so about the baby." Alice held her stomach.

"Honey, are you feeling all right? Jesse asked.

"Oh yes. I'm just looking forward to being a mother."

Jesse hugged Alice. "And you're going to be a good one."

***

Jesse, Alice, and Gus settled into their homes and for the next three months their lives were somewhat of a routine. The three of them continued to attend church, while the work at the mill became easier for both Jesse and Gus. They became physically stronger and grew more confident about doing their work. Although confident, each month they contacted the Lighthouse Board regarding a new lighthouse. Alice and Jennifer visited each other when possible, and during that time Alice became good friends with Jennifer and her mother, Lucille. At least once a month Jesse and Alice would have Gus over for supper.

At 6:00 one Friday night, Jesse and Alice were in the kitchen when they heard a knock at the front door. "I'll get it," Jesse said. "It's probably Gus." He opened the door and there stood Gus. "Come in. Supper is almost ready."

"Thanks for having me." Gus laid his hand on Jesse's back. "I always look forward to being with you guys."

"We enjoy having you. Come on into the kitchen." Jesse led the way.

Alice smiled and hugged Gus. "It's so good to see you again. How are you?"

"I'm doing good, but I'm not having a baby." Gus grinned. "How are you doing?"

"I think my time is close. I've been having pain." Alice picked up a towel and pulled a hot pan of bread out of the oven. "You men get washed up, it's ready."

Jesse shook his head. "No offense, but I told Alice we should cancel having you over tonight, but she insisted she'd be all right." He poured water in a pan. "Gus, you go ahead and wash up." Jesse turned and saw Alice holding her lower stomach. "Honey, what's wrong!" He ran toward her.

"My water just broke. Get Lucille, quick."

"I'll help you to the bedroom first." Jesse put one arm around Alice's back.

Gus dried his hands and threw down the towel. "Let me help you, Jesse." He held Alice by her other arm.

Alice frowned and rolled her eyes. "The pain is getting worse."

"Breathe, deep," Jesse said. "We're almost there."

They sat Alice down on the edge of the bed.

Gus pointed at Jesse. "You stay here with Alice. I'll get Lucille."

***

Outside the bedroom door Jesse paced back and forth while Gus sat wringing his hands. Occasionally, Jesse would stop pacing and listen at the door. They had waited two hours when Jesse heard the sweetest noise. "Did you hear that? I heard the baby cry. It's here. I hope Alice is all right." He smiled from ear to ear and slapped himself on the side of his leg. "I'm a father!"

"Congratulations, Dad." Gus laid his hand on Jesse's back. "Do you want a boy or a girl?"

"It doesn't matter. I just hope Alice is all right." Jesse wiped his forehead.

Lucille opened the bedroom door. "Congratulations, Jesse, it's a girl. Come in and see your beautiful daughter."

Jesse and Gus smiled as they entered the bedroom.

"Honey, are you all right?" Jesse asked. He bent over and kissed Alice on the forehead.

"I'm just tired, but it was worth it. Just look at our daughter." Alice smiled as she adjusted the blanket to reveal more of the baby.

Jesse reached over and held the tiny hand of his daughter. "Hi there, pretty girl." He looked back at Alice. "She's beautiful. Alice, I love you so much." He turned toward Gus. "Look how beautiful she is!"

Gus stepped closer to the bed. "She sure is. She looks a lot like you, Alice. Have you picked a name?"

"We decided on Lucinda if the baby was a girl." Alice touched Lucinda's cheek.

"That's a pretty name," Gus said.

Lucille moved over to the side of the bed. "You fellows should leave now and let these ladies get some rest."

Alice looked up at Jesse. "Did you and Gus get anything to eat?"

"No. We were too excited, but I'll warm up something now." Jesse kissed Alice. He reached over and touched Lucinda's chin with his finger.

Gus patted Alice on the hand. "You and Lucinda get some rest.

***

Months later, Jesse was awakened in the early morning by the sound of a bell ringing. *It's the town bell. I wonder what the emergency is.* He knew this sound was a call for all available help to report to the town hall. Jesse jumped out of bed and lit the lamp.

Alice rose up in bed. "What's wrong?"

"There's an emergency," Jesse said as he dressed.

"You be careful."

"I will." He kissed Alice and went to the barn to saddle Molly.

***

Jesse rode down the hill toward the town hall. On the next street over he could see flames coming from the Saw Tooth Boarding House. *That's the emergency. Flames are already coming out of the roof. I hope everyone got out. I hope Gus got out!* He stopped two houses before getting to the fire and tied Molly to a hitching rail. He ran toward the boarding house and approached one of the men who were fighting the fire. "Have you seen Gus Crosby anywhere?

"I haven't seen him. I've been busy fighting the fire."

Jesse ran to another man and asked him about Gus.

"I haven't seen him, and if he didn't get out when the fire started, he may not have been able to get out. This is a big fire and a hot one.

"There's Mr. and Mrs. Franks. They made it out!" Somebody yelled.

Jesse ran up to Mr. Franks. "Have you seen Gus?"

"Not yet, but I've seen five other boarders so far."

"I'll go look on the other side. Maybe he's over there." Jesse hurried. *Where are you, Gus? God, help me find him!* "Anyone seen

Gus? Gus! Gus, where are you?" *Please, God, help me find him.* Tears pooled in Jesse's eyes from emotion and smoke. He searched all around the burning building but couldn't find Gus. The heat from the flames was intense, and he realized the fire was now out of control. The boarding house could not be saved with the buckets of water being thrown on the fire. He knew no one could survive the inferno. Just then the top floor toppled over. *Oh, Gus!* Tears streamed down Jesse's face. He fell to his knees and sobbed. *Why? Why, God? Why did you let this happen to Gus?*

***

Daylight came and Jesse, like several of the town's people, had stayed and watched with disbelief while the fire burned down the boarding house and reportedly took four human lives. By now the fire had reduced enough in size that those fighting it were able to extinguish the flames.

Jesse moved to the side of the boarding house where Gus' room was located. He was able to get closer to the smoldering timbers. While he thought about Gus, he noticed something lying outside the main area of debris that caught his eye. He stepped closer. *It can't be. I don't believe it. It's his lighthouse!* With his foot, Jesse brushed at the statue turning it over. *It's charred a little, but it is the lighthouse Rusty carved for Gus. It must have been thrown here from the window sill when the second floor toppled.* Jesse picked up the little statue with his handkerchief, then hung his head for a minute before returning to Molly. *I dread telling Alice about Gus.*

***

"Oh, I'm glad you're back," Alice said. "I could see flames from the kitchen window. Are you all right?"

"Gus is gone!" Tears welled up in Jesse's eyes as he reached for Alice.

"What?" Tears filled Alice's eyes. She grabbed onto Jesse, and they held each other.

"He was killed in the fire."

Alice pulled herself closer to Jesse. "Oh, no! Our dear sweet

Gus."

Jesse shook his head. "I can't believe he's gone. That's a horrible way to die. Why did this happen?"

"We may never know." Alice wiped the tears from her cheeks. She looked up at Jesse. "I hope he didn't suffer."

"Me, too."

Just then the baby started crying.

Alice released Jesse. "I need to go check on Lucinda, and then I'll fix you some breakfast."

"I'm not hungry." Jesse cupped his hands over his face.

"You need to eat to keep up your strength."

"I don't feel like going to work today. I want to go talk to Preacher Haley about a service for Gus."

Alice held onto Jesse's arm as she wiped her tears. "Honey, promise me you won't go until after you eat some breakfast. It may be too early to talk to him anyway."

Jesse wiped his tears. "All right."

***

Jesse got up from the table. "Thanks for breakfast, honey. I'm going to saddle Molly, then go see Preacher Haley."

"Are you sure you feel like doing that right now?" Alice asked.

Jesse frowned. "It's not going to be easy no matter when I do it. Gus didn't have any living relatives, so it's up to me to arrange something."

"What arrangements can you make since Gus's body is gone?"

Jesse shook his head. "I don't know, but I think there should be some kind of service to remember him."

"That would be nice. Maybe Preacher Haley will know what to do."

***

Jesse rode toward the preacher's house, and as he approached Main Street, he noticed a group of eight men gathered in front of the doctor's office. *I wonder what's going on at the Doc's?* He stopped Molly in front of the office, then saw Morgan

Usher who was part of the group.

"Morgan, what's all the excitement about?" Jesse asked.

"Doc White has Gus in there!"

"*What?*" Jesse jumped down from Molly's back and grabbed Morgan by the arm. "Are you sure?"

Morgan shrugged. "Well, I didn't see him myself, but four of those men over there claim they carried Gus into the doc's office."

Oh, thank you, God! "I want to see him." Jesse started to move toward the group.

"It's no use," Morgan said. "Doc White has the door locked, and he won't let anyone in."

Jesse turned back toward Morgan. "I was sure he died in the fire. Where was he?"

Morgan pointed to a man in a dark blue shirt. "He found Gus behind the boarding house, lying in the weeds across the alley."

"I'm glad he found him." Jesse rubbed the side of his face. "I wonder how he got over there?"

"That man said it looked like Gus had come down the back stairs of the boarding house, but tripped and fell into the weeds as he was running across the alley. He said Gus was unconscious and had a cut on his head.'"

"I hope the doc can fix him up."

"Yeah, me, too. Looks like you're not the only one who is going to be late for work today. A couple of those men waiting to see Gus also work at the mill."

"Well, to be honest with you, I wasn't going to work. I was headed to see Preacher Haley about a funeral service for Gus."

Morgan grinned. "I'll bet you're glad you don't have to do that now."

"Yeah, but I still want to find out if Gus is going to be all right."

"I understand how you and these other men feel about Gus, but don't take off any longer than necessary. We lost two of our workers in that fire, and with others taking time off it will affect production at the mill. Guess I'll need to hire someone to replace those two."

"Instead of making arrangements for Gus' funeral, now I need to find a place for him to live."

Morgan shook his head. "That won't be easy. All of the houses in town are occupied and now the boarding house is gone."

"Alice and I don't have an extra room, but maybe we could put Gus up temporarily until we can find something more permanent. I think Jennifer and her mother might have an extra room. I may ask them."

Morgan's eyes widened. "People around here wouldn't think that's proper, and Gus might not either."

Jesse lowered his head. "You're probably right. I'll figure out something. I'm just glad he didn't die."

"Here comes the doc," said someone on the doctor's porch.

Doctor White stepped out on the porch. "Gus is now conscious, but he'll need to rest here for a while. He must have hit his head on something hard, and it knocked him out. There's a nasty cut on his head. It took four stitches."

Jesse pushed through to the front of the group and stepped up on the porch. "Doc, can I come in and see him?"

Doctor White shook his head. "Not now. Gus needs rest. Everyone may as well go home. You've done all you can do for him, right now."

The group began to leave, but Jesse stood still.

"Doc, you don't understand. Gus has to stay with me now. He doesn't have any place to live.

Doctor White sighed. "That's fine with me, but he's not going anywhere until I say he's ready. I suggest you come back in three or four hours."

Jesse frowned. "All right, I'll be back."

***

Alice was sitting in her rocking chair breastfeeding Lucinda when she heard an unusual noise from outside. She stood up, holding Lucinda, and looked out the front window. Jesse was waving his arm and yelling as he rode toward the back of the house.

"Gus is alive! Gus is alive!" Jesse said as he burst in the back door and headed for the front room.

Alice approached Jesse. "Gus is alive?"

"He is alive!" Jesse smiled from ear to ear.

"That's wonderful?" Alice pulled away from Lucinda, which made her cry. She adjusted Lucinda's head. "I'm sorry sweetheart, mommy didn't mean to cut you off." Alice looked at Jesse. "What happened to Gus?"

Jesse filled her in on the details. "Honey, we have to help Gus."

"Certainly." Alice said. She gently rubbed Lucinda on the shoulder. "What can we do to help him?"

Jesse sat down on the end of the daybed. "He needs a place to live."

"Yes, but we don't have extra room." She sat down in the rocking chair.

"I know, but until he can find something, I thought we could let him sleep here on the daybed."

"Well … I can't say no to Gus, but it's going to be crowded."

Jesse reached over and touched Alice on the arm. "We'll have to make some adjustments, but so will Gus."

"For sure, he'll have to get used to Lucinda crying in the middle of the night." Alice finished nursing Lucinda, then held her up to her shoulder.

Jesse grinned. "Gus won't complain. When he finds out how close he came to losing his life, he'll be glad he's alive and would stay just about any place."

"From what you said about the fire, he must have lost everything."

"The only things he has now are the clothes on his back and the lighthouse I found."

"Lighthouse?"

"Remember the one Rusty carved and gave to Gus?"

"Oh, yes. Where is it?"

"It's out in the barn. I didn't think you would like the smell of charred wood in here."

Alice nodded. "You mentioned lighthouse and it reminded me of the telegram the two of you sent to the Lighthouse Board the other day."

"We should hear from them soon. After all that Gus has been through, I'm sure some good news would be welcome."

A knock at the front door.

"I wonder who that could be," Alice said.

"I'll get it." Jesse opened the door. "Hello Preacher Haley. Good to see you." Jesse smiled and shook his hand. "Come in. Did you hear about Gus?"

"Yes. He was very lucky. Matter of fact, he's part of the reason I'm here. I'm trying to let everyone in Gardiner's know the church is collecting items for those who lost everything in the fire."

"That's good. I'm not the right size to be of help to Gus, but maybe we can give something that may help some of the others."

"Anything you can give will be appreciated. Just drop it at the church." Preacher Haley turned toward Alice and grinned. "Looks like Lucinda has gone to sleep."

"I need to go lay her down." Alice got up from the rocking chair. "I think it's great that the church is leading in the effort to help those people."

"Well, it's good to see most people in Gardiner's put on a heart of compassion and kindness to help those who lost everything."

Jesse brushed the side of his face. "Don't know yet what we'll give, but we'll come up with something."

"Thanks. I better go. I have more people to contact."

Chapter 25

Near Completion

GUS WOKE TO the sound of Lucinda crying. *She must be hungry again.* He turned over on the daybed. *Almost time to get up. Oh, Lord. It's not that I don't appreciate Jesse and Alice taking me in, but after three months of this every night, I'm ready to live by myself again. A couple of more weeks and the new boarding house should be finished.* Gus pushed the covers off. *I may as well get up. As soon as Alice feeds Lucinda, she'll go to the kitchen to fix breakfast.*

***

"Jesse, Gus, breakfast is ready," Alice said from the kitchen.

Jesse walked into the kitchen and kissed Alice. "The bacon smells good."

"Thanks." Alice turned over eggs in the skillet.

"Morning," Gus said. He stood in the doorway to the kitchen.

Alice grinned. "How did you sleep?"

"Just fine," Gus said, then lowered his head.

Alice pulled a pan of biscuits from the oven and set it on top of the stove. "I wondered if Lucinda woke you. You men have a seat. It's ready. Jesse, would you pour the coffee?"

He poured Gus' coffee. "Now that the Lighthouse Board has started construction on the new lighthouse, how long do you think it will take to finish it?"

"I don't know, but it took about two years to build the first one."

Alice handed Gus the biscuits. "Watch out; they're hot."

Jesse looked at Gus and frowned. "Sure hope it doesn't take that long for this one. Work in the lighthouse was more satisfying than working here at the mill."

"Yeah, and work at the lighthouse was not as dangerous either. I've been thinking about going over there to see how construction is coming."

"Do you want more bacon, Gus?" Alice asked.

"I've got enough."

Jesse lifted his cup. "When are you going?"

"Maybe Sunday."

Jesse quickly set his cup down. "I'd like to go with you."

"Can both of you get off work?" Alice asked.

"Honey, pass me the biscuits and another piece of that bacon. It's so good." Jesse looked at Alice. "We don't work on Sunday."

"I think Alice is talking about Monday," Gus said. "Remember, the boat won't leave Harvey's Landing to come back here until Monday afternoon, so we would miss work."

Jesse touched his forehead. "Oh, yeah. I'd still like to go if I can get off work."

"All right. Let's plan to go next Sunday.

"Either of you want more coffee? Alice asked.

"I'll take some," Jesse said.

Alice handed the coffee to Jesse. "You could stay with Daddy and Nellie, but you should send a telegram to let them know you're coming." Alice looked up at the clock. "Eat up. You don't want to be late for work. Your boss may let you off permanently."

***

Sunday morning, Jesse and Gus hurried to the front of the *Melissa* as it arrived at Harvey's Landing. They had looked forward to this trip to the lighthouse all week, and now they were about to dock.

Gus pointed. "Look, there's Lloyd and Nellie to meet us."

Jesse nodded.

The *Melissa* docked and they walked down the gangplank.

"It's sure good to see you fellows again." Lloyd said and shook their hands.

"We have really missed you." Nellie hugged each of them. "Jesse, how are Alice and Lucinda?"

"They're just fine. Alice sends her love."

"I hope they finish the lighthouse real soon," Nellie said. "I can't wait until you guys get moved back here so I can see Alice and Lucinda more often."

"That Lucinda is such a beautiful baby. You're going to love her." Gus pulled at his shoulder to straighten his shirt sleeve.

"Nellie and I can't wait to meet our granddaughter."

"We've been excited ever since Alice's letter came, telling us about Lucinda's birth," Nellie said.

Gus rubbed his chin. "We can't wait to see the progress of the new lighthouse. The sooner it's built, the sooner we can get moved back here."

"I've got the team and wagon ready for you," Lloyd said.

"We appreciate you letting us use them," Jesse said.

"Do you want something to eat before you go?" Nellie asked.

"Thanks, but we've got food here." Jesse pointed to a box under his arm. "Alice fixed this so we wouldn't be a bother to you until breakfast."

Nellie grinned. "You're no bother. Whatever it takes to help you guys get moved back here. Oh, by the way. We're getting a church. A young preacher moved here and is starting it."

Jesse nodded. "That's good. I'll have more news to tell Alice when I get back."

"Whenever you're ready, the team is tied over there." Lloyd pointed to the hitching rail in front of the corral. "When do you think you'll be back?"

"Before dark," Gus said. "Thanks again for use of your team."

***

Gus and Jesse traveled the road alongside the river that led through tall pines toward the location of the old lighthouse.

Jesse pointed to where the old lighthouse used to be as the wagon came out into a clearing. "Remember, you used to be able to see the lighthouse from here."

"Yeah, it seems strange not to see it. And I don't see any signs of where they've started building the new one."

"Remember the suggestion you made to Mr. Bronson? If the board listened to you, the new lighthouse would be built on a hill not far from the old one."

"Yeah." Gus pointed to the left of the old lighthouse. "It would be on that hill over there. That's why we can't see anything. It's hidden behind the trees up there."

They continued on the same road and came to the junction of a new dirt road on the left.

Jesse pointed. "That must be the road they built up to the new lighthouse."

Gus nodded. "Looks like it." He drove the team up the new road. It cut through tall pine trees to the top of the hill and then came out into a clearing.

As they entered the clearing, Jesse stood up. "Look, there it is!"

"I see it. Sit down before you fall and break your neck." Gus stopped the team a few yards from the construction site, and they climbed down from the wagon.

Jesse turned toward Gus. "You know, you had a good idea for a location to build the lighthouse. Look!" Jesse pointed out to the ocean. "You can see both the ocean and the mouth of the river from here."

Gus smiled. "This location is even better than I thought. I'm surprised the Lighthouse Board used my suggestion. I wish the men were working today. We could talk to them and maybe get an idea of how long they think it will take to finish the tower."

They walked closer to get a better look at the construction.

"In the three months they've been working, the tower walls appear to be about half done," Jesse said.

"Close to it. But even after they finish the walls, it'll take time to put the lantern room and the roof on top. Then there's the stairway to build, and the lens to be installed in the lantern room."

"That could take a while." Jesse picked up a small rock and threw it back into the trees.

"Remember, the board said they were also going to build separate two-story homes for the head keeper and his assistant.

"It'll be great to have separate homes. But I wonder what they think you're going to do with all that room."

"Maybe they think I'll get married again and have lots of children." Gus chuckled. "We'll both have more room than we've got right now."

"I hope Alice will like it out here."

"At least she'll get to see Nellie and Lloyd more often."

"That'll help." Jesse pointed to the woods. "Do you think they'll have to cut more trees to make room for the houses?"

"Yeah." Gus took out his pipe and after he lit it, he stood gazing at the size of the property. "You know, between the tower and the two houses, it'll take up a lot more land than the old lighthouse."

"This'll be great. To see this tower being built makes me more anxious than ever to see it finished, and for us to get moved in here."

"Wickie, I feel the same way." Gus puffed on his pipe and touched his beard.

"It's been a long time since you called me Wickie."

"It makes me feel like we're closer to operating the lighthouse, and helping the mariners."

"If it was in operation, we'd have to light the lantern. The sun will soon be going down."

"Guess we better head back to the Landing," Gus said. "I told Lloyd we'd be back before dark."

They walked toward the team and wagon.

"It's hard to think about going back to work at the mill after being here." Jesse said. "I wish this were already finished."

"Me, too." Gus said. He climbed up to the wagon seat and picked up the reins. "At least we know they're making progress."

***

Several months passed, and late on one Saturday afternoon there was a knock at Jesse's door. Both Jesse and Alice were playing with Lucinda.

Alice looked at Jesse and frowned. "Who could that be?"

"Don't know. I'll see." Jesse opened the door. "Well, what a nice surprise, Jennifer. It's good to see you. Come in."

Jennifer stepped in carrying a folded paper in her hand.

Alice picked up Lucinda. "We haven't seen you for a few weeks. Are you all right?"

"Yes. I've just been busy working at the restaurant and helping mother." Jennifer smiled as she reached over and touched Lucinda on the cheek. "She is such a beautiful child."

Alice smiled. "Thanks. How is Lucille?"

"She's good. She said to tell you hello." Jennifer unfolded the paper. "I have something to show you. When I read this article about the lighthouse, I thought of you, Jesse. You may have already seen it."

"What article?" Jesse's eyes widened.

Jennifer handed the paper to Jesse and pointed to a picture.

Jesse smiled. "Wow. That's great. I wonder if Gus has seen this." Jesse moved over next to Alice and held up the paper.

Alice leaned forward a little. "Look at that! It's almost finished."

"Will you be moving soon?" Jennifer asked.

"Not for quite a while." Jesse handed the paper back to Jennifer. "They still have to build two houses yet, in addition to finishing the tower and the workroom."

"You've been such good neighbors. I'm going to miss you."

"We'll miss you, too." Alice stepped forward holding Lucinda and hugged Jennifer. "I'm going to miss you being just down the street from us."

"I appreciate that," Jennifer hugged Alice again. "Would you like to keep the paper?"

"Yes, thank you. I'm sure Jesse will want to show Gus."

"Well, I better go. I still have dishes to do."

Jesse waved to Jennifer. “Thanks for the paper. The news made it a better day for me.”

COAST GUARD MUSEUM NORTHWEST

Workers celebrate the near-completion of the second tower in 1892.

Umpqua Lighthouse Tower Near Completion

Chapter 26

Good News All Around

ALICE AWOKE AND went to the kitchen in her night clothes to start preparing breakfast. She made coffee, sliced some bacon and potatoes, and began to fry them. Soon the aroma of bacon filled the kitchen. "I don't feel so good," she said to herself.

Jesse walked in. "Good morning." He kissed Alice. "That bacon sure smells good."

Alice frowned. "Morning. It doesn't smell so good to me."

"What's wrong?" Jesse asked.

"I'm a little sick to my stomach, but I'll be all right." Alice turned the potatoes over to finish frying them.

Jesse poured himself a cup of coffee. "I remember the last time you were sick in the mornings and you said you would be all right."

"You mean when I was pregnant with Lucinda?"

Jesse grinned. "Neither one of us knew why you were sick until Nellie told us."

"It's ready. Sit down and eat. You don't want to be late for work."

"Honey, you need to eat, too."

"I'll eat later when I feel better."

"I hope it's soon. If we're right about why you're sick, then you need your strength."

Alice moved over by Jesse and laid her hand on his shoulder. "Yes, but it will be worth it, just like it was with our beautiful

Lucinda. How do you feel about us having another baby?"

Jesse looked up at Alice and smiled. "I think it's great. Lucinda shouldn't grow up by herself."

"I agree, but let's wait and see. We don't know for sure that I'm pregnant."

"No offense, but I hope you aren't. I'd rather not be moving again when you are pregnant."

"How long do you think it will be before we move?" Alice asked.

"Don't know for sure, but it shouldn't be real long. It's been six months since we saw the lighthouse tower in the paper. They should have made a lot of progress by now."

***

After work that afternoon, Jesse was saddling Molly for the ride home when Gus rode up. "Hi Gus. How was your day?"

"Another hard one." Gus dismounted. "But after seeing what I saw today, I can handle it."

Jesse's eyebrows raised. "What did you see?"

"I got a copy of the paper today and there's a picture of the lighthouse in it." Gus pulled the paper from his back pocket and unfolded it. "Look at that."

Umpqua River Lighthouse Under Construction – Attached Workroom –Tower –Asst. Keepers House

"It's a beauty. The tower and one of the houses are almost finished."

"Yeah. They should have the construction completed

before long." Gus folded the paper and started to return it to his pocket.

"Could I take the paper home and show Alice?" Jesse asked.

"Sure."

Jesse tightened the cinch of his saddle. "I wonder how long it will be before the Lighthouse Board is ready for us to start work?"

"The way things look it shouldn't be much longer. We need to contact Mr. Bronson and find out."

Jesse mounted his horse. "Let's go send a telegram to him."

"Good idea," Gus said. He put his foot in the stirrup. "Then we can plan a time for our move."

They rode the narrow dirt road toward the Landing.

Jesse looked over at Gus. "We'll also need to notify the mill foreman about us leaving the job."

"It won't be a surprise to him. I'm sure someone in town has already told him. Half of Gardiner's City already knows we've talked about going to work at the lighthouse."

Jesse grinned. "You mean because of Jennifer?"

"Yeah. She's a sweet lady and a hard worker, but she does like to talk. You know what I mean."

"I guess it gives her something to talk about while she's waiting tables."

Gus pointed to the Landing. "Hey look. There's Morgan Usher standing outside the office."

"I wonder if he knows about the lighthouse."

Gus shrugged. "We may find out real soon."

Gus and Jesse dismounted their horses in front of the office. As they tied them to the hitching rail Morgan Usher stepped toward them.

"Hi, Mr. Usher," Jesse said. "How's your day going?"

"Real good. How's the job going for you men?"

Gus looked at Jesse and then back to Mr. Usher. "It's going good, but I'm always glad when the day is done."

"It's tough work, but from what I hear, both of you men are doing a good job."

"Thanks, Mr. Usher," Gus said.

The door of the Landing office opened and the telegrapher stepped out. “Mr. Usher, here’s the telegram you’ve been waiting for.”

“Thanks.” He turned back toward Gus and Jesse. “Well, I’ve got what I came for, so I’m going home. See you later.”

As Mr. Usher drove away in his buggy, Gus frowned at Jesse. “You know, he didn’t act like he knew anything about the lighthouse.”

“I was surprised he didn’t ask us about it.”

“We’d better send the telegram.” Gus opened the door. “I need to get on to the boarding house. Mrs. Franks will get upset if I’m late for supper.”

“Me, too. Alice will have my supper ready.” Jesse tapped Gus on the arm. “This morning she couldn’t eat breakfast. Remember how she got sick before Lucinda was born?”

“It sounds to me like you’re going to be a father again. Are you ready for that?”

“Yeah. Lucinda shouldn’t grow up by herself, and I think Alice agrees with me.”

They moved over to the telegrapher’s counter.

“Good to see you fellows again. Can I help you?”

“We need to send a telegram to the Lighthouse Board in Scottsburg,” Gus said.

“Just tell me what you want to say, and I’ll have it sent in no time.”

Gus held his bearded chin as he thought. “Send this, ‘When will houses be ready for us to move in? Need time to tell our boss and pack.’ Sign it Gus Crosby and Jesse Fayette.”

The telegrapher counted the words then looked at Gus. “That’ll be fifty-five cents.”

“I got it.” Jesse reached into his pocket and pulled out the money before Gus could get to his.

“Thanks.” The telegrapher said.

“We’ll check for a reply after work tomorrow,” Gus said.

They walked out of the Landing office and Gus reached in his pocket. “Here, let me pay you for the telegram.”

Jesse held up his hand. "Keep it. I think you paid for the last one. How long do you think it'll be before the board is ready for us to move in?"

Gus shrugged. "Your guess would be as good as mine."

"I hope they don't take a week to answer our telegram. I want to tell the boss and get packed."

***

Like the previous three days, Gus and Jesse met after work to go check with the telegrapher about a reply to their telegram. They had ridden only a short distance from the mill when they saw Morgan Usher coming down the road in his buggy.

"I think we should stop Mr. Usher and tell him that we'll be leaving in the near future," Gus said.

"We can't tell him when, but at least he will know." Jesse stopped Molly and patted her on the neck.

Morgan Usher stopped. "I just heard at the restaurant that you fellows are leaving to work at the lighthouse. Is that true?"

"We were just about to tell you." Jesse touched the back of his neck. "We're waiting to hear from the Lighthouse Board. Right now, we don't know exactly when we'll leave."

"So you *will be* leaving. It was only a few days ago I was telling you fellows I had heard how good a job you were doing for us at the mill."

"Sorry, Mr. Usher," Gus said. "We held off telling you because we weren't sure."

Mr. Usher turned up the palm of his free hand. "I shouldn't be surprised. I remember when you fellows hired on. You had just come from the lighthouse that fell over."

"Did you see the picture of the new lighthouse in the paper?" Jesse asked.

Mr. Usher nodded. "Yeah, but it never occurred to me that you fellows would want to work there."

"We're on our way to the Landing office now," Gus said. "Maybe we'll hear something today."

"Let me know as soon as you can when you're leaving." Mr.

Usher waved and drove on.

Gus and Jesse continued their short ride on to the Landing office.

They walked inside to the telegrapher's counter.

"Do you have a telegram for us today?" Jesse asked

"Sure do. It came in about an hour ago." The telegrapher handed it to Jesse.

"Thanks for your help," Jesse said. He and Gus walked back outside. Jesse opened the telegram and held it up between Gus and himself to read.

"Hmm." Jesse smiled. "Three weeks and one keeper's house will be ready to occupy."

"And they want us there to help with cleanup, stocking stores, the oil, and preparing the light for operation."

"I can't wait to tell Alice." Jesse's smile widened as he patted Gus on the arm. "We're going to be *Wickies* again!"

"But it sounds like we'll all have to live in one house for a while. Can you and Alice adjust to that again?"

"Yeah, but it's more like you'll have to adjust to us. At least the house is big enough that you can have your own bedroom this time."

They moved to the hitching rail and untied their horses. Gus frowned. "I wonder why they can't finish the other keeper's house by the time the first one is done."

"The telegram didn't say. We may not know until after we get moved over there."

They mounted their horses and Jake nickered.

"Steady boy." Gus patted Jake on the neck. "At least we can give Morgan Usher a day when we'll be leaving the mill."

"Now we can start packing some stuff and plan our move."

"I don't have much to pack because of the fire, so I can give you and Alice a hand."

Chapter 27

She's Beautiful

THE *MELISSA* MOVED slowly toward the dock at Harvey's Landing as gray smoke bellowed from her stack toward the sky. The air was crisp that November afternoon as Gus, Jesse, and his family stood waiting for the boat to dock and the gangplank to be lowered.

Alice's face beamed with joy as she smiled and waved to Lloyd and Nellie waiting on the dock. She held up Lucinda. "Your granddaughter," she said across the water.

"I can't wait to hold her!" Nellie said.

Jesse gently took Alice by the arm. "Let's get in the buggy. They're ready to lower the gangplank."

"I know we're in a hurry to unload the boat, but I'd like some time for Nellie and Daddy to visit with Lucinda."

Gus climbed up in his buggy. "Could I make a suggestion?" he asked Jesse.

"Sure."

"While Ike and Seth help us unload, Alice could spend time with Nellie and Lloyd."

"Good idea." Jesse turned toward Alice. "There's no need for you and Lucinda staying out here in the cold."

Jesse drove his buggy down the gangplank and Gus followed in his. After they got off the dock they stopped, climbed out, and moved over to where Lloyd and Nellie were standing. Meanwhile, Ike and Seth moved onto the boat to start unloading.

With her arms wide open, Nellie moved quickly toward Alice then hugged her and Lucinda. "Let me hold her." Nellie picked up

Lucinda and looked into her face. "You're so pretty. You have your mother's beautiful brown eyes and brown hair."

"This is your Grandma," Alice whispered. "Can you say thank you?"

Lucinda was silent, but smiled out from under her beige knitted cap. She wore mittens and was wrapped in a blanket.

After the men had shaken hands and greeted each other, Lloyd moved over to Alice and hugged her. "We sure missed you guys. You've been gone now close to three years and this is our first time to see this pretty little girl." Lloyd touched Lucinda under the chin.

"We're sorry Daddy, but it was just as hard for us to get away from our work as it is for you and Nellie to get away from yours here at the Landing.

Lloyd nodded. "I know. Guess I should be thankful we're back together."

"Now that we're back, we should be able to visit more often," Jesse said.

"That sounds good to me." Lloyd looked toward the *Melissa*. "Right now, Ike and Seth could use some help unloading your stuff, or I'll be hearing from Webster about his schedule."

Gus looked around. "I wonder why Gunther is late. His telegram said he'd be here to help."

"I have no idea, but we need him and his wagon." Jesse looked at Lloyd. "We appreciate you loaning us Ike and Seth." He moved toward the gangplank.

Lloyd smiled. "It's the least I can do to help my granddaughter move back home."

Nellie turned toward Lloyd. "I'll take Alice and Lucinda to the house while the men unload the boat."

"All right," Lloyd said. He looked around and saw Gunther driving up. "Hey, Gus. Gunther is here."

Gunther climbed down from his wagon and shook hands with Gus. "Sorry I'm late. I had to finish digging a grave, which took longer than normal."

"Anyone I know?" Gus asked.

"I doubt it. Mr. Slogan lived up river a ways and didn't come around here much."

"Never heard of him." Gus patted Gunther on the shoulder. "But I'm glad you're here. It's good to see you again, old friend."

Gunther grinned. "It's good to see you too. I sure missed you and I'm glad you're back."

"Jesse and me appreciate you helping us move our stuff to the lighthouse."

"Glad to help." Gunther looked around and saw Jesse carrying a big wooden box down the gangplank. "Looks like Jesse could use some help. I better get to work."

"We need to unload the *Melissa* as soon as possible so the captain can get her back up river," Gus said.

Jesse and Gunther met and shook hands. Jesse smiled. "You're a welcome sight. Gus was concerned that something may have happened to you."

Gus looked at Jesse. "I just forgot he may have had to dig a grave."

"I didn't mean to worry you." Gunther said. "Anyway, it's good to see both of you back here."

"Thanks. We better get to work." Gus rubbed his hands together. "After we unload the boat, we'll load the beds on the wagons first, and then other things that we'll need for tonight at the lighthouse."

Gunther rolled his eyes. "Sounds like you don't think we can get everything moved this afternoon."

Gus looked at Gunther. "I figure by the time we get this boat unloaded we'll only have about three good hours of daylight."

"I have a funeral tomorrow morning, so I can't help until after noon," Gunther said.

Jesse touched the side of his face. "Maybe Lloyd will let us use Ike and Seth again tomorrow."

Gus pointed at Jesse. "That's good. We could probably finish the move by noon, and then Gunther wouldn't have to come back."

"That would help," Gunther said. "I feel bad though. I told you

I would help you move, but now I can't finish the job."

"Oh, don't worry about it," Gus said. "We'll get moved."

"And you're still saving us a lot of time and trips," Jesse said.

"I need to get to work." Gunther said. "It's too cold to just stand here and talk."

After several minutes they finished loading the wagons, and stacked the rest of their furniture and belongings in a small shed adjacent to the dock.

***

Nellie was carrying an iron kettle as she, Alice, and Lucinda came out of the Landing office. They joined Lloyd and the other men standing by the loaded wagons.

"What've you got in the kettle?" Lloyd asked.

"Beef stew."

"Look, Jesse!" Alice pointed to the kettle. "Nellie fixed supper for us." Alice smiled looking back at Jesse. "You know, I think it's time we start calling her Mom."

"*Mom* sounds good." Jesse looked at Nellie. "Thank you, Mom, for the stew. It will go real good with the fresh bread Alice baked yesterday morning,"

Nellie smiled and handed the kettle to Jesse. "Well, it's hot right now, but it probably won't be by the time you get to the lighthouse." She turned toward Lloyd, gently took him by the arm, and looked him in the eyes. "And we're going to be grandparents again."

"What?" Lloyd asked. "You're kidding!"

"Alice just told me in the house."

"It's true, Daddy," Alice said smiling.

Lloyd moved over to Alice and hugged her. "That's great." He turned toward Jesse. "Hey, why didn't you tell me?"

Jesse shook his head. "We were busy working and I didn't know for sure."

"I'm sure now." Alice said.

"I hope it's a boy." Jesse touched Alice on the cheek.

Gus moved over by Jesse. "I'm happy for both of you." He slapped him on the back then cleared his throat. "We should leave. Darkness will be here before we're ready."

"Do you think you can get the rest of your stuff on one wagon load tomorrow?" Lloyd asked Gus.

"It might be tight. We'll bring our buggies to load some of the small stuff."

"Honey, it's time to go to our new home." Jesse escorted Alice and Lucinda to the buggy and pulled it up alongside Gus' buggy. He looked at Gus. "If you want to take the lead, we'll follow the wagons in case there's a problem.

"That's fine."

They waved goodbye and departed the Landing.

***

They traveled along the road that followed the river. Anticipation built with each passing minute.

Alice looked at Jesse. "I've always enjoyed traveling this road. There's something beautiful and magic about this area."

"Yeah, it's good to be back."

"Even though it's cold, I still enjoy looking at the water. It's so

Umpqua River with tree covered hill in background

calm today, and the pine trees make a beautiful background to the peaceful looking river. The trees smell so good.

The ground to the right side of the road sloped down sharply for twenty feet to the river's edge. The slope was covered with frozen brush and weeds while the edge of the river was lined with jagged rocks and boulders. The ground to the left of the road sloped up gradually for thirty feet, and was covered in brush in a similar fashion to the other side. However, beyond the weeds, the slope quickly rose and became the foothills of a mountain covered with a thick stand of tall green pines.

A few minutes later, both buggies and wagons turned onto the sandy-based narrow road that led up the hill to the lighthouse. As they entered the road, shadows blanketed them.

"Those pine trees are so thick and tall they block out the sun," Jesse said.

"It looks like it's almost night time and feels much colder among all these trees," Alice said.

"Honey, this won't last long. When we get to the top of this hill, we'll be out of this and into a clearing where we'll be able to see the lighthouse."

Two or three minutes later Jesse's buggy rolled out of the trees into the clearing.

"The light is much brighter out here," Alice said. She held Lucinda close.

Jesse pointed. "Look, there's the lighthouse. And workers are still there."

"The lighthouse is beautiful, but it's not as tall as the other one."

"That's because it sits on this hill, so they didn't have to build it as high."

Alice pointed. "Look! There's smoke coming from the chimney on one of the houses."

"It's probably the one we're moving into. Gus is talking to one of the construction workers there by the bonfire." Jesse pulled his buggy up behind Gus' and got out.

Alice turned toward Jesse. "If that's the house, it was nice of someone to start a fire for us."

"Yeah, honey, I'll be right back." Jesse moved toward Gus and the worker, but before he could get there, they met him halfway.

Gus laid his hand on Jesse's shoulder. "This is Alexander. Mr. Bronson had him build a fire in the house next to where we're parked. And tomorrow afternoon Mr. Bronson will be here to meet with us."

Jesse shook Alexander's hand. "Thanks for the fire. My wife and I really appreciate it. When I saw the smoke rising from the chimney it gave me a warm feeling inside."

Alexander pulled his hand away and grinned. "I just did what I was told to do."

"My wife and little girl will appreciate moving into a warm house," Jesse said.

"I thank you too." Gus shook Alexander's hand before he went back to the bonfire.

"Gus, I'm going to get Alice and Lucinda out of this cold."

"I'll start unloading the wagons with Gunther and the other men. We have to get them back home before dark."

"I'll be back in a couple of minutes. By the way, did you notice there are two oil houses behind the lighthouse?

"Yeah. It looks like we'll be stocking more oil than we did before,"

Jesse returned to his buggy and helped Alice up the steps and onto the front porch of the house. He opened the front door and they stepped inside.

"Oh, my goodness!" Alice said smiling. "This is a nice sized room, and the fireplace makes it feel so cozy. I like this."

"Me, too. You and Lucinda can stay here by the fire. I'm going upstairs to look at the bedrooms."

"I want to see them too," Alice said. She moved toward the stairs with Jesse. "Lucinda and I will go with you."

"All right," Jesse said.

They went up the stairs to a hallway that ran through the center of the upstairs, and peeked into the rooms as they went.

"There are four bedrooms here," Alice said.

"We'll have more than enough room, and there's a place for a heating stove in each bedroom."

A few minutes later Jesse and Alice returned downstairs. Gus and Gunther entered the front room carrying a mattress.

"What bedroom do you want me to take, Jesse?" Gus asked. "This is part of my bed."

Jesse pointed toward the stairway. "Up those stairs and down the hallway to the second room on the left. Alice and me will take the first one on the right."

"All right. Ike and Seth should be right behind us with your bed."

"Jesse, how long do you think it'll take to unload everything?" Alice asked.

"Thirty or forty minutes. Why?"

"If you unload the dishes from our buggy, then I can unpack some bowls. That way, when you fellows finish unloading, we can all have some of Nellie's stew.

***

An hour later, the men had finished unloading everything and assembled the beds. Alice had given each one of them a bowl of stew, sliced bread, and coffee.

They sat on the floor in the front room, eating the meal.

"What's the tall skinny building between here and the other keeper's house?" Gunther asked Gus.

"I think that's a water tower," Gus said. "Mr. Bronson's coming tomorrow, so I'll find out for sure then."

Seth finished his stew and stood up. "Ike, we should go. It's going to be dark before long." He turned toward Alice. "Thanks for the good supper."

"You're welcome, but Nellie made the stew," Alice said.

Everyone took Seth's comment as his cue to leave.

Gus and Jesse walked out on the porch with everyone.

"Nice barn they built for you, Jesse" Gunther said.

"Yeah. Someday we'll get us a cow and a few chickens," Jesse said.

"When you're ready, maybe I can help with the chickens,"

Gunther said.

"Hey," Ike said. "I've got a couple of extra cats I'll give you. They'll help keep the mice population down."

"Sounds great!" Jesse said.

Gus and Jesse made arrangements with Ike and Seth to meet them back at the Landing the next morning at 8:00 to finish moving.

***

Around noon the next day, Gus and Jesse stood in front of the keeper's house and waved goodbye to Ike and Seth as they drove away in the wagon.

"It feels good to have everything moved," Jesse said.

Gus rubbed the back of his neck. "Yeah, but it took us two trips to haul the stuff because I misjudged the amount of space in our buggies.

"We still have time to unpack some of our things before Mr. Bronson gets here."

They moved toward the house. Gus suddenly stopped and drew in a breath. "I can't wait any longer. I want to see the inside of the lighthouse."

"Me, too!" Jesse rubbed the side of his face. "We can work on unpacking after Mr. Bronson leaves."

They walked up the few steps leading to the door of the workroom and Gus opened the door. "This is the only door to get in the lighthouse."

Jesse stepped inside the workroom and looked around. "There's a fireplace in here."

"Yeah, and a window too. The tools there in the corner must be for working on the light and clock mechanism."

"One thing I don't see is a desk," Jesse said. "We need one for working on the records."

"We'll see about getting one." Gus turned away. "Let's go look at the weight room."

They walked through a hallway six feet long that joined the work and weight rooms together.

Jesse entered the room and rubbed the top of the weight with his hand. "This weight looks a little bigger than the one in the old lighthouse."

Gus nodded. "I thought so too. There must be a reason." He looked up the stairway. "Let's go up and see the rest of the lighthouse."

They walked up the narrow steps and came to a landing with a window looking toward the assistant keeper's home. "Look Gus, I can see my house."

Clock Mechanism

"That's a good view of it."

Jesse took the lead as they continued climbing up the steps. "Looks like another landing further up." Jesse stopped. "Here's another window. Hey, Gus, I can see *your house* from here."

"You're blocking my view. I can't see. There's not room for both of us in front of that window."

"All right." Jesse walked up three steps and waited for Gus.

"Wow! This is a good view of my house." Gus followed Jesse up the stairs and a few steps later they came to another landing.

Jesse pointed to the center of the floor. "Look how they've threaded the cable through that hole in the floor for the weight." He looked above them. "It's through the floor of the room above us too."

"That must be the watch room up there." Gus nudged Jesse. "Don't just stand there, we've got more to see."

They walked up a few more steps and entered the watch room.

"This clock mechanism is bigger than the one in the old lighthouse," Jesse said.

Gus nodded. "That may explain why the weight is also larger. Look, there are four windows in here." He moved over by the one facing the Pacific. "I can see both the ocean and the mouth of the river from here."

Jesse quickly moved across the room next to Gus. "This view is fantastic! I can see for miles toward the horizon. The ocean looks so blue against the white waves coming in and pounding the shore. It's like the ocean is whispering to the land, 'Glad you're here to catch me.'"

Gus rolled his eyes. "It's the same ocean I've watched for years and those waves never made me think of that. You sound like some poet who's seeing the ocean for the first time." He turned away from the window, and looked up at the lantern room. "Look how big that running gear is for the bottom of the lens. It's much bigger than the first light." Gus tilted his head. "There must be about ten feet of empty space from that gear up to the top of the lantern room."

Jesse stepped away from the window and looked up at the empty space. "Once the lens is assembled, it won't be so empty up there."

Gus pulled his pipe from his pocket. "This is going to be a big lens."

Jesse looked around. "It looks like we've seen everything for now."

"I think so." Gus lit his pipe but stood looking out the window for a short time. *Those waves are beautiful.* "Guess we should go unpack our stuff."

***

They stepped up onto the front porch. "I'm hungry," Jesse said. He opened the front door.

As they entered Jesse's new house, Alice met them.

"Aren't you glad the moving is done?" Alice picked up Lucinda. She had been playing with wooden blocks that Jesse made for her.

"I sure am. Now if we just had everything unpacked." Jesse touched Lucinda's hair. "Are you being good for mama?"

Lucinda smiled. "Yes, Papa."

"She's been good." Alice gently squeezed her. "You're probably getting hungry. I should have dinner ready by the time you finish setting up the kitchen table." Alice winked.

Gus looked at Jesse. "Let's do it. I'm hungry too."

***

Later that afternoon Gus and Jesse were watching from the front room as Mr. Bronson arrived on horseback. They walked out to greet him as he stepped up onto the front porch.

Gus shook Mr. Bronson's hand. "It's good to see you again."

Jesse reached for Mr. Bronson's hand. "We want to thank you for hiring us back."

Mr. Bronson removed his hat and rubbed the brim. "I try to be a man of my word, but it took the board longer to get the money than I thought."

"Well, things worked out," Gus said. "We're just glad to be here."

"We sure are," Jesse said. "And this house is so roomy and comfortable,"

Gus rubbed his chin. "Speaking of the house. When will the other keeper's house be finished?"

Mr. Bronson shook his head. "It could be as long as two weeks. We're waiting for some windows and the cook stove to come in."

"I was wondering ..." Gus pointed to the lighthouse. "Jesse and me couldn't wait. We've already seen the inside of her."

"I figured that," Mr. Bronson said. "You probably noticed some differences. We're not using the lens from the old lighthouse. Instead, a much bigger one will be installed. It's a first order Fresnel lens made in France. It requires a bigger clock mechanism and weight. The lens should be here in a couple of days."

"We noticed they were bigger," Gus said.

“We did have a problem with the clock mechanism running gear,” Mr. Bronson said. “It wouldn’t protrude high enough into the lantern room to mesh with the running gear for the lens.”

“So how’d you fix it?” Gus asked.

“One of our engineers designed an add-on floor.”

Jesse frowned. “What do you mean add-on?”

“They built up part of the watch room floor by almost a foot. Did you notice how the walkway around the clock mechanism is lower than the floor where the mechanism sits?”

“I remember seeing that,” Jesse said.

“The lower walkway is the original floor level, and the higher floor is the add-on,” Mr. Bronson said.

“That was clever of the engineer. I hope it works after the lens is installed,” Jesse said.

“Speaking of the lens, there are over six hundred pieces to the lens. We want your help to carry them up to the lantern room.”

Gus frowned. “Sure, but we’re not qualified to put it together.”

“The engineers will assemble it,” Mr. Bronson said. “You just have to help us get the pieces up there. Another thing you need to know. The lens also requires a bigger burner head and it will use more oil.”

Gus looked at Jesse. “That explains the two oil houses.”

Jesse pointed toward the other keeper’s house. “We were wondering about that tall slim building that sits between here and the other house.”

“It’s your water tower.” Mr. Bronson rubbed his hands together. “The engineers figured out a way to capture water in the tank as it runs off the roof.”

“That’s a good idea.” Jesse reached for the doorknob. “Let’s get inside out of this cold air.”

“Tomorrow, you’ll get a delivery of stores, then next week the oil,” Mr. Bronson said.

“Alice will be glad to hear about the stores. She mentioned to me earlier that we were getting low on some things.”

They stepped inside.

"What's the height of the lighthouse?" Gus asked.

"Sixty-five feet," Mr. Bronson said.

"She's beautiful," Jesse said.

Completed Lighthouse with Workroom – Tower – Asst. Keepers House

"We think so, too." Mr. Bronson said. "We were lucky to get the painting done before it got so cold."

"Would you like a cup of coffee?" Jesse asked.

"Thanks." Mr. Bronson removed his gloves. "That would taste

good about now."

Jesse pointed to a chair next to the fireplace. "Have a seat, Mr. Bronson. I'll be right back."

As Mr. Bronson and Gus sat down, they heard Lucinda in the distance. "Mommy."

"Sounds like Lucinda just woke up from her nap," Gus said.

"How many children does Jesse have?"

"Just one for now, but they are expecting again."

"Good for them. They've got plenty of room here. The board planned ahead and expected the keepers would probably have big families."

"That makes sense," Gus said. "But what about me? I don't plan to marry again."

"The board didn't know that. We planned for—"

Jesse returned with coffee and handed the cup to him.

"Thanks, Jesse." Mr. Bronson took a sip of coffee and looked back at Gus. "I started to say, the board planned for *this* lighthouse to have a long life. We figured you might marry, but if not, when you retire, we wouldn't have to build on to a small house to accommodate the next keeper with a family."

"The board did a good job planning and building these houses." Jesse said. "This one is well built and very roomy compared to where we lived in Gardiner's City."

"Thanks. I'll tell the board." Mr. Bronson took another sip of coffee then looked up at Jesse. "Gus tells me you're going to be a father again."

Jesse grinned. "Yeah. I'd like a boy this time."

"Congratulations." Mr. Bronson stood up. "Thanks for the coffee. Now, I need to go. I have a meeting with the foreman."

"Thanks for everything, Mr. Bronson," Gus accompanied Mr. Bronson toward the front door.

Jesse followed them. "We're looking forward to seeing the light in operation."

"So are we," Mr. Bronson said. "But there's more work to be done before that can happen."

Chapter 28

Anticipation

AT 2:00 p.m. THE NEXT day a wagon pulled up and stopped outside Jesse's house. One of the two men on board climbed down and moved toward the front door. Before he could reach the porch, Jesse was out the door to meet him. "Do you fellows have our stores?"

"Sure do. Where do you want to unload?"

Gus stepped out onto the porch.

Jesse turned toward Gus, "They've got our stores."

Gus nodded.

Jesse pointed toward the back of the house. "Pull back there by the kitchen."

Gus and Jesse followed the men and met them as they climbed down from the wagon.

"Which one of you is Gus?" one of the men said.

"I'm Gus."

"Here's a list of everything we've got on here. When we finish unloading, I'll need your signature to verify you received it all."

"No problem." Gus looked at the list, then at Jesse and the men. "Let me know what you carry in so I can keep track of the stuff."

Jesse moved closer to Gus. "What's on the list?"

"Beef, pork, flour, rice, beans, potatoes, coffee, vinegar, laundry soap, toilet paper, brass polish, mops, and brooms."

"Sounds like some of the same items we used to get at the other lighthouse."

"Maybe we could plant a garden come spring and have more vegetables to go with this," Gus said.

"We'll eat good anyway. You know Alice is a great cook."

The driver removed the backboard of the wagon. "Can we start unloading? We have to get back before dark."

"Sure," Jesse said. "But those barrels are too heavy for me to lift by myself."

"That's what I found out when we loaded them," the driver said.

Forty minutes later the four men finished unloading the wagon and Gus signed the paperwork. "Here you go." He handed it to the driver.

The two men climbed up into the wagon and the driver picked up the reins.

Gus waved. "Thanks."

***

Two days later Jesse was helping Alice hang curtains in the sitting room when Gus came in. "Sorry to interrupt you. I think the lens is here. A wagon just pulled up by the lighthouse."

Jesse stepped down from the ladder and turned toward Alice. "Honey, I have to go, but I'll finish this when I get back."

"Go ahead. I can do it."

Jesse frowned. "I don't want you on the ladder. You could fall."

"All right, but you worry too much."

Jesse and Gus went to the lighthouse and were met at the wagon by the construction foreman.

"The lens is here. You fellows ready to go to work?"

"Yeah, Bart," Gus said. "Anything we need to know before we start?"

Bart nodded. "Let me show you." He climbed up inside the back of the wagon and removed the lid from one of the wooden boxes. "Be careful and don't drop any of these prisms. They came all the way from France, so it would take a long time to get a replacement."

"Don't worry," Jesse said. "We've handled prisms before."

The foreman pushed back some of the sawdust packed around the prisms. "But if you notice, these are bigger than the prisms of the lens in the first lighthouse."

Gus stepped closer to the back of the wagon and looked inside the box, then turned toward Jesse. "He's right."

"It doesn't look like there are over 600 pieces on this wagon," Jesse said.

"There isn't." Bart climbed down from the wagon. "There should be three other wagons arriving here soon with the rest of the prisms."

Jesse shook his head. "This will keep us busy for a while. If there's nothing else, we should get started."

"One more thing. Take the first few boxes up to the second landing so we can start unpacking them there. The remainder of the boxes will be stacked on the first landing and in the weight room. There won't be enough room for all the boxes inside. You'll have to stack some of them out here next to the building. My men will help you carry the boxes."

"Thanks. How long do you think it'll take to assemble the lens? Gus asked.

"One of the engineers told me it could take a couple weeks," Bart said. "He said this is a very unique lens, and it's the first time they've ever assembled one like this."

Jesse brushed the side of his face. "What do you mean unique?"

"You'll see when you unpack the boxes. There are both white and red prisms."

"*That is* unique," Jesse said. "I'm looking forward to seeing this lens in operation."

"Me, too," Gus said. "So the quicker we get to work, the sooner we'll see it."

***

Five hours later they finished unloading the wagons. Gus and Jesse began to unpack the boxes.

"Before you take any prisms up to the lantern room, make sure you remove all sawdust from them," Bart said. "The sawdust will prevent the prisms from fitting together properly."

"It'll be easier to sweep up the sawdust from this landing floor than from up there in the lantern room," Jesse said.

"You'll be able to carry the prisms up there faster than the engineers can assemble them. They'll show you where to lay them and how many to stock."

"It sounds simple enough." Gus rubbed his bearded chin. "But will it take four of us to carry the prisms since the engineers will assemble them slower than we can supply?"

"No. You'll work by yourselves. I received notice that the materials to finish the other keeper's house will be here tomorrow. I'll put men over there to work on that house."

Gus' eyes widened. "How long before that house will be ready?"

"Couple of days," Bart said. "You'll still have pieces of the lens to carry upstairs, but you might be able to move some of your personal stuff while you're waiting to restock."

"I don't have much, so it shouldn't take long for me to move."

***

Three days later, while Alice was preparing breakfast, Jesse came into the kitchen. "Morning, honey. It looks like we got about four inches of snow last night."

Alice smiled. "The way it covers the pine trees is so beautiful."

"What's for breakfast? Something smells good."

"I fixed biscuits, gravy, fried potatoes, and bacon."

Jesse kissed Alice, and picked up Lucinda who was standing nearby. "How's my girl this morning?"

Lucinda giggled. "I love you, Papa." She hugged his neck. "Can I play in the snow?"

Jesse hugged her. "I love you too. You can go out after breakfast." He moved next to Alice at the stove. "Well, this is Gus' last breakfast with us."

Alice nodded. "I know he only moved next door, but I'm going to miss him being in this house. I enjoyed cooking for him and having him at our table. And he treats Lucinda as though she were his granddaughter."

Jesse nodded. "Maybe we could talk him into eating with us, at least until the lighthouse is completed."

"That would be nice."

There was a knock at the kitchen door.

"I'll get it." Jesse opened it. "Morning, Gus. Come in out of the snow."

"Morning, Jesse." Gus stomped the snow off his boots before stepping inside. "Good morning, Alice."

"Morning."

Gus held out his arms to take Lucinda from Jesse. "How are you this morning, sweetheart?"

Lucinda leaned forward into Gus' arms, and then put her arm around his neck. "Why you move, Gus?"

"It's best if I live in my house. You have your house. We'll still see each other almost every day. I'm just next door."

Alice set hot biscuits on the table. "Sit down, breakfast is ready."

As they sat down Jesse looked at Gus. "Alice and I were talking about this being your last breakfast with us."

Gus touched his chin and looked at Alice. "Yeah. I'll miss your good cooking, but I hate to make extra work for you."

Jesse took some bacon and passed the plate to Gus. "I was thinking you should continue eating your meals with us until after the lighthouse is finished. It'll make more sense then, because we'll be working separate shifts."

Gus looked back at Alice.

"I agree with Jesse." Alice grinned. "It's not any more work for me to cook for four than for three. Besides, we enjoy your company."

"Let me think about it," Gus said.

"All right." Alice said. "I'll expect you for dinner."

Gus chuckled.

Alice leaned toward Jesse. "You know, with all that's been happening, I almost forgot about Christmas. It's only three weeks away."

Jesse frowned. "That *soon*?"

Gus cleared his throat. "Yesterday, I was talking to Bart, and he said the Lighthouse Board would like the lighthouse operational by then."

Jesse set down his coffee cup and looked across the table at Gus. "If they can make that schedule, it would be a great Christmas present to the mariners."

"That's what I thought when Bart told me."

Alice touched Jesse's arm. "Honey, could you cut a Christmas tree when you have time?"

"Sure, I'll make the time." He took a bite of his bacon.

"Papa, I want one this big." Lucinda stretched out her arms.

Jesse smiled. "I'll try, sweetheart."

Gus set down his cup. "She's old enough to enjoy Christmas this year."

"Yes," Alice said. "I'm going to let her help decorate the tree. We may cut out some paper snowmen, and string some popcorn. She still has the little star you gave her last Christmas, Gus. We'll use it too."

Jesse reached for another biscuit. "If it's all right with you, Gus, I'd like to cut the Christmas tree before I go to the lighthouse this morning. However, I don't want to be responsible for holding up assembly of the lens. If you think it'll jeopardize the work, I'll cut the tree later."

"It shouldn't be a problem," Gus said. "The workers may be late anyway because of the snow."

Lucinda's eyes widened. "Papa can I go out and play in the snow?"

"Have you finished eating?"

"Yes." She climbed down from her chair.

"All right." Jesse said. "But put on your coat and boots before you go out."

"I don't think you'll want her to go out there by herself," Gus said. "When I came to breakfast, I saw wolf tracks in the snow. I've not heard of them attacking anyone around here, but no sense of taking a chance."

"Guess I'll postpone cutting that tree."

Alice got up from the table. "I need to help her with her boots, anyway. I'll go out with her for a while. Besides, it's Lucinda's first time in the snow, so I don't think it'll take her long to get her fill of it."

"Well, if you're going with her, then I'll go now and cut the tree," Jesse said.

"Keep a watch out for that wolf," Gus said. He got up from the table. "I'll see you at the lighthouse."

"I'll be there as quickly as I can."

***

A short time later, Alice and Lucinda stepped out onto the front porch.

Lucinda headed for the steps. "Mama, look at the snow piled up on the railing."

"Wait for me. You'll fall on the steps." Alice hurried to catch up with Lucinda at the top of the stairs and took her by the hand.

As they walked down the steps Lucinda drug her hand on top of the rail, pushing the snow off. She smiled. "The snow is pretty and soft, Mama."

"Yes, but it can be slippery on these steps. Be careful not to fall."

Lucinda drug Alice by the hand into the yard. She started picking up snow and throwing it up in the air. Lucinda giggled with each handful. She made tracks in the snow with her boots and tried to roll up a big snowball on the ground.

Alice stepped back for a moment, feeling a sense of contentment she had never experienced before. God had blessed her with a husband, a beautiful new home, a daughter, and another little one on the way. She wiped a tear from her eye, and then taught Lucinda how to make a snowball.

***

Jesse went to the barn, picked up his axe and slung it over his shoulder. He headed for the edge of the pine forest behind the barn. He moved along the edge of the forest looking for a tree small enough to use as a Christmas tree, but big enough to satisfy Lucinda's desires. Beyond the water tower, he glanced down and saw tracks. *Those tracks must be the ones Gus saw. They come from the other side of the water tower, across here, and then go toward the forest.* Jesse stopped, surveyed the area at the edge of the forest. He saw something move. *It's the wolf. I have to scare him away.* Jesse clapped his hands and yelled. "Get! Get away from here! Go chase a rabbit! Get!"

The wolf ran back into the forest.

Jesse continued walking along the edge of the forest and soon passed behind Gus' house. About fifty yards beyond the house, he saw small trees. *I remembered seeing smaller trees at the edge of this clearing the first time Gus and I came to the lighthouse.* Jesse chose a tree about four feet tall and chopped it down. He retraced his path in the snow while he pulled the tree with him toward his house. Several yards ahead of him, he saw two deer slowly moving through the pine trees along the edge of the forest. *I guess they haven't seen or heard me yet or they would be long gone.* A minute later they were spooked by something and took off running into the forest.

Jesse arrived at his house and laid the tree outside next to the kitchen door. Inside he found Alice cleaning off the table from breakfast. "Hi honey, I'm back." He rubbed his hands together. "Did Lucinda have a good time playing in the snow?

Alice smiled. "Oh yes, and I was wrong about her not taking long to get her fill of the snow. She didn't want to come in, but I had housework and needed to start something for dinner."

"Now we know Lucinda likes to play in the snow. Did you see or hear anything of a wolf while you were outside with her?"

"No wolf." Alice said. "But I heard you yelling at something beyond the water tower."

"I saw the wolf and was able to scare it off."

Lucinda entered the kitchen. "Papa, where is the tree?"

"It's lying outside and it's beautiful." Jesse touched her on the shoulder.

Lucinda's eyes gleamed and she grabbed Jesse by the hand. "Papa, can we put it up right now?"

"We'll have to do it later. Right now, I have to go to work." Jesse hugged Lucinda. "Sweetheart, we have several days yet before Christmas."

***

The morning before Christmas, Gus and Jesse were waiting impatiently for the foreman when he finally arrived at the lighthouse. Bart stepped down from his buggy and frowned. "Morning. You fellows seem a little nervous."

"We may be." Gus said. "As you know, tomorrow is Christmas, and there are still several pieces of the lens and some of the burner unit to be assembled before the light is ready for operation. Do you think it'll be ready by tomorrow?"

Bart rolled his eyes. "I think you already know the answer to that question. Everyone has worked hard to achieve the board's goal to have the light operating by Christmas. However, I never expected so many workers to get sick, and then we had those eight inches of snow."

"What's your best estimate as to how much longer?" Jesse asked.

Bart held the back of his neck. "Well, we don't work tomorrow, but if the weather holds out and my men stay well, I think we can finish in four or five more days."

Gus rubbed his beard. "After you finish the job, we still have to fill the oil reservoir, then test the light and clock mechanism."

"We want to test them as soon as possible," Jesse said. "We're really looking forward to seeing this light in operation."

Bart pointed at Jesse. "I'm just as anxious as you guys, but it's part of our job to test the equipment before we leave. When it comes time, you can carry oil and fill the reservoir. I appreciate the work you have done already. Without your help we wouldn't be as far along as we are now. Believe me, as soon as it looks like we're almost ready to test, I'll let you know when to start carrying the oil."

Gus shook his hand. "If we can do anything to help let us

know."

"I will, but for now continue to unpack and carry those prisms." Bart went inside the lighthouse.

***

The next morning, at the usual time, Gus knocked on the kitchen door for breakfast.

"Come in, Gus," Jesse said.

He stepped inside. "Merry Christmas."

Gus exchanged Christmas greetings with Alice and Jesse. He walked around the table and patted Lucinda on the head. "Merry Christmas."

Lucinda smiled as she turned her head toward him. "Merry Christmas, Gus."

"Have a seat and I'll serve these eggs," Alice said.

Gus sat down and looked across the table at Lucinda. "Did you get any gifts this morning?"

Jesse passed a plate of biscuits to Gus and then the bacon.

Lucinda's eyes sparkled. "I got a dolly, but she's asleep right now."

"Thanks Jesse." Gus took two biscuits and some bacon and passed the plates on to Alice.

"Take some of these fried potatoes," Alice said. She passed the dish to Gus.

"You sure have fed me good all these weeks. After the lighthouse is finished, I'll have to learn how to cook all over again, but it still won't taste as good as yours."

Alice chuckled. "Thanks, but you know you're welcome at our table anytime."

Lucinda looked at her mother. "Mama, can I show Gus my doll?"

"After you finish eating."

A few minutes later, everyone finished breakfast. Lucinda led Gus into the front room while Jesse and Alice followed. Lucinda headed straight for the Christmas tree.

The tree was decorated with paper snowmen and strings of

popcorn which lay across the limbs and encircled the entire tree. Small white candles nestled in the pine needles while the tree stood stately with Lucinda's star on top.

Gus looked under the tree and saw a small rag doll lying in a little cradle filled with hay. "You have a beautiful doll," Gus said.

Lucinda looked up at Gus and smiled. "Thanks Gus. I love her."

"It looks like she enjoys sleeping in the cradle."

"Mama said my dolly reminded her of baby Jesus."

Gus winked at Jesse and Alice as he sat down on the daybed. "What do you mean, baby Jesus?

Lucinda's eyes sparkled as she looked at Gus. "You *know*, baby Jesus."

Gus grinned and looked at Lucinda. "Tell me what you mean about him."

"'Cause baby Jesus was born in a manger. He had to sleep on hay just like my dolly."

Gus looked at Jesse and then back to Lucinda. "Do you think baby Jesus slept on the hay as good as your baby does?"

"Oh yes! He was a good baby too." Lucinda leaned over and picked up her doll from under the tree.

"That's interesting." Gus said. "Why do you think Jesus was a good baby?"

Holding her doll, Lucinda moved over to Jesse and cuddled between his legs. "Papa read a story from the Bible this morning about baby Jesus. He didn't cry about having to sleep in that manger, so I know he was a good baby."

Jesse hugged Lucinda. "You got more out of the story than I thought you did."

"Mama's proud of you." Alice leaned over and kissed Lucinda on the cheek.

Gus smiled at Lucinda. "I'm proud of you, too. I've read the story of Jesus' birth, but you told me something I've never thought about before."

"You make me feel good, Gus." Lucinda turned toward Alice. "Mama, can I go play?"

"Aren't you forgetting something?" Alice asked.

Lucinda frowned. "Oh." She moved over to the Christmas tree and picked up a piece of paper from beneath it, then handed it to Gus. "This is for you."

Gus unfolded the paper and found what appeared to be a drawing of a man standing next to a lighthouse. "This is beautiful, Lucinda," he said. "Did you draw this?"

"Yes." Lucinda pointed to the picture. "That's you by the lighthouse. I made one for Papa too."

"Thank you very much," Gus said. "I'll hang this in my sitting room, and then I can look at it every day."

Lucinda smiled. "Mama, now can I go play?"

Alice brushed her hand across Lucinda's shoulders. "Yes, but stay inside the house."

Jesse stood up from the daybed. "Gus, Alice and I have a little something for you. It's not much, but we wanted you to know we appreciate your friendship, and we're glad you're a part of our lives."

Alice picked up a package from under the tree and handed it to Gus.

"Well, thank you." Gus tore open the package and found two pair of socks and a scarf inside. "Thanks. I especially needed socks. Not just to keep my feet warm, but some of mine have holes in them."

"I can't take credit for knitting them," Jesse said. "Alice did all the work."

"Well, thank you both for your thoughtfulness and for the gifts." Gus lowered his head. "I have a gift for the both of you, but I didn't get it completed."

"We didn't expect anything," Alice said.

"That's right, Gus. Having you here to celebrate Christmas with us is gift enough."

Gus smiled. "I appreciate that, but I wanted to have something for today to give you. However, since I couldn't move into my house sooner, I got a late start in making your hall tree."

"Hall tree!" Jesse said.

Alice smiled. “We sure could use one. We’re always tossing our coats on the furniture”

“I thought it would be useful to you. I should have it done sometime tomorrow if I work on it today.”

Jesse shook his head. “Where in the world did you find materials to build us a hall tree?”

Gus chuckled. “Well, some of the pieces were left by the workers after they finished my house. I talked to Bart about how I would like to use that wood, and he approved me using it. However, I did have to make a quick trip to the general store the other day for the rest of the materials.”

“You’re pretty sneaky,” Jesse said. “We had no idea you were building anything.”

Gus rubbed his cheek. “I was afraid you would hear me.”

“I never heard anything,” Alice said.

Gus stood up. “Thanks for breakfast and the gifts. Now, I better go work on your gift. I’ll need your help, Jesse, to carry it over here tomorrow.”

“Sure, just let me know when you’re ready.”

***

The foreman walked up the lighthouse steps behind Gus and Jesse to the second landing. They set down a box of prisms to unpack.

“How many boxes do you have left?”

Gus looked around at Bart. “This is the last one.”

“That’s good. We’re already four days behind the completion schedule. But if things keep going this well, we might be able to run the start-up test tomorrow.”

“Great.” Jesse said.

“When you finish with these prisms, I might be able to use your help with the burner unit.”

Jesse’s eyes lit up. “You mean after that you’ll be ready for us to carry the oil?”

Bart frowned. “Absolutely not. I don’t want any oil in that reservoir until after they finish assembling the lens. If they should drop a prism or tools in there, we'd have a mess."

Jesse lowered his eyes. "Guess I'm too anxious and I misunderstood what you said."

Bart nodded. "We're all anxious. Let's get back to work."

"We'll be ready to help with the burner unit as soon as we finish with this box," Gus said.

"I'll let you know." Bart walked past them and up the stairs.

Gus and Jesse went back to unpacking the box of prisms. They cleaned the sawdust from each piece, then carried them up to the lantern room and carefully laid the prisms on crushed paper.

"Now that the lens is almost assembled, you can see how huge that thing is going to be," Gus said on their second trip down from the lantern room.

"Yeah, and it's beautiful too. I remember the first time we came up here and talked about the big open space at the top of the tower. Well, it's not open anymore."

"I'd like to know how big the lens is," Gus said.

"Me, too."

They leaned over and picked up another prism to clean.

"Let's ask one of the engineers on our next trip up there," Jesse said.

They cleaned the prisms and took them up to the lantern room.

Gus looked up at the engineer working closest to him. "We were wondering about the size of this lens. Do you know how big it's going to be when completed?"

The engineer looked down from the scaffold. "According to the specifications, the lens will be nine feet, seven inches tall, and six feet across at the bottom."

Gus waved at the engineer. "Thanks for your help."

"Thank *you,*" The engineer said.

As Gus and Jesse started to walk down the stairs, Bart stopped them. "We're further along on assembly of the burner unit than I thought. I'll only need one of you to help us finish it. When you're done with the prisms, I need one of you to help load empty boxes and haul them to the Landing. Gus, you decide which one of you will stay here and who will load boxes."

"Why are empty boxes being hauled to the Landing?" Jesse asked.

"Mr. Bronson said the Lighthouse Board wanted to keep the ones that are in good condition. They may use them later for something else."

Jesse rubbed the side of his face. "Does someone have to go to Scottsburg with the boxes?"

Bart shook his head. "Only to Lloyd's Landing. People there will load the boxes on the boat, and then the board will provide workers to unload at Scottsburg."

Jesse looked at Gus. "If you want me too, I'll load boxes."

"You made my decision easy," Gus said.

"Jesse, you and my man on the wagon will probably only have enough time for two loads today. By the time you finish tomorrow with the boxes, we should have things ready here to carry the oil and start testing."

Jesse smiled. "That's what I've been waiting to hear."

"Me, too," Gus said.

Bart rubbed his hands together. "Alright, we're close to finishing. Let's make it happen."

***

Gus pushed back from the table after the evening meal. "Thanks for another great supper, Alice. I ate more of your beans and pork than I should've, but they were so good and the mashed potatoes too."

Jesse stood up. "And the apple pie was great too, honey."

Alice smiled. "Well, Gus, since you decided this would be your last meal with us, I wanted to fix something I knew you really liked."

"I appreciate you, Alice, and I'll start missing your cooking in the morning. Remember, the agreement was that I would start doing my own cooking when the lighthouse was operational. And tonight is the night."

"I can hardly wait," Jesse said. "We have to finish filling the burner unit reservoir, and it's ready to go. All the testing of equipment was completed this morning."

Alice smiled. "I'm happy for both of you. I know you've been anxious for a long time to see the light operational."

"Yeah," Gus said. "But mainly for the safety of the mariners coming into the river."

"It is December 31," Jesse said. "The light was supposed to be operational by Christmas."

Alice frowned. "Have there been any shipwrecks since Christmas?"

Jesse's eyebrows curled. "No, but I don't understand your question."

"Well, if there were no shipwrecks during that time, then you shouldn't feel bad because the light wasn't operational."

Gus looked at Alice. "I understand what you're saying. But just because there were no wrecks doesn't mean the light wasn't needed. If the light had been operational, it would have made the job much easier for those captains who had to navigate to the mouth of the river."

Alice held her head up higher. "I didn't mean to say the light wasn't needed during that time. I was just trying to get you men to not worry about when it was *supposed* to be operational, and focus on tonight."

Jesse grinned. "You're always trying to stay positive. Guess that's another reason I love you." He moved over to Alice and hugged her.

"The truth of the matter is, I'm also looking forward to seeing the light," Alice grinned. "The combination of both red and white lenses should make it a spectacular sight."

"Indeed, it should." Gus looked back at Alice as he moved toward the door. "Thanks again for a great meal. Now we need to go make final preparation for tonight."

Alice moved toward the door with Gus and Jesse. "Are you working first or second shift, Jesse?"

"I'm working second shift, but I'm not going to bed until I see the light working in total darkness."

Alice touched Jesse on the shoulder. “I’ll be up with you, and maybe Lucinda too. She’s been asking when the light is going to shine.”

“This first lighting of the lighthouse will make history,” Jesse said. “It’s going to be a big occasion, and there’ll be more people here tonight than us. Bart told me he was going to be here, as well as Mr. Bronson and other board members.”

“They’re not the only ones,” Gus said. “I didn’t want to tell you about going to the store the other day for those materials, but I also stopped by the Landing office and briefly talked to Lloyd. He said Nellie and him plan to be here for the big event.”

Alice’s mouth gaped open as her hands touched the sides of her face. “Oh, my. I had no idea there would be so many visitors here. I better bake some sugar cookies to serve with coffee.”

***

At dusk, Mr. Bronson walked up the stairs leading to the door of the lighthouse workroom. He stood on the top step looking out over the numerous people standing there with lanterns. He cleared his throat. “I would like to thank everyone for coming to celebrate with us the reopening of the Umpqua River Lighthouse. Thanks to the engineers, the construction team, and to everyone else who worked so hard to help build this lighthouse. It has taken us a few years to get to this point. We know how important this lighthouse will be to the safety of all mariners, their ships, and the products and people they bring to the Umpqua River.”

The crowd applauded.

“I would also like to thank Mrs. Fayette for providing the coffee and cookies for our refreshment this evening.”

More applause.

“This is the big moment we’ve all been waiting for.” Mr. Bronson smiled down at Gus and Jesse standing at the bottom of the steps. “Are you men ready?”

“We’re ready.”

“I’ve given Gus and Jesse the privilege of lighting the light together.” Mr. Bronson beckoned both of them up the steps. “Go light that light."

Gus and Jesse opened the workroom door and entered the lighthouse.

Mr. Bronson moved down the steps. "Let's move away from the lighthouse so we can see the light better when it comes on."

Everyone followed Mr. Bronson to a spot he had selected about seventy-five feet away from the base of the lighthouse. "We should be able to see good from here," he said.

Five minutes later the light began to shine through the lens, and the people saw the Umpqua River Light shine for the first time. The light coming through the prisms of the lens projected light beams of red and white.

"Ohh."

"Wow!"

"It's *beautiful.*"

"*What* a sight."

"Look at that!"

Lantern Room lighted at night – Red and White Light

A few minutes later, Gus and Jesse came out of the lighthouse and joined Alice, Lucinda, and the rest of the crowd.

Jesse pointed to the light. "Look Gus, from out here you can see both red and white lights."

"Why do you say that?" Alice asked. "You already know it has both red and white prisms."

"Jesse is right," Gus said. "After we lit the burner head we looked inside the lens and all the prisms looked crystal clear. It's strange. We didn't see any red."

"I wonder why?" Jesse asked.

"I can't explain it for sure, but it must have something to do with it being dark outside and there was no light coming through the lens from the outside toward us."

Lucinda tugged on Jesse's pant leg. "Papa, I like the light."

Jesse picked up Lucinda and hugged her. He put his other arm around Alice's shoulders. "Just like the lighthouse lights up the night sky and provides joy and hope to the mariners, the two of you provide joy and hope to me."

Alice squeezed Jesse's hand. "Thanks, that's sweet of you."

"I'm so happy right now, I could burst," Jesse said.

"Me, too," Gus said. "It's not just the beauty of the light, but to realize all the work that went into building this lighthouse."

"Yeah, and we helped," Jesse said.

Mr. Bronson moved over next to Gus and Jesse. "Congratulations, men. This is a proud moment for the board. Thanks for all your help to make this happen."

"Thanks," Gus said. "We're also proud, but more important, the light is providing the navigational assistance needed for the mariners."

"Has the board decided about leaving the light on during rainy days? Jesse asked.

"Not yet.

"The light is beautiful," Alice said. "But now it's time for me to take Lucinda home for bed, and I need to get off my feet." She slipped away from Jesse's arm.

Jesse turned toward Gus. "Unless you need me for something, I'm going home with Alice. I'll see you at midnight."

Gus patted Jesse on the shoulder. "See you then."

Chapter 29

Life Saved – Life Given

A FEW MINUTES before midnight, Jesse walked up the steps to the workroom and opened the door. Gus was sitting at the small desk, smoking his pipe, and writing in the record book. Hot wood embers glowed in the fireplace at the end of the room. *It feels good in here. I'm glad to be out of the cold night air.* "Evening, Gus. How'd it go?"

"Everything worked good and I had no problems. How's Alice doing?" Gus asked.

"Alice?" He blew out the flame in his lantern.

"She said her feet were hurting."

"She felt better before we went to bed. She just stood up too long."

Gus puffed on his pipe. "When do you think you'll be a father again?"

Jesse touched the side of his face. "The new doctor at the Landing figured sometime in July."

"That's still seven months away. I hope she doesn't have this problem very often."

"Me, too." Jesse stretched his arms over his head. "Did you see any ships?"

"One entered the river about 8:00 p.m."

Jesse grinned. "I'd like to have been on board that ship to hear the crew's conversation when they saw the light. I'll bet they were more excited than we were."

"It's possible." Gus took the pipe out of his mouth, then looked up at Jesse. "I know I felt good when I saw that ship coming in. I knew the light was shining toward them, and it had to be of help to the captain and crew to find the mouth of the river. It brought back memories of our times in the old lighthouse."

"That may be what has driven us to want to stay as keepers. Our jobs seemed thankless, but I know the work we did to maintain the light helped to save lives."

Gus nodded. "You're right. Well, I better go to the house." He stood up from the desk and picked up his lantern. "In addition to recording no problems with the equipment and seeing the ship, I also made entries in the book to show the celebration and startup of the lighthouse on December 31."

"Good idea."

Gus opened the door. "I hope you have a good night." He stepped out the door, but before it could close behind him, he turned and stepped back inside. "Hey Wickie, I just realized it's a new year."

"You're right. Guess we forgot about the new year due to all the excitement about the light last night."

"Yeah. Anyway, happy new year." Gus opened the door again.

"Happy new year to you, too." Jesse turned toward the weight room. *I better check the equipment to make sure everything is still operating properly.* He walked through the short hallway that connected the workroom to the weight room, and climbed up the winding stairway leading to the watch room. He looked at the clock mechanism. *It looks like I'll need to rewind the clock in about an hour.* He checked the level of oil in the reservoir. *I'm glad this lantern has a big reservoir. There should be enough oil to last through the night.* He took a few steps across the watch room to the short stairway that led up alongside the lens into the lantern room. He arrived in the lantern room, looked at the windows and frowned. *What in the world is that?* He looked closer. *It looks like a huge splatter of bird dung. Gus must not have seen that. I'll have to clean it off in the morning.*

Jesse returned downstairs to the workroom and made an entry in the record book about the dung. He worked the rest of his shift without any problems, and saw one ship. About an hour after daybreak, Jesse shut down the light and pulled the curtain around the lens.

He returned to the workroom and dipped a bucket of water from the water barrel sitting behind the door. He picked up a few rags and a window scraper and went back up the stairway to the lantern room. *I need to open that glass door to get out on the catwalk.* He unscrewed the large wing nuts that fastened the heavy metal frame of the door and stepped out onto the catwalk. *This thing is narrow. I'm glad the railing is here to hold on to, and I'm glad we removed the snow.* Jesse crept around to where the windows were splattered and set down the bucket of water. *It's freezing cold out here this morning.* He scraped off the worst of the dung, and while washing off the remainder with rags, he spilled some water.

Jesse finished washing the windows and picked up the bucket. As he turned to go back inside, he slipped on the icy catwalk and fell. He reached for the railing but missed it and grabbed on to an upright support just as he was about to fall off the edge of the catwalk. *Oh, thank you God.* Jesse's heart pounded as he grasped the support. He took a deep breath, then exhaled. *Oh, man! That was close.* I *didn't think water would freeze that fast. My hands are freezing. I have to get up from here. It's about a fifty-foot drop to the ground.*

***

Alice walked out of the bedroom and down the stairs to go fix breakfast. As she moved through the front room she glanced toward the lighthouse and saw a dark object at the edge of the catwalk. *What's that?* She moved closer to the window and saw a man hanging from the railing of the catwalk. *It's Jesse!* She grabbed her coat from the hall tree as she ran out the front door. *Oh God, please don't let him fall!* As she ran across the yard, she yelled, "Hold on Jesse, I'm coming!"

***

Short of breath, Alice arrived in the lantern room. She stepped out onto the catwalk. "I'm here Jesse, hold on!"

"Watch for ice!" Jesse said. "Hold on to the railing."

"I am." Alice crept toward Jesse where he was dangling off the side of the lighthouse. She held to the railing with one hand while she knelt down. "What can I do to help you?"

Jesse grunted between gasps of air. "I'll swing my leg up there and you hold it down to the catwalk deck while I pull myself up. I hope this works. My arms are tired."

"You can do it!" Alice held her hand ready at the edge of the catwalk.

He swung his leg onto the catwalk and she grabbed his leg by the ankle, pressing it to the deck. Jesse pulled himself up on the deck and then got to his knees.

Breathing deeply, he hugged Alice. "Thanks, honey. You may have saved my life." He stood up and helped her to her feet. "Let's get back inside, but be very careful."

They stepped back inside the lantern room.

"What was wrong that you had to go out there?" Alice asked.

"I needed to clean bird dung off the windows."

"You almost lost your life for that? She shook her head. "Next time you better wait for Gus to go out there with you."

"That's probably a good idea." Jesse fastened the glass door.

Alice hugged him again, and sighed. "Let's go to the house. I need to check on Lucinda and fix your breakfast."

"I've worked up an appetite, but first I need to stop in the work- room and make an entry in the record book."

"All right. I'll see you at the house."

Later, Jesse told Gus about his experience on the catwalk and they agreed that neither of them would ever go out there by themselves in the winter. For the next several months, they settled into a routine. There were no accidents or significant incidents that occurred. They performed their jobs and were happy to be back doing most of the same duties they had performed in the old lighthouse. They were pleased with their jobs and daily operation of the light, especially as they watched ships safely enter and leave the mouth of the Umpqua River.

***

One beautiful morning in late spring, Jesse had finished breakfast and decided to dig up an area of soil behind the house for a garden. A couple of days later, after he and Alice finished breaking up the soil, they planted a variety of vegetables. As the garden grew Alice helped hoe weeds and pick vegetables for the first few weeks. By the first of July, she was great with child, and Jesse didn't want her working in the garden, so Gus volunteered to help tend to it.

***

Early afternoon of July 24, Jesse and Gus were picking beans when they heard Alice yell from the kitchen door.

"Jesse, I need you!"

She sounds afraid. Jesse dropped his bucket of beans and ran toward the house. A couple of minutes later he came back out the kitchen door and waved at Gus. "Alice is ready to have her baby!"

Gus ran to Jesse. "Say no more." He handed Jesse both buckets of beans. "I'll get Doctor Radcliff." He hurried to the barn and hitched Jake to the buggy and drove off toward the Landing with his horse at a trot.

Jesse went back into the house with Alice and Lucinda.

***

Forty-five minutes later, Gus and Doctor Radcliff returned. They stepped inside the front door. "Jesse, the doctor is here," Gus said.

"Get him up here, quick!"

Gus pointed the way upstairs to the doctor. They arrived in the hallway and Lucinda ran toward them.

"Papa needs *you*, Gus." Lucinda pointed to the bedroom.

"*Me*?" Gus asked. "The doctor's here."

"But I heard Papa say, 'Come on Gus, I need your help now,' and then Mama screamed some more."

Gus patted Lucinda on the head. "You go ahead, doc. I'll stay here with Lucinda."

Doctor Radcliff knocked on the door, announced himself, and entered the bedroom.

Although the door was closed, Gus could hear almost everything through the door.

"Quick doctor, I need help with the head," Jesse said.

"Looks like I got here just in time."

Then Gus heard a loud moan.

Five minutes later the door opened and Doctor Radcliff smiled at Lucinda. "Young lady, you have a beautiful baby brother."

Lucinda frowned. "Is Mama all right?"

"Your mama is fine."

Jesse came to the door smiling. "Lucinda, come in and see your mama and the baby." He beckoned to Gus. "Come in, see my son."

They gathered around Alice's bed and Doctor Radcliff picked up his bag. "Jesse, you did a good job delivering your son. Mother is doing fine, so you don't need me anymore, at least for now. But if anything changes, let me know."

Jesse shook Doctor Radcliff's hand. "Thank you. I couldn't have done it without you. I'll walk you downstairs."

"You stay here with your family. I know my way out."

Jesse moved back by the bed.

"Mama, are you all right?" Lucinda asked.

Alice looked at Lucinda and smiled. "Mama's fine, and so is your brother." She pulled the blanket back from the baby's head.

"Can I touch him?" Lucinda reached toward his cheek.

"Yes, but be gentle," Alice said.

Gus looked at Jesse. "You delivered your son?"

Jesse shrugged. "Well, I had no choice. You and the doc took too long to get here. I couldn't just stand here and not try to help Alice."

Alice looked up at Jesse and smiled. "You did great, and now we have a little boy."

"What are you going to name him?" Gus asked.

Jesse looked at Alice. "We picked out the name Lane, if it was a boy. Do we want to stick with that name?"

"Yes. I like Lane."

"Lane Fayette," Gus said. "That has a nice ring to it."

Lucinda smiled at her mother. "I like it too, Mama."

"Congratulations, Alice. You have a good-looking boy there."

Alice smiled. "Thanks, Gus."

Gus stepped back from the bedside. "I need to go unhitch Jake from the buggy. Jesse, don't you worry about helping to get things ready at the lighthouse tonight. You spend the time with Alice."

"I appreciate the extra time to help her. I'll see you at midnight, then." Jesse walked with Gus out to the hallway. "Thanks for all your help, Gus."

Gus put his hand on Jesse's shoulder. "Hey, you're welcome. You know, this makes me feel like I'm getting old."

"What do you mean? Jesse asked.

"Time has gone by so fast. It seems like only a few months ago that Lucinda was born. Now, here's Lane. If he grows up as fast as Lucinda did, he'll be running around here before you know it."

"I look forward to him being as much help to me as Lucinda is to Alice."

The sound of Lane crying came from the bedroom.

Gus grinned. "Right now, it sounds like he needs your help. I'll see you later."

***

Five years later . . .

Gus finished breakfast and set his dishes on the kitchen counter. He looked out the window and saw Lane standing in Gus' yard with his chin down on his chest. Curious as to what might be wrong, Gus walked outside and approached him. "Morning, Lane. Is everything all right?"

Lane was silent for a few seconds. "Lucinda won't play with me again."

"Why?

"She said she has work to do."

"Work?"

Lane frowned. "Will you play with me?"

"Well, we can throw the ball again if you want. But I think you need a friend to play with."

"A friend?" Lane looked up at Gus. "You're my friend!"

Gus smiled. "Yeah, but I'm talking about a friend who would be there for you any time of day or night."

Lane rolled his eyes. "Who's that?"

"I think you need a dog."

Lane's eyes widened. "A dog? I would like that!"

"You would have to do more than play with it, though. You'd need to give it food and water, too."

"I can take care of it. When can I get it?"

"I know someone who has a dog, but you need to ask your papa first if you can have one."

"I'll go now." Lane took off running toward his house.

Gus walked up onto the porch and sat down in his chair. He lit his pipe and after a few puffs he saw Lane and Jesse come out of the house. Lane quickened his steps as he got closer to Gus, and ran the rest of the way to Gus' porch.

Lane's smile said it all. "Papa said I could have a dog!"

"Good for him." Gus patted Lane on the shoulder. "I'm glad for you."

Jesse walked onto the porch with a grin on his face. "You've really got Lane excited about a dog. Would it happen to be one from Gunther?"

Gus nodded. "Yeah, he told me the other day the pups were about ready to be weaned."

Jesse rubbed his cheek. "Do you have time to go with us and help pick out one?

Lane pulled on Gus' arm. "Come with us, Gus."

Gus smiled as he got up from his chair. "Sure. It'll give me a chance to visit with Gunther again."

***

Jesse pulled his buggy to a stop in front of Gunther's house. Gus got out. "I'll get Gunther while you tie Molly to the hitching rail."

"All right." He tied his horse and helped Lane down. As they arrived at the front porch, Gunther opened the door.

"Hi, Gus. Good to see y—well there's Lane and Jesse, too." Gunther stepped out onto the porch and shook hands with them. He patted Lane on the head. "What brings you fellows here?"

"Lane's looking for a dog," Gus said.

Lane looked up at Gunther and grinned.

"I've got three of the best-looking Beagle pups in the county. You'll have fun trying to pick a favorite. Are you ready to see them?"

Lane smiled. "Oh yes."

"Let's go around back and you'll see what I mean."

Everyone followed Gunther to the back of the house. Against the woodshed was a medium sized dog house. The mother dog was peacefully lying on the sparse clumps of thin grass. She immediately stood up when everyone came around the corner of the house. The pups were not concerned and continued to play around her.

Gunther pointed. "There they are."

Lane's eyes lit up and a big smile appeared on his face. "Oh, Papa, they are beautiful."

Jesse smiled. "They sure are."

Gus looked at Lane. "It could be tough picking out one. They all appear to have the same markings and color, but they'll each have different personalities."

"Look again, Gus." Gunther pointed to one of the pups that had been lying down with another pup that was lying over its back end.

"Oh, I see what you mean," Gus, said.

Lane moved toward the pups. "I know the one I want!" The pup whose back end was covered hurried over to Lane. Lane picked up the pup and it began licking him on the chin. "I like this one, Gunther."

Gunther chuckled. "Well, it looks to me as though he likes you, too."

Jesse kneeled down next to Lane. "Are you sure you want this dog? You hardly looked at the other two."

Lane smiled. "I like this one, Papa." The pup licked him on the nose.

"Well, he is different." Jesse scratched the pup behind its ear. "The markings on the other two are the same, but this little guy's legs are white. Look how it runs all the way up and covers his rear end."

Gus chuckled. "He has more spark than the others."

"Well, Jesse," Gunther said. "It looks like Lane has made his choice."

Jesse stood up. "I think you're right."

Gus looked at Lane. "Now you've got yourself a dog. What are you going to name him?"

Lane looked at the pup and then up at Gus. "I'll call him Sparky."

"I like that name!"

Gunther kneeled down in front of Lane. "He's your dog now. You call him whatever you want." Gunther hugged Lane and the dog together. "All I ask is that you be good to him and take good care of him."

Lane smiled. "I will, Gunther."

Gunther stood up and looked at Jesse. "You've got a fine boy there. I believe he will be good to the pup, and they'll become great friends."

Jesse smiled. "I have no doubt. What do I owe you for the dog?"

Gunther shook his head. "Let it be my gift to you and Alice for being good friends over the years."

Jesse shook Gunther's hand. "Thanks."

"You've done a good thing, Gunther, and made that boy very happy," Gus said.

"We should go," Jesse said. "It won't be long until it's time to start work at the lighthouse."

They traveled back to the house and were met on the front porch by Alice and Lucinda.

As Lane held his dog close to him, he turned up his nose at Lucinda. "Now I have someone who will play with me."

Chapter 30

Hard Thing to Do

TWO YEARS LATER, early one summer afternoon Gus pulled up in his buggy while Jesse was working in the garden, and Lane was playing in the dirt with Sparky

"Hey, Wickie, I'm going fishing. You fellers want to come along?"

Jesse stopped hoeing and leaned on the hoe handle. "Yeah, but I want to finish these weeds first. We'll catch up to you in a little while."

"I'll be at my favorite spot." Gus waved and drove away.

Several minutes later Jesse finished with the weeds. He and Lane went into the house. As they entered the kitchen, Alice was mixing dough to bake bread.

Lane ran over to Alice. "Mama, I'm going fishing with Papa."

Alice stopped mixing and turned toward Lane. "That river is too dangerous for you." She looked at Jesse. "I think he's too young to be around that river yet. Wait till next year."

Lane's lower lip curled. "But I want to go fishing with, Papa."

Jesse put his hand on Lane's head. "Mama's right about the river. You'll be big enough next summer."

"Oh Papa." Lane was almost in tears.

Alice wiped the flour from her hands. "We haven't had fish for several days now, so bring home a nice one."

"I hope they're biting." Jesse kissed Alice and turned toward Lane. "You'll be all right, and before you know it, it'll be time for you to go fishing."

Lane rolled his eyes as he made circles in the flour lying on the table.

***

In the barn Jesse gathered his fishing tackle, then saddled Molly and rode toward the river. As he approached Gus' favorite fishing spot, he saw his horse and buggy. *I don't see Gus. He must be fishing further down the bank.* Jesse stopped, dismounted Molly, and tied her to Gus' buggy. Jesse cupped his hands around his mouth to enable his voice to carry. "Hey Gus! Where are you?"

No answer.

He walked a little farther along the river bank, then suddenly stopped. He saw the body of a man. "Oh, God no!" Jesse took off running across the rocks and splashed through the shallow water. It was Gus. He was lying on his back in the water.

"No, God! Please!" He knelt down and lifted Gus' head and shoulders out of the water. "Gus, wake up!" Jesse brushed his hand across Gus' face to wipe off the water and attempted to wake him. "Wickie, don't you die on me!" Jesse's voice trembled.

Gus didn't respond. He lay still in Jesse's arms.

"Please, God, don't take him!" Tears trickled down Jesse's face. *God, help me. I have to get him to the Landing.* Jesse stepped behind Gus and placed his hands under Gus' arms and shoulders. He lifted him up and struggled to drag Gus backwards up the bank. When he reached the top, Jesse gently laid Gus on the ground. "Hold on Gus, I'll be right back." He ran back to the buggy, and returned with it. He loaded Gus in the back. Jesse's hands were trembling as he grabbed the reins. *God! Don't let him die.* Jesse cracked the reins and drove the buggy toward the Landing. "Hang on, Gus. We're going to the doctor."

***

Jesse stopped the buggy in front of Doctor Radcliff's office and ran inside. "Come quick, Doc! Gus is hurt."

Doctor Radcliff stopped writing and stood up from behind his desk. He hurried to follow Jesse back to the buggy.

"What happened?"

"I found him on his back in the river." Jesse's voice quivered. "He must have slipped and fallen on a rock."

Doctor Radcliff took Gus' pulse and listened for his heartbeat. He looked at Jesse. "Jesse, I'm sorry. I found no sign of life. Gus is dead."

Tears ran down Jesse's face. "He can't be dead. Are you sure?"

Doctor Radcliff reached over and touched Jesse's shoulder. "I'm sorry. He must have drowned after he hit his head."

Jesse sobbed and hid his face in his hands. "What am I going to do?"

"You have to do the hard thing. Take Gus to the undertaker."

Jesse climbed in the buggy and picked up the reins. Tears trickled down his cheeks. *I can't believe Gus is gone.*

***

Jesse drove the short distance to the undertaker's office and arranged for Gus' funeral. When he left the undertaker, he started back toward the lighthouse, but then he stopped. *I need help.* He turned the buggy around and drove back to the Landing office. Jesse walked inside and was met by Lloyd.

Lloyd frowned. "You don't look so good, Jesse. What's wrong?"

Jesse could barely say the words. "Gus is dead."

"He's what?" Lloyd's mouth dropped open. "What happened?"

Jesse explained the circumstances of Gus' death to Lloyd. "I need to send a telegram to the Lighthouse Board."

"Sure, but I have to tell Nellie first." Lloyd darted through the doorway leading to his quarters. "Nellie, come here quick!"

Nellie appeared. "What are you yelling about?"

Lloyd put his arm around Nellie's shoulders. "Gus is dead. He drowned in the river."

Nellie gasped, and tears pooled in her eyes. "He can't be!"

Lloyd shook his head. "I can't believe it either."

Nellie wiped the tears that rolled down her cheeks. She turned toward Jesse. "What are you going to do?"

Jesse looked at the floor. "I'm not sure. Somehow, I have to keep the lighthouse going, but I'll need the board's help."

Lloyd moved behind the counter and picked up his pencil and paper. "What do you want your telegram to say?"

Jesse held the back of his neck. "'Gus died. His funeral day after tomorrow. Need help at lighthouse.' Sign it, Jesse Fayette."

Lloyd read the message back to Jesse. "Is that correct?"

Jesse nodded.

While Lloyd sent the telegram, nothing could be heard except the clicking of the telegraph key. "It's hard to believe that Gus is gone," Lloyd said.

"Things will never be the same without him," Jesse said. "Oh! I need to go. Alice doesn't know yet. She thinks I'm still fishing."

Lloyd moved out from behind the counter, and laid his hand on Jesse's shoulder. "What time is the funeral?"

Jesse cleared his throat. "The undertaker agreed to 11:00 a.m. and said he would arrange everything with the preacher."

"Nellie and I will try to be there. I'll see if I can get Ike or Seth to watch things here while we're gone. If not, I'll close the office."

"I appreciate it." Jesse shook Lloyd's hand. "Thanks for your help." He turned to walk out, but stopped. "I didn't pay you for the telegram."

Lloyd waved him off. "This one's on me. It's for my old friend."

***

Jesse was silent as he met Alice in the kitchen.

"You look terrible." Alice frowned. "Was fishing that bad?"

Jesse took Alice by the hand.

She looked at him. "What's wrong?"

"It's Gus." Jesse swallowed. Tears pooled in his eyes.

"What's wrong with Gus?" She laid her hand on Jesse's shoulder.

"He's dead."

"What? He can't be!" Alice hugged Jesse. She began to sob. "What happened?"

Jesse told Alice about Gus' accident, the funeral

arrangements, and the telegram he sent. Alice was still wiping tears when Lucinda walked into the kitchen.

"Mama, why are you crying?"

Alice looked back at Jesse. "I can't tell her."

Jesse put both hands on Lucinda's shoulders. "We're sad because Gus had an accident."

"Accident!" Wrinkles appeared on Lucinda's forehead. "What happened?"

"He fell into the river."

Lucinda touched Jesse's arm. "Will he be all right, Papa?"

"Honey, I'm sorry. Gus is gone." Jesse put his arms around Lucinda.

"Is he coming back?" Lucinda asked.

Jesse held her tight. "No."

She began to sob.

Alice put her hand on Lucinda's head trying to comfort her. "Gus is all right. He's safe with the angels in heaven."

"I'm glad he's safe, Mama, but I miss him so much."

"We all miss him," Alice said. "He was like family."

Jesse released his hold on Lucinda and looked her in the face. "Gus would want us to go on with our lives. It'll be hard without him, but we have to do it."

"Papa's right. Can you do that?" Alice asked.

Lucinda wiped a tear. "I'll try."

"Mama and I miss him too, and we'll never forget him. We have great memories of our time together. He was a good friend and human being."

"He was my friend, too," Lucinda said.

Alice looked at Jesse. "We need to tell Lane."

"I'll go outside and get him," Lucinda said.

"All right," Jesse said.

Alice shook her head. "He's been out there playing in the dirt with Sparky ever since you left to go fishing."

"I saw them when I came back. I think he's mad at me, 'cause he didn't come to me."

"Maybe this is not a good time to tell him about Gus." She

touched Jesse on the arm.

Jesse shook his head. "We have to tell him. You know he looks for Gus almost every afternoon by the lighthouse, and he'll know something's wrong if he doesn't see him."

"You're right, and speaking of the lighthouse. How are you going to take care of it by yourself?"

"I'm not sure, but regardless, I'll have to keep it operating until help gets here."

The kitchen door opened and Lucinda walked in with Lane who was crying. He ran over to Jesse and hugged his legs.

"Why are you crying?" Alice asked.

"I told him about Gus," Lucinda said. She played with strands of her hair.

"You what?" Alice said.

Tears rolled from Lane's brown eyes. He looked up at Jesse. "Papa, I'm sorry I got mad about fishing. I don't want to lose you, too. I love you."

Jesse reached down and picked up Lane. "I love you, too. You're not going to lose me."

Alice patted Lane on the back. "You're taking Gus's death like a big boy. Mama's proud of you."

Lane's lower lip curled. "I really miss Gus and I know Sparky will miss him, too." He wiped the rest of his tears. "Papa, will you have to do all the work by yourself now?"

Jesse adjusted his hold on Lane. "Yeah, until they send me some help."

"Papa, I can help you," Lane said.

"Me, too," Lucinda said.

Jesse smiled. "Thanks. I have to do it, but you make me proud 'cause you want to help."

Alice grinned. "You know I'm here for you, too."

Jesse leaned forward and kissed her.

***

A few minutes later, Jesse went to the lighthouse to begin preparation for the evening. His first stop was the workroom. *I need to make an entry in the record book about Gus before I do anything else.* Jesse sat down at the desk and opened the book. He stared at the page and tears pooled in his eyes. *This is a hard thing to do. I can't believe you're not here, Gus.* He wrote: "August 17, 1875 — 5:10 p.m. — Gus Crosby died today around 2:00 p.m. in a river accident while fishing. Requested help from board — JF." Jesse laid down the pen. *I better get started, Gus. It won't be long until it's time to light the lantern. I've got a lot to do before then.*

Jesse walked up the narrow spiral stairway to the watch room. Every step reminded him of Gus. He climbed inside the lens and trimmed wicks on the lantern burner head that needed to be trimmed. He returned downstairs and went out to the oil house. He made a trip back to the watch room with a five-gallon can of oil and filled the lantern reservoir. On his trip to return the can to the oil house, it started to rain. Jesse went back upstairs to the watch room and wound the clock mechanism. By now, it was thirty minutes before dusk. He climbed up into the lantern room and pulled back the curtain from around the lens. He finished there, and descended the short stairway to the watch room. *It's raining harder.* Jesse climbed inside the lens again and lit the lantern wicks.

Since the rain was more intense, Jesse decided to stay in the lighthouse instead of going back to the house until time to check the equipment and the lookout. He sat down at the desk and began to read a book.

***

Jesse jerked as the door opened. He looked around and saw Alice standing there, water dripping from her hat and coat. "What are you doing here?"

"I got worried when you didn't come back to the house."

"I'm all right." Jesse stood. "I must have dozed off for a couple of minutes."

"Couple of minutes? It's past 8:00."

"Oh my! I was out longer than I thought."

"Well, you're tired." Alice laid her hand on his shoulder. "It's been a stressful day. You and Gus normally worked together to get the lighthouse ready for the night."

"I need to check the equipment and the lookout."

"Can I help?"

"You've already helped by waking me up." Jesse held Alice's wet hand. "Honey, I'd feel better if you go back to the house with the children."

"All right, but if you don't come over soon, I'll be back to check on you.

Jesse grinned. "I'll be fine. I've had a nap."

"I know, but that wasn't enough to keep you going all night. If you come to the house, you can nap between equipment checks and I can wake you when it's time for the next check."

"But I need to check it every hour. You won't get any rest if you have to get up to wake me."

"If I have to, I'll take a nap during the day." Alice took Jesse by the arm. "You don't know how long it'll be before you get help. Until then, it's just you and me. So, let me help you this way."

Jesse looked down at the floor and back up at Alice. "All right, but go back to the house and I'll be there as soon as I can."

Alice helped Jesse that night as well as the next by waking him after naps. This enabled him to keep the lighthouse operating throughout the night. During the day, Alice would take a nap while Jesse took care of the children.

***

After Jesse completed work at the lighthouse the second night, he walked into the kitchen carrying a Bible. Alice and the children were there to greet him. "Morning everyone," Jesse said.

"Morning, honey. Breakfast is almost ready. Lucinda, you need to set a knife with Papa's plate."

"Sorry, Mama."

Lane looked up at his father as he walked by the table. "Did you have a hard night, Papa?"

"Not really hard, but I've been doing a lot of thinking." Jesse set the Bible down on the corner of the cupboard and washed his hands.

Lucinda moved over next to her mother and whispered. "Papa doesn't seem like himself this morning."

Alice put her arm around Lucinda's shoulder, and choked back tears. "Well, today is Gus's funeral. I'm sure that's on his mind. I know it's on mine. Now, pour Papa's coffee."

Jesse finished washing his hands and sat down at the table.

Alice plated fried eggs and set them on the table with the bacon and biscuits already there. "It's ready."

Jesse held hands with his family to ask a blessing, which had been his practice since moving to the lighthouse. "Heavenly Father, we thank you for this food and ask you bless it to the needs of our bodies. Help us through this day and to do your will as we go. Amen."

Alice passed the bacon to Jesse. "What were you thinking about last night?"

"About Gus. Now I know how he must have felt when he had to work by himself all night at the other lighthouse."

"I think about Gus too," Lane said. "Sparky and me really miss him."

Alice touched Lane on the arm. "Honey, we all miss him. He was like a part of our family." She passed the biscuits to Jesse. "I'll never forget the time when Gus gave us the baby cradle for our wedding gift. He said he had made it for his wife, but she died before they had any children."

"I didn't think of that, but I remember the first time I met Gus at the Landing. He appeared disappointed with me, and I think he thought I was too young to replace Wyatt."

Lane looked at his Papa. "Who's Wyatt?"

"He was the first assistant keeper to work for Gus."

"What happened to him, Papa?" Lucinda asked.

"He died in a storm."

Alice shook her head. "Children, stop the questions and eat your breakfast."

Jesse took a sip of coffee. "I remembered the time when I thought we lost Gus to the boarding house fire. We were devastated until we found out he survived."

"I remember that, and how afterwards he couldn't find a place to live, so we let him live with us in our little house." Alice took a bite of biscuit.

Lane frowned and looked at his Mama. "I don't remember a little house."

"You weren't born yet," Alice said, "But it's the same house where Lucinda was born."

"Mama, I don't remember it either," Lucinda said.

"You might not. You were just a little over three years old when we moved from there."

Jesse sat up straight. "Speaking of that little house, it reminds me of why we moved to Gardiner's City. Honey, do you remember the look on Gus's face when he saw the lighthouse tower lying in the river?"

"Yes. He looked like he had lost an old friend."

Jesse took a bite of egg. "That's the way we feel and why it'll be a hard day for all of us."

Lucinda looked at Jesse. "Papa, is that your Bible over there?"

Jesse shook his head. "No. It was Gus'."

"Why do you have it?" Alice asked.

"I was thinking of asking the preacher to read from it during Gus' service."

"Why? I'm sure Preacher Avery has already prepared something."

"Probably so, but I found something in Gus' Bible that I believe is appropriate for his funeral."

Alice looked at Jesse. "How did you get Gus' Bible, anyway?"

"I found it in the desk drawer at the lighthouse. He kept it there so he could read when he had time."

"What did you find, Papa?" Lucinda asked.

"I found a couple of passages of scripture that Gus had underlined. I think because of the way he lived his life and treated people those scriptures were a guiding light for him."

"What do they say, Papa?" Lucinda asked.

Jesse swallowed. "You'll have to wait until the funeral. Finish your breakfast. You have to help Mama clean up the table, and you still need to get ready to go."

***

Jesse and his family were the first to arrive at the graveyard that morning. He parked his buggy inside the entrance and climbed down. "Stay in the buggy for now. We're early."

"I want to get out," Lane said.

"All right, but you stay close to the buggy." Jesse turned and saw Gunther coming toward him from under a big pine tree. Jesse waved to him as he approached and they shook hands.

"I'm really sorry about Gus," Gunther said. "He was a good man and friend."

Jesse patted Gunther on the shoulder. "You were his best friend."

"Thanks." He stepped over to the buggy.

As Jesse followed, he saw the undertaker's wagon coming with the pine box in it. Behind the wagon were Preacher Avery and other people in their buggies from the Landing.

Gunther reached into Jesse's buggy and gently took Alice by the hand. "I'm sorry about Gus. We're going to miss him. He was a great friend to all of us."

"Yes, he was," Alice said. "And I know he would appreciate everything you've done for his funeral."

Gunther lowered his head. "It's a sad time, but I'm glad I could help."

"I hate to interrupt," Jesse said, "but they're here. Alice, let me help you down, and then I need to go talk to Preacher Avery before he starts the service."

"I can help her," Gunther said. "I've got time before I have to be over there at the wagon. The undertaker asked me and others to help carry Gus' coffin."

"Thanks, Gunther." Jesse looked at Alice. "You and the children wait here. I'll be right back and we'll go together."

***

Minutes later, Jesse and his family arrived at graveside with the other mourners and they exchanged greetings. The preacher began to speak as Nellie released her hug on Lane.

"I would like to thank you all for coming out today for this sad occasion," Preacher Avery said. "We are gathered here to bury our dear friend, Gus Crosby." The preacher opened his Bible and removed a piece of paper. "Gus was born February 16, 1817 and died August 17, 1875. During Mr. Crosby's fifty-eight years, he was loved and respected by everyone who knew him."

Preacher Avery continued and reminded everyone of how Gus died. He told them about a meeting he had with Gus not long after he moved back from Gardiner's City. It was then, Gus told him of the different jobs he had worked at over the years. A dock worker, hotel clerk, and a lumber mill worker, but his favorite job was lighthouse keeper. "We all knew Gus and the kind of person he was. Jesse found Gus' Bible, and he has asked me to read two verses that Gus had underlined in it. This may help us understand the light that Gus used to guide his personal life." The preacher opened Gus' Bible and he turned several pages. "The verses are from the book of Matthew, chapter five. Verse eight is the first one." The preacher began to read. "'Blessed are the pure in heart: for they shall see God.' "The second is verse sixteen. 'Let your light so shine before men, that they may see your good works, and glorify your Father which is in heaven.'"

Preacher Avery closed the Bible and bowed his head. "Heavenly Father, thank you for Gus' life and his time here with us. We will miss our dear friend, but we know his spirit is with you and we commit his body to this place. May he rest in peace. Amen. This concludes the service. Thank you all for coming."

Everyone milled around for a few minutes afterward talking to each other. Then, except for Gunther, the rest of them went to their buggies and drove away. Gunther continued his unpleasant job by having to shovel dirt over the coffin of his old friend.

***

Four days later, a young man and woman stopped in front of the lighthouse in the afternoon. The man stepped down from their buggy which was loaded with a few boxes. He turned and gazed up toward the top of the tower. *I must be dreaming.*

Jesse stepped out of the oil house carrying a can of oil and saw them. "Can I help you?"

The young man turned toward Jesse. "I'm looking for Jesse Fayette."

"I'm Jesse." He moved closer and set down the can of oil.

They shook hands. "I'm Red Saunders. The Lighthouse Board sent me to be a light keeper." He turned toward the buggy. "This is my wife."

Jesse nodded and touched the bill of his hat. "I'm glad to meet you Mrs. Saunders. It's good that you could get here as soon as you did. I need the help. Come on inside."

Red helped his wife down from the buggy while Jesse picked up the can, and opened the door to the workroom.

As Red stepped inside, he noticed a charred miniature statue of a lighthouse sitting on the window sill.

Jesse set the can down. "Where's your furniture and belongings?"

"They're still at the Landing," Red said. "But I've hired a man to haul everything out here tomorrow."

"We don't have very much," Mrs. Saunders said.

"My old friend and head keeper ..." Jesse swallowed. "He had no next of kin, so all of his furniture and things are still over there in the house." He pointed and looked back at Red. "You can use his stuff if you want. But Gus' clothes may be too big for you."

Red grinned. "Thanks. I've got enough clothing." He reached over to the window sill and picked up the statue. "You said Gus?"

"Yeah. That lighthouse carving was his."

Red rubbed his thumb over the middle of the statue and pulled a white bone handle pen knife from his pocket. He started to shave off some of the charred wood when Jesse stopped him.

"Hold it! What are you doing?"

"I was checking to see if I might be able to fix this." Red quickly placed the statue back on the window sill. "Sorry." He folded his knife and returned it to his pocket.

Jesse looked at the floor, then back at Red. "That's good of you to offer, but I don't want it fixed." He looked at the statue. "You see, that statue reminds me of the young boy who made it for Gus, and the love and respect he showed for him. It's also a reminder of the years I worked with Gus in the lighthouse that it represents." Jesse looked back at Red. "The charred wood on the statue reminds me of the time when I thought I'd lost Gus to a fire." Jesse looked down at the floor.

Mrs. Saunders looked at her husband and shook her head. "Rusty, he doesn't recognize you."

Jesse raised his head and his eyes widened.

The End

Made in the USA
Columbia, SC
11 August 2019